About the author

Lindzi Mayann almost always has her nose in a book whether she is reading or writing it! She loves to create vibrant, relatable characters, expose gritty truths, explore real life scenarios and use humour to create light heartedness.

Lindzi is also a specialist tutor, blogger and columnist. In what spare time she has, she enjoys upcycling furniture and clothes, travelling, festivals and challenging herself in the name of charity. Visit www.lindzi.co.uk to find out more!

By Lindzi Mayann

Educating Jodie is part of the '**Jodie Trilogy**' and is the sequel to **Maga High**, already available on Amazon. The prequel, **Pub Life** can also be purchased via Amazon.

Maga Rush is also available on Amazon for Kindle only- short stories linked to Maga High. These stories can be enjoyed without reading Maga High although feature smaller characters including Tanya, Gemma, Beth and Face.

Follow Lindzi and stay up to date with book news:

Lindzi Mayann

Twitter: @magahighmayann

Instagram and Facebook: @Lindzimayann

Lindzi Mayann

Educating Jodie

By Lindzi Mayann

Lindzi Mayann

Dedications

Once again a huge shout out to my ever loyal friends, family and new fans who continue to share the word about my books.

Thanks to my chief readers and their input on this and Maga High. Editing my books has been an ongoing learning curve and your help is very much appreciated.

To everyone who got involved with #magahigh and #magahighbook THANK YOU for supporting Maga High in its quest to travel the world. Feel free to join in the fun and share your Jodie book pictures- I will add all locations to my world map!

Contents

Prologue

My mum picks me up from the airport and I speak to her non-stop during the journey home.

Six weeks in Magaluf has felt like so much longer, a lifetime, and the stories fall from my mouth in an unrelenting stream. I have missed her and although she has missed me, I think she wishes I would stop telling her about my close-calls and near-misses!

I try to keep the tales light and censored but it's difficult considering Maga proved itself to be so untamed and I'd been so easily whisked away by it all.

I keep reminding myself that what was normal there, is far from ordinary here! Some of the things I say do really sound outrageous in the dull, grey light of the Midlands and I find myself questioning if they really happened like I remember at all.

The familiar sign for my village summons a mixed bag of feelings in my gut, my heart thuds and it makes me feel sick, nervous and excited all at once.

I can't wait to see Leila and Cat, my brother George and my other friends. I have my new job to look forward to; training starts on Thursday, in just a few days. Plus, my own bed! I am genuinely excited about sleeping in my own bed.

How do I feel about returning to this place where everybody knows my business? Knows that I was cheated on, lied to, taken for a fool... it was only months ago.

It had all felt so much more important back then though!

Trust mistakenly placed is surely something which will happen again if I am living with an open heart, I won't be changing that. Mistakes are something I will not regret- I made a few in Magaluf too. I will try not to repeat mistakes which hurt me, or others and I will take opportunity from them where I can.

The decision to go on the holiday to Magaluf in the first place is a prime example. The journey it led me to is now the start of a new era.

Although the centre of Anstige village looks a little boring in comparison to the popping Maga strip, I don't feel as claustrophobic being home as I thought I would.

There are just a few things to get in order over the next couple of days and then the next chapter really can begin!

Firstly, the STD clinic needs a visit. I'm not proud to have risked my sexual health for an unprotected fling with one of the most gorgeous guys I have ever seen- ok, I'm not completely disgusted with myself either, *but* I have learnt my lesson from fooling about.

It is all fun and games so long as you're safe! Because the 'Maga-banging' attitude will be hard to shake I'll definitely be stocking up on condoms!

Secondly, I need to detox. My gums are bleeding, my stomach aching and my throat raw from the persistent drinking of- poisonous- vodka, if the stories are to be believed! Fruit, vegetables, water and green tea, it's all on the list.

Physical health aside I undoubtedly look the best I ever have and mentally feel it too. I'm tanned, toned, confident and sure of my inner strength and ability to succeed. So much has changed around me *and* within me, just in this past year.

I am feeling motivated to make this next year the best yet.

If, when, I see my ex Dane, I know I'll feel nothing at all. I won't even need to say anything at all. Actions speak louder than words. Let my happiness and success be the only form of revenge I seek.

I will be saying yes more, I want to travel more, experience more and learn more!

A new job in Specialist Education will be teaching me enough and I'm sure there'll be other life lessons too. I don't think I'll ever stop learning.

Ultimately though, I've decided to make the best of it along the way! My eyes have been opened and there is no way back now anyway.

Teacher Training- Day 1

"Now lower them to the ground. Remember they'll probably be thrashing around, upset, spitting etcetera... Volunteers, could you start to role play a little?" Sam, the trainer, calls out the instruction.

My cheeks grow hot with tingling embarrassment, I *am* a volunteer currently and I try to wiggle a little. The men embracing an arm each resist me easily and I feel too uncomfortable to react with more vigour.

I literally only met these people a few hours ago. I suppose it's one way to get acquainted!

"Come on Jodie, you're an angry, young boy!" Troy murmurs at my side and I giggle.

"I'm glad I'm not!" I declare as they swing me forward to the ground with ease.

"Yeah Jodie, I expected more of a fight from you!" Gilbert drawls from my other side.

I'm now pinned face down to the floor by two hunky men, this should not feel sexual! This restraints training is the first proper session of today and I must concentrate. But my brain has obviously and irreparably been altered by Magaluf. I think about a certain conversation I had about how I fight, with *that* particularly gorgeous guy- wow it does not help things.

"Once in a ground hold, the observer will take notes. Remember the observations? Remember the signs..." Sam once again goes into details of how to recognise asphyxiation, it is actually very serious, and I try to forget my numbing arms and Troy holding onto one of them.

I suppose having us endure each 'hold' is as important as learning how to safely execute them. Not that I need to feel added sympathy, it already doesn't seem right to have to restrain children let alone in a school.

"Gently release your volunteer and carefully get back to your feet please." Sam announces finally. "You probably all feel a little stiff."

Troy catches my eye meaningfully and I barely contain my smirk. I should not be swooning over him. I keep telling myself, sternly, because mixing my professional life with my personal life is a mistake I have made before. It should be completely out of the question especially considering the consequences!

But when he walked into the staff room earlier…

"It's time to swap positions." Sam announces earnestly, and I raise my eyebrows. It's hard to control my inappropriate mind with all these innuendoes! Or is it just me and Troy who think so?

Giving me the subtlest of winks which makes my heart skitter, he stands between Gilbert and me.

"My turn." He says in his soft voice and gives me a lazy, lingering look.

"Give us a challenge Troy." Gilbert's voice is incredibly deep but his laughter high-pitched as he brushes his own muscled arms. "If you can!" He adds.

A set of dimples appear in Troy's cheeks, his eyes sparkle at the dare. I look away.

"Don't go too mad." I mutter worriedly. "*I* won't be able to handle it!"

I see grins widen on both of their faces and realise what they're thinking with another blush.

"I'm sure you will." Gilbert remarks dryly and I briefly search his handsome features for intention.

"We'll see!" Troy answers one of us, both of us maybe and flexes a bicep to reveal a bulge which fills and stretches out his t-shirt sleeve. I swallow hard. He's much easier to read than Gilbert; playful, likeable, desirable…

"We'll see." I echo. His eyes are like rich coffee beans and full of mischief when I meet them.

"Remember the steps!" Sam pipes up. "A firm grip. A little pressure as you guide them…"

I'm so close to Troy it's hard to miss the glance he gives me. But I concentrate dutifully on the positioning of my fingers on his arm, ensuring I'm using 'caring C's' how I've been shown because thumbs are powerful and can cause bruising. Seeing my hands, one wrapped around his tattooed wrist, the other just above his elbow where his arm becomes thicker does nothing to diminish my growing lust towards him.

"Struggle a little guys, come on, this won't be easy!" Sam is snapping as he walks around the groups. "There won't be time to hesitate, you've got to be confident and quick!"

Troy starts to throw his torso around and I catch Gilbert's eye as we wrestle to control him between us. We're on our feet still, somehow we must transfer him to the floor without slamming or crushing him or tripping accidently or scratching him!

My heart is whirring for different reasons now. The effort to maintain our grip is one thing but I also feel panicked by a sudden wave of realisation.

"Jodie?" Gilbert barks above rising noise levels. "Ready to go on your knees?"

I nod. There's no creeping smirk this time. Next week when the kids start back, I could be expected to put this into practise for real. No sexual chemistry, no jokes!

I step forward in unison with Gilbert, lowering a knee. We then tuck the other leg under and lean our hips together, slightly trapping Troy's body which still jerks and thrashes.

"Ready to go to ground?" Gilbert checks and I again nod.

We have to force Troy into position, but I know he is withholding his true strength on account of my own.

"Well done!" Gilbert gives me a satisfactory nod once we have him secured and I feel a mixture of pride and unease.

What if the students are stronger than me? Most of them here are lads. Are teenage boys stronger than grown women? What if I forget how to do a hold properly and hurt someone? More likely I'll be the one getting hurt.

Without Troy's flirting making the whole thing seem frisky, the responsibility is suddenly enormous.

"Ok, on your feet again, we'll take a quick ten-minute break." Sam tells the room. "And then we'll run through the basic moves one more time and have a small assessment before its lunch."

Instantly the room bustles into life. A test! I think I've taken it all in but there's literally been so much to consider already. Around a third of the staff-group is in here. For a relatively small school there are a lot of us.

I'm beginning to understand why though. The students are described as 'challenging' for a reason it seems and adult-child ratio is way higher than usual.

There is a cluster of chairs in the corner of the hall, so I head there for now. I purposely don't look around to see what Troy is doing. Once seated, I can scan the faces and test how many names I've learned so far.

"Where are you sneaking off to?" He has followed me.

"I'm not sneaking anywhere." I reply. If he insists on accompanying me I will at least use him to get to know my peers. I plonk myself down and he sits right beside me, too close to even turn and face him, I can't help but notice.

When I arrived this morning, it had been busy and chaotic. Del, the Deputy Head, gave me a timetable to follow for the training days and we had an assembly welcome meeting first thing with Julie, the Headmistress. Then I got stuck into the learning of restraints and rapid defence moves to attacks such as chair throwing and hair pulling!

I had been cringing at the idea of getting physical with complete strangers but then Troy had pounced on me to partner him for most of it and, well, I'm not complaining.

"So, tell me names and job roles and things." I say staring at the milling bodies, some chat in groups whilst others are leaving and re-entering the room.

"Gilbert, who we were just with, he's in charge of behaviour. Lewis who we worked with before? He's an artist, supports the teacher Helen. In Art, *obviously*. Dom over there, that's his brother, he'll support the Year 9's this year. Jess, Leanne, Lacey, Eric they're pretty much all mentors or some kind of support staff in here."

I nod along as Troy continues matching the names with the subject or year group that they work with. I don't know where I'll fit in yet. Del said I'll find out in the morning when my permanent timetable has been confirmed.

My head is spinning with it all, new sights, smells, people, routines and systems. It is overwhelming to my senses but Magaluf prepared me to expect the unexpected and so far, the day has already far outlived any preconceptions I'd had about the place.

I'm mildly concerned over the nature of the students, considering my first task has included a quick round of self-defence. But overall, I am intrigued! Once again, I feel like I'm peeking behind curtains, uncovering a new and unruly world. And admittedly I did get a cheeky, childish thrill when allowed into the 'Staff Room' earlier.

"Harishma, over there, she works with the year 10's. And that girl with the dark hair, Lucy, she's a professional athlete! It's a good bunch to work with. We go out sometimes. You'll like it here."

I already suspect that I will! And *go out sometimes*, like, when! He said that on purpose, right?

This is not Magaluf it is real life, I remind myself and nod along smiling politely.

The mentors all look around my age, Troy isn't the only good looking one either. I think of single Leila and the 'we go out sometimes'. There are also a bunch of pretty girls, all different. They look fun and sound interesting; an artist and an athlete! Plus, there's Troy with his quirky tattoos and funky afro hair. New work friends!

"Is everybody back?" Sam asks anybody, loudly, retaking his place at the front. "Has everybody got their partner back?"

There are murmured responses and Troy and I stand up ready. I must give this refresher my undivided attention.

"I'm going to enjoy this." Troy purrs and I grin all the same. My attention can handle an eighty-twenty split.

***

Lunch is provided in the form of a large buffet. It's been laid out in the staffroom and I line up with Troy. Surrounded by strangers, I'm grateful he's taken me under his wing regardless of the fact that he's also gorgeous and sexy and a serious distraction. A constant turnover of faces file in and out of the room, some wear lanyards displaying their names but next week there'll be students to remember too!

I passed the assessment earlier and even got a certificate stating I can now officially restrain children. It feels very surreal! I,

Jodie, am allowed to manhandle a child, although holds are only used as a last resort- if there is an imminent threat of danger or damage to themselves, others and/ or property. Still, I hope the situation doesn't come around too often.

"Don't get used to this." Troy breaks into my thoughts, gesturing the spread as we take our plates. "After tomorrow it won't happen again for another year!"

"Doesn't stop *us* going out though does it?" A voice croons from behind me. I turn to find a lanky guy with grey eyes waiting for me to respond.

"Erm!" I falter. "That's good."

"You'll come out with us, won't you?" He stares at me beadily.

Wow invite number two! Ok, so Troy's wasn't official but this one definitely is.

"Yes! I *love* a night out! I've been out every night for the past six weeks actually!" I joke.

"Hard-core!" He exclaims and balls both hands into rock and roll gestures. "Why?"

"I was working in Magaluf." I tell him. We're all plucking food now moving along in a conveyor belt fashion.

"Awesome!" He cries. "Bet you did loads of shagging!"

My breath snags in my throat and I almost drop the mini sausage I'm retrieving before quickly checking around me. Troy is laughing loudly.

"The boys did." I counter, hiding behind sexism shamelessly. It's about time it proved useful.

"I bet!" He guffaws. "I'd love to do that, well done you!"

The heat is off, and we leave the buffet table. I'm slightly taken aback, definitely amused, but what if somebody had overheard and been offended? We're in a school now!

"You'll get used to Sean." Troy tells me as we take a seat. Sean has taken a place elsewhere and I recognise Eric, Dom, Lewis and Lacey amongst others already at our table.

Existing conversations continue, and my eyes wander around the room as I eavesdrop. Yet again I feel swamped with alarming insights as they discuss particular students and previous incidents. We have 'Safeguarding' training next. As a waitress I did Data Protection and Health and Safety. This will be much more personal I expect.

Once I've eaten, I excuse myself and fetch my phone from my locker before visiting the bathroom. Leila and Cat get the same message declaring I LOVE it and I CANNOT WAIT to tell them ALL ABOUT IT! Then I'm once again following Troy, and the same crowd as before, to a different part of the school.

Claire is already at the front of this room which vaguely resembles a library. She's the 'Senco'. I know her title, but I don't know what it means. Gilbert is loitering beside her, his smile like a Cheshire cat greeting us as we filter in.

I find myself seated between Troy and Lacey at a desk and there are print-outs of a PowerPoint presentation in front of us. I begin to look through it: What Are the Forms of Abuse, How Can You Recognise Abuse?

"Geek!" Lacey hisses from my side and I find her grinning at me.

"I am actually, I don't mind admitting it." I laugh but the word 'abuse' is etched into my mind. "Actually, it's my first school job, so this is all... new to me."

I don't want to describe it as 'downright crazy!'

"Oh well I'm sure you'll be just fine." She flicks her golden locks. "We have to do safeguarding *every* term to keep it all fresh in our mind. My advice is just record *everything*!"

Troy laughs from my other side.

"Everything?" He repeats. "You'd be here all day with what our lot come out with!"

"True!" Lacey agrees.

I don't really understand what they mean but smile along anyway. Lacey is glamourous looking with long, blonde hair loosely curled at the ends, thick eyelashes and a deep tan. She seems out of place in this environment. But then so many of the staff don't look like how I'd expected.

When I was at school many of the teachers seemed ancient, stuffy and certainly not cool. Perhaps I'm getting old myself and my perceptions have changed!

"Good afternoon and welcome everybody." Claire's voice is gentle, and a hush descends respectfully. "Before we begin, Jodie, please don't be afraid to ask questions. These guys have done this training a few times before, but discussions are always handy, and I want you to feel confident with the processes ok?"

"Yes, fine thanks." A few people turn to look at me and I randomly give out smiles.

"In that case..."

The session begins, and slides fill the screen one after another. I scribble notes onto my own version of the presentation.

Lacey remarks, "you weren't joking were you, you nerd!"

I don't mind, I know she's kidding. When we stop to deliberate over certain situations, Lacey and I take the opportunity to chat about other things too, mainly blokes and going out. She is a rebel. I've picked up on that about her already, and indeed, I like it!

I also learn that the outcome to any issue includes recording the concern and alerting Claire or Gilbert; makes sense now why he was in here acting so smug when we arrived. I get the impression he likes having power.

After another hour my brain actually hurts. I can handle the workload and remembering of rules but the truth behind some kids' lives is raw and utterly heart-breaking. A severe lump forms in my throat after a number of case-studies towards the close. I suppose I knew somewhere deep down that these things go on. At least working here, I might be able to improve on a life.

I can only assume that Troy's remark earlier means I should be expecting to record worrying comments and instances daily. I turn my concentration back to Claire who is wrapping up. All will be revealed next week I suppose.

"Well, that's it for the day!" Lacey trills gleefully. Undeniably I also feel elated to be finishing now- it feels like half a day after shifts in hospitality.

"How have you found it?" She's jumping to her feet, so I follow suit.

"Good. Yeah. It's a lot to take on, completely different!"

"You'll soon get used to it."

"I'm not sure I *want* to be used to it after hearing some of that stuff." I tell her honestly, gathering my things.

"It's not so bad day-to-day." Troy joins us as we exit the classroom. I almost call bye to Claire, she's on my timetable to be giving me a 'Tour and Induction' in the morning. But Gilbert is talking to her intently, so I don't interrupt.

"So how often do these holds happen?" I ask as casually as I can. It's probably the thing that has played on my mind the most.

"We don't really have to get involved Jodie." Lacey says. "The boys can be quite sweet."

"Sweet!" Troy cries before conceding. "Well there are some who wouldn't want to hurt a woman. But generally, they don't want to be held by a *girl* because it would look bad wouldn't it? There's a lot of male bravado."

I have to laugh, it makes some macho sense. "And what about the girls?"

Troy and Lacey exchange a glance.

"We'll have to wait and see won't we!" Lacey shrugs. "I'll see you tomorrow anyway Jodie, nice meeting you."

"You too!" I reply and she's already dashing off. "What does she mean, wait and see, about the girls?"

"They're not here yet. This will be the first year we've taken on girls." Troy is busy grabbing belongings from his locker and misses my confusion and shock.

"So, you don't know yet then?" I ask dumbly.

He straightens up and gives me the most serious look of the day.

"The men aren't exactly feeling great about the idea of holding females. You know, 'safeguarding' and all that." He shrugs but then his bright smile returns. "Anyway, I'm off. I'll see you tomorrow."

"See you tomorrow." I manage but I'm once again overwhelmed, and a dawning realisation is seeping over me. Del spoke to me about the 'Girls Unit' this morning, a lot, which did seem strange because there's only one class in comparison to six classes of boys. But the way he told me all about it, I just thought he was proud of it, making an example of it. It seems very likely now my role is going to include being with the girls; in this completely new territory.

Oh shit. I take a deep breath.

I always knew my role would be fully decided once the term began. The offer was for a position as a mentor and I will support wherever they ultimately decide is best. It will be ok. Of course it'll be ok. I just handled myself for six weeks in a foreign country, herding drunken hooligans- I can manage a couple of teenage girls with behavioural problems, can't I? The prospect is still unnerving.

"Jodie?" I turn from my declining thoughts to find a man of around my age, Asian and wearing a crisp white shirt with his hand outstretched. Taking it, I nod. "I'm Iqbal. Some people call me Iggy."

"Hi Iqbal. Iggy!"

"Well actually nobody calls me Iggy, I don't know why I said that!"

We're still shaking hands, his pumping mine energetically and I can't help but giggle at him.

"Anyway!" He lets go and his hand drops to his side. Then he runs it through his thick shock of black hair. "I'm Iqbal, the I.T teacher."

Iggy the IT teacher, it's got a ring to it! I return his genuine, wide smile.

"I think, well I hope, that you'll be working with me for some of the week, I wanted you full time. Not *you*! *Whoever* got the job!" He almost shrieks and another grin escapes from me.

"I get it." I ease him. He has none of the sexy charisma which oozes from Troy's every pore, but he has a friendly, kind aura.

"I was just wondering if they're going to use me in the Girls Unit?" I hope he'll laugh and say no way! But instead he nods, and my heart sinks a touch.

"I think that might be the plan. Some of the time in there, some of the time with me, in I.T. You don't need to look so unhappy, it's not as boring as it sounds!"

"No, sorry it's not that! I'm worn out, first day taking it all in." I bluff, snapping out of my reverie.

"Ok, well I would like to talk to you tomorrow, about my lesson plans and rules and everything for this term."

"Of course." I retrieve my timetable and we scan the columns. There is a slot before and after lunch labelled 'Prep/ Meeting Time'.

"Here or here?" I point, and he peers closer before nodding.

"After lunch. I'll meet you in here at one fifteen."

"Ok, nice meeting you." I tell him quickly feeling a little guilty he thought I disapproved of him, or I.T, or both! Actually, my mind is humming at the thought of working with the girls more so than the boys. The fact they're uncharted feels so much more nerve-wracking.

The staff room is almost empty of mentors now and as I turn to leave I catch Julie staring at me. I've barely seen the Head today and smile but she doesn't return it, so feeling like a naughty school-girl myself, I scurry out of the room.

***

I drive home with my music blaring and the windows down just because there are some milky rays of sunshine fighting through the clouds. It's August still, just, but the weather is cool and inconsistent in comparison to sunny Spain, so I'll take whatever of summer is left.

Today has been exhilarating and demanding I'm shattered and yet buzzing. My mind won't stop ticking over information, questions and what-ifs over tomorrow, next week and beyond. The new faces of the staff members float behind my eyes, mainly Troy's, but I keep pushing it aside and I think of beautiful Lacey, pleasant Iggy and Julie with her weird, robotic trance-like stare.

George has text saying he will be at the Trap, our local, if I fancy a drink this afternoon. I'm sorely tempted despite the fact that I'm supposed to be thoroughly detoxing but ultimately, I decide to save myself for tomorrow night.

A weekend, a *real* weekend, looms ahead of me. I have been working non-stop over the summer, albeit drinking and partying along the way. And prior to this, I worked 'unsociable hours' waitressing. I have only *ever* had a weekend off due to a special occasion since leaving school and now Friday night, Saturday and Sunday loom enticingly.

It actually feels like a special occasion!

Today has been so much more than I'd dared to hope. It's been shocking in places. Safeguarding was an eye-opener never mind the restraints training and this revelation about the Girls Unit. Gilbert exudes arrogance, Sean was full-on and Julie creeps me out but overall, I have good vibes about this new job thing.

Tonight, for the first time in yonks it feels, I'll be sensible. I have 'holds' to practise, notes to run over and I want to Google tactics for behaviour management. I want to do these things.

I'm already looking forward to tomorrow for so many reasons. I'll get my timetable and therefore clarification of my actual role- eek will it include the girls? I have my 'Tour and Induction' with Claire, the meeting with Iqbal, Troy's hot company and Lacey's mischievous chat! And of course, Gilbert, Sean, Julie, Claire, Lewis, Dom, Eric and many more to get to know; although some more inviting than others.

And it'll be Friday. I can go out for drinks maybe with George, or message Chantelle. Leila and Cat will both be working at the Trap anyhow.

Wow it's good to be happy. Sometimes I was scared my happiness in Magaluf was only temporary due to being so far away from home. But the reality is great, and that feels fantastic!

Teacher Training, Round 2!

I arrive at Belfry Lodge and have to wait to be buzzed in again by Terri, the receptionist. Her pudgy face grins at me warmly through the glass as she taps away at her computer and I make my way to the staff room.

The door isn't propped open today and I haven't got a key to let myself in. I look around, but the corridor is deserted. Opposite is another locked door with SLT stamped into the silver plaque. I have no idea what this means. Stock, Laundry and Toiletries springs to mind but I am barking up the wrong industry. I knock on the staffroom door feeling stupid but without another logical option.

Nobody answers so I knock a little louder and wait again. I can hear voices on the inside and I raise my hand to bash my fist into the wood with force when the door swings open. I almost bop Del on the end of his nose and his eyes widen in his bald head.

"God sorry!" I cry. "I haven't got a key, I was knocking…"

"Good morning to you too Jodie!" He blusters. "Come on, I wanted to see you anyway." He steps past me and lets himself into the SLT room. Inside Julie is sat at a desk, leaning back in a chair. Gilbert is sitting *on* her desk and I wonder what his purpose is here. Sitting, Lounging, Talking- SLT?

Neither of them bothers to look at me and they lower their voices to an inaudible level. Serious Legal Teacher-talk? There's another man, at a separate desk. I've seen him but don't know his name and he throws me a small wave which I bat back.

I loiter awkwardly by the door, still in my coat and holding my bag, whilst Del fishes around in a drawer. Finally, he straightens up with a digital camera in his hand.

"I need to take your picture for your ID badge." He tells me lurching forward. "That's fine against the white wall."

I've been lightly sweating in my discomfit and as I quickly unzip my coat, he's already raising the camera. Feeling seriously stupid with Julie and Gilbert as an audience, I swipe at my face and paste on a smile.

He takes one and I don't ask to look at the outcome. Julie is watching me, I can sense her scrutiny and I don't meet her eye.

"Claire is going to take you on the official induction this morning. Here's your starter kit. Your badge will be printed today. I'll get it to you later on." Del babbles gathering several items together. "There's your timetable too, you'll work it out, meet with the teachers, I'll catch up with you later."

"Thanks." I take the bundle of goodies from his clammy hands and I'm ushered from the room without time for questions. But I do now have a key and with it I let myself into the staffroom with an idiotic proud grin. I belong here!

I greedily study the timetable he's given me, I'm sure I'll 'work it out'. I should take the freedom as a compliment. Yes, lots of IT, a few other subjects all with the year 10's plus a full day and a half with the girls. It could be worse. I'm sure it'll be fine. I'm too preoccupied to grasp a commotion behind me but then Lacey grabs my shoulder.

"Are you in with the girls too? What days?" Her eyes are shining, she seems excited.

"Yes." I show her the page. "Tuesday afternoon and all-day Friday."

"I'm in there Wednesday, Thursday, Friday!" She holds up a manicured hand to be high-fived, so I do so.

"Yay!" I add not wanting to repeat yesterday's mistake with Iqbal. Plus, Lacey's elation suddenly makes me feel a whole lot better.

"We're meeting the new teacher after break. She couldn't make it yesterday. I'm a bit gutted *she* isn't a *he*, but you know, I understand why." She gives me a wicked smirk and I know already I'm going to enjoy working with her.

"What's her name?" I ask.

"Lizzy. I don't know anything else. I only got told just now that I'm actually working in there."

"I didn't even get told!" I laugh. "You know more than me."

"Harishma is too." She points out a girl with shoulder-length black hair and a pointy nose making a drink.

"Jodie?" Claire has come to fetch me, and I pack my things away into my locker.

"I'll speak to you at break." Lacey tells me and rushes to Harishma who's taking a seat at the table.

"Have you seen the whole place yet?" Claire asks me. She's round and pale with bobbed brown hair and caring eyes.

I shake my head, putting the key in my pocket.

"Let's start with that then, a full tour and I'll tell you all about it as we look."

***

Talk about mind blown. I'm sipping a coffee and trying to process everything I've just learned about values, rules, rewards and consequences, points for prizes, statuses. I feel like I could go home and nap!

Lacey is chatting animatedly beside me to Harishma, we're all meeting Lizzy soon and I'm wondering how she must be feeling about meeting us. What will she be like? We'll be working so closely together and on a sensitive, potentially explosive project.

"I wonder if we'll get to read their statements!" Harishma marvels rubbing her hands together.

"Of course we will." Lacey answers. "There have been six girls confirmed, so we'll have them."

Six doesn't sound too bad.

"What's a statement?" I ask them.

"It explains their background, their traits and needs." Harishma tells me.

'Traits' means characteristics and I presume 'needs' mean special circumstances in the classroom- but I couldn't guess what these might include. There really is so much to learn! With a silent groan I jot down a few more bullet points in my notebook.

"This one is such a geek!" Lacey exclaims happily thumbing in my direction. "I love her, she's so sweet."

She wraps an arm around my shoulder and side-hugs me with a surprising grip. I'm not usually one for hugging unless it's a close pal- or I'm very drunk. But I don't care, actually it makes me feel like one of the clan.

"Ahhh," Harishma grins sarcastically. "You can take all the notes then and we can have a copy of them."

"Fine." I tell her laughing. "I'd be making them anyway!"

This whole experience is becoming more and more like returning to school. I'm now 'in' with rebel Lacey, I've got a raging 'crush' on Troy, I'm scared of my head teacher and now bossy, lazy Harishma wants me to do the written work for her.

"Come on anyway, it's time!" Lacey tells us her blue eyes dancing. And now I'm about to meet another 'new girl', like me.

I visited the Girls Unit this morning as part of my tour. It's separated from the main school by two locked doors. Inside it feels calm and welcoming with two small 'pods' branching off from the large main classroom. The notice boards are boldly papered but bare of any work. It has its own little reception area with a glass panel and buzzer to let people in from the outside.

Is Lizzy sat in there right now, waiting for us?

As we approach the first of the doors Del appears, letting himself back out.

"She's all yours." He holds it open and smiles at us all as we pass him.

Harishma and Lacey are bursting with delight I can feel it. I hold my breath feeling nervous for myself and the other newbie as they unlock the other door separating us. We almost fall through it into a heap and a woman glances up before jumping to her feet.

She has cropped blonde hair and brown eyes. She's taller than all three of us with an athletic build and a makeup-less, pretty face. I automatically think 'Tom-boy'. I was a bit of one as a kid and can spot a fellow a mile off.

"Hi!" Her voice is feminine in comparison to her style. "I'm Lizzy. So, tell me- who's who?" She smiles openly, glancing from face to face and my insides flare, I instantly like her.

"I'm Lacey, this is Harishma and this is Jodie. We're all *so* excited about this!" Lacey cries.

"Me too!" Lizzy claps. Her voice has the subtlest southern twang. She turns to one of the two round tables, there are files piled on it. "Shall we?"

She gestures toward them with a roguish expression. I surmise she'd be *that friend* who I gaily follow into trouble because they make it sound like such a fun idea.

"I cannot wait to see who we've got." Harishma divulges. "I think that's the best part, unpicking them and finding out what makes them tick!"

"You're just a nosey bitch." Lacey calls her out.

"I must admit, I've been *obsessing* over it!" Lizzy inputs without embarrassment.

"I didn't even know I was working in here until this morning." I tell her. "But I *am* quite intrigued!"

Understatement of the year! My eyes are roving from Lizzy's fascinated face to the folders beside her filled with determining information.

"Ok, do you want one each or shall we do each one together?" We're skipping any further introductions for now in favour of discovering who our students will be.

"One each!" Harishma cries.

"No, don't be rude." Lacey chastises her. "We're in this together. Ignore her Lizzy, she's got no manners. And *this* one is a total nerd."

"And *she's* a rebel." I add playfully to which Lacey pretends to be shocked.

"And I'm… just me!" Lizzy bursts into laughter.

"We'll find out what you are." I tell her giggling and her eyes twinkle when they meet mine.

We take a seat and Lizzy finally takes the top file and opens it. Like a jigsaw puzzle, pictures become clearer in time as each piece falls into place.

***

"Well! I feel like I need a drink after uncovering that lot." Lizzy concludes to my unspoken but roaring agreement.

Not only have I had an unbarred introduction to the girls themselves but also a gruesome introduction to 'statements'. They're so invasive, detailing every aspect of their lives. In some respects, I'd rather not know everything I now do. I can no longer go in with a clean slate, yet I must avert judgements and preconceptions.

The last thing these kids need to see in my eyes is pity- or fear!

"That was some hard-core shit." Harishma comments her eyes glazed over.

They range from living with foster carers to aunties to drug-dependent mothers. All have suffered some kind of abuse in their childhood. All have been expelled numerous times for one incident or another.

"Poor sods." Lacey sighs and pulls Eve's details toward her. "This one is going to be tough. Out of school for four years! She'll need a long transition."

"Most of them will need a part-time timetable to begin with." Lizzy adds.

"I think she'll be a handful." Harishma points out the Year 10, Jayde.

I'm thinking they're all going to be a handful. The colourful selection of students might already be down to five since Camden is currently awaiting trial for assault. It's expected she'll receive a sentence, this time, so we're not sure if or when she will join us!

"I think we should go for lunch, all this thinking has given me an appetite." Lizzy suggests. "Can I tag on to you guys?"

"You can tag onto me." I laugh. "I'm also a tag-along! I only started yesterday."

"Really? Great! We're newbies together except you're one day older than me."

Lacey shoots us an exasperated look and rolls her eyes. "Come on you pair of tits."

We exit the double set of doors together and stroll up the corridor to the staff room. After lunch I have my meeting with Iqbal. It seems implausible there is yet more to discuss and take on board. Lizzy is right, a stiff drink is definitely in order later to help soak it all up.

"Oh Jodie." I turn to find Del scampering over. He has a plastic rectangle wrapped in a lanyard which he passes over. "Your badge. Are you getting on ok? Meeting relevant staff?"

I nod and he mirrors me, he's awkward, blithering. "Great, great, ok great. See you later."

He hurries away, and I catch the others up, untwining the ID. This is what the staff attach their key to and wanting to look the part I quickly fasten on my own. It's only then I look at the picture and let out a horrified gasp.

"What is it?" Harishma is immediately in my face and I dissolve into a fit of giggles. I don't want to show her, but I have no choice, Lacey is looking at us curiously now too.

"It's my badge, look!" I hold it out for them to see and Harishma grabs it to keep it steady.

She throws back her head and lets out an enormous bellow of laughter. This has Lizzy unashamedly galloping closer and she and Lacey take a good look too before also bursting with mirth.

Troy trots over. "What is it?"

He is also passed the card. One set of giggles after another emerges as Sean then Eric, Dom, Lewis, every one of the mentors takes a look. My face looks like a spooked beetroot, not helped by a flustered tan and emphasized by the white wall. The whites of my eyes are visible all the way around the iris and my teeth look vivid. I look awful.

It is that bad.

"I cannot wear it!" I splutter. It's making its second round now and a few more eruptions occur. "Just think what Eve will say!"

Our upcoming year 9 student was labelled as 'insulting and abusive' and Lizzy howls holding onto her side. Harishma is positively gleeful with all the fuss and Lacey finds it utterly hilarious. I can safely say I am fully inducted in this group.

***

For the remainder of the day I keep my badge in my pocket.

The meeting with Iqbal goes well. It is subdued in comparison to a lively lunchtime gossiping and squealing. We attracted a number of looks from other teachers and when Julie had come in we hushed suitably in unison. I notice she makes everybody feel uncomfortable to a degree, it seems our boss favours ruling by sheer terror.

Iqbal mentions, Julie 'runs a tight ship'. Lacey had described her as 'needing a dildo up her arse'. I'm unsure of her meaning, but overall she's obviously a bit of a stiff bitch. Teamed with her icy hair, steely eyes and overall cold demeanour, I think I'll just try and keep out of her way.

I enthusiastically thank Iqbal for the in-depth intro to IT and classroom life when he wraps up his latest spiel. I genuinely have been lapping it up, he was complimentary about my habit of note-taking and I also want him to realise yesterday's reaction was not personal.

"I'll see you Monday morning!" I call to him when I exit his classroom almost two hours after I first stepped in.

I find Troy loitering in the staff room. It's just gone three in the afternoon and I stifle the hope he is there waiting for me. I've barely seen him today. His presence appeals to my every sense. I tingle all over as he raises his eyes and smiles.

"Good day?" He asks casually and approaches me. He *has* been waiting for me I decide, and inwardly applause.

"Fantastic thanks. Except for the badge, you know! How about you?"

"Yes, fine thanks. Actually, I was thinking about the badge. I'm, erm, into photography and..." He holds up his hands, this shyness only makes him all the more attractive. "Not in a weird way, but I can take your picture. We could nip into a classroom now and on Monday I'll bring in a copy and we'll paste it over the top of *that*."

"Will it work?" I ask giggling nervously. Smiling for the camera will be awkward with this totty behind it but the alternative is worse.

"Yeah! It's still you isn't it? Nobody will even notice."

"Let me grab my things."

Decision made we dart into a classroom close by and I try not to dwell on that feeling of being alone with Troy in the still room. I fluff my hair, then pat it down and quickly smooth on some lip balm.

"Smile!" He singsongs and begins snapping away. His hobby doesn't surprise me, he looks 'arty' and completely natural behind a lens. "Here."

He hands me his phone and I scroll through a couple, they're all a dramatic improvement on the original and I pick one easily.

"Thanks." I tell him as he puts it away and opens the door for me.

"No problem." He holds my eye a second too long and my tummy fizzes.

The SLT door opens up-ahead, breaking the connection. The unnamed man, who waved at me this morning, steps out along with Julie.

"Have a great weekend!" Troy calls to them confidently as we cross their paths. I can't imagine ever addressing Julie like that.

"What does SLT mean?" I ask him before we split to our cars.

"Senior Leadership Team." He replies.

"And who *is* the *Senior Leadership Team*?"

"Julie and Neil who we just saw, plus Del and Claire."

"And what is a Senco?" I laugh. "Sorry, final question!"

"It's cool. It means 'special educational needs coordinator."

"Ok. Thanks. Bye!" I climb into my car. That's more pieces of the puzzle collected. I can only hope Neil is the 'alright one' of the SLT because so far Julie is a cow, Del seems drippy and Claire nice but a bit soft!

But Lizzy and Lacey are awesome. Troy just divine, Iqbal is sound, Harishma funny and Sean a little absurd. I'm almost looking forward to work on Monday! How weird is that?

Almost! Up until now *that* 'Friday Feeling' has been all but an elusive sensation. I find it raging through my veins now as I hoick up my music and cruise the route home on an utter high.

That Friday Feeling!

My phone beeps and I take a break from prancing half-naked around my room to find it's my mum.

Can you turn it down please?

I tut and smirk. What's she like? I'm two floors up in my attic bedroom but I can hear her now maintaining *the bass carries.*

If I had my own place I could play my music as loud as I wanted but I respectfully adjust the knob of my stereo, just a touch. I did move out before, with a boyfriend, Scott. Then I moved back in again, in May last year. Really I'm grateful for her giving me that option, plus I can't afford rent on my wage alone. Belfry Lodge pays less than my job before and I no longer have the luxury of cash-in-the-hand tips either.

I continue with my jig, the tunes are hardly quiet even now, and get back to browsing my wardrobe.

What to wear when I want to show off my tan before it completely fades and yet I'm only going to the village pubs, with my brother. Last week 'showing off' would have been my bare chest to a range of blokes. This week it'll have to be much tamer! I'll get away with a pair of shorts, but a boob tube is out of the question. I finger a denim skirt with a rip below the pocket. Dane loved me in that one. Of course, he could be out tonight amongst the samey faces.

When I left for Magaluf he was in an already rocky relationship. If they're still together he won't be there. If not, then who knows? I won't wear that skirt. I wouldn't want him thinking it's a subliminal message.

His face lingers for a moment in my minds-eye. I used to trust it, love it so much. I can visualise every facial expression. It's funny how where once there was so much feeling- true affection, crushing hurt, then burning anger. Now I find nothingness.

It's sad I suppose. It hadn't been all bad, I suppose.

I dismiss the creeping melancholy and select a stripy cotton playsuit. His actions will not define who I am. I let my mind fill once again with the here and now and set about preening my hair and face.

"I'm meeting George at the Trap." My voice sounds imposing on the quiet living room. My mum is ironing and looks at me, screwing up her nose.

"I thought you were *detoxing!*"

"It'll only be a couple. *And* it's a Friday!" I tell her resenting having to justify myself. She knows I've worked every Friday night for yonks and George doesn't get half the lectures I seem to. Never mind her boyfriend Keith. Needless to ask where he is!

She shrugs as if to say *it's your choice*. Which I could remind her, it is! I say bye and shake off the huff as I stride down the street and guilt replaces annoyance. She shouldn't be cooped up alone whilst her other half gallivants the night away, every night. But, it's *her* choice!

The streets look just the same as I left them. It's getting on for seven, there's barely anybody on foot and the evening light is becoming golden. Before I went away I'd gotten skittish walking alone and especially in the dark thanks to certain events, yes Dane related. There's a skip to my step though and I just know such feelings of foreboding have gone.

Both Leila and Cat are working behind the bar tonight. Through them I hear all manner of gossip about the regulars, myself included up until recently. I virtually stopped going out just after the break-up. Mortified at what people might be thinking.

It is a con but also a pro of living in a close community. Because I actually don't mind indulging in questionable whisperings about other people! Our village is seamed together with talk. Rumours knit alliances and rivals alike. Now I am no longer one of the central focuses, I can go back to enjoying the excitement from the side-lines.

Up-a-head my destination looms into view. It is a large period building, sitting on one edge of a roundabout, providing a snapshot of the goings-on in the centre of the village. There are figures loitering in the front doorway smoking, even though there's an equipped outdoor area behind.

I wonder if George is round the back or playing pool. He could be watching me approach from behind the rectangle, glinting windows. All manner of eyes could be watching me; the 'Rugby lot', the 'cowboys' and the 'hillbillies', the 'younger lot' and the 'old-boys'.

The men in the doorway nod at me as I pass them. I don't know their names. They could know me as Jodie the karaoke singer or Jodie the div that went out with that twat Dane. I pull the wooden door open and enter a crowded bar.

Considering it is only early evening there are plenty of people about. There's a cricket match on the dusty TV screens, and a crowd playing cards, another couple chucking darts and the pool table is surrounded. I can't see George.

"Jodie!" Leila exclaims from behind the bar. I give her a little wave and head over. Cat comes barrelling out of the glass-wash room and squeals when she sees me.

"Hello darlings." I beam at them.

"It seems so strange you being in here!" Cat cries.

"I was only gone for six weeks." I remind her.

"It felt like forever!" She groans. We've not known each other a year but she's become a firm friend. "What you drinking?"

"George got her one in." Leila tells us and begins pouring a pint of cider. I smile gratefully. Once upon a time I tried sticking to spirits because they're less calories, but I can't face them yet even if it isn't Rushkinoff vodka.

"Where is he?" I ask them.

"Outside." Cat replies before gushing. "Tell us all about today! What did you do? Quick!"

"Yes, who's the fitty? Are there more?" Leila questions. I giggle at her because I'm sure before she came to visit me in Magaluf she was never this forward. Just a few days in that intoxicating place were perhaps enough to coax her into peeking out of her shell.

"Yes, there are and they go out together sometimes, so you'll definitely be coming with me."

She claps her hands together. Customers are gathering around us so there's no more time to enthuse.

"I'll chat to you both later." I tell them and leave them to work, in search of George. I find him sitting at a table on the terrace outside and he calls over.

"Hey!"

"Thanks for the drink." I say as I take a seat. His mates, Mark, Russ and Jag welcome me retrospectively.

"So how was it?" Russ refers to Magaluf, not my first days at work. Like most people they haven't seen me since my return.

"Amazing!" I admit. "I thought I didn't want to come home, but it isn't so bad."

"What, mum isn't doing your head in yet?" George laughs, and I roll my eyes. She's lovely but it's our shared joke that her constant fretting is annoying.

"I think I could do it." Mark says taking a decisive glug of his drink. "Next year maybe."

"Go for it." I advise. He has all three PR attributes; he's attractive, he can be an incredible dickhead at times and he'll whip his sizeable penis out at the drop of a hat. "You'll fit right in."

"I'm going to take that as a compliment Jodie." He tells me, and I grin nodding.

"You can tell me if it is or not next year, can't you?"

It isn't long before we have all revisited the bar to fetch in a round. The drinks I played down to mum as being a 'couple' is rapidly exceeding a 'fair-few' and when we move inside I take the opportunity to catch up with Leila some more.

"I cannot believe you've already bagged another fitty!" She cries talking about Troy.

"I've *not* bagged him." I retaliate giggling but I'm not blind, the signs were all there.

"You so are going to though aren't you?" It's a rhetorical question but I shake my head anyway. "Do not be a fool!" She says flippantly.

Since when was she the pushy one? I like her new attitude but I'm feeling far from foolish.

"A fool repeats their mistakes and expects a different outcome." I retort firmly.

"Touché!" She giggles. "So, is he fitter than Justin?"

She is referring to *that* absolutely gorgeous guy from Magaluf; this is her marker of godliness.

"As fit." I tell her and whip out my phone. I took the time to observe Troy's full name and find his profile on Facebook. It's on complete privacy lockdown- *safeguarding*- but I've got a screenshot of the one available picture. Stalking him in this way is merely to prove a point, obviously. She takes a look and agrees eagerly.

"Yes, Jodie! You have *got* to go for it *if* you get the chance."

"Go for what?" Cat appears and Leila darts to serve a customer leaving me to explain.

"Is he as fit as Justin?" She asks now, and I stare at her for a moment, staggered. When did my friends decide on this as the new ratings scheme?

"Leila showed me him on Facebook, I've been looking at his pictures ever since when I need a boost!" She yelps with laughter and I can't help but giggle myself and I show her the same image of Troy that I showed Leila. She lets out a low whistle.

"Girl, he is fine!" She puts on a crappy American accent and I nod grinning.

"Yup." But I'm still not going there.

"Shall we go up the road?" Jag asks George from my side. His jaw has been swinging for the past hour and 'up the road' is the Sports Bar (or *Snorts* Bar if you like) it is renowned for attracting dealers and users alike.

"Yeah man, why not?" George is happy to go wherever the ladies might be and admittedly it does draw an all-round younger crowd due to the weekend DJ's and its reputation.

I bid farewell to Leila and Cat promising to see them both tomorrow and we leave the noisy pub for the hushed night time street.

It is stuffy, dark and loud in the Sports Bar. There are bodies busily dancing, playing pool and leaning around the circumference of the room.

"What do you want?" George asks me. I spy the 'Cocktail of the Weekend', Cheeky Vimto, and immediately point. It's got to be done! Whilst I wait for my drink I quickly scan for faces I recognise. Poll, Tyler; old school friends and some of Dane's mates but no Dane himself.

Nods are exchanged. The news will travel to him that I'm back in the village like molten lava. I think of his sister, I haven't spoken to her in ages and I ought to message. It isn't her fault he's a twat and we had become quite good friends.

"Here."

I take the blue-black liquid from George and taste it. Sickly, sweet, blue WKD and port, not a cheap imitation like Blush had me selling toward the end. It tastes delicious and reminds me of the Maga strip.

My surroundings almost match the memories and my nerves fire up with pleasure. I let my hips swing to the music and glance at the DJ, Ashley Tyler. I used to have such a crush on him! He's a few years older than me and never would have looked twice at me back then. I doubt he'd look twice now either, he's still gorgeous and undoubtedly not short of offers.

"Fancy a game?" George is calling into my ear. "Doubles, me and you stick Mark and Russ."

Signalling agreement, I ask. "Where's Jag?"

"Where'd you think?" He nods to the toilet door.

"I'll cock block you!" I tease him as he puts a coin down on the table. It's an ongoing joke that I get in the way of him pulling.

"Nah, I've already shagged the fitties in here." He casts his eyes around and drops out a few cute smiles to lingering girls. If he wasn't my brother I'd possibly dislike his cocky arrogance. As it stands I find him entertaining, and a helpful insight into man logic which involves football, drinking, cash and sex in no particular order.

"She's fuckin' getting it tonight!" Russ pipes up beside us and rubs his hands together hungrily eyeing a girl nearby. I raise my eyebrows and side glance him.

"Does she have a choice in the matter?" I joke dryly.

"Who could possibly turn down this strapping specimen?" His words are slurred, and I eye up the numerous beer stains on his shirt.

I choose not to burst his bubble.

"I'm gunna have a quick go on the bandit while we're waiting." Mark mutters and eyeing the flashing machine with the same lust, he wanders off.

"That's him skint." George remarks watching his back retreat.

"And I'm gunna go and make advances!" Russ announces. We watch him half trip in the brunette's direction. A guy from the 'younger lot' taps George and hands him a cue.

"Looks like it's just us then. Watch out for the seven-baller!" He cries in glee and begins setting up our game.

Despite growing up here and sporting similar features, people often mistake us for a couple. We're close for siblings. I feel lucky he's one of my best friends. But as happy as I am for him to play the main man in my life, he can't satisfy my craving for contact.

Neither, I am aware, can Troy. I've tried to push thoughts of him from my mind telling myself I got hurt before. But there is so much more to it than just a physical attraction, there's no point denying it, I already like so much about him. He's ticking boxes for things I didn't even know I'd created. Creative hobby- check, natural vitality, charm and charisma- check. Tattoos, unique style- check.

"Your break or mine?" George asks.

"You take it." I offer but he's already shaking his head and pulling out a coin. "Heads or tails?"

Tails I don't pursue this with Troy, I think.

"Heads." I say.

"Tails!" He bounds to the other end of the table to take his shot. The reaction in my heart tells me I still want to go there. What if ignoring it is a mistake?

I watch as numbered balls scatter over the blue felt. Life can't be lived on the result of a coin toss after all!

George chats to me about various dates and tells me juicy morsels of gossip from his circle of friends as we play. I finish off a variety of drinks and allow myself to appreciate some of the less wasted guys in here. I notice Russ seems to have successfully hit his target and wonder what state she must be in to find him an option. It doesn't matter how horny I feel, I'll still choose wisely.

Once back home, I clumsily peel off my outfit and reflect. My first night out in public has been Dane-free and it has been nice to find my feet before facing a chance reunion. Nobody approached me and demanded to know the gory details, which isn't an unrealistic worry in this village. Plus George is still friendly with him, I know that, but he stayed away from the subject and ultimately, I'm glad.

I'll probably be out again tomorrow so plenty of time for prying questions and unwelcome details yet. And I'm sure mum will be vocally disapproving of a second night out!

It would be so cool to have my own place. I really do love my mum but I'm single and ready to mingle and she will be privy to my every coming and going. There'll be no option to bring a man back here either.

I suppose living in Magaluf gave me a taste of freedom and independence, reminded me of what moving out the first time was like. Although I lived with a boyfriend then so there were no bringing back men for a cheeky fumble! No thought of it even.

But anyway, there's no option of moving out just yet anyway.

I climb under the covers and set an alarm. I don't want to wake up too late tomorrow. I've got things to do and people to see.

I know where I want to be headed, that's the main thing. I'm rid of toxic energy and instead full of positivity. I will get my own place eventually and I'm going to be the best I possibly can be in this new role.

I lie content and allow the room to gently spin me into a deep sleep.

Saturday Surprises

I'm reading and re-reading the Facebook message I've just received from Aaron. I met him during my last couple of days in Magaluf, we hit it off and now he wants me to go and meet him. In Madrid. For a dirty weekend! So, he hasn't actually described it like *that* but how else can it be labelled?

It's his friend's apartment, he's suggesting two nights. In Madrid! It sounds so glam, these things don't really happen to me. Well they do now! I grin to myself, picturing the look on Leila's face when I drop this in.

Aaron is from the UK but he lives in Barcelona, and obviously also has friends in Madrid. My heart vibrates against my ribcage, I promised myself I'd say yes and travel more. This is both!

Flights to Madrid, I type into Google and results ping up from in the region of forty pounds. One hundred max then once petrol and parking are booked in too.

Oh, sod it, just go for it!

Sound's great, thanks for the invite ☺ When are you thinking?x

I'm smiling like a lunatic now. I've imagined the adventures meeting so many new people could lead to. Madrid, I'm going to Madrid!

By the time I've showered and been for breakfast with George at the local greasy spoon, it's all arranged. In merely three weeks I'll be jetting off, again.

"I hope he's not some weirdo, that's all I'm saying." George gives me a grim look.

"Don't be daft, I *have* met him before, he had friends with him and everything. Plus, I've seen his Facebook profile since, he goes to work, he's got a dog, he's *normal*!"

His eyebrows raise at my choice of word and I know what he's thinking- what *is* normal?

"What about this *friend* where you're staying?" He asks.

"He's going on holiday with his girlfriend." I reply and trusting my judgement he nods.

"Fair enough. Mum's gunna have kittens. Just saying!" He stands up now we're finished. "I'm going bookies then for a lunchtime pint, you can come if you want?"

"I'm going to see Leila, she's got the day off. She doesn't know, I'm going to Madrid! With a fit boy!" I clap my hands gleefully and George grins.

"You're nuts. But fair play to ya, why not ay?"

We split paths and I half-jog to Leila's. I'm not a complete moron and obviously George's concerns struck chords. There's a crowd of what-ifs lurking in the shadows of my mind but all in all the likeliest negative is he's actually a twat, we fall out on the first night and I have to book a room elsewhere on my credit card.

I wonder how reformed Leila will take the news. Pre-Maga Leila's first response would definitely be panicked shock. Reaching the shared house, I buzz for her room.

The lock on the frame crackles telling me to enter and I rush up the stairs and along the hall.

"Oh Leila!" I cry as I burst into her room. "What the hell?"

She looks like a wilted daisy perched on the edge of her bed and I can see from her blotchy skin she's been crying.

"Babe, what's happened?" I rush to her, forgetting my glory and kneel so I can see her face.

"We're being evicted! Jodie, what am I going to do? There's nothing out there! I can't afford rent!" She immediately breaks into alarmed chirruping. "Six weeks! I've been searching, and I haven't saved as much as I wanted! In six weeks, we've got to be out!"

"Woah, Leila." I soothe knowing if I say 'calm down' or 'chill out' it will likely induce a red-headed rage. "Take a breath honey. Let's think this through together."

There's a tiny scratch at my brain. I could move out with her, couldn't I? I was only thinking about it last night...

"Jodie, there's nothing!" She stresses. "Well, ok I *can* afford a room in *some* areas but they're really not nice and-"

Desperate to put a stop to her frantic hysterics when I have a solution I blurt out.

"We could get a place together."

She stops dead and looks me squarely in the face.

"Say again?" She squeaks and cocks her head to one side. I can't help but dissolve into manic giggles at her pinched expression.

"I said," my voice wavers with mirth, "we could get a place together."

She bursts into tears and to my astonishment so do I. I'm just so overcome. Things keep on taking turns for the better.

"I am so fucking happy!" Leila exclaims when snivelling we finally pull ourselves together.

"Me too! And, guess what?" Before we can begin house hunting, exciting enough, I have to tell her about Aaron! Getting a place with Leila could mean no spare cash for whimsical future holidays, however it provides a place for visitors to come to me.

50

I spill the beans about Madrid, she reacts ecstatically (Maga transformation confirmed) and we return to the very pressing topic of a shared abode.

"So, I wasn't going to mention this until it was all more official." Leila begins looking intently at her duvet. "I'm going for key holder at the Trap, which means I'll be part of the management team." She meets my eye and I'm smiling from ear to ear. "So, although I'll be getting a pay rise it still won't be much!"

"Leila, that's such awesome news, well done!"

"Well, it just got me thinking when I visited you. I said didn't I, after that day India got beaten up, I want more from my job. I want more from my life!" I'm nodding enthusiastically as she cries. "Oh my god, moving in with you will be the best thing! I can't afford a lot though, even paying half."

"Me neither." I concede, forgetting for a moment my thrill. "My monthly pay is a pittance because it's spread across twelve months and we only actually work thirty-nine weeks a year."

"Ok, I don't think I can share with you. I'll be *so* jealous of you when it's the school holidays!"

"I won't have any money to do anything." I assure her.

"Yeah but you'll be able to chill. In our house! I wonder if we'll have a big garden?"

"Do you want to live locally still?" I ask her now extracting my phone and loading up a search engine.

"I do really. But I understand with Dane and that, if you want to-"

"No." I cut her off. "Thanks, but you want to stay here, you work down the street and my mum, brother, grandad… they're here too, it makes sense to me."

It only takes a few minutes of browsing to realise there's nothing in our price range available through a letting agent. I set up several alerts just in case.

"I'll ask around." Leila says positively. "Somebody might know somebody."

She is right, and I physically cross my fingers.

We leave to visit Cat together and bring her the latest instalments. She's such an excitable person I fear she'll pop with news of Aaron, Madrid, Leila's promotion and a potential housemate situation. I think of Cat like my wise owl. She's only a few years older yet runs a family household of two kids and a partner and manages their eldest daughter's autism with superhuman energy. She has vested interest in my new role at Belfry because she knows Esmay will not attend a mainstream school. Since meeting her around Christmas last year she's been an emotional rock and a cheerleader of my triumphs, despite going through challenging times herself.

"Boobies squeam! Ello Aya! Hiiiiaaa Oh Deee!" Daniel chatters hilariously referring to his mum as 'boobies'. Nobody knows why, and the irony is she's completely flat chested! But he's right, Boobies does scream. So do me and Leila.

"This is all so amazing!" Cat yells. "You're going to be my boss Leila! Do you want a tea to celebrate?"

She clicks on the kettle anyway and Esmay comes into the room on her tiptoes with her hands clasped over her ears.

She hollers loudly, clearly unimpressed with the commotion.

"Sorry baby girl are we being too loud?" Cat doesn't expect Es to answer; she's still non-verbal at almost five and instead she switches on the radio and goes over to her.

"It's these crazy aunties of yours, they have good news! Shall we dance?" She asks and holds out her hands. I watch transfixed as Es lowers her own arms and takes her up on the offer.

"Are we dancing Es?" She asks laughing now, swinging her elbows back and forth.

Their bond is so pure they don't need words to communicate.

"Me wan oo dance!" Daniel cries from my kneecaps so I sweep him up and join in with the impromptu boogying.

Leila makes the celebration teas, we've already decided to toast things properly later, and eventually we settle down for a chat with the kids occupied in the living room. With two under-fives we're rarely without interruption for long and over a second mug we finally finish up covering details of Belfry Lodge.

"Sounds like it is going to be completely new and challenging but in a really good way." Cat concludes.

"Exactly. Like living with Leila!" I jibe, and she swots me.

"Speaking of which, we'd better get off, gel ready and put the word out that we're looking! You never know, by tonight we could have somewhere." She grins at us both.

It seems wishful thinking for it to happen so fast but crazier things have happened and I don't knock her positive mental attitude. I'm so pleased she's found her confidence and motivation, the admission earlier sealed it, Magaluf did have some kind of effect on her too.

We leave Cat's and stand on the corner which will divide us, talking for a further twenty minutes.

"Come to mine at six and bring a bottle of wine?" She instructs. "We'll drink that and then go out."

"Ok." I agree, and we finally split ways. I now not only have to tell my mum I'm off to Madrid to meet a virtual stranger but also that I've decided to move out. I drop George a text explaining so that he's heard it from me first.

"You just don't see the danger Jodie! You watch those grisly programmes about murderers, how can you be so sure he's safe?"

"Mum!" I cry exasperatedly for the third time. "I've told you, I'll get you the address. I'll be in contact with you! I looked after myself in Magaluf didn't I?"

"Only just by the sounds of some of your stories!" She huffs and stomps into the kitchen. She's so predictable, I fume.

"I worry Jodes." She turns to look at me intensely and I see only affection.

"Well you won't have to when I've moved out will you? You won't know what I'm getting up to then!" I pout virtually reverting to a teenager.

She gives me a lingering look and then a small smile. "I'm glad you're open with me Jodie. I think! I'll always worry about you though."

"Well I wish you wouldn't because I don't plan on settling down anytime soon." I stubbornly retort, and she gives off a withering sigh.

"I'm going for a shower." I say. "And you don't need to worry! Honestly mum, it's pointless."

What *is* pointless is me telling her this and I leave her to it. She's taken the moving out news well. She likes Leila and knew I'd leave again sooner or later. Possibly once the shock of my impromptu trip dies down she'll have time to conjure some worries about that too.

Time for a hot shower and then I'll be getting ready to hit the tiles again. I don't plan on making a habit of this in my oh-so-fabulous new life, I won't be able to afford to once plans come to fruition, but things are just calling to be celebrated. Plus, like Leila said, something could turn up tonight!

***

"Oh, frigging hell!" I declare.

We've entered the Trap which is heaving, it's almost nine and the Saturday night crowd are going full swing to a live band, but there is Dane. Slumped in a seat his eyes are blurred, skin pasty and mouth sagging.

"Gross!" I giggle feeling a little tipsy on the wine we already drank. He hasn't seen us. I doubt he could focus even if he did look in our direction.

"You want to go somewhere else?" Leila calls in my ear. "We could go up the road?"

I look across at her. "Shall we?"

We nod in unison, turn on our heel and leave again. It doesn't bother me really, him being there, but people will be reminded of our history seeing us both and I just can't be bothered to revisit it. And the state of him! He's likely had a bust-up with his girlfriend, history repeating itself. Talk about love being blind.

We reach the Fox and it is also busy. They have a DJ and karaoke and Leila gives me a knowing smile.

"I'm not singing!" I tell her but she just grins. I say it every time and then I have a few drinks and start feeling brave. To be honest I haven't done it for a while. Just another thing Dane didn't like so I stopped doing. Ironic really when only the second time we met I was singing!

I feel the first inklings of defiant temptation. I do enjoy it. I admit I must be a bit of an exhibitionist at heart. I get such a thrill belting out lyrics, performing.

We decide to share another bottle of wine. Dennis is propping up the bar and he gives us a near toothless grin.

"Hello beautiful ladies!" He greets and leans in to kiss Leila's cheek. "Let me get this for you." He tugs out a twenty.

"Aww Den, are you sure?" Leila coos.

"Course I am, it's no good to me when I'm dead is it?" He hands over the cash for our bottle.

"Thanks Dennis." I pat his arm and we turn with our glasses to find a spot to loiter.

"Bless him, he's so sweet." I say in her ear as we push through the mob.

"Hiya Helen! Alright Mick?" Leila greets punters and I offer my own share of hellos.

"Den's a good guy." She says as we find a ledge to put our drinks on. "And he's absolutely loaded! He barely has to buy a drink in the Trap he gets bought so many because everyone loves him. I wouldn't have let him pay otherwise, and he insists on it."

I acknowledge her reasoning and sway to the music whilst taking stock of who's present. The thing with a village is I recognise most people but only know most by the nicknames we've made up.

"Leila, looking gorgeous as usual." Shane sidles up to our sides with a few cronies in tow. "You too Jodie, you've been somewhere hot." He comments taking in my tan.

"Been working in Magaluf." I reply smirking.

"You dirty bitch!" He assumes the details. "So, what brings you both out looking all glammed up?"

"We're celebrating!" Leila declares.

"Me too!" He holds up his pint to be chinked. "So, what's your news?"

"Well there's quite a lot really." She grins widely. "Jodie started her new job this week. I'm doing some training with work, so I'll be promoted. *And* we've decided to get a place together!"

"Congratulations, both of you. So have you got somewhere?"

"Not yet." Leila takes a swig of wine. "We're keeping our ear to the ground. So, what's your news?"

"Well my news could help you pair out!"

"How?" I ask him my ears pricking up. Leila's eyes have lit up in anticipation.

"Moving out aren't I. Johnno is off to Australia and you know I've lived at the flat with him for seven years. Time to get on the property ladder. Sooo…"

I understand in an instant what he's suggesting.

"Oh my god," I virtually whisper, my mind going into overdrive. Whatever actually caused Dane to get sloshed at the Trap tonight, I'm thankful of it for sending us up here.

"Oh my god!" Leila shouts. "*The* flat! I've been to some banging parties there!"

I don't know where it is and turn to her. "Where is it? What's it like?"

"It's just up the road from the Trap, it's alright, it'll need a good clean!" She shoots Shane a playful look. "Only kidding darling. So, can you put us in touch with the Landlord?"

"Landlady." He corrects. "Jane's lovely. In fact, I'll text her right now and put in a good word."

"Thank you!" Leila cries.

"Yeah thanks." I add meaningfully. "And congratulations on buying a house! Have you got anything yet?"

"No but I'll be out the flat in less than a month. I'm moving in with the 'rents because I don't want to rush into a decision."

"This is so perfect!" Leila squawks.

"When's the housewarming?" Shane's friend pipes up and she winks at him.

"Your invite will be in the post, obviously!"

My heart is pounding. It's a sign, it's meant to be! Please, please let this happen. This is going to happen, even if not here, somewhere. But I've got such a good feeling already, it's like it's a definite!

"I'm going for a smoke girls. Leila is your number still the same?" She nods, and he continues. "I'll message you when I hear back."

"Awesome!" She claps, unable to contain her excitement. I feel the same, my face might split with the smile on it.

"I knew it! I knew something would come up!" She tells me as they leave.

"When did you party there?" I ask her.

"Oh, years back, when they first moved in really. I've shagged him you know." She giggles and my eyes boggle.

"No way! He's loads older than us!"

"Only ten years on me!" She responds pursing her lips.

"You secret hoe." I tease her, but I am a little shocked at the revelation. Since I befriended Leila she's been my project. Broken hearted and unwilling to give dating a go I just kind of assumed she hadn't had a sex life previous to her failed relationship.

"It wasn't a secret back then." She cries. "We were at it for a few months actually."

"So you've already christened our flat?" I giggle.

"He's slept with the whole village in there since! That flat has seen more action than a brothel."

"Well hopefully your rendezvous has come in handy!" I muse and we both go quiet amid the lively atmosphere.

"Guess what?" Shane returns, grinning from ear to ear. "She says I can give you a tour and if you like it, it's yours!"

"Wow!" I gasp as elation floods me. This is unbelievable and yet it is really happening. "When can we go?"

"Tonight if you want baby, spend your first night there, with me." He flirts, and I cringe imagining him with Leila. I vaguely remember his sister babysat me a few times, he's way too old!

"Tomorrow?" He suggests realising it's not happening. I happily would go and look tonight but not with a stopover on the cards.

"Yes, we can do tomorrow can't we Jodie?" I nod, and Leila continues. "My shift starts at three, so it will have to be before then."

"I'll be up from midday." He tells us. "Just bell me Leila? It looks a bit scruffy because there are boxes everywhere, but you'll get the idea."

Everything has become hazy. I'm slightly intoxicated, yes, but the natural high of today's events is taking its toll.

"I reckon I am going to sing after all!" I exclaim overcome. I've not even been home a week. I never expected things to be this great!

I belt out a rendition of Upside Down by Paloma Faith and silently salute Dane for being the catalyst which caused this turn of events. I'd secretly thanked him in Maga too, maybe without his destructive influence I never would have just thought *fuck it* and stayed. He's helped me along in the right direction, paid above and beyond his penance and he doesn't even know it.

Lindzi Mayann

'The Tales of Jodie and Leila'

I open my eyes and feel enveloped in an instant happy buzz. My mouth tastes like shit but I did bring a glass of water to bed with me so I quickly down it.

What time is it? Not ten yet. It's an amazing feeling to not be getting ready for a shift serving Sunday lunches. It's even great not whipping on a pair of shorts and hitting the strip for a shift in the sunshine. Lying in my bed, genuine pleasure rumbles around my stomach and I tap open Facebook to check how the weekend has panned out for everyone else.

I have a number of messages and notifications. I know Aaron will have been messaging and I click the icon to see who else has.

My heart thumps. Ashley Tyler. Sent at one o'clock this morning.

Hey how you doing? Was good to see you Friday ☺

I literally cannot believe it. We have never even spoken before. We've managed being Facebook friends somehow, we have plenty of mutual friends. But I didn't think he really knew I existed. I used to virtually drool when I saw him as a youngster! Thinking of him now makes me feel a little breathless and I exit that screen thinking what the hell do I reply?

Even though I scroll the newsfeed, I barely take in what I read. All I can think is Ashley Tyler has messaged me. In the end, I bring up his most recent profile picture. Those blueish eyes against light brown skin, neatly shaved hair, a nose piercing and designer stubble, yep does it for me. After looking at a number of his pictures I go back to his message.

I'm good thanks, how are you? I spotted you DJ-ing ☺ *it was a good night*

I hit send and try not to overthink it. Instead, I reply to Aaron agreeing I'm looking forward to seeing him too. What a hussy!

But seriously Ashley is gorgeous and he's just the distraction I need to keep my mind off Troy. Although the thought of seeing *him* tomorrow causes another torrent of tingling within me. Magaluf has created a monster!

I just need to get to Tuesday without hearing back from the STD clinic and I'm officially all clear. I send another prayer to anybody listening, promising I will never have unprotected sex ever again if I get away with it this time.

I type Leila a quick message, so she knows not only I am awake but that I've received yet another exciting message. And I am actually gagging at the bit to see the flat, despite being side-tracked. I tell her I will be at hers for midday on the dot.

My phone vibrates in my hand and I see Ashley has replied. Luckily, I can see the message without needing to open it. Being too keen is not a good look.

All is well ta ☺ Yeah been DJ-ing there a while now. Glad you're not with that twat anymore, I always thought you were too good for him. What you doing today?

I'm floored. He not only acknowledges me, but he's taken note of my relationship status and is obviously referring to Dane since he *is* a twat plus I rarely went out locally with Scott. I climb out of bed and gather things I'll need for a shower, I eventually reply.

Haha, thanks yeah took me too long to figure it out! I'm viewing a flat today, hopefully moving out soon ☺ how about you?

By the time I've washed and changed there's another message waiting for me.

That's great news! See what happens when you get rid of bad vibes?! ☺ When's the housewarming, haha. I'm just chilling, if you fancy a film or something later…

Well that's forward, I can't help but think. I'm not naïve, he's after something and not a full-blown relationship I assume. Would I even want that though, another relationship so soon? I barely know him, but I like the *vibes* comment and his beautiful face is welcome in my life regardless of his intentions.

***

"He's alright to be fair." Leila is telling me since revealing she almost slept with Ashley! *Almost* thankfully else it wouldn't have felt right for me to do the same. There's literally so much I don't know about her I realise. I'm intrigued to know who else she had relations with in her pre-me life.

"He's easy to chat to. You could have actually gone round and watched a film and it not been awkward."

"That's not why I turned him down!" I laugh. "I just didn't want to jump in the sack with him on a Sunday afternoon, if that's what he'd tried. It seems slutty."

"But waiting until Saturday night is ok?"

I shrug giggling. "Well a Saturday will involve alcohol and then it doesn't seem as bad! Plus, I'll need Dutch courage, bloody hell he's so fit!"

"He is, I suppose I've got used to him because I knew him so well."

"I can't imagine getting used to him." I muse before pushing aside thoughts of the newly arranged 'date'.

We're on our way to Shane's flat. Possibly our new home! Leila called him earlier and woke him up. The rent is way cheaper than a house but he thinks Jane might increase it slightly before we takeover. Still it is within our budget, just. There's not much that's going to put me off.

"It's there." Leila is pointing ahead.

"Where?" The street is full of detached houses and I frown.

"The one with a van on the front."

I'm not sure what I was imagining but the magnificent, red-brick property was not it.

"Marshamonvilla." I read the plaque above the peeling black door aloud. "I love it!"

Leila knocks. "The flat is upstairs, the guy who lives down here uses the back door. If things haven't changed, since *then*."

Shane swings the door open and beams. His eyes are bloodshot, and he croaks.

"Good morning."

"Afternoon." I reply.

"Only just!" He yawns as if to prove a point and thumbs a door behind him. "That door leads to Billo's flat, but he never uses it."

He confirms things haven't changed since *then* and I smirk.

"Right this way." We follow him through the tiny porch and up a narrow flight of stairs.

"Bathroom," he points to a door on our left. "Living room. Bedroom number one. Kitchen." He points down the dingy hallway. "And the second bedroom comes off the kitchen. Help yourself, Johno's out. Sorry about the mess."

I poke my head into the first door. A small bathroom, a little worse for wear but not a touch on what I saw in the Magaluf worker apartments. Living room is spacious, first bedroom large too. The kitchen is a good enough size and I spy a stable-style door at the other end.

"There's a bedroom through there?" I ask as we approach it.

"My bedroom!" Shane calls out from another room.

I give it a shove and it comes undone with a click. We have to duck to enter but there's a step down and we can straighten up again once inside.

"I love it." I whisper. "It's like a secret cave!"

It isn't much smaller than the other bedroom, but the low ceiling gives the impression it's tiny. I think it's charming!

"You can have this room if you want mate." Leila tells me, and I envision it full of my own things.

"Did you, *do it*, in here?" I murmur.

"We did it everywhere!" She hisses back giggling and I think how it sounds like another standard set; blokes as fit as Magaluf-Justin and bonking all over the place. I'm up that.

"So, are we going for it?" I ask.

"If you're up for it?"

I look at her twinkling green eyes and nod in agreement, a large smile creeping onto my face. "Yes, definitely am!"

"Eeeek!" She jazz hands and we leave *my* bedroom seeking out Shane in the living room. I try not to imagine him and Leila going at it on the mangy sofa behind him.

"You gunna go for it?" He grins.

"Yep!" Leila declares. "Can you text Jane, or do you want to give me her number?"

"I'll do both." He ferrets for his phone, types out a short message and then reads the digits to her. It's happening!

"This is cool." Shane guffaws. "I feel like I'm handing this place down to the next generation!"

I stifle my true laughter thinking you've handed more than *that* to the *next generation*!

There's nothing to hang about for and thanking Shane we leave.

"Well, I'm going to head home and get ready for work. How about you?"

I glance at the Trap, not far down the street from us. George is possibly in there. I could go and let him know the latest but then I'll have a pint, possibly more than one.

"I'm going home too. I'm going to chill today. Maybe read a book."

"You should start writing again, the *Tales of Jodie and Leila*!"

"We don't know what's coming yet." I tell her and the thought of what is to come makes my heart flutter.

"Best make sure we get up to lots of naughty adventures then."

"Well, if it's in the name of research!" I concede jokily. She's referring to another of my on-off hobbies. I always liked story-telling and I started penning a few before Magaluf. I hadn't even thought about my writing since I'd got home. Dane ripped me for it, surprise surprise! He's not around to critique me anymore though is he? He'd make a great villain actually.

"I'll let you know as soon as I hear anything from Jane." Leila tells me before swooping me into a hug. "I'm so glad we're doing this, it's going to be the best!"

"I know!" I tell her genuinely excited. Just what will the Tales of Jodie and Leila behold?

Once upon a time two best friends decided to move in together... I envision a series of Happy Ever After's, all equally as fantastic.

We bid farewell and I briskly walk home typing out a message to my brother and dad telling them the news. Mum will be waiting to hear how it's gone, no doubt she'll be in the kitchen right now cooking up a full roast dinner. Now that's something I'll miss!

Even so, I can't wait! First Magaluf. Now I have Belfry as my new venture, Madrid, an upcoming adventure and the journey is continuing with Marshamonvilla; what exactly does this place have in store for me? I suspect whatever it is won't be dull.

Proper First Day

I'm so nervous my tummy rolls over on itself and my palms are clammy against the steering wheel. I keep taking deep, steadying breaths and telling myself they're just kids but it isn't helping.

In five minutes, I'll be there. The students will begin arriving at half past. I'm just so thankful to have already met the staff; at least it isn't a double whammy.

As I turn off the ignition I realise I'm shaking slightly. Chill out! I give myself a firm talking to but I'm just so desperate for them to like me! *And* not attack me, I suppose.

Today feels like a proper first day and I realise any 'new kid' feelings last week were watery in comparison to today's greasy fear. Other cars are rolling in to spaces around me and I realise I can't just stay in the car looking disturbed.

"Morning!" I warble to Leanne and a lady I don't know.

"Morning!" They reply and I trot inside behind them.

Troy is already here. As soon we enter the staff room our eyes meet and he comes over to me immediately.

"Here." He hands over the passport sized picture and a glue stick.

"I'd forgotten all about that." I admit feeling giddy in his presence. I didn't even tell anyone over the weekend about the badge, and now they'll never see it because I'm covering it permanently. "Thanks again!"

I've definitely spent my days off underplaying the effect he has on me. He smells like sweet cotton and my fingertips ache to touch his chest. I busy them with affixing the picture.

"Good weekend?" He asks me and my mind flits to Ashley and Aaron and Madrid.

"Brilliant thanks. Me and my friend are getting a flat together! How was yours?" I return the question, batting the attention away and inspect my handy work- well Troy's mainly- the badge looks fine.

"Yeah, same old." He shrugs.

"Which is?"

He doesn't get chance to answer because Julie sweeps in at that moment causing a quick hush all-around.

"Morning brief." Troy mutters and I slip into a nearby seat not wanting to be easily spotted. I'd also forgotten about the horrid feeling I get around her.

"Good morning." She states to a few murmured responses. "Today will be busy. The kids will undoubtedly be lively. No girls are due on site today but be honest with the boys. They'll have heard one way or another that they're due and they'll be rampant with curiosity."

Julie continues to deliver information in quick succession including snippets of news about particular students. There have been changes to living arrangements for some, minor misdemeanours for others and a couple of complete newbies to watch too. I like the idea of there being other new kid's onsite; I might seek them out and try to form bonds on this basis.

Every morning there's a rollcall in assembly. From there lessons will begin and a register is also taken in every class throughout the day. Attendance is closely monitored.

I spot Iqbal and give him a wave. I have IT for almost the whole day today. What a way to start the week! I'm determined to give the classes a chance but if my memories of school are anything to go on the subject is dull and tedious.

"It's breakfast clubs first." Troy tells me once Julie's finished. "There's a rota over there which tells you your duties for morning, break and lunch."

He helpfully points out a section of the notice board and next to my name I find: hall, hardcourt, clubs.

"What does this even mean?" I point out the words.

"First thing you're in the hall, me too. At break you'll be out on the hardcourt so fetch your drink and go straight out the back door, near the girls unit. Then at lunch, clubs start at ten to one. Lucy will be able to tell you which one to monitor. Clubs change depending what they're into. You're never alone either there are usually three staff at each post."

I thought I had everything covered but I absorb all of this new information realising I've encountered just a tip of the iceberg so far.

"Come on, we've got to get to the hall now."

I leave the staff room feeling at least confident that my badge resembles my regular face and enter the hall to find thirty-or-so boys already. They're a loud, boisterous mass of dark trousers, bright jackets, a range of heights and builds, some have backpacks. Some look scruffy and some pristine with fresh haircuts. It generally smells manly in here, liberally used aftershave mixed with sweat.

Other members of staff already loiter around the edges, making sure the students remain composed despite the general hype. I notice now some lads are sat down already; one talks to himself, one stares into the distance he's so pale, malnourished even.

Troy's presence turns heads and a number of lads surround him. Their voices are a mixture of unbroken, breaking and broken all battling to be heard. They're definitely entering their teens. I guess they're the class Troy supports; the year 8's.

"Who's she?" A blonde demands as he takes me in. He has clear blue eyes, is chewing gum and wears a gold and black Adidas jacket.

"That's rude. Why don't you try, hello, I'm Mason, what's your name?"

He rolls his eyes and pastes on a smile.

"Hi, I'm Mason, who are you?"

"I'm Jodie." I reply. "Nice to meet you. What are your-"

"I'm Josh!" A voice rings out from a tiny skin head.

"Hi Josh!"

"I'm Keon." A kid with an impressive fluffy afro steps forward. His eyes are sharp like a bird of prey and he flashes a wicked smile. "I'm in charge."

He thumbs his chest confidently and Mason steps up to him but then places himself beside him and I wonder what his thought process was.

"This is Kyron and Shay." Keon continues, indicating two Asian boys. Kyron gives me a shy grin and Shay stares straight through me as he smiles.

"Nice to meet you all. I hope I can remember all of your names, you might need to remind me."

"They've got IT before dinner." Troy states.

"Not Iqbal!" Keon exclaims and with a shared groan they mooch away.

"Are you in there then?" He asks me, and I nod thinking *does that mean you'll be in there too?* Maybe reading my eyes, he nods and continues, "Eyeball does an alright job keeping it light."

"*Eyeball*?" I repeat.

"Shhh!" He giggles. "Don't let Mason hear you, I'm wondering how long until he clocks on himself."

"Clocks on to what?"

"Don't you think Iqbal sounds like Eyeball? We used to call him that, we were at the same school. I wouldn't say it to his face now though."

"How grown up!" I retort feeling a bit sorry for Iggy. Perhaps that's the reason he dreamed of a nickname. It must feel strange being back in a school together. I keep experiencing deja-vous myself. Just by looking at the students and staff alike I can pick out 'popular' kids, bully-types, 'oddballs', those that don't care, those that do.

The hall continues to fill, and I follow example and unload stacks of chairs before dragging them forwards to create a large, loose circle. Most of the lads help and take a seat without needing to be told.

"Sit there." Troy directs me before taking a place further along. Within only moments Julie enters and there is a definite change in atmosphere. I check the time and make a mental note to always be ready for now.

"Good morning." She utters stiffly and takes a chair herself before scanning the room with a laser stare. This woman is truly a scary force. The boys feel it too, I can tell. Satisfied everybody has glued their lips closed she begins with a 'welcome' before moving on to the register. Now is my chance to begin matching up more names to faces!

***

I'm pleased to find out Troy is more than right about Iqbal livening up potentially dreary IT classes. His genuine enthusiasm for the subject appeals to my geeky side. I easily fall into the swing of trying to excite an array of students into giving the tasks a go.

We had the year 7's first. A new kid, Ryan, had a huge tantrum and Laura and I had to escort him to the Behaviour Support room. This was technically my first experience of a 'hold' although he didn't resist or fight back. I think he was merely afraid and overwhelmed, I felt sorry for him. By sharing that I too am new, I managed to coax him back for the last part of the lesson.

I gave myself a pat on the back for that. Now though, it's after break and the year 10's turn.

At the start of the lesson Iqbal talks to them at the front of the classroom, introducing the topic and allowing conversation to wonder at times to football and films. Then they hit the computers and try for themselves to reproduce the document discussed.

Break time had come around quickly but approaching third lesson, it's dragging. Possibly because I'm wishing the time away! Not long and the year 8's, and therefore Troy, hit the classroom.

"Miss?" A gangly, freckled boy calls and I swiftly approach Ben. It is funny being called *Miss*, but it's happened numerously already and isn't necessarily a respect thing. Learning just one name is too much effort for some, they've told me so and Iqbal has given up reminding them.

"Why have you got Minecraft loaded Ben?" Iqbal calls from his own computer. He already showed me the software which allows him to view all of the students' screens to check they're working on what they should be.

"Oh shit!" He blushes and titters behind his hand. "I forgot about that!"

Iqbal raises his eyebrows. "Language. Do you want me to block the site?"

"No." He admits and rolls his eyes at me with a goofy, abashed smile.

"If you get your work finished you can go on for five minutes. Keep going on when you shouldn't be and I'll block it."

"Yeah and ruin it for everybody!" Sam barks from where he has been tapping away quietly.

"Ok, hush now. Sam you're doing really well. Maybe on track for Star of the Class!" He smiles at him proudly.

Sam tuts, and I hear him mutter. "*Star* of the *Class*." But his cheeks have flushed pink and I suspect he's enjoyed the recognition.

I get Ben back on track and catch Iqbal's eye. He motions me to go over to him.

"I know it's only been a few classes but you're a real natural Jodie. Keep going!"

"Thanks." I feel a little embarrassed, but like Sam, pleased of the acknowledgement. The moody nature of this group is exceptionally different to the needy Year 7's but both have required me to be consistently on the ball. Made more difficult when *everything* feels completely new, even the computer programmes they're using!

I check the clock, ten minutes to go.

"Well done Sam, Jon and Mo." Iqbal announces eventually. "You've all made a really good start. Ben, next time I want a little more from you. Shaniq, Liam- you did *enough*... Nothing wrong with pushing yourselves. Please save your work- Jodie can you check they're doing it how I showed you?"

I obediently begin to circle the room, flicking my eyes across the screens. I feel so naughty being this excited about the next class. It feels inappropriate to be experiencing such wayward thoughts, perhaps magnified when surrounded by children!

Iqbal encourages everyone back to the front of the room to round up and give out his Star of the Class. He's told me I can pick one too once I get to know them better and understand the reasons behind his choices. Oh, the responsibility.

"Jodie- walk them to their next class will you. They're all on bronze still." He adds pointedly referring to their individual statuses. A Silver student doesn't have to be escorted everywhere so this is an initial motivation to follow school rules and begin 'climbing in status'. I'm intrigued to see who goes up and who stays put next week.

"What you got lads?" I ask enthusiastically.

"History." Sam mumbles but the others don't even meet my eye.

"Lead the way." I offer him because I actually don't know where we're going.

Harishma was assumed to be their designated mentor but I've picked up a few slots with them, I suppose she must be doing jobs in the Girls Unit and splitting her time.

"I'll see you again later, in English." I tell them.

"English is shit." Shaniq pipes up.

"Well I love English so hopefully I can show you otherwise." I retort.

"Hmph!" Sam snorts unbelievably.

I leave them at their next class and head back the way I came, acutely aware that Troy will have walked to IT in the meantime.

Everybody had those crushes at school didn't they? That made certain classes ridiculously exciting... this is the very adult version of that. Who knew coming back to school would be this much fun!

Iqbal has started by the time I'm back. I don't stare at Troy who's sitting right there and take a seat close by, behind the class.

But they all turn and spotting it is me, give up listening. Josh and Keon both begin talking at the same time.

"Is your name Jodie?" "You're the girl from this morning."

Instead of coming down like a ton of bricks, Iqbal accepts their interest and folds his arms smiling. I breathe a quiet sigh of relief because I've caused the interruption and he isn't blaming me.

"Boys, this is Jodie, she will be working in IT a lot of the time."

"Wicked!" "Cool!"

I'm genuinely pleased at the reaction and catch Troy's eye, he grins at me.

"I'll be making you work extra hard!" I joke winking at Keon. "Don't think I'll go easy on you."

"I work hard anyway, don't I Troy?" Keon looks to his mentor for support and receives a dubious look in return.

"I couldn't give a flying fuck about IT if I'm honest!"

"Mason." Iqbal's voice is firm but not raised. "Glad you're *honest*. But unfortunately no choice, remember." He shrugs casually, dismissing the outburst. "Right lads. Who can explain to Jodie what topic we're covering?"

They all fall quiet now, not so eager to answer and I note Mason still scowling.

"We're going to design a shop remember?" Iqbal's characteristic passion shines through. "Just wait until you see some of the work you'll be doing! Buying stock, designing logo's..."

He goes to sit at his chair and click through the presentation when Mason sighs loudly.

"Rather not thanks!" He stands and turns on his heel. The other lads snigger as he stalks out the room with his middle finger held aloft. Troy immediately follows him, and Iqbal merely resumes not giving the incident any more attention than it needs.

I'm not so shocked after dealing with year 7 Ryan earlier and I wonder if Mason is struggling to find his place amongst the others after the six-week break. Surely I can relate to that, six weeks can do a lot to somebody.

As with the other classes, Iqbal allows conversations to ebb and flow around his introduction. Troy comes back after a while and collects a worksheet for Mason. He leaves again but returns soon after, just as the others are dashing for a computer each.

Mason isn't with him; he must be working with Gilbert or Sean who man the Behaviour Support room between them. The year 8's easily take up our time but we exchange continual smirks and snatched comments when we're having banter with the students.

For the first time today Iqbal even joins in with the chatter as they work and the atmosphere crackles with liveliness. The year 8's are easily my favourite class so far. And, no, it doesn't have everything to do with Troy being with them.

***

By the time I'm heading home after my real first day I feel absolutely shattered but in a truly content way. The students at Belfry are as much of an eclectic mix as the staff and I'm already seeing cracks of personality glowing through their actions. I'm proud of myself for navigating successfully through more rules, responsibilities and situations including the kind-of hold with Ryan!

I am, however, aware there is so much more to come. I have been thrown in at the deep end in many respects and the next few weeks will be sink or swim.

This afternoon after seeing the year 10's again I met the year 9's. They are a handful as a class with three lads competing for a Top

Dog role. Tomorrow I have an afternoon timetabled with the girls and I wonder if there will be any students in attendance.

Once home I have messages to reply to; Aaron, Ashley- both asking after my day and making general small-talk. I also message Leila and Cat and type out a hello to Jem, Dane's sister. I feel bad for not speaking to her sooner. We used to go to Pole Dancing lessons together, I wonder if she still does.

What to do with a Monday evening? The shift I used to work as a waitress every Monday night was usually tedious and slow. I feel privileged to have another evening all to myself and decide perhaps I should think more about Leila's suggestion- my writing.

I've never been one to just sit and watch TV. I like to be doing something. Reading, singing, pole dancing and writing, they were all on-off hobbies before Magaluf, I should be taking them back with both hands.

I pick up a notebook and pen and begin to brainstorm. What type of Happy Ever After could I dream up? Who would be the characters and what would be their experiences?

The Way the Cookie Crumbles

After another round of IT until lunch with the year 7's and 9's again plus the year 11's, I'm now off to the girl's unit for the afternoon. We were told this morning to expect a visit from both Mollie and Bonnie, our youngest students. There won't be any classes, just a chance to get to know them. My stomach is tingling with nerves and curiosity as I clutch my lunch box and approach the double locked doors.

Harishma and Lizzy are both seated as I enter, about to tuck into their food, but Harishma immediately dashes over to me and plucks up my lanyard ogling the ID.

"Wha? Did you get a new one?" She cries sounding disappointed and staring at my actual face. Trust her to notice!

"Troy helped me out." As I say his name I feel hot blood creeping around my neck. We've spent another day flirting at every opportunity; he'd been gutted when I said I wasn't eating with him today.

"Wow, you can't even tell!" She slides it from its casing and waves it in Lizzy's direction.

"How's it going sister newbie?" She greets me good-naturedly. "I'm glad you got it sorted. It looks *so* much better."

"Sister newbie!" Harishma scoffs. "There are no nuns in here. I hope!"

Neither agreeing nor disagreeing Lizzy hands me the card back and I take a seat.

"So, what have I missed? Is Lacey coming down?"

"Nope!" Harishma says gleefully. "She's like *so* annoyed to be missing out on the first meeting! Just the way the cookie crumbles!"

She takes a huge bite of her sandwich and chews happily.

"We've got files set up, but obviously there's not a lot in them yet." Lizzy tells me. "Once we meet them we'll be able to decide what their targets should be, what level they're at academically. There's a lot to work out before we can even begin."

Her voice has a layer of patience and she sounds methodical like she's got it all thought out, which is a good job because I'm way out of my depth. I gaze at the details we do have on Mollie and Bonnie as I tuck in to my food. At least we're all in this together, they have more experience than me but none of us know what to expect really.

"What time are they coming?" I ask them.

"Any time after one but I expect Mollie will be here first and for longer." Lizzy answers and taps on Bonnie's statement. The line she has indicated reads;

Extremely anxious, highly nervous and easily scared.

"Bless her." I mumble.

After I've eaten I busy myself getting to know the classroom. Everything is new; the furniture, the stationery, there is a stock cupboard brimming with crafty items. It is geek heaven and I breathe in stacks of exercise books! Lizzy tells me about her last post, in a mainstream school but working specifically with the 'difficult' kids. She has a natural energy about her, loads of really cool ideas and just gives life to the room.

"See that noticeboard?" She's saying. "They'll have a section each, they're going to make name badges and then fill their space with things important to them like photos or pictures of things they like."

"That's a wicked idea!" I exclaim and scope out the little areas which will soon represent our girls. I feel a tad jealous actually, I wouldn't have minded having my own section of cool things.

"We'll all have one too, of course." Lizzy adds indicating the smaller board next to it.

Could this really get any better?

"I love making and drawing!" She enthuses touching the tips of her fingers together.

"Me too!" I laugh. "I waitressed before this, I was always doodling, I like graffiti art." I tell her.

Harishma looks up from the box of DVD's she's found and says, "If you like drawing so much, you can do my name tag for me."

Forty-five minutes later and we're still waiting so we've decided to make a start on our names for the 'All About Me' wall. Harishma watches on, demanding how she wants hers to look. With a start we glance at the windows when figures suddenly pass by and enter into our reception. Lizzy springs to her feet and marches to the wall where the buzzer is located, already beaming at the lady and girl through the glass panel separating us.

"Hello to both of you," Lizzy says warmly. "Come on in and make yourself at home! I'm Lizzy."

I look over at Harishma who is staring without shame at the newcomers. It is Mollie and her Auntie Shelly, I know because Bonnie will be with two people. Her statement told us she always is when she visits somewhere new.

"Hiya!" I wave to the girl who barely meets my shoulder and has curly blonde hair in pigtails. She lowers her eyes shyly and I wonder how she has possibly been expelled so many times. She's eleven years old and looks every inch of it virtually cowering into her Auntie's side.

"I'm Jodie." I tell her then look at Shelly and smile at her too. "Nice to meet you both."

Once Harishma has gathered her manners we take a seat and Mollie instantly begins to look more comfortable. Lizzy leads the introductory conversation and I watch as the small girl's eyes dart and rove. Before long she joins in where she can.

"I'm a good dancer." She inputs when Lizzy mentions drama. "*And* actress. I can sing, dance and act. I'll probably be famous." Her cutie mask slips and I glimpse more; a domineering edge, deep-rooted insecurity.

"That's great! We'll-"

"I want to look around now." Mollie interrupts Lizzy and without waiting for an answer plops from the chair and saunters in the direction of the pods.

Should we leave her to wander? Should I follow her and attempt to talk? I look to Harishma but she's eyeing Shelly eagerly.

"So, how *is* she? Is she excited about starting?" She enquires.

I turn back to Mollie who is pulling drawers open and peering inside of them, with none of the excitement I'd experienced earlier. She tugs out numerous items, drops them on the floor, moves onto the next thing.

I stir, annoyed at her actions. She's out of sight now, fully inside the pod. I walk over and enter the room to find her switching on a computer.

"Can you get onto Minecraft?" She asks not deterred by me appearing. I take a seat.

"You'll have to try won't you?" I tell her casually and make a mental note to ask Iqbal how we go about limiting access. She would have gone on to try with or without my permission, I know that, and follow the advice of choosing my battles wisely.

I glance at the discarded items on the floor.

"What do you think then?" I ask her.

"Of what?" She mutters tutting and clicking things on the screen.

"This place. Your new school?"

"S'ok. Nice." She shrugs.

"You see all the new stuff, ready for you guys?" I point in the direction of the cupboards and she nods.

"Yeah. It's nice."

"Well, we've got to make sure it stays tidy. We don't want it looking all scruffy like the boy's classrooms!"

She meets my eye conspiratorially.

"Have you seen their classrooms, where are they?" She stands up, intrigue propelling her and I quickly slow her down by blocking her way.

"Let's pick these things up first, look." I crouch as I say it and slowly pick up a rubber. "Then I'll show you something."

Mollie mirrors me and picks up two things. "What is it? Can we go now?"

"You'll see soon, come on just a few more!"

Once the objects are stashed away I triumphantly lead her to the internal doors.

"What? A door?" She's nonplussed but this was my only handle.

"Look," I unlock it. "The toilet is through here and this door…"

I point to the door with a glass window and she dashes toward it and on tiptoes can see into the corridor beyond.

"That's always locked so you know, this is really special, your very own section of school."

"Is that the boy's part?" She asks suitably awed.

"Yep." I nod. "They're all in lessons at the minute. What's your favourite subject?"

She screws up her nose. "*None* of them!"

I can't help but giggle. I was the complete opposite at her age. I might have been cheeky occasionally but in general I enjoyed school. I show her the toilets before we re-enter the classroom. Mollie skips over to Shelly, who is looking relaxed now her niece is at ease.

"There's no reason for her not to start straight away." Lizzy is explaining. "There'll be six girls, we think, but not all will be fulltime at the minute. We could start with a half day tomorrow and Thursday and a full day Friday… see how you get on, Mollie?"

"What do you think Mol?" Shelly also looks at her, but she just shrugs idly. At that moment more people arrive.

"I'll get it." I say but Harishma dives out of her chair in the direction of the intercom. It's Bonnie and two women. I know she lives with her mum, so this other lady could be a family member or friend.

"Hi! Thanks." One lady greets Harishma and ushers the other pair through the open door. Bonnie has long hair which is greasy and tangled, swiped behind her ears. Her eyes are large and wary, and she whimpers loudly as she takes us in causing Mollie to giggle.

"Good afternoon." Lizzy greets them all. "Why don't you take a seat over there, on the comfy chairs?"

I sense she's purposely giving Bonnie some space to acclimatise. I'm in charge of my senses, for the most part, and I find meeting a room of new people daunting. She continues to make low whining noises and Mollie continues to find her a source of intriguing entertainment.

"So, Mollie, will we be seeing you tomorrow?" I attempt to divert her attention.

"Will *she* be here?" She thumbs in Bonnie's direction and I shrug my shoulders.

"Maybe. *Especially* if she knows there's a girl she can make friends with. You're the kind of girl people can be friends with aren't you?"

She nods eagerly. Lizzy has sat beside Bonnie and mum, Reena. The other lady introduces herself as a social worker and takes a seat at the table. The moaning sounds have virtually subsided as Lizzy expertly soothes Bonnie.

"See those little classrooms, we can go in there for a bit of quiet. And see that cupboard, that's full of crafty things, we're going to have lots of fun. All the staff are really nice, this is Jodie…"

Bonnie raises eyes like a scared deer to mine. I give her a small smile. Her mouth contorts into a petrified grimace.

"And this is Harishma."

Harishma waves and coos. "Hello Bonnie."

"Mollie?" Lizzy catches our other new student's eye. "Say hi to Bonnie."

I also give her an encouraging smile and to my relief she switches into her cutesy role and sweetly says. "Hiya Bonnie. I'm a bit scared too. But we can be friends."

At this Bonnie looks momentarily elated but then an almighty groan escapes her causing Mollie to burst into childish hysterics.

"What's *wrong* with her?" She asks me loudly. Ok, that backfired.

"Bonnie is just nervous, some people feel more shy than others." I look at Shelly wondering when she will intervene. "We can all help each other settle in though can't we?"

Thankfully, for whatever reason, Mollie bites her lip but she gives me a huge eye roll and throws another smirk in Bonnie's direction for good measure.

"Ok, so, Jodie do you want to sit with Bonnie for a minute and I'll wrap up with Shelly and Mollie?" Lizzy motions for us to swap places.

"Will. You. Be friends. With me?" Bonnie's voice is stilted and booming. We all turn to find her looking at Mollie. Mollie looks at me and I hold my breath but then she giggles and nods.

"Yes, we can be friends."

It's another mini win and I take my place beside a newly revitalised Bonnie. She's a year older than Mollie, year 8, but her nature already resembles a child far younger and she now flings herself to the carpet toward a pile of books.

"I've been. Learning to read!" She reports and sniggers wetly.

"Wow, that's great. Pick a book, we can look together?"

She snorts and I smile. I have a soft spot for her already, for both girls. Mollie has shown already there is such potential.

The afternoon easily rolls away and by the time both sets of girls and caregivers have left, it is home time for us too.

"Well, two down ladies! They seem alright don't they?" Lizzy pats the files that represented them but couldn't do their intricate characters justice.

"That Bonnie, poor thing." Harishma comments pulling a face. "And Mollie, she's a madam isn't she! Wait until her feet are under the table, she'll be a monster."

"So what about the others?" I probe. I won't be back until Friday so presumably I'll miss out on a few first meetings now. Just the way the cookie crumbles, as Harishma said.

Lizzy checks her diary. "I have Holly and Jayde tomorrow afternoon. Lacey will be with me then."

"I'll see if I can come by." Harishma says reassuringly putting her hand on Lizzy's arm. I'm not sure who she's comforting but most likely herself that she won't be missing out and I inwardly smile.

"The 10's are really settled," she's continuing. "And I've told them I want more hours in here anyway."

"Lacey will be going offsite to meet Eve, Wednesday and Thursday morning." Lizzy explains.

"What? Oh, well." Harishma flounders.

"She's been attending a temporary unit, we need to coax her into coming here instead."

"But. I'm- but. Well." Harishma finally gives in looking dismayed. I'm so tempted to add, *just the way the cookie crumbles mate!*

***

As is becoming ritual, I bomb homeward, music blasting and in high spirits. Today has been just as exhausting as yesterday but it is exhilarating, and I've never felt so alive. Each child I am meeting I can actually do something to help. This is so much more than fetching somebody a sauce to go with their chips.

I was a proud waitress, worked hard and climbed the ranks. I'm going to do just the same here at Belfry. Work hard, watch Iqbal and Lizzy, learn the ropes, make a real difference and although it will be tough, it should also be massively fun too.

Tuesdays used to equal a night out at the Trap. There'll be a karaoke and I used to have Wednesdays off so it was like my Friday.

Leila will be working and George will be heading out for a couple of pints. I could tag along, I probably won't.

Once home I prep some chicken and veg for dinner. Mum will be home soon, and I like to help her out. In under a month's time, I'll be moved out, and she'll have to go back to serving George and Keith alone!

Friday Discoveries

The girl's unit is a hub of activity. Both Mollie and Bonnie have been here since this morning and Lacey, Lizzy and I are getting on like a house on fire. Obviously Harishma has found a number of reasons to visit throughout the day and up until now both of the girls in attendance have been manageable. It's after lunch now though and their moods are shifting.

"Stop. STOP! She keeps. Taking. MY pen!" Bonnie hollers and Mollie grins as though suitably rewarded.

"They're *our* pens. We have to share! *Don't* we Lizzy?"

We all know she is manipulating the situation in order to get at Bonnie but technically she is right.

"Why don't you sit there with Jodie?" Lizzy suggests to Mollie. "I bet she'll help you put patterns on your letters like she has on hers. Bonnie, remember they aren't just your pens." She gently reminds her.

They've been working on their nametags on and off all day and Mollie stands now to move over to me.

"That's. Not. Fair!" Bonnie cries. Typical, she didn't want me to touch her work of art five minutes ago.

We've been expecting Jayde, the Year 10, I haven't met her yet and Lacey told me earlier Mollie plays up a treat when she's around- but I'm looking forward to her getting here anyway. It'll break up the monotony.

"I'll help you." Lizzy appeases Bonnie, but she screws up her face *and* the picture she's been so carefully working on before bursting into angry, wailing tears.

Mollie looks at me and shrugs. Bonnie is prone to these outbursts, they've been occurring all week apparently but are only natural. Given the circumstances, she's actually doing really well. Her emotions and responses are on par with a toddler so she's handling all of this change and pressure the only way she knows how.

I busy Mollie with decorating her name whilst Lizzy and Lacey calm Bonnie. She's howling now, regretting ruining the picture.

"I'll draw you another one, Bonnie. Let me get Mollie sorted." I say it matter-of-factly and with a number of shaky sobs she quietens a touch.

"Look it's Jayde!" Mollie exclaims causing Bonnie to throw herself from the table onto the floor. From here she does a strange half-crawl to the padded chairs and buries her face in a cushion.

"She. Doesn't. Like. Me!" She bawls and I'm unsure who she's talking about, Mollie, Jayde, one of us. Lizzy tends to her again, Lacey lets Jayde enter and I smile at the peroxide girl with long slim legs and a humongous round chest. How old is she again? How unfair is the world when a fourteen-year-old girl is rocking a Page-3 worthy pair and I'm making do with these lumps. I think boobs should start small and expand as you get older until you don't want or need them any longer.

"Hiya Jayde, I'm Jodie!"

"Hiya." She replies in a friendly enough way and plonks herself at the table. "What's her problem?"

She throws a teenage look of disgust to where Bonnie is now lying on her back with the pillow over her face.

"She's a weirdo, she's always doing it." Mollie answers and I frown at her. "*What*? She is!"

She's definitely showing off. All day she's been fairly patient but now it'll win her brownie points with the older, cool girl.

"You must have felt nervous before?" I play to Jayde's empathetic side, hoping she has one. "You know, coming to a new school and stuff?"

"Nah." She bites at the skin around one of her nails. "I've been to loads of different schools, doesn't bother me."

Ok.

"Well, we're the girls team, we've got to stick together." I try again.

Mollie shoots me a sneering look and I resist rising. The last thing I need is a staff versus student situation.

"So, have you started a name tag yet Jayde?" I change tact. "I'm just helping Mollie. Then I'm doing one for Bonnie." I say this loud enough for her to overhear, if she is indeed listening from her safe place.

Before long there're three students and three staff spread across the two round tables. Bonnie is once again happily colouring in and Mollie hasn't stopped sucking up to Jayde. It's hard to imagine there being two more in the mix. It's been confirmed Camden has been sentenced to fifteen months so we likely won't meet her now.

The year 11, Holly, came yesterday. She's sullen by all accounts and is starting properly next week. Eve, the girl Lacey visited offsite- described on paper as 'unteachable'- spat at her and refused to interact both times. She's scheduled to try again next week.

"Have you got a boyfriend?" Mollie is asking Jayde having declared she's already got six ex boyfriends of her own. I think of mine, not something I'll be discussing.

Jayde smirks coyly.

"I've met someone recently." She confides.

Mollie is all ears, virtually climbing into her lap.

"Is he sexy?" She asks and I cringe. It doesn't sound right coming out of her young mouth and I'm unsure if we should halt the conversation.

"*Well* sexy." She clarifies, and I look to Lacey for guidance.

"Come on girls," Lacey takes me up on the silent SOS. "Jayde, remember the girls are younger than you."

"I know all about sex and everything!" Mollie pouts not enjoying being labelled as a child. I wonder if this is something we should record. Troy was right about the amount of potential safeguarding paperwork. I fill out an amber form at least daily explaining one thing or another a student has declared.

"Well now isn't the place to be discussing it." Lacey says firmly.

"We will have some Sex Ed lessons." Lizzy tells them. "So if you have any questions that will be the time to talk about it."

"Like if I should spit or swallow?" Jayde asks smirking and I nearly choke. Did I know this type of thing at fourteen? Yes, I think I did, but it just sounds so wrong, I certainly wouldn't have spoken to teachers like this.

"Spit or swallow what?" Mollie asks confused. She doesn't know *all about everything* then.

"Right girls." Lizzy stands up. "That's enough now please. Jayde, can I have a word?"

She disappears into the pod with the teen following her. Lacey throws me a subtle smile and I give her a teeny wink to acknowledge it.

"What did you say to Jayde?" I ask Lizzy once we're waving the girls off at just gone three.

"I asked her who had said that to her about spit or swallow but she clammed up, said she heard a friend say it." She pauses and sighs, runs her fingers through her hair. "The guy she said she's seeing… her social worker asked us to feedback any information she tells us about him, but she's not really said a lot. She isn't daft. She told me he's nineteen but-." She stops.

"But what?"

"They think he's older. Twenty-five."

I gasp, that's my age! Ok, Jayde is a fully-developed woman physically but underneath that she's a child still. It makes me feel sick.

"Vile." Lacey comments. "Needs his dick chopping off."

I nod in agreement, my mind conjuring images of what he might look like. Probably completely normal, *well sexy,* Jayde described him.

"She's protecting him." Lizzy continues. "She knows it's wrong, I think, else why lie? She must love having the attention of an older guy, flattered!"

I shake my head as though attempting to dislodge the uncomfortable truth. This is my first week and any innocence I'd unknowingly harboured about children is completely shattered. I feel naïve for ever underestimating the depth of the role.

"I'll record it anyway." Lizzy tells us. "Thanks for your help today guys, it was mostly a good day and I think we're going to make a good team!"

The teachers don't finish when us mentors do, they have meetings, planning and prep to do. We bid her a good weekend and leave her in the unit. Having spent virtually the whole day cooped up in there, the main school feels sprawling and surreal as we head to the staff room.

"Did I miss anything?" Harishma comes skipping to our side. Troy also approaches us.

"How was your day?" He asks us smoothly and I drink him in, almost glad for the weekend to put some space between us.

"Not bad thanks, how was yours?" I answer him whilst Lacey fills Harishma in on this afternoon.

"Ah Mason and Keon had a fight earlier. Both got sent home."

"Oh no!" I had actually sensed that brewing and looking back should have predicted it.

"Who won?" Harishma inquires obviously listening to both low-downs and I suppress an eye role.

"Mason started it. Neither of them finished it before they were split up. So anyway, who's coming pub?"

"Pub?" I echo, did I hear him correctly?

To my surprise Lacey shakes her head saying no but I'm not surprised that Harishma is a definite yes.

"Jodie?"

"Yeah why not. Do you drive there?"

"Yeah it's not far, you can follow me. We only have a couple, you know... end of the week tradition."

"You coming for a pint?" Sean lollops to our sides, his grey eyes sweeping over all of the female faces.

"Yep, come on." Harishma and Troy turn with Sean and I follow them beside Lacey.

"Why aren't you coming?" I ask her.

"Gym babe. It's the weekend, I need to be looking my best!" She smooths her hands over her tight stomach and right down over her pelvis. "I've got a date tomorrow!"

Me too! I think but don't exclaim. I know it's naughty, but I don't want Troy to know. Basically, I'm hedging my bets.

"That's cool, who with?" I say instead.

"He's nothing special really. I'm just sleeping with him."

We're at our cars now and Troy looks over his shoulder calling to me.

"Jodie, follow me yeah?"

I nod, a little dreamy eyed thinking *I would follow you anywhere!*

"Gorgeous isn't he." Lacey picks up on my expression and I nod honestly. "His bird must be constantly on edge."

His WHAT! My brain literally melts in my head and I'm unsure why, but I don't want Lacey to know I'm shocked by this news.

"I've only ever seen her twice. She's a stunner. I don't think he brings her out on purpose." She winks. "You get what I mean?"

Unfortunately, I do. And now I'm wondering if Lacey has slept with him; cheated with him on his beautiful girlfriend. It adds up that he's taken. Why would this godly man be single? Why hadn't I questioned it!

"I haven't been there." She admits. "Given half the chance I would though."

"Come on Jodes!" Troy rolls close to our cars in his own and I force a smile for them both.

"I've loved today." I tell Lacey. "Hope your date goes well."

I hop into my car and kind of want to just drive home. Another part of me rationalises that at least I know now. Let's see how long it takes him to tell me himself! I stare at the bumper of his car as we weave through the streets.

What a snake! I'm angry at him for leading me on, if Lacey hadn't mentioned it I would have continued to fantasise about us getting together. Perhaps even going further than just a one-night stand because I'd fully accepted we would sleep together. Not now though and I am bitterly disappointed.

But I can hardly talk can I? Ashley lined up for tomorrow, Aaron for the weekend after next. We're pulling into a carpark now. There's a crowd of mentors waiting; Sean, Harishma, Dom, Lewis, Jess, Laura and more. I cast my eyes over the guys, are they single? Not that it matters. It's Troy I'm totally besotted with. None of these could ever match up to him.

I climb from the car and lock the door along with my heart. Troy is off the cards. It isn't that bad. There's plenty more fish in the sea, blah, blah.

"What you drinking babe?" Troy's eyes are like liquid chocolate and I guard my feelings as I meet them. *Babe.*

"I'll get it, thanks." I don't let on that I'm annoyed. I'm confused. I'm still smiling at him with gooey eyes and I still want him so badly. I give myself a hard, mental kick. He's got a girlfriend Jodie! I already knew I should stay away; this is the definitive barrier I needed. I am not a cheat. I was cheated on and know how it feels, how can I even still be considering him!

***

The news of Troy's other half doesn't completely dampen my Friday vibes. I've arranged to see Chantelle tonight and Alexa will be there. It'll be fab to catch up with her too. We weren't necessarily 'friends' before Magaluf but our holiday bonded us. She wasn't so lucky on the unprotected sex front and copped out with an STD after sleeping with a PR. Now it is Friday- a whole ten days since my test- I dare to accept that I've gotten away with it. I will not be repeating that mistake!

Girly giggles and gossip over a bottle of Prosecco is just the way to launch the weekend. And quench the nerves that are beginning to consume me over tomorrow night! Date night with the gorgeous Ashley; it's just the thing I need to help me forget about Troy.

***

"I'm telling you Jodie!" Alexa is drawling in her confident, slow fashion that I came to know so well. "Chantelle here is an anomaly. *Trust* me!"

Ironic really because whilst we were away together she inadvertently helped me to see that opinions should be treated with caution, being just that; an opinion. But I do agree with her and eye our beautiful friend, Chantelle. She shakes her head impatiently.

"Come on girls, there's somebody out there for everybody, you pair have just been…" She stumbles for the right word and I meet Alexa's eye.

"Unlucky?" I infill.

"Pah, *they're* unlucky!" Alexa trills. "Can't recognise a good woman when they grab them by their balls!"

I laugh and scoff, "More like can't resist *any* woman who grabs them by their balls! They're all cheats!"

I glug the fizzy wine, thinking of Troy. Oh Troy. If only I'd known from the start it might be easier to accept.

"Not *all*." Chantelle says quietly, and I feel bad.

"No, not Perry." I agree. "Alexa is right though, you pair are an anomaly. Here's us normal girls trying to get what you've got with Perry, it's not going to happen for everyone."

"It will Jodie." She tells me firmly. We've been best friends since we were two and are more like sisters. I think I want to believe her but then I question myself.

"I'm not sure when I'll ever want a relationship again." I tell them.

"That's the way forward, it's what I'm telling you!" Alexa reaffirms. "Since breaking up with Garth I've just realised! It's me, myself and I from now on!"

Chantelle, who is topping up our glasses, puts her hand on her hip and tuts.

"You were mad about him last week. And next week there'll be somebody else."

Alexa is not affronted, she smiles heartily. "We'll see! I'm not saying I'm not open to 'the one' but he'd have to be pretty fucking special for me to quit singledom now I've had this epiphany. Serial dater, that's me."

I ponder her outlook. I suppose it resembles my own to a degree. If, *if,* Troy had been single even then would I want him as a boyfriend? And Ashley, although I'm pleased as punch to be meeting up with him tomorrow, I'm under no allusions. He isn't seeking a relationship, not with me! I mean, he could have anybody. I'll just be a notch on his bedpost and actually, I am fine with that because he will be a notch on my own.

"I want to get to the magic one hundred." Alexa announces.

"One hundred what? Men?" I ask curious.

"Darling, there've been far more than one hundred men!" She rolls her eyes and I have to admire her record. I thought reaching double figures was provocative. "No, one hundred orgasms, before I settle down."

"You haven't had one hundred orgasms before?" I ask her.

"Not with a man. I average one full blown orgasm every ten or so. Sometimes even twenty! *This* year I'm soul searching."

"I'm not sure that's exactly what soul-searching means!" Chantelle quips and I tally my own experiences.

"I'm more like one in three." I tell them, and Alexa gives me an approving look.

"You must be lucky honey, you can cum easy."

"Mines every time!" Chantelle states.

"It's different for you." She dismisses her. "That's probably the *one* good thing about a long-term relationship, he knows exactly how to flick your bean."

Chantelle looks momentarily hurt and I can see they're at complete opposing ends of the spectrum. They maintain a friendship even though so much about them is chalk and cheese, but I guess that's also why it works. I'd say I'm somewhere in the middle-personality wise- but also in my opinion on this elusive Happy Ever After scenario.

Alexa continues unperturbed. "I've realised I enjoy my own time, I have my own hobbies and I don't need somebody stamping all over that."

I know she feels like she's right, she always does, but I am actually silently agreeing. I sense Chantelle is beginning to feel annoyed though.

"So, are you still pole dancing?" I ask Alexa. A subject change is needed and because it still places her as central topic she easily takes the bait.

"Are you going to start coming again?" She's asking now having explained she's been teaching since having a pole of her own installed at home.

"I want to. I've messaged Jem, who I went with before."

"You could come to mine one night, we'll have a session and a few drinks."

"I'm definitely up for that!" I've been doing some soul searching of my own and I want this hobby back.

Alexa goes on to relish in exposing some particularly gory details about a recent encounter involving anal beads. And my mind returns to the possible, more likely inevitable, sex with Ashley tomorrow night.

There's no need to walk the streets when we call it a night way past one. After we've all hugged and squawked in the doorway about the hilarious evening, Perry drops Alexa and I off at our homes. He doesn't drink often and has spent the evening online gaming in their converted garage away from the estrogen-fuelled commotion.

I thank him for the lift and climb the stairs to my room with a hazy head and thinking over the evening's conversations. Chantelle and Perry have a lovely home and settled life, good sex by all accounts and a future possibly including marriage and kids. My life is so far removed from that.

I'm neither jealous nor proud in the way Alexa spouts. I'm happy and I'm single. I don't know if I'm happy *because* I'm single. But I know one thing; men have their cake and eat it all the time and I'm not averse to taking a slice of no-strings, just-for-fun dates, kissing and sex. Whatever the menu offers I am free to try. At least, until I find out otherwise, like Troy and his secret, stunning girlfriend.

But Aaron is single, and Ashley, plus plenty of others and I don't see the harm in playing around whilst I wait for this Mr Right who Chantelle seems certain exists. Maybe I already know him I just don't know *it* yet!

Maybe I'll fall head over heels in love tomorrow night or maybe so in Madrid. Maybe I'll fall in love a little with every man I have relations with and maybe I won't ever find love again.

The prospect doesn't scare me. I'm not intimidated. I'm excited and looking forward to finding out.

Date Night

After another blissful Saturday morning lounging and having breakfast at the cafe, I am now strolling home from visiting Cat to begin prep for this evening. I told her the latest with Troy. She seemed as disappointed as me with the news and agrees that I should continue as though I don't know, just to see how long he will play me for; a sort of social experiment.

Bubbles of anticipation fill my stomach as Ashley's face fills my mind instead. He might be a player but at least he's in a position to participate. What will it be like to kiss him? Will I sleep with him? It's too much to even think about; that caramel skin, the contours of his muscled arms.

In my bedroom I'm busy tossing suitable clothes for a 'house-date' onto my bed when my phone pings. I check it immediately just in case Ashley has changed his mind and is calling the whole thing off. But it's Jem.

I'm ok thanks, same old! I quit and bought a pole so I could practise but I never go on it! That's great news about the flat! Going up in the world girl. So, do you want to buy the pole?

I read the question over and over, an excited giggle escaping my lips.

Yes, how much?

I add some other niceties but all I can think about is buying that pole. The flat's living room is way big enough to house it and I can't see Leila having a problem with it. I won't allow her to! Wow, my very own pole! The possibilities dance in my mind along with a carousel of images; me performing each move with well executed grace and style. I could get Alexa round to give me a refresher lesson.

With renewed zest I narrow down my outfits and a half hour later I have also haggled the pole for a price of sixty pounds. I text Leila to tell her the good news, not ask her *if* we can put it up! I cannot wait to move into Marshamonvilla even more now which I didn't think was possible. Taking a last look at the oversized, flimsy grey jumper I've finally chosen, I head to the bathroom.

It's amazing how much prep goes into a date. I can't remember ever making this much effort for Dane or Scott but I assume I must have at some point when things were still fresh and exciting. There is definitely something in this 'player' business. I'll never have to worry about things getting stale. There might be times the sex is crap but nothing worthwhile is without a risk. And I just can't see Ashley being crap in the sack!

As I shower I think this through. Experience doesn't always equal skill. He has very good looks on his side though and even if he is crap I suspect I'd be back for round two! Shameless *and* shallow I know!

***

The walk to Ashley's is as daunting as walking into Belfry was on Monday morning. I have to pep talk myself all the way there. *You've been with just as hot men in the past. And far worse! It will all be fine.*

I knock on his door tentatively and swallow my heart which is pumping in my throat. I hear the latch click and there he is, stepping aside to let me enter.

"Hey, how are you?" His voice is softer than I expected and I'm instantly at ease. He smells amazing.

"I'm good thank you. How are you?"

"Come through," he ushers me to the middle room. "Yeah I'm really good thanks. Have you been up to much today?"

His living room has a pale wooden floor, dark blues walls, there's music playing and a couple of candles lit in the window sill. I award him a point immediately for effort.

"Not really." I answer him. "Went to see my friend earlier. Chilled this afternoon." I don't tell him it took me four hours to get ready to come here.

"You hang around with Leila don't you?"

I nod thinking about the time they almost slept together. Maybe he didn't light candles for her.

"Wine?" He's holding a bottle of something pink.

"Yes, please. I should've bought one with me." I add.

"No, I told you to just bring yourself." He grins and my insides swish with desire.

Leila was right about him being easy to chat to. Hours while away as we discuss various village people and families. He obviously keeps his ear to the ground. He knows more about mine and Dane's relationship than I did! He also divulges hearsay I almost wish I could un-hear; dangerous gossip including questionable paternities and apparent affairs going on right under people's noses!

This type of talk requires bodies close. Mouths directed at ears and hushed voices even though nobody is around to hear. I'm not complaining, perhaps it is a tactic. His hand now lies permanently on my thigh. I'm giddy with attraction. The wine has undone any coyness.

As I look into those unusual blue eyes once again, his face finally draws to mine and we kiss. It is slow and seductive, his soft lips linger and toy with mine making me want more, more, more. Hands begin to wander and I appreciate his full pecs, smooth arms. His touch is gentle, but his fingers could be red-hot pokers as they trace a scorching sensation across my skin.

"Do you want to come upstairs?" He murmurs into my neck.

"Yeah, ok." I reply breathily, too caught up to feel awkward.

"Are you sure, because we can wait." He tells me planting light kisses around my mouth. Wait for what? For not the first time this evening I flirt with the idea he is looking for something a bit more long-term than I first assumed.

"It's cool." I smirk shrugging. "I kind of thought it might happen."

Why sugar the pill? We're consenting adults and it's incredibly gentlemanly of him to double check that I actually want to do it. I wonder if Leila made it this far and she chose to opt out. She must've been mad!

He takes my hand and stands up. I feel a rush of excitement. This is going to be my first *home* 'bang'. Ashley already made it clear he doesn't want us to end up as village gossip. And I assured him he is far from a rebound. I have no desire to spread the news to make Dane jealous; which he would be because that's just his nature. Other than Leila and Cat, Chantelle, and maybe George and Lacey, I won't tell a soul.

His bedroom is in darkness and remains this way so I can't tell if it's messy, but I suspect not if the rest of his home is anything to go by. The bed is squidgy when he guides me over to it and we lie on top of the quilt. The kissing continues and we only break to take off our tops. I'm not taking any of this for granted and I try to commit the pleasure I'm feeling to memory. Who knows if it will happen again? Who am I kidding, if I have anything to do with it of course it will happen again!

He's stroking my legs, hips and all that's in-between through my leggings. I begin working them down and he takes the hint stripping off his remaining clothes. Virtually naked the playing and teasing floods me with fire. I'm so aroused I'm going to cum soon!

Alexa thinks I'm lucky, but the way he touches me has nothing to do with luck.

Satisfied that I'm satisfied, he rolls me over and he's so much bigger than me as he squeezes between my legs. His cock is hard, short and seriously thick (yes wrapped in rubber) and he gradually pushes himself all the way in making me gasp at how wide I'm stretched. He thrusts slowly, once, twice.

"You're so tight." He groans. "It feels so good!"

He isn't wrong. I feel pinned to the bed by his weight, crammed full of his throbbing cock and my hips scream with the strain of being forced so wide open but I don't care it does feel oh so good. I couldn't move, even if I wanted to, and I get a kick out feeling that I'm being dominated by him.

Another slow drive of his hips, I'm gasping again, he is dominating me! Then he whimpers before muttering.

"Fuck. I just couldn't stop it, sorry."

He climbs off me and busies himself disposing of the condom. Is a speedy ejaculation a sign he enjoyed it as much as me? I hope so! I don't understand the apology when I clearly had a good time. I can't imagine a woman ever saying, 'oh sorry, I came too quick!'

"I'm going to the bathroom." I slip out of the room, padding along the hall in socked feet but nothing else. I look round the smallish room and my eyes rest on his single toothbrush. My mind flits to his comment before; we can wait. If I'd come into this wanting a boyfriend I would've made him wait. But I don't want one really and I didn't make him wait so I've probably blown it now anyway.

Back in the bedroom Ashley isn't there. The only light comes from the landing but I can see the outlines of a huge wardrobe and dresser. I can hear him downstairs, the music has gone off, glasses clank their way into the kitchen. He's house-proud, I like that. He is a lot more mature than the men I usually end up with.

Soon I know the delicate smell from extinguished candles will drift into the room and I hover unsure whether I'm supposed to be getting dressed and leaving or stopping the night. It suddenly seems like the answer will determine a lot about any future I have with him.

I put on my underwear so that he doesn't return to find me naked and assuming. I hear him taking the stairs lightly and pick up the discarded jumper-dress as he reappears.

"Not leaving are you?" He asks.

"Not if you don't want me to."

"Cause not, it's late! I wouldn't make you walk the streets even if I *didn't* like you!"

My heart melts. He's kind *and* he basically just said he likes me!

"Well in that case." I unfasten my bra. "I can't sleep in this thing."

"I'd rather you didn't anyway." He grins cheekily. "I'll just use the bathroom then I'll switch off the light out there. Make yourself comfy."

I do as he says and clamber under the puffy mass of duvet, snuggling down into a pillow. I hope he hasn't got a specific side he prefers to sleep on.

Minutes later he slides into the bed and loosely spoons me. His breathing becomes rhythmic almost immediately and I concentrate on this sound, congratulating myself that I've just slept with Ashley Tyler!

I mentally give myself a pat on the back and don't resist the happy, gormy smile settling on my face as I fall into a content sleep.

Sunday Wake Up Calls

I wake with a start. A loud fart still reverberates in the dimly lit room. I'm not facing Ashley thankfully; my eyes are pinged wide-open with shock. I genuinely don't think it was me. I'm hoping it wasn't me!

I don't know if it's woken him too, but I lie completely still anyway under the marshmallow of a quilt. I want to giggle, it can't be helped, and it somehow normalises this beautiful creature behind me. Everybody has bodily functions! It's easy to forget that when faced with somebody so divinely handsome. I know already he'd be embarrassed though, last night we really connected. It felt like he bared his soul, like we suddenly know each other really well. I pretend to continue sleeping.

Behind me Ashley rises and leaves the room. He has probably been doing the same as me for the past few minutes and assumes I've missed it. Or he could think it was me!

Now I feel mortified.

I quickly write the incident off and replay last night instead. I wonder if he's a morning sex kind of guy. Last night we were safe in a tiddly state, today would be sober, hungover, I bet my breath stinks actually.

"Morning." Ashley says gently and I feel his weight return to the mattress. "Jodie? I've made you a tea."

I stir, simulating a rousing.

"Morning." I say quietly and wish I'd had chance to look in the mirror before being confronted with him. He looks just as delicious in the watery light of day. I could have mascara under my eyes and a lopsided eyebrow.

"Thanks. I'll just nip loo." I slip from the bed without giving him too much time to inspect me and hope my bum at least looks perky as I leave.

The mirror reflects an ok face and I swill some water around my mouth before returning.

"I didn't know how you take it, so I guessed and put a sugar in it."

"I don't really have a preference to be honest." I take the mug from him once I've sat beside him and he gives me a horrified look.

"What?" I giggle.

"You don't have a preference! Jodie, I am a tea connoisseur! It has to be PG tips for a start."

I laugh at him but his eyes widen and he looks at me earnestly.

"I'm not kidding, you have got to take this serious!"

Despite the absence of alcohol we still get along easily. We don't have sex, but we finish our tea and another stream of conversations about anything and everything before getting dressed.

"Well, thanks for having me." I say as he walks me to his door.

"It's been great!" He tells me openly, those eyes like calm oceans pouring straight into mine. "I hope it's not the only time I'll be seeing you?"

I blush and smirk. "Well, when I get my own place I can return the favour."

I think of the pole, delighted at the possibilities and he raises his eyebrows.

"Nah, I know where it is and you can see everything from the windows of the Trap." He laughs casually and adds. "People would talk!"

I try to act like I haven't been stung by the comment and resume the farewell. The door clicks shut behind me and I march down the street, it's Autumn and already the air has a cold edge to it. Like Ashley perhaps?

People would talk.

He's right, if he was spotted then of course they would. I don't want that and he already told me he doesn't either so why am I annoyed by it, hurt even.

I've taken it far more personally than it was meant, I'm sure. Ashley has been the ultimate gent and host. He didn't mean it to offend me. He is the one missing out after all. He could have had free lap dance shows for the foreseeable.

I let myself in just as mum is coming down the stairs with a bundle of laundry.

"Where have you been?" She has a way of asking things in an accusatory tone regardless if she means to be.

"At a guy's house, Ashley." I could lie and say Leila's, but I've always been honest with her, often to her disapproval. I'm truthful all the same. I'm an adult plus she *made* me didn't she, she should know what I am!

"Oh?" She's interested, assuming a new relationship.

"It's not like that."

"Didn't go well?" She brushes by me and I follow her to the kitchen.

"It went really well!"

"Just a friend then?" I've always had male friends so this wouldn't be an odd occurrence.

"No! I mean, it's not a boyfriend thing. You know, just sex."

She swivels her eyes towards me, mouth forming an O.

"Well!" She sniffs and carries on stuffing the clothes into the washer. "You'll get a name for yourself."

This is something I've always been wary of. I've been reported to have had sex with plenty of people in the past, Chinese whispers, I've been called a slag. I suppose technically I am now but I wasn't then! And I still got labelled anyway. I shrug.

"We're keeping it secret."

"Nothing stays secret in this village!" She counters, and I snort.

"Well it's hard to tell what's true and what isn't mum. People think I've slept with every guy I talk to anyway and it's not like we'll be seen together."

He made that clear just now!

I can at least be sneaky about my encounters, hide the evidence. I do indeed *love* sleeping with fit blokes and some just because they're nice and funny. Why shouldn't I and if I can't shout it loud and proud, society dictates that, I can still do it in relative secrecy.

Mum isn't convinced. She's at the fridge now plucking out meat, onions and other root veg.

"It could work well." I say and click on the kettle, thinking of Ashley and his quirky tea obsession. "Every couple of weeks I'll get to pretend I have the most perfect boyfriend and there's none of the stress attached."

"Wasn't like that in my day." She comments.

"Your day! Mum, you're not even twenty years older than me."

"Well I mean we couldn't just go around... *having flings*. You had to move out to have... you know, *sex,* and that meant marrying the first guy you dated."

"Bloody hell!" I gasp laughing. "That sounds awful. No wonder you ended up with dad!" I tease her and that familiar cloud fills her eyes.

"I fancied him for months before he finally noticed me and asked me out."

"Then you married him so you could move out with him and have sex to your heart's content?"

"I married him because I fell pregnant with you!" She retorts with a small smile.

"What an accident I turned out to be!"

"You weren't an accident." She tuts. "But you know, it *was* different back then."

"Well now there's a field to play. There could be for you too, if you wanted to..." I let the suggestion linger and notice her back stiffen. She doesn't take me up on the reference so I ask instead, "Where is he anyway, in bed still?"

"Mmmm." She answers and doesn't look at me from where she's prepping. I've made us both a hot drink and I'm about to leave the kitchen when she carries on speaking.

"I have regrets Jodie. I don't want you to. I'm glad you're..." she pauses. "Doing your research. I know when you left Scott and moved home I didn't understand but I do now. And I'm glad you got rid of that Dane. You're so special Jodie, you deserve a man who is every bit as special as you. Don't settle for second best!"

We both have eyes glistening with sentimental tears and I wish she'd take her own advice. Keith does nothing for her; she's more like tenth best behind the pub, drinking, his friends, work and hobbies.

"Ditto." I mumble but I feel choked. It means a lot to have her unwavering support especially when the subject is fairly controversial. "I am happy mum. I want you to be too." I add.

She looks at me and it crushes me to see sadness.

"I'm not like you Jodes. My priorities are different. I am really proud of you sweetheart."

"Shut up now else you'll make me cry! I'm going for a shower anyway." I tell her and give her a swift hug. "Thanks for being the best mum always."

"I don't know about that." She mumbles going back to her roasting dish.

"You are. I'm your only daughter so it's definite. And I know George thinks so too! I mean who would make his packed lunches for him?" I drop in the dig with a grin and leave her shaking her head.

I could list her qualities, but it won't change a thing. I feel genuinely gutted that she's so at ease living without excitement and passion. She thinks she isn't worthy of a man helping her round the house, taking her out for dinner and treating her with respect and I don't know how to open her eyes. You don't miss what you haven't got that's the trouble.

Freshly showered I lie on my bed and write some more. Just paragraphs, chapters, ideas. At least this thing with Troy having a girlfriend has given me some perspective. Before that I'd been conjuring ridiculous scenarios of romance; unrealistic and wishful. Even with Ashley fresh in my mind it still makes my stomach ache to acknowledge my chances with Troy are officially over.

A sneaky one-time kiss wouldn't hurt would it?

I quash the inner voice chastising it for the suggestion. Instead I channel the possibility into a story. What kind of character goes with a man they know is taken?

***

It's evening. I'm no longer full to bursting with the Sunday lunch I devoured and I'm off to meet Leila. Her shifts have been all over the place since starting this training and she's finishing shortly. Usually she works Sunday night so she's thrilled and suggested we have a few drinks then go for a curry later. I'm game!

She wants to hear all about Ashley. I don't know whether she's been to his house, experienced his fabulous kiss, I don't care! It's all new to me and highly thrilling. I'll also tell her about the wake-up call because it is funny, even if he does think it was me.

And it hasn't put him off anyway. He's been messaging me all day about this and that. It really isn't a one-time thing!

The Trap, as usual, is pretty busy. Cat is behind the bar and I give her a wave.

"Has Leila finished?" I ask her.

She motions for me to go closer.

"*He's* here!" She hisses. I don't need to ask who, I've guessed right because I hear Dane's familiar cackle of a laugh and he walks around the edge of the bar. I look at him and he spots me instantly.

"Jodie." He approaches me.

"For fuck sake." I mutter. "Where is Leila?" I ask Cat because why didn't *she* warn me, she knew I was coming to meet her!

"Jodie. I'm so sorry." He says loudly and I cringe for us both glancing at those closest to us. He stinks of ale and sways slightly from side to side.

"Ok." I shrug and look around him for signs of Leila.

"Jodie?" He lines his face up with my vision. "I said I'm sorry!"

"And I said ok." I reply quietly without anger. "What do you want me to say? *Thank you*?"

Cat titters from my side. She's busy ignoring customers in favour of witnessing the exchange. His face contorts as if to say, *how dare you* and I have to giggle at the irony.

"Is Leila outside?" I ask Cat.

"Yeah she is. I saw her go out there." Dane answers for her looking dismayed. I feel a twinge of guilt. I need to get away from him, how can I feel sorry for him after what he did to me?

"I'm not with *her* anymore." He follows me as I walk. I don't know how to respond, so I don't. "Jodie, talk to me *please*."

"I've got nothing to say." I reply coolly.

"You hate me don't you?" He cries. It's still all about him I realise.

"I don't feel *anything* for you." I tell him pausing at the door. "Leave me alone, you don't know me."

He looks at me in disbelief as though I have slapped him. I praise myself for staying gracious and leave him frozen in the doorway.

"Oh Jodes!" Leila flies to me as soon as I walk outside. "Didn't you get my messages? I've been waiting for you out here."

I pull my phone from my pocket and scan the text instructing me to go around the back because Dane is inside. I'm actually pleased I didn't avoid him. I fully put him in his place just now and I grin from ear to ear.

"You'll never guess what I just said to him!" I begin with my heart racing as it fully sinks in.

"That's awesome! *I don't feel anything*! I bet that got to him." Leila is positively gleeful after hearing the rundown.

"I wasn't trying to get to him, it's the truth, it just came out. If I hate him I still have feelings for him! There's just no place for him in my life."

"Good riddance to rotten eggs!" She exclaims. "I'm gutted I missed it though."

A squeal of laughter and a flash of Cat bursts through the door before she launches herself into a hug.

"You were amazing!" She shrieks into my ear.

"Oh, shut up!" Leila howls. "It's not fair!"

"Both of you." I try to tell them off but they're so animated and my adrenalin has spiked because of the meeting making me light-headed and giggly.

"Jodes, we should go up the road for drinks instead, sorry Cat." Leila suggests but I shake my head.

"I've got no reason to avoid him. And if he's got any sense, he'll leave now."

Leila raises an eyebrow and sighs exasperatedly. "Of course he has no sense, else he wouldn't have thrown away his chance with you, would he?"

"He is still in there." Cat confirms nodding. "Bought another double JD as soon as you came out here."

"Someone's in the money." I murmur.

"It's on a tab." Cat smirks and I groan.

"I really was a fool wasn't I? Come on, he can torture himself then and watch me from afar."

Leila and I grab a bottle of wine from the bar and head to the pool table. We're only minutes into our game when Dane comes stumbling around the corner, a miserable face plastered on. I hope he'll pass straight by us to the toilets, but he begins to slow and stares at me glumly.

This is really awkward because we were talking about Ashley- in detail- and we do our best to fake a conversation and continue the game. He lurks for a while before shuffling off again and we can't help but burst into laughter at his back.

"Are you kidding me?" I giggle. "He's a mess."

"He always will be Jodie, you're so much better off without him."

"You do not have to tell me that!"

We're wrapping up our second game and deciding whether to have another bottle of wine when Dane decides to approach us again. His eyes are bleary and he stumbles into a little table for support upon reaching us.

"Jodie." He slurs. "Look at me Jodie."

I ignore him at first, but he says my name again and again and I finally do as he keeps asking. It feels good to hear him beg.

Other than breaking it off with him I feel like he controlled our entire relationship. Well now I'm in the driving seat.

"What do you want Dane?" I ask him using his name in return. He stares at me as if he's never seen me before. As if he's finally recognising everything I stood for when we were still together. And in many ways he really is looking at me for the first time.

He scratches around in a befuddled brain trying to remember what he wanted.

"Jem says you're buying her pole." He finally manages, each word a task.

117

He's trying to make small talk? He never even liked the pole thing. I don't think so! I'm about to tell him where to go when I'm distracted by a group of lads entering. I glance over before physically swooning. Even Dane, in his intoxicated state, spots my pupils dilate to saucers.

"No way!" I hiss beside myself with delight. The smile is instantaneous and huge. It always is when I see Luca.

"Who is it?" Leila is beside me, Dane forgotten.

"It's Luca!" I hiss. "The model guy I told you about."

I collect myself to head over and just catch the look on Dane's face as I pass him. Again, I feel a stab in my heart. Wounding people doesn't come naturally to me even when they have hurt me and making him party to my reaction is callous. But almost uncontrollable!

Luca was a childhood sweetheart; before the part-fame came along. Our paths rarely cross these days but when they do it's at random times like this and seeing him fills me with a racing, heated energy. As a youngster I always thought he was gorgeous. But since he grew into his large grin and long-lashed eyes, everybody else in the world thinks so too.

"Hey." I greet him with swiftly mustered casualness. Leila has followed me and arrives by my side.

"This is Leila." I introduce her to Luca.

"Hi Leila," he croons, turning on the beam he knows makes most women, and many men, weak at the knees. She doesn't reply, breathless I expect, but manages a smile.

I greet the others he's with. His friends are local and I see them around pretty often. My eyes are instead drawn to Luca's face.

"So, what brings you down here?" I ask him.

"I was at a shoot nearby. The boys were moaning they hadn't linked up in ages."

"Working on anything good?" I ask and notice Cat ogling him as she serves them, a little star-struck.

"*Always* baby." He winks and my heart explodes in my chest even if he does ooze cocky confidence. "Want a drink?"

"We're good, it's my round." I order another bottle of wine, any hints of appetite rapidly disintegrated. I'd drink petrol if it meant staying here and Leila hasn't got a choice.

"So what's new?" He asks.

"Everything!" I grin. "New job, new flat."

"New man?" He asks.

"No. *No* man." I clarify and he holds my eye allowing his to twinkle flirtatiously. Last time I saw him I'd still been with Scott. The time before that we'd had clumsy drunken sex on a park bench, we were twenty.

"Well that's good news." He grins and I return it for as long as I can manage before I feel dizzy and have to look away.

"So how long are you around for?" I ask him before the word spreads and the pub becomes inundated with adoring fans.

"Long enough." Allusive as ever; but that's part of the attraction.

"Long enough for what?" I rise to the remark. Every part of me is vibrating with excitement. Every girl wants him, I've had him before numerous times and now I'm going to do my best to have him again.

"You, me, we can see what happens..." He looks away from me as the first swarm of hangers-on buzz hungrily through the door. "Facebook me, yeah?"

"Ok." We share one more electric gaze and my time is up. Initially we're separated by a tangle of bodies, moments later the Trap is swamped.

"What the actual FUCK!" Leila screams over the commotion. "He is even better looking in real life! Wow Jodie!"

She's overwhelmed having seen him on the TV and modelling various accessories; sunglasses, hats, boxers- yes, I have all the pictures stashed under my bed. It was strange seeing him in print at first, but I'm stunned by just him, we met when we were thirteen and I remember every single meeting since.

"Wow, Jodes, sorry but Dane really was just a blip wasn't he! *Wow!*"

I glance around suddenly remembering Dane but there's no way I'd spot him, even if he is still amongst this utter chaos that my forever-crush has caused. I still feel bad he had to see that but, well, he wasn't thinking about my feelings back then was he?

Let this be his wake-up call. Hopefully he'll go on to learn from his mistakes. All the times he put me down, the accusations and the disrespect. Look where it's gotten him.

And as for the boy who has caused this ruckus. He's ridiculously boyish, arrogant as hell and smooth as they come. Women fall at his feet. But there's something extra between us, a history and a connection to a world before he didn't know who to trust.

"Come on, drink up, let's go for that food." I tell Leila who's tiptoeing to get another look.

"I can't see him!" She complains. "Who are all these people, they aren't his friends!"

"Don't worry, we'll be having bacon sarnies with him when we've got the flat."

"Oh my god Jodie!" She yells as we turn to leave. "Don't even *say* that I can't cope! He's so beautiful."

I obviously feel chuffed that she is so in awe of him. I feel proud to know the man behind the mayhem and truth be told when I first met him other girls thought he was annoying. I didn't though and now look at him, women decorating him wherever he steps foot. He told me to message him!

I'll need a Little Black Book at this rate. Men are coming along like buses!

"Why didn't you let him buy us our wine?" Leila asks as we walk to the curry house. This is nothing like when Den treated us before and I explain my reasoning.

"I'm not interested in his money. I don't *need* his money and I want him to *know* that. I'm different." I wink at her. "I'm playing the game."

***

I'm home and propped up on my bed nursing my tummy wondering if I am too greedy. My body is filled to the brim with pure glee as well as curry and I half-heartedly watch the TV.

I've replied to messages from Aaron and Ashley and Facebook stalked Luca to the point of making myself giddy with desire, but I won't message him tonight. It'll look too keen and he could be entertaining another floozy right now.

I can't blame him. I know the feeling of being like a kid in a candy store; I tasted it in Magaluf.

I turn my mind to tomorrow and Belfry. It's the opposite end of the spectrum to Maga and I've got to adjust my mind-frame ready for the next week at school.

Monday meetings are now on the timetable. After the students have gone home, each one will be discussed and their new 'status' decided. Some kids will go up to Silver One, earning them the first tier of extra privileges.

I am feeling way more confident about everything, if I were a student I'd definitely be moving up to the next level. Except, I'm also looking forward to seeing Troy again- way too much.

I'm still pissed at him for not letting on about his relationship status. And between Aaron, Ashley and Luca I've got plenty to concentrate on.

But Troy...

I decide I perhaps do have a greedy streak after all. I've heard of one piece never being enough, this is taking it to a whole new dimension.

Monday Meeting

The school day has passed by with a regular occurrence of tantrums and holds. It would seem that five days is enough for the students to find their feet and not all lessons run as smoothly as they did last week.

By the time I'm heading to the staffroom for the end of day meeting I feel utterly drained and looking forward to sitting down with a hot drink. I enter to find Troy immediately flagging me over to the seat he's saved. He's made me a coffee too.

Resisting his charm is difficult considering he seems to have turned the notch to 'full'. I wonder how well he and his girlfriend actually get on. If he was happy at home, why would he make such a play for me? And it is just me. I've watched how he is with the other females. He does flirt a bit naturally but not like how he does with me. And Lacey said herself she hasn't been there because the chance hasn't arisen.

I plop beside him and gratefully take the cup returning his smile wearily.

"Tough day huh." He comments. The whole school has been lively and when I haven't been somehow involved in an incident, I've been able to at least hear another going on.

"Let's make a start, there's a lot to get through." Neil is announcing and I relax further realising I haven't got to sit facing Julie for the next hour. "Year 6's- Jenni."

He has a kind voice and knowing the protocol, Jenni, the year 6 teacher begins.

"Alfie, Cameron, Areeb, Dexter, Kai all moving up to Silver One please. Isaac and Dante staying the same."

"That's a shame." Julie's voice pipes up from behind me. No such luck of escaping her all together then.

"Yeah they've both had a really tough week." Jenni says disappointedly and her assistant Leanne nods looking equally as gutted.

"Ok, any objections?" Neil looks at Iqbal and Helen the art teacher, the only others to teach the 6's. They have their own unit a bit like the girls and are nurtured virtually fulltime by Jenni for their first year. "No? Moving on, year 7's."

Del steps forwards and like Jenni reels off the names of those moving up. No protests. Next it's Troy's year 8's and the class teacher, Debra, stands up.

"Ok. Mason, Keon, Josh staying down obviously." She states to murmurs around the room. "I'd like Shay and Kyron to move up. But I don't know what you guys think?"

"Well, Shay was really rude to me." Gilbert's deep voice announces.

"He did time for that though didn't he?" Claire counters. She's referring to a punishment where they lose minutes at their breaks, not hard time in prison.

"Yeah but it's not really silver behaviour is it?"

"Silver two or three maybe." Claire huffs. "Shouldn't we focus on all the positives he's had? He's under a lot of stress at home."

Gilbert shrugs as if bored of the conversation and looks away. Claire has a flustered flush rising from her collar.

"He has had a good week." Troy adds from beside me.

"Has he been in BS much?" Julie asks flatly. BS equals Behaviour Support, not 'bull shit' which immediately sprang to my mind when I first heard the abbreviation.

"Not that I'm aware of." Debra answers looking down at the notes she holds. "Nothing on here. He's had mostly fours."

The best score to achieve per lesson.

"Move him up." Julie makes the decision and I watch Gilbert's odd reaction of a smirk. Perhaps he feels embarrassed being stood up to by the seniors because he does have an irritating air of inflated self-importance.

"What about Kyron?" Debra asks almost meekly having just caused the little debate.

Nobody argues and the procedure moves on. It's almost therapeutic listening to names being rattled off and not being called upon to do any real thinking.

The statuses, now decided, will be announced in tomorrow's assembly. The race for gold is on!

"Safeguarding?" Neil nods towards Claire and they swap seats.

"Just a few bits. Mason's step-dad has been sentenced to twelve years. We'll be monitoring him as the dust settles. We're not sure how much he witnessed, the next couple of months are crucial..."

I had no idea he was enduring this kind of turmoil, or of any explicit details, but my mind races with possibilities. Whatever comes out of Claire's mouth during this part of the meeting, I realise, is going to be tough to hear but important and necessary for their wellbeing.

"Ben is still being closely monitored however it is on a *need to know* basis. Those involved need to be vigilant. And now Jay, year 7 Jay," she confirms because there are number of duplicate names. "The decision has been made to remove him from his home. It will be happening this evening and he'll be taken to a foster family."

There are a few intakes of breath. I've worked with Jay today. He's on the scrawny side which could indicate neglect. He's also energetic, witty and flamboyant, I wouldn't have judged him as unhappy and I wonder how he'll handle such news; heart-break, distress, relief? Could circumstances ever be so bad a child feels relief at being removed from their parents?

"He'll be in tomorrow, nothing about his routine should change here but he'll need a lot of support to get through this. As always there's a lot going on in the background with the others. If you're unsure about anything we would rather you report it to us."

She looks at Gilbert and smiles stiffly. His eyes crinkle easily.

"Yes. Drop into BS anytime and speak to me."

I think I hear Claire utter '*us*' and I'm sure there's some sort of rivalry going on there.

"Any other business?" Neil is announcing. "No?"

He looks around the room. "Ok, thanks and have a good evening."

"Thanks Neil." Julie coos loudly. She doesn't thank Claire. I watch Gilbert watch Julie as she waltzes out of the room.

"Jodie?" Lizzy has bounded up to me. "Tomorrow afternoon, I want you to try with Eve."

125

I quickly rack my brains and place her.

"As in Eve who spat at Lacey and refused to even talk to her?"

"Yes. Her." She smiles apologetically. "I honestly think you'll make headway with her! A change of face will help, and I've seen how you are with the others, not just the girls, *all* of them."

Her praise makes my heart dance. Admittedly I do feel like I have a knack with the students, but I've been putting it down to beginner's luck. Maybe it is, but then perhaps I should go for it whilst it's on my side!

"Ok." I swallow hard. I've only ever been asked to fetch bits from the local supermarket if the bar ran out of lemons or Tabasco sauce. "You'll have to tell me exactly what to do because I've never done anything like this."

Troy vacates the chair beside me, using my thigh to push himself up. He looks back and smirks, taking both our empty mugs to the sink and Lizzy plonks into his spot. The warmth of his palm is etched into my skin and I resist rubbing at the spot.

"So, you'll have your lunch then whizz down to the industrial estate off Eastside Way…" Lizzy gives me all of the details, I take notes.

"Honestly, I've got a good feeling, I think you'll do it." She finishes kindly.

"Fingers crossed!"

Driving home, my mind is busy turning over all the stones today presented; Jay being told he's got to leave his home and his mum, Mason witnessing things that got his dad banged up for twelve years and what about Ben that needs vigilance and secrecy? It must be something dire, but he seems so jolly! Plus, Eve, and this visit to her tomorrow.

It's hard to just switch off and I stand under a hot shower trying to wash the sympathy and helplessness and fretful questions out of my head. I need to start thinking about packing up my room. I've still got boxes of stuff from the house I shared with Scott and teamed with the bits Leila has got, we're in good stead for our new abode.

Once back in my bedroom, my mind turns to Luca. Today has been manic, and I've been mildly distracted by Troy, I've barely dwelled. I message him now though, keeping it short and casual.

Good to see you yesterday ☺

Then I busy myself with packing away DVD's and knick-knacks and pretend I'm not going to spend every second waiting until he replies.

The Unteachable Eve

I drive away from Belfry with Google maps loaded on my phone and instructing me just a little too late when to take a turn. The journey is only predicted to take ten minutes and I feel tense and apprehensive. Lizzy told me to remind myself of the details on Eve and having re-read her statement I feel far less-equipped for this than I had done this morning.

Abusive, unteachable, unpredictable, volatile and more; the kid's been labelled them all. I feel a strange sense of sympathy. How does she stand a chance when this is the first impression given about her?

The building is a non-descript warehouse and I head to the entrance. There's a buzzer with a little camera and I press the button waiting for the electronic ringing to be answered.

"Hello?" A male voice picks up.

"Hi, it's Jodie from Belfry, I'm here to see Eve." I tell the speckled metal.

"Come in." The door hums and I pull it open.

I'm met with a large reception room. A couple of plants and foam chairs and a coffee table littered with magazines. A small man, tufty greying hair rimming his head, tumbles through a door and meets my eye beadily.

"Hi. I'm Pete. I run Intervene."

"Hi Pete, nice to meet you."

"She's through here. I must say I don't know how well you'll do." He looks me up and down and I feel a wave of dogged determination.

"I'm sure we'll be fine." I smile. He harrumphs and my suspicions of people judging Eve are confirmed. "Does she know I'm here?"

"Yeah. She's already threatened to throw a chair at you."

"Great!" I try to laugh off what I'm sure isn't a joke and my optimism diminishes.

"Right this way."

I follow him, remaining a little behind just in case she makes good on her proposal. Eve is sat at a desk, facing the door and we lock eyes immediately. I give her a small smile and her lips curl into a menacing grin.

"Hey Eve." I say, and her glinting slate blue eyes don't leave mine. "I'm Jodie. Can I sit down?"

"If you want!" She surprises me by answering but jumps up herself. "I'm going in there though."

She's almost my height, has mousy hair and an untidy fringe, an upturned chin with a scar across it. I sit as I suggested I would, and she flounces into another room slamming the door behind her.

Well, at least no spit- or a flying chair. Yet!

"Told you." Pete has his arms folded and a smug look on his ferrety face.

"She doesn't want to leave here." Another man sidles out of a side room from where he's obviously been lurking. "I'm her keyworker here, Giles."

He's younger than Pete, not by much, but his sandy hair is yet to recede or grey. I now have a man standing to both my left and right, mimicking bouncers- although the only resemblance is their stance. I catch the smirk and filter out a professional smile instead.

"Hi Giles, I'm Jodie. So how long has Eve been here?" I ask and glance at the door where I spot her peeking through the window.

"Two months. Before that she was out of education for four years. She's basically feral. She is unteachable and won't ever be able to access a proper curriculum."

"I read that." I say coolly and follow my instincts heading toward the room Eve is in.

"I wouldn't if I were you. The last one they sent got spat at."

"I know." I growl undeterred. There's something about these guys and the possessive way in which they're acting, I want to rescue her.

I knock and hear a muffled. "Fuck off."

Not completely unexpected so I enter anyway. She must be fed up with people talking about her rather than to her.

"Hey. What you doing in here?" I slip inside purposely leaving Vile Giles and Sneaky Pete behind. I want to talk to her alone. She still hasn't answered me but there's a vivarium with a lizard inside on a rock and she watches it intently.

"Cool pet." I comment and slide into a chair. "What's his name?"

"Andy." She says without looking and I can't help it, I laugh out loud. Ironic really, the namesake I met in Magaluf was scaly to say the least.

"Did you name him?"

"Yeah." She glances at me and a shimmer of humour titivates her features.

"Nice one. Does he move much?" I look away from her back to Andy the lizard.

"Not really. Sometimes I poke him."

"And *then* does he move?"

"If I poke him hard enough." She answers confidently. I feel sorry for Andy.

"I bet you feel bad about leaving him?" I use him as an avenue and she flicks her eyes to me again.

"You want me to go to that school!" She fires and her expression snaps from placid to rage in an instant.

"Don't you like school?" I don't twitch a muscle and keep my voice just as calm as before.

"I *hate* it!" She shouts and I hope against hope neither of the men come in and ruin this for us now. I want Eve to co-operate for her sake as much as I know the accomplishment of convincing her to come into Belfry will bring me inevitable glory.

"What do you hate about it?" I continue to lead her along.

"The teachers." She snaps.

"Well I'm a teacher, do you hate me yet?" I ask and sensing her wit flash her a grin. I know it's bending the truth, but it trips her.

She returns the smirk then shakes her head. "I hate the other kids."

"There's just four others." I say shortly and allow this information to dissolve. Then I add. "There's a school for boys joined on but you don't have to see them."

I can actually see her warming to the idea.

"You're ok aren't you Eve?" Giles enters the room and I curse him inwardly. She jumps and looks from me to him before marching out of the room without a second glance.

"She really doesn't like the idea." Giles says loudly. "It won't work, this won't."

I want to retaliate but for the sake of Eve, and my mission, I hold it all in. I don't like this man, why doesn't he want to let her go? Letting her come to us will give her the best opportunity.

"It will take time but she'll come around." I dismiss him and go to find her.

"Why are you following me?" Eve demands when I catch up with her. She's twisting the dials on a keyboard.

"I just wanted to see what other stuff you've got here." I reply and touch the screen beside her fingers. "Can you play?"

"No!" She admits and laughs. The titter is like music to my ears.

"I can't either." I tell her. "What do you like doing then?"

She shrugs and throws herself down onto a nearby couch.

"Do you like Minecraft?" I ask and she thinks it over.

"It's ok." She says eventually. I know there isn't much time before Giles comes to intervene again, so I have to rush along.

"You know, I'm new at the school. Belfry. The place I want to show you." I choose my words purposefully and she listens.

"What's it like?" She finally nibbles.

"It's really nice. Everything in our girls part is brand new. I can't wait to show you!" I add, mimicking Iqbal's excitement for his subject.

Eve ponders what I've said and as I predicted both Pete and Giles now enter the space we're occupying.

"Best to keep you company." Pete tells me. "She isn't good with new people. Are you Eve?"

Eve tuts and rolls her eyes. I project a silent voice willing her to trust me and take the leap.

"Well, I think Eve would like to at least visit." I jump, will she follow? "You know so she can decide properly if she doesn't like it."

My invisible hand is extended, please take hold Eve.

"When? Today?" She snaps. I don't know whether she means she wants to now or hopes not.

"Yes." I say at the same time as Pete and Giles chorus;

"No."

"If you want to Eve, you can. We can go for ten minutes and come back." I tell her.

"I'll come with you as well." Giles adds recognising that Eve does not look taken aback by the suggestion.

I'm already being more forceful than I think I should be, so I don't object. I have no idea if I can ban his presence, but I'm legally covered to take her, part of my contract was to upgrade my car insurance.

"Let me go for a think first. Then we'll go." Eve tells me before skipping out of sight.

A *think*, how mature! This is definitely something we can accommodate at the unit. Not only will it make the transition more effective but the others could learn a thing or two!

"Where does she go for a think?" I ask them and they exchange a look. "We could do something similar if it's something that works for her." I explain.

The pods are perfect for creating quiet, calm spaces and I look from one face to another before eventually Pete answers.

"When she says a 'think', what she means is. What she means is… A *think* is…" He stops and starts before looking at Giles.

"She means a fag. She's gone for a fag break and frankly I'm going to join her." Giles ups and leaves and so does my ability to speak. I'm flabbergasted by not only the news they allow a thirteen-year-old to openly smoke but he's *joining* her.

"She's a smoker Jodie." Pete tells me with a shrug. "If we didn't let her she'd walk out and do it anyway."

I cannot imagine Julie taking such a lenient stance. The students in year 10 and 11 can go offsite at break times *if* they're above bronze status. It's no secret some of them do so to slip in a crafty cigarette.

Eve is year 9. I'm unsure how we can accommodate this. *If* we can! Our work is truly cut out but already we've- I've- managed a massive hurdle.

Once Eve and Giles have finished their 'think' we pile into my small car and head back to Belfry. I've called ahead to tell Lizzy we're coming, she is over the moon! Harishma will be just ecstatically frantic and I'm sure Mollie will be easily whipped into a frenzy. Bonnie will melt down and Jayde stay as cool as a cucumber, filing her nails at the desk.

"We've got our own section of noticeboard and we can decorate it with anything we like." I'm gushing all of the positives about the unit as I drive and Giles is doing his best to scatter seeds of doubt.

"I don't think a box of Richmond Super Kings will be allowed." He comments. "Do you Eve? Bet they won't like that."

I cringe. It's so inappropriate; my safeguarding alarm bells are ringing. What is his problem?

There's pretty much a welcome party waiting at the door for Eve. Giles finally loses his confidence since he's outnumbered seven to one and he loiters in the reception as introductions are made.

Just as I suspected Jayde is laid-back, Lizzy her usual calm and Mollie panting at the sight of fresh meat followed closely behind by Harishma. Bonnie has disappeared into a pod wailing.

"Hi, hello." Eve greets everyone with small smiles and wary eyes and I glimpse a regular year 9 meeting her classmates for the first time.

"Mollie, do you want to show Eve around?" I suggest, and she doesn't need convincing.

"Come and look over here!" She guides her off and I linger but give them a chance to sightsee and chat together.

"Well done!" Lizzy silently mouths and gives me a double thumbs up. "Harishma, can you check on Bonnie?"

"Hmm?" Harishma is roused from where she's staring at Eve.

"Bonnie." Lizzy reminds her. "Can you see to her please whilst we keep an eye on things here?"

"Oh. Bonnie. Yep, sure."

She scuttles away and I catch Lizzy's eye, she smirks and I know she's on my wavelength.

Eve explores with Mollie for ten minutes and then they begin to examine the 'All About Me' board. I hold my breath praying she doesn't repeat the Vile Giles comment about Richmond packets. Mollie will thrive on that.

But instead the arty names intrigue her.

"Who's Jayde?" She asks eyeing the pictures of intricate manicures and pretty frocks.

"Me." Jayde raises a hand but doesn't look over, still engrossed in her own nails.

"Me and Jayde are friends, aren't we Jayde?" Mollie coos and beckons for Eve to follow her to the table. Jayde rolls her eyes and briefly catches mine.

Please behave Jayde, is all I can think. But she can't fit a word in edgeways over Mollie gushing about her- amazing, beautiful, clever- better words than those used by their statements I realise wryly. Even if it is a little cringe-worthy to watch!

Eve gazes at Jayde's face in adoration. They could all prove such positive influences on each other- or quite the opposite if they choose to. The conversation does however stay suitably tame and for a few moments I enjoy witnessing new bonds bloom. I also love noticing Giles squirm. You've lost her mate!

Bonnie has finally dared to reappear and her and Eve lock eyes on one another. They're both defensive but in completely different ways. Bonnie whimpers and Eve snarls.

"Eve, this is Bonnie. Bonnie, Eve." I say taking the lead. "Bonnie, you still feel a bit nervous about being in school don't you? Well Eve is new and she is feeling the same."

"Am not!" She scoffs. "I'm fine about this." She flings herself back into the chair and pulls her best 'I'm cool' face. I rejoice inside because despite this being bravado she's agreeing to come again.

Giles decides now is the time to exit and her eyes find him through the glass, leaving reception and into the carpark.

"I need a think!" She declares. I haven't had chance to explain this quirk to Lizzy and I don't want the girls picking up on anything before we've had time to make a plan.

"Me too." I add much to her approval. "Come on, we'll go to my car and I'll take you and Giles back."

He hasn't even interacted with any of us, never mind her. Surely Lizzy will have noticed that. He's weird. And I'm under no illusion he timed the walk out purposefully.

"How did you like it then?" I ask Eve the obvious question as she skips, hops and leaps on the way to my car.

"Fucking good yeah!"

"Ay, remember one of our goals, you've got to try and watch that language, *especially* around the younger ones."

"She's got a potty mouth." Giles meekly attempts to derail, but it's clear he knows he's lost whatever battle he waged.

"You'll try and remember though won't you, don't want them learning words that only teenagers should use!" I play up to her yet again and she smiles and bashes her shoulder into mine. I take the contact as a positive sign.

"Can I smoke in your car?" She asks once we're pulling onto the road.

"We'll be back soon. Wait until then please."

I'm chuffed she actually does.

"So, are you happy to come back tomorrow?" I ask as we draw up to the Intervene building.

"Yeah! Are you coming to get me?"

"It'll be Lacey tomorrow and Thursday. But then me again on Friday."

"I spat at her!" She guffaws. "A big greenie!"

She giggles and I try to mask my revulsion.

"It missed her!" She assures me not fooled. "Will you be there when I get there tomorrow?"

"I'll be working with the boys. But I'll try and come and see you. I'll definitely see you Friday though. Gives us both something to look forward to, I can't wait for you to tell me all about it."

She smiles at me and I resist grinning victoriously at Giles, I won't stoop to his level. I'm just glad to be getting her out of this freaky place.

"Thanks Eve." I say as they get out. I suspect she isn't thanked often and I'm rewarded with the biggest grin yet. She's a gawky kid under all of the nasty labels. I'm sure we'll be privy to some of that behaviour but I'm feeling hopeful as I make the return journey.

"Glory, glory sister newbie! Glory, glory sister newbie!"

I'm literally crying with laughter as Lizzy hails my return in the tune of a football song. Mollie, Bonnie and Jayde have gone home since it's past three.

"I told you!" Harishma chastises. "*Sister* newbie makes it sound like we're running a finishing school!"

"We kind of are!" I giggle.

"But we're not nuns. Are we?" She says it affixing my eye and I have no choice but to answer this time.

"Well no, I'm not really. But the girls don't need to know that!" I laugh and we both turn to Lizzy who has fallen quiet.

"I'm, erm, I'm… gay."

"I knew it!" Harishma cries gleefully. "I could tell!"

Admittedly the football song had added to the subtle hints I'd been collecting already.

"Have you got a girlfriend?" She asks her.

"No!" She paws the air. "I'm not a nun either, as you keep putting it. You do make me laugh!"

"So anyway…" I have to change the course of this conversation to an altogether less jovial direction. "There's something odd about Intervene, the place Eve is at? Did Lacey say anything?"

"She said they were weirdos." She clarifies and I feel better. "Go on."

She doesn't feed me with what else Lacey said and I take a breath as Harishma leans forward ready to gulp in my next words.

"They just seemed like they don't want her to go. Not in a, *I care about your future and I'm not sure this is right for you*, type of way. In a strange, jealous kind of way. Like they didn't want me to succeed."

Lizzy nods and sighs.

"Unfortunately." She begins and my heart sinks. "There's a lot of funding surrounding these kids. In business terms Eve is worth big bucks, I mean *a lot* of Government money. If she attends Belfry they lose a massive chunk of income."

"Ok." I understand and feel a tad relieved because the picture I'd been painting was far more sinister than that. Still it is seriously manipulative behaviour on their part.

"One more thing." I go on to explain about the 'think' and how Giles also smoked with her.

"You need to report all of this Jodie." Lizzy tells me. "Go and find Claire. If she's busy, find Gilbert."

I scoot off hunting for Claire first because I'm not keen on Gilbert and head to her small office.

There's a screaming coming from another classroom. I can hear year 7 Jay yelling, "I don't want to go! It isn't my home!"

My heart sinks through the floor and I physically shudder at his retching cry. Poor, poor kid. In the high of this afternoon I'd forgotten all about the other battles going on. I glance through the doorway, Sean is overseeing a ground hold and he returns my nod signalling it is under control.

I leave behind the anguished rage but not the feeling of despair it evokes and slowly approach Claire's office. I can hear

Gilbert's deep voice reverberating and he swings open the door announcing.

"You mark my words, *Claire*." He enunciates her name and I freeze instinctively feeling like I shouldn't have overheard. His eyes clap on my face and stay there as he sweeps his sneer past and away down the corridor.

I knock on the door and hear a clearing of a throat.

"Come in." Claire calls breezily and I enter to find her shuffling paperwork. She doesn't look up immediately.

"Claire?"

"Ah Jodie. Everything ok?"

I could ask her the same thing; her face reveals she's upset, and I politely ignore the obvious pink eyes.

By the time I have explained and Claire has recorded everything, her face is back to normal.

"You've done the right thing telling me about this Jodie." Claire reassures me as I stand. "We'll try to sort something with the smoking and you're right, Giles should not be smoking with her it's unprofessional." Her eyes cloud momentarily and she shudders. "Unfortunately you'll come across this too often."

I stand to leave thanking her and saying bye, and unlike my unsettled mind, the school is quiet now. Jay has gone and so have the mentors. There is just quiet rustling drifting from the classrooms, teachers still hard at work.

I fetch my things from the staff room, Troy must have given up waiting and I try not to feel disappointed. I exit and abruptly come across Julie.

"Jodie." She says my name like it leaves a bad taste in her mouth. "Next time you *decide* to bring a student into Belfry you call reception and check. With *me*. I am in charge here."

Her eyes are hooked into mine almost painfully.

"I called Lizzy." I explain hoping I'm not throwing her under the bus. Perhaps she forgot to ring in her attendance.

"Lizzy is your supervisor. *I* am your *boss*."

She could be physically whipping me as she says this and I feel like a ton of bricks has been dropped onto my head. The only positive right now is that nobody is witnessing my dressing down.

"I never meant to do the wrong thing." I tell her feeling as pathetic as a puppy and she gives me a disdain filled look.

"Goodnight Jodie."

"Goodnight." I croak and walk away with my tail firmly between my legs. By the time I'm halfway home my embarrassment and upset has been replaced by anger. How dare she? I did exactly what was asked of me and in rapid time. I thought she'd be proud, that it would make my manager notice me. And she has! But it seems for all the wrong reasons.

I can't fathom a reason she'd be annoyed at the success. As if she really wanted to be personally alerted. She knew Eve would appear as soon as a connection was formed; that was the aim of the visits. It seems a thinly veiled excuse to have a go and if that is the case, her message was loud and clear. She is my boss and she is in charge.

I'm scared stiff of her as it is. As if I'd purposely put a foot out of place!

Her mean tactics have certainly taken the shine off my glory, glory. But on the other hand, I noticed the messenger icon flashing on my phone. It could be Ashley or Aaron and it could be Luca!

I drive home allowing the thrill of wondering to tickle my mind amid the rampage of irritated thoughts. By the time I'm parked up I fully push the school events to one side in favour of divulging my curiosity and unlock my phone whilst I'm still in my car.

It's all three of my current men!

I giggle to myself at the absurdity. If there is an angel and a devil on a shoulder each right now, one shakes her head as the other jumps for joy.

Obviously, Luca gets my attention first. I read his short reply as I walk from my car to the house.

Wanna see me again? ;-)

I quiver, yes, yes, YES! But the golden rule is to hold back. Just a little! I flick to the message from Ashley instead. He wants to see me again too, on Friday this time. I briefly wonder if I've been relegated from prime weekend slot to warm-up gig. Although he would make a tasty appetiser, Luca can be my Saturday main course.

I agree to Friday with Ashley because, well, why not! He's as good to chat to as a mate, the sex is erotic in an RnB music video kind of way and he has a very comfortable bed.

Hopefully no morning farts this time!

Leila texts interrupting me as I gleefully read through Aaron's message outlining his plans for me in Madrid- not dirty- genuine tourist attractions and so forth. I've not paid him much thought and I feel a bit guilty because he's put a lot of effort into the details.

Leila wants to know if I'm free to meet with her and Jane, our landlady, this weekend to sign contracts. I can't think of a better invite and visions of us living in Marshamonvilla are like smoke in my mind, tantalising but I can't capture them to take a better look.

A respectable number of hours have passed since Luca replied to my message so I type a response to him too.

I'm free Saturday.

Let's see how seriously he takes me. He'll no-doubt be busy but I try my luck anyway and press send. I just hope he doesn't suggest Friday now. That would be a serious bummer. And finally I reply to Aaron. It's mad how the Madrid thing has become the least of my excitements.

I think about work once again as I go through the motions of showering, changing and eating. I'm back to IT for most of the day tomorrow. I can't wait to tell Iqbal about the Eve achievement. Unlike Giles and Pete, I view her as an individual with potential and rights and needs. Not a monetary pawn in the accounts department.

The encounter with Julie plays on my mind, should I confide in Iqbal? And what about the Gilbert and Claire scenario, what is going on there?

I decide to give my poor brain a rest from the scrutinizing and pay Cat a visit. I also need to take my mind off Luca, buzzing like a fly is the notion he might just say yes.

Friday Tactics

Lacey has gone offsite with Mollie. Eve has been and gone- managing almost two hours- her longest so far before kicking off royally. Bonnie and Holly both went home at lunch for differing reasons- Holly is yet to complete a full day. And Lizzy and I now sit with Jayde and her social worker.

"You aren't in trouble." The stout lady repeats. "It's him that's in the wrong."

"How is he in the wrong?" She retaliates with a venomous lip curl.

"Because he's twenty-five Jayde. Over ten years older than you!"

I think of Leila admitting she slept with Shane, but then she wasn't fourteen when it happened.

"He's not twenty-five anyway." She hasn't been swayed to concede but she does giggle as she says it. "And, there was ten years between my mum and dad."

"It's not wrong that a guy finds you attractive Jayde." I try a different tactic. "You're a good-looking girl. It's just whilst you're still in your teens you should date somebody in your teens."

"Well he is, he's nineteen."

We're not getting anywhere.

"Jayde, he isn't a nice person. He has convictions for violent offences. He's a danger to you!" Davina, her social worker, tries again.

"Is not!" She retorts with the know-it-all confidence of a teen. She shakes her head clearly amused because we just don't get it.

"What's his name?" I ask Davina. She tells me and I head to the nearby computer typing it into Google.

"What are you doing?" Jayde asks me but before she's finished her sentence the evidence is in black and white on the screen.

"Blah blah, lives in South side, numerous offences, Asbo and look, aged twenty-four and this was from…" I scroll up checking the date of the newspaper report. "January this year. Jayde, you're better off with a guy your own age, I promise you. He'll bring you nothing but trouble."

I look at her imploringly, but she looks away.

Davina breaks the silence. "Jayde, I've got to alert the Police to this. I'm sorry but-"

"You're a fuckin bitch! You're a fuckin two-faced, fat, ugly bitch! Coming in my mum's house, eating all her biscuits and you're just trying to ruin everything for me!"

As the torrent of abuse escapes her mouth she jumps to her feet and pulls on her jacket.

"Lizzy let me out, I need a fag."

The girls weren't awarded new statuses this week because they've barely had a chance to start. She's on bronze and Lizzy looks at me nodding.

"Go with her please. Just this once Jayde because I know you're stressed. Talk to Jodie about it and then I want you to come back and we'll finish properly."

Jayde reluctantly nods, and I join her by the door where we're buzzed out and free to walk offsite.

"Where did you meet him?" I ask as a way of making conversation.

"When I was walking to the shops." She answers, and I'm surprised, I thought she'd say Facebook!

"They're wrong about him. He really cares for me." She sparks up and takes a long drag.

"I'm sure he does care for you." I soothe her.

"He buys me loads of nice things! The first time I met him he gave me a tenner and bought me some fags."

Grooming, I realise grimly. She looks so pleased and I smile weakly. I make a mental note to write all of this down for the social worker's report.

"He got me some trainers this week." She adds. "I don't want the police to know, what if they take back my stuff?"

"They won't." If I can eliminate this worry maybe she'll cooperate. "Davina wouldn't do this if it wasn't best for you."

She tuts and mutters, "She's a twat."

"You said some mean things back there Jayde, I think you should apologise for being rude."

"Whatever." She huffs. "How did you know to Google him anyway?"

I catch a glimmer of respect in her hazel eyes and wonder if I should be truthful.

"Because this boy I know is a model and I Google him all the time." I admit hoping the admission will seal our bond.

"That's sick! But what's that got to do with it?" She means sick as in *really good* not sick-in-the-head.

"Because he used to get into trouble, when he was younger. And the newspaper reports come up from back then sometimes. I'll show you."

I'm using Luca to gain brownie points just how Mollie does. But I hope by offering some 'sick' information about myself she will open up to me again in the future. It is better she tells me however disturbing the reality is.

Once back inside, Jayde eyes Davina before mumbling, "Sorry about what I said."

Lizzy catches my eye and I know she's happy with me. I told her about Julie and her words regarding Eve, she told me to ignore her; she's met bullies like her before apparently. So I'm resigned to do my best, with a tyrant for a boss. Iqbal is happy with me, so is Lizzy and as long as they both remain pleased with my efforts I have to stay positive.

Once Davina has explained to Jayde she's heading to the police station I use Luca once again to distract her from dwelling. I pull up a picture of him exhibiting a sports cap.

"He's well nice Jodie! When did you meet him?"

"I was thirteen." I explain to her about our relationship and put emphasis on the fact we were even younger than her when we first met. "That's why it's best to stick with your own age- at least when *you* get to my age he's not all old and crinkly."

I can see my admissions adding dimension to her view of me, maybe us 'teachers' as a whole.

"And what is old and crinkly to you my dear?" Lizzy pipes up and raises her eyebrows.

"What you on about, you look my age."

"I'm twenty-nine."

"Not much older then."

"I feel ancient. You're still young and fresh." She grins at me, a spark in her eye and I wonder if she's flirting.

"So, do you still see him?" Jayde asks looking from me to the beautiful Luca onscreen.

"Sometimes." I tell her. "Maybe this Saturday."

In truth he hasn't messaged back but this doesn't mean no so I cling to that. I'm seeing Ashley again tonight. Regardless of tomorrow I am getting laid this weekend!

Not something to share with her though, I have boundaries and reasons for disclosing the Luca thing. I want to be a role model and being promiscuous is not something I want her to idolise, not at her age anyway. I've spoken about Luca to gain her trust and it seems to have worked.

Lacey returns from the walk with Mollie and she and Jayde are packed off home.

"You did a really good job with Jayde back there. It's tricky knowing how to handle things and get the real message across." Lizzy congratulates me. I feel happy hearing she thinks so, but the war is far from won.

"What happened?" Lacey asks and I tell her everything. She is just as gutted as us about the issue but demands to see Luca for herself once I've finished. I show her to murmurs of appreciation.

"And what about Ashely you little tart?" She teases me gleefully. As Harishma keeps pointing out we're not nuns and in this haven not expected to be.

"I'm seeing him tonight." I answer and she nods approvingly. "So, will you go to the pub after work still?

I've been contemplating this but my mind is made up. "No, I want to get ready properly before I go round."

It's a difficult decision to stick by especially with Troy brushing against me as he asks the same question when I'm in the staff room.

I look into his hypnotic gaze cursing him for being taken but stick to my guns. I'm betting he will never voluntarily come clean about having a girlfriend. We've spoken enough this week and I now notice the little manoeuvres that allow our conversations to leave her out of it.

I leave him to chat with the pub-going staff and Sean frowns at me for not joining them.

I manage to exit the school without any sightings of Julie or Gilbert which I am pleased about. I resolutely avoid both where possible. I feel like Julie is looking for any excuse to reprimand me and Gilbert seems the type to drop a banana skin on purpose. Both of them give me the creeps when I have to meet their eyes.

Driving home, I use the time to chew over the week. On a Friday I try to resolve my thoughts and shut them down for the weekend. It's the only way I can see to remain sane; the pressure of Belfry is *in*sane! I can't help but worry about all of the kids and if I can't learn to manage the emotional distress, I'll be no good to anybody.

Troy is my final issue for the week. Another week of flirting gone by except this time I've known the truth of the situation all along and my inner voices are rabid with contradicting arguments.

He's not lied. I haven't asked him outright. He is crossing the line. I am too because I'm giving him the opportunity. It's just an experiment! An experiment I enjoy too much! Somebody is going to end up hurt...

It's not the first time I've had the conversation with myself. I know any barriers I form melt like sugar in hot water as soon as he's near. I need him to back off. I could cause him to do so by calling him out. But whatever my reasoning, I won't yet, I know that too.

For now I change the record. It's time for the weekend vibes to seep in. I think of Ashley, tonight's entertainment and inwardly smile gloatingly.

One thing is for sure, I have more stress and concerns than I ever had before and that's saying something because the past year at least has been rocky! But I most certainly feel the best I ever have.

I am slowly uncovering that unknown potential I knew existed within me. I took a risk when I ended things with Scott (my first 'proper' relationship) and moved home. I followed an elusive 'feeling' of something else being my destiny. Working with kids, meeting all these new people and experiencing new places has made me sure I was right.

I'm more honest with myself about exactly what it is I want. I'm less hard on myself when I realise too late it wasn't good for me and well, go-getting has panned out brilliantly so far!

For now though, I just want my make-up to go on easily, so I can have a fun night with the gorgeous Ashley.

Saturday Shambles

I leave Ashley's house on Saturday morning and float home on cloud nine. Date number two (and it *can* be called that if candles, wine and gentlemanly manners suggest it) went even better than the first! Our conversation improved, we're at ease in each other's company. He acted like my boyfriend, he felt like a boyfriend, as if it's been going on for years.

Whilst we're shut up in his home it feels like nothing else matters and I've fully relished in that feeling.

He's at a gig tonight. That's the reason he invited me for a Friday. There's a twinge of guilt regarding the Luca situation and a twinge of doubt about Ashley's true feelings for me. But Luca probably won't message me now anyway and there's no point worrying over how Ashley really feels.

I let myself in at home and get ready for the meeting with Leila and Jane, our landlady-to-be.

We've decided the Trap is easiest because there's no need to impose on Shane and by early afternoon we're sitting at a table together with the documents between us.

"I know it seems very formal girls." The extremely attractive woman of early fifties is telling us. "But the contract is you know, just to cover everyone's backs. Those flats have been occupied by the same tenants for years and I've never done a spot check. Shane says you're good girls and if I'm honest I prefer renting to females."

I watch her painted lips moving, she winks at me and smiles displaying even, pearly teeth.

"I need you both to sign and date every page to show you've read it all. The rent is going up by twenty quid as we already discussed. Once them pair move out the decorators need a couple of days to jazz it up and then it's all yours. Have you thought about a moving date?"

Leila and I look at each other.

"No," she answers for us. "I mean, I've got to be out within the next four weeks."

"Well Johno is already gone." She enlightens us. "Shane will be gone this weekend. There's no point in hanging around, shall we say next weekend?"

"Yes!" Leila agrees.

"I'll be in Madrid until Sunday." I remind her and she looks crestfallen.

"Well I'll give you the keys on Saturday Leila. You can make a start and Jodie, you just join in when you're home."

"I like your style!" I grin. "You can have the kettle on ready for me, I'll be home by the afternoon!"

I nudge Leila who's beaming starry eyed. "I'll wait for you! I can't go in without you. We'll just sleep on the floor or something Sunday night."

Jane cackles with warm laughter. "I'm so happy for you girls. You're going to have so much fun!"

So we are! I can't wait to tell Leila how well it's gone with Ashley, but we've still got to etch our names onto every page of the lengthy contract. And the moving date is set!

Jane finally leaves us to it and we're left clutching a copy for ourselves. It's done! Next weekend we'll be moving in together!

Leila is working from three today which is a blessing else we'd be drunk on wine as well as exhilaration. We talk animatedly and I tell her all about last night before we return to the subject of our flat; Marshamonvilla.

"You'll be back by afternoon, we'll move in at least one mattress." Leila plots. "We can just move in properly through the week if we're too excited to do it all Sunday."

"Oh, I reckon we'll manage a fair bit!" I giggle giddily imagining us like a pair of squatters with only one mattress between us. "It's all just too good to be true!"

"What will be too good to be true, is you inviting Luca for breakfast."

"Babe if he's there for breakfast it's because I invited him the night before." I quip and think of Ashley and last night. I don't feel too bad for joking. After all he did turn down my invite to visit himself. She whoops in favour and I'm buoyed by her glee. We begin to say our goodbyes and my phone pings.

The 'speak of the devil' saying springs to mind. Luca!

I spin the screen to Leila.

"Look who it is!" I grin and click open.

Get ready for 8 ye

I don't care that he's being presumptuous and my heart springs into action, my palms sweating instantaneously. I feel every inch the teenage girl who fell head over heels for this striking boy.

"What you going to say?" Leila asks breathily.

I give her a withering *what-do-you-think* look but really, I can't engage my brain to speak.

"Well go on then, reply!" She demands and I forget all rules on not responding too quickly. I don't want to miss my slot. I know how busy he is.

Ye ok ☺

I hit send and smile crazily at Leila.

"I think I'm going to faint." I finally manage.

"Don't be silly…" But she trails off realising how I must feel and I raise my eyebrows smirking.

"You're gorgeous Jodie." She falls back on the timeless classic in bestie encouragement. "You'll rock it. And you already know him. Just be excited!"

When we finally part ways I energetically march home and try to ignore Leila's advice. If I allow myself to get excited I will just combust right here and now. The thought of seeing Luca genuinely electrifies me.

There is a real attraction with Ashley and I have real chemistry with Troy. This connection I feel to Luca isn't necessarily *better*, it is all-encompassing and almost too overwhelming to be pleasurable. But it's *different* and I've never felt this way over another man.

I contemplate how genuine any of my feelings can be if I can just switch the heat like this. They exist. They affect me physically, consume my mind. And for now, however absurd, they happen despite of each other.

Perhaps the limited availability of time with Luca explains the power of my emotion toward him. Maybe the fact Troy is taken has made him even more desirable. Who knows, whatever the reasons, I like it! I'm truly having my cake and eating it!

Once home I wish I could sit still long enough to write. This sensation pulsating throughout me would be amazing on paper, I'd like to at least try and capture it in words. I'm far too fidgety however so instead I clean, tidy and pack up some more of my room.

The whole ritual of preening and beautifying must shortly begin again. And of course, the looming prospect of what to bloody wear!

***

By eight o'clock I'm ready and waiting in my bedroom. Actually, I've been ready since half past seven, just in case, which is definitely not like me.

I've decided on a suitably sexy black dress with wedged, black boots. Simple yet effective and perfect for subtly showing Luca the figure that lurks beneath the stretchy fabric.

By half past eight I'm busy distracting myself, staring at a page in a book, staring at my phone and staring at the TV screen. My heart beats above its usual rhythm and I do my best to keep my mind clear of Luca related thought.

By nine o'clock my cheeks are tingling with annoyance. I'm really trying not to dwell on it but it's consuming my mind, I'm going stir crazy.

By nine-twenty I have my phone in my sweaty palm and I'm humming with disappointment instead of any feelings of anger.

Last seen online, ten minutes ago.

So where is he? What's he doing online when he's arranged to meet me!

Another three minutes crawl through my temples and I begin to type. At this instant he appears 'online' and also begins typing.

Postcode?

Coming now

Both ping through and I rapidly delete what I had been typing and reply with my address. I should be angry, I know that. But I'm not, I'm ecstatic. My throat is tight, a pulse rages in my ears, I feel like I'm rushing from a parachute jump.

He's coming! Luca is coming!

Thrill effortlessly overrides irritation and quickly I check my reflection. After reapplying blusher and lip gloss I bound down the stairs and fling open the living room door.

"I'm going out!" My voice is raspy and mum eyes me curiously.

"To… that *boy's*?" She suggests.

I genuinely hesitate.

"Oh *Jodie*!" She rightly guesses. My pause has said it all and then my phone begins to vibrate. Luca is calling me via Facebook. I've never even answered one of these calls and I squeal at her.

"Gotta go!"

The night air is cool and dark, the only sound on the street comes from the purring engine of a black Audi. It's parked a few houses up and I half trot to it, putting effort into steadying my breathing. My skin feels refreshed by the cold and by the time I reach the passenger side I'm ready to step into the role of collected.

"Hey!" We greet each other, his smile wide and eyes sparkling how they always do. I clamber in and shut the door. The interior light lingers and fades as I click my belt on. The music drowns out my hammering heartbeat.

"Where shall we go babe? I'll take you wherever you want." He pats my thigh and the unexpected contact sends a shock straight to my pants.

To bed, I think.

"For a drink somewhere?" I say.

He nods and pulls the car away. "So what you been up to?"

We make general conversation as we leave the village and join the dual carriageway to town. There are no nerves, any amount of time can pass between us and we still click right back into the companionship we built as teens.

"Vodka Revs?" He suggests as the car crawls down a city street. I agree and look through the tinted windows, watching the milling bodies exiting and entering bars.

"Can you park here?" I ask when he pulls up outside our destination.

"Do you know who I am?" He laughs boldly. "I can park wherever I want!"

He really is a cocky shit, he's not *that* well known! But the car is not mine and I'm sure if it does get clamped Luca is flush enough to sort it.

I step onto the curb feeling a surge of importance.

Look who I'm with! My mind screams at the people nearby who gawk as we abandon the flashy vessel without a bother. I swagger into the club on Luca's arm enjoying every bit of the attention.

"Wanna share a jug?" He calls once we're at the crowded bar and points out the 'Shambles'. I giggle at the name, I hope it isn't an omen but nod my head anyway and he gets served as soon as he catches a barmaid's eye.

We're gaining a fair few admiring glances from those around us. Whether they do recognise Luca or just wonder who the fitty is I'm unsure and don't care.

"Here you are babe." I find him brandishing a pink shot toward me and my eyes linger heavily on his.

"Thanks." I tip the liquid back. It burns and I don't even flinch.

"Come on." He has the large jug in one hand and two stacked glasses in the other and flicks his head toward the dark, cave like seating area.

This section is for paying VIPs and Luca knows the bouncer who lets us in without issue. The exclusive treatment is such a far cry from my usual life and I feel a huge wave of sentimental pride for Luca. As a youngster he boasted he would be famous. Nobody believed him really except maybe his Mamma, and me. I always knew he would do it. His charisma is undeniable and teamed with his bolshie determination it was only a matter of time until he got himself noticed.

"What a coincidence we're both single." Luca says in his usual forthcoming way. We're sat opposite at a small round table and he leans forwards, placing his elbows on his knees. His smile is wide and his eyes glitter.

"I know." I return the grin and shrug. "Must be fate."

He doesn't remove his intense gaze and I hold him steady.

"It's weird isn't it," he muses. "How we keep crossing paths."

"Just the universe's way of reminding us where we come from." I tell him casually. We do come from the same area, it isn't *that* weird we bumped into one another again. But I'll drink to letting him believe we're meant to be or something. I raise my glass to suck the straw suggestively. I learnt this trick from Alexa.

His eyes flash, he hasn't missed the hint and early memories of us experimenting with each other's body visit me. I wonder if he remembers the same.

"Well, don't rush into another relationship." He says smiling.

"It will take a pretty special bloke to convince me." I reply evenly.

He sits back and stretches his arms out.

"I can't see myself settling down anytime soon." He pauses and takes a look around. "I've got it good."

"So have I." I smirk truthfully but I know he won't hear me- or at least won't break his stride to contemplate this- he's on a roll.

"I've seen so much, you know? Been to so many places, partied with so many faces!" He smiles as he's talking, using his hands to mould his words. He really is beautiful. "I come back here, and you know, nothing's changed! I just feel so, so... *different*."

"I know exactly what you mean since returning from Magaluf! I'd love to see as much as you but-"

"You do like a week holiday, I'm jetting off every *month*!"

"I did almost six weeks this year!" I laugh. "Working out there, it was crazy!"

He raises his eyebrows and nods looking at me afresh. "Fair play! I bet that was mad. I've been there four times. I prefer Ibiza…"

Luca goes on to regale which venues are the best and I listen. Ibiza is on my hit-list. I met a guy in Maga, Shaun, and he was off to Ibiza on his dad's boat, lucky sod.

"Europe is underrated man." Luca informs me now. "Especially Spain, there are some swish places! You just gotta be in the know!"

He rests a finger on the side of his nose, giving me that playful look once again.

"I'm going to Madrid, next weekend." I tell him and pick up my drink once again. I notice I am doing a majority of drinking the Shambles; although I think I'm holding my own pretty well. I know I can never compete with Luca's adventures, but it feels so good to at least have some conversation which shows I'm not the girl he bumped in to two years ago.

"Nice! I'll be in America next week."

"Awesome." I enthuse. "I'd love to go to America."

"It'll be my fifth time. I've been going at least once a year; did I tell you about when I met Snoop Dog?"

I sit back and enjoy the company and the cocktail. His tales are ripped straight from glossy, gossip magazines; he's smoking weed with musicians, having pool parties with cat-walk models and partying with film stars.

"I like hooking up with you." Luca tells me now as I finish off the jug. "You're the girl who makes me feel normal."

I feel a strange combination of pleasure and pain. I might not still be the waitress, living with her tame boyfriend but I will never be the girl who blows him away either.

"You know who I really am." He says matter-of-factly. I drink in his face savouring the compliment. Just you remember that, I think. But I know I will never be enough for him.

In a sea of faces starry eyed, he sees me as his familiar. And that will have to be enough.

"I'm so happy for you. I really am. You always said you'd do it, and now look at you, you really are doing it!" I'm fuelled by shambles and desire and a genuine heartfelt glow towards him. I feel admiration of his achievements and only sheer determination to continue growing my own. Time to drop the big one!

"You're getting a pole!" He exclaims. He's impressed again.

"Yep, we're moving in next weekend. You'll have to come round and see it."

"See you on it!" He corrects. "So you ready? Shall we go to a hotel?"

I was drunk on lust the moment I got in the car, added to that this champagne cocktail. I all but splutter, "Yes, ok. Yes!"

Remember you're his normal, I chastise myself.

I nip to the toilet and type a hasty message to Leila telling her the news. In Magaluf going back to a hotel was standard, but here in the UK I have never done it before! A hotel! It's seedy and raunchy and how it's done in the films and it's happening to me, right now.

"Fucking hell." Luca curses when he sees the yellow and black plastic wallet stuck to his windscreen. He pulls it off and grins wryly, shrugging.

"Do you want to stop and get wine?" He asks as we climb in. "I've got some green if you fancy a smoke?"

For old time's sake! I hear Tanya's happy voice back in Maga and remember the warm, delicious buzz from her joint.

"Both?" I giggle, then I remember the omen; *shambles*. "Actually, just the weed."

He puts his hand on my thigh again.

"My little home-girl." His eyes glint from within his thick lashes. I know he can't use this line on anybody but me. I also know he has a girl, or six, in every city globally so possibly I'm in a long queue of home-girls. But at least I *am* home. I know him for the real him, he said so himself.

"Have you got your bank card?" We're parked in the large carpark of a chain hotel at a motorway junction. I nod, thinking surely he isn't going to make me pay?

"Go and check us in, use your details." He hands me a wad of cash. "And I'll skin us one up, come back when you have the key."

It's not very gentlemanly making me do the deed. But then Luca gets what he wants and I totter away obediently. Typical him to hype himself up this way, as though he can't leave a trail for the media to sniff out. The reception area is brightly lit. I feel very self-conscious booking a double room at this time of night and in my sexy black dress. The man doesn't hide his judgement, I don't hide the details.

"Room for two. Check out before ten." He simpers and hands me the plastic card.

The process and payment took a painfully long time and my excitement has eased as I head back to the car. When I see the fat cone Luca has rolled for us though I'm glad for the momentary lull in ferocious electricity. Surely otherwise, smoking this would've induced a heart attack.

"Do you remember how Dan used to be with me?" Luca asks as he lights the end causing whirling grey smoke to fill the car.

I nod and guffaw. "He was a dick!"

"He wants me to put in a good word for him now. About his t-shirt designs."

"Oh, how the tables turn." I reply dreamily.

As we pass the spliff back and forth we chat about old acquaintances. It's like time has stood still and although so much has happened since then, we're right back there, laughing easily, fantasizing about what might have been.

My body is wrapped in a warm haze. I can't tell what's affecting me most; the drugs, alcohol or Luca. He alone is a highly powerful substance altering my reactions and moods drastically.

I feel so close to him, this feels so right.

"Ready?" He grins widely, his eyes narrow. Even stoned he's gorgeous and I return the goofy smile. "Go make yourself comfortable, I'll be up in ten minutes."

"Ok." I shrug. I've never done this before and have no idea of the rules. I teeter over the carpark, my legs feel like jelly and questions rapidly plague my mind.

What does *make yourself comfortable* even mean? Should I strip to my underwear and drape myself seductively on the bed? Should I shower? Get in bed? Make us a tea?

I resolutely avoid the receptionist's eyes and head for the stairs. We're only on the second floor but I don't do lifts anyway.

The room is bog-standard; fresh, white pressed linen, pine fittings, a long mirror and dressing table. I quickly flip at all of the lights until I find a suitable ambience and then panic all over again about if Luca is even coming up to me. Perhaps having the smoke wasn't such a good idea. My brain races paralysing me to the spot; strip, shower, leave, get into bed? Is he coming or has he left me here? I just don't know!

Minutes pass and I decide I shouldn't behave like a total idiot and take off my shoes. I'm wearing trainer socks and realise this does not look sexy at all, so I take them off too before looking around frantically for somewhere to stash them.

There's a light knock at the door and startled I ram them into a slot by the bed with a bible.

"Luca?" I call out softly.

"No." He replies and I open the door giggling.

"Had to make a few calls." He says importantly and strides to the TV. "These were in my boot too."

He throws me a bottle of Oasis.

"Thanks." I slug some gratefully then return my gaze to Luca. He is swaying to the music channel he's found, his eyes closed and miming the words.

"So, tell me Jodie, where do you see yourself in five years?" No conversation is out of the ordinary with Luca; just one of many things I love about him. He stands, opposite to where I'm sitting on the bed and I give the topic careful thought. Obviously I want to impress him.

"I want to have travelled, and be full of memories. So I need to get my head down and earn some real money. I don't care where I end up living, as long as I'm happy. This can't be it."

"No, it isn't." He replies meaningfully and I shiver at his expression. He approves of my answer and our easy flow of conversation takes hold once more. Luca paces the room as he asks and answers questions and I commit every detail of *us* to memory.

"What about religion?" He suddenly cries and reaches out for the book by the bed. He plucks it out and my inside-out socks fly out too, landing on the floor either side of him. "Are they yours?"

He must guess by the look of sheer horror on my face. I'd actually forgotten they were in there and I feel hot mortification for hiding them in the first place.

I can't lie so I nod. I can't have him complaining to reception about unclean rooms and undeterred, he carries on with his subject. Inwardly I thank him for not teasing me. It's not a complete shambles!

What an idiot, I inwardly giggle. I can't believe that's just happened, but it's already forgotten it seems as he begins indulging me to a number of dramatic readings, randomly plucked from the pages of the bible. Suddenly he shuts the book with a thump and slides it back in its rightful place. The socks remain on the floor.

He steps toward me, a serious look passing over his features.

"Do you remember the last time we did it?" He steps closer again and instinctively I slide further onto the bed. I can't cope with him coming any nearer, my ears roar with adrenalin.

"Yeah." I simper and my eyes blur as I picture the clumsy and quick but urgent and hot encounter. I remember the first time we did it too- and every time in between that. He peels up his shirt and takes another step forward. I slide back again, my legs now fully on the bed and sticking out between us.

164

His bare torso is something I haven't seen in the flesh since we were teens and he had a pigeon chest. I've seen the photos of his six-pack and inked art. In real life it is devastating and I stare at his belly button, the trail of hair leading to his pecs and then his face.

The closeness and familiarity I felt for him earlier diminishes. This beautiful man is not just the gawky boy I met twelve years ago. My heart pounds and I suddenly feel completely star-struck. I have stacks of publications under my bed of his image. And now here he stands before me like a lovingly carved statue.

"Come here Jodie." He presses himself right up to the edge of the bed and the soles of my feet.

"I can't!" I begin to giggle overwhelmed. He's so crazily desirable, the pressure is too much. He must have been with a thousand women. And a thousand more would give an arm to be in my position right now.

"I'm too shy!" I wail.

He smirks and grabs my ankles. The touch is like a spark to gas and I explode on the inside. With a firm tug he pulls me toward him and wraps my legs around his hips. His groin presses firmly into mine, I can feel his erection and my whole body is already sizzling in arousal as he begins to kiss me.

"You always were a slow kisser." He mumbles into my cheek. My heart clatters so hard it's making me feel woozy.

"Take off your dress." He commands and straightens up again. I watch him, watching me, as I slip it off. He takes in my lingering tan, my stomach which is still flat even if it has lost some tone.

He licks his lips and slides down his trousers revealing white boxers and a lengthy cock straining to be released. I'd forgotten how well-endowed he is. Fleeting memories of us, young, unsure and experimenting, again decorate my mind.

He lies down beside me, and his fingers begin to play with the lace of my thong. I return the teasing and stroke him through soft fabric.

"I've got condoms." I mutter eventually as the lingerie comes off.

"I've got my own." He jumps off the bed and retrieves a cardboard strip, peeling back a tab and taking out what looks like a small, folded bag.

"What *is* that?"

He carefully pulls it on.

"These are the only ones I'll use." He explains. "Latex free, large, extra thin. They're unique."

"Are you being sponsored by them?" I joke. He chucks the credit card style packaging at me. There are two out of three gone.

"Save it. For next time."

I lie back and open my legs. I wonder who he used the other with. The comment though has washed me in confidence- *next time*- and I smile at him as he climbs onto the bed, between my knees.

Some blissful, mind-racing time later, Luca lets himself go with a guttural grunt. The sound of him coming invites another flurry of pleasure to contract my muscles around him. I've managed to orgasm, twice.

At this rate I'll reach the magic one hundred in under a year! Poor Alexa, is she shagging the right guys, or is an orgasm really that elusive for others? Perhaps it's why I like sex so much!

I'd love my brain to have a 'record' option, I want to remember this forever. I soak in the vision of Luca as he glides about the room, smiling dopily.

"Do you like murder shows?" He asks picking up the TV remote. "I can't fall asleep in silence."

He hasn't redressed, just disposed of the condom and I wish I could somehow project this image for Leila and Cat to see right now!

"Love them." I answer, and he chooses one about couples who go on a killing spree. I read the tattoo on his arm; *ride or die*. There's a portrait too of a blue-eyed girl. I allow myself to fantasise that it's me and that deep down he knows we're destined to be Bonnie and Clyde. Loyal lovers that go way back and are prepared to fight the world to be together.

We climb under the covers and I snuggle beside him allowing my leg to rest against his and I don't want to fall asleep because then the moment will end.

It Suits Me Sunday

I wake up at eight. I'd fallen asleep virtually right away last night, thanks to a combination of spent exhilaration and narcotics consumed. Luca is still asleep beside me and I realise for all my imagining last night, it was just that, wishful, fanciful thinking.

Today he will drop me home and I possibly won't see him again for months, maybe years! But he did give me the extra condom. I'll check its expiry date. I'll use it as an excuse to contact him and suggest he comes to see me again; and me on my pole!

I leave the bed still barely believing how perfectly last night unfolded and head to the bathroom. There are complimentary toiletries and fluffy towels and I decide to take a shower. I'm naked still and step into the compartment once it's steamy and close the glass door behind me.

Only minutes later I hear a click and feel a suck of cold air. Luca squeezes in beside me looking sleepy and cute, standing a head and shoulders above me.

"Morning." He grins.

Without any more words we lather each other in the soapy suds of coconut shower gel. The foam looks extra white against our wet skin and I pay extra attention to making sure he's washed *all over*. Over and over!

The hot water doesn't last and we're forced to jump out squealing when it changes to cool, then icy droplets. Naked and dripping we stare at each other. My mind is torn. If we have sex we use the condom. If we don't I might not see him again anyway! I know my erect nipples are making my boobs look great, this is a bonus at least.

"I've got to get going." He breaks the hush and I'm partly relieved. My lifeline remains intact. *Maybe* he was thinking the same thing. Maybe I'm wishful thinking again.

We dry and dress, chatting about Luca's upcoming work in America. *Any* thing is better than *no* thing, I tell myself- *over and over*- as I realise more and more the chances are slim of seeing him again anytime soon.

"Hola ye." Luca tells me as I clamber from his car outside of my home. I shut the door and blow him a kiss before smirking and sauntering away best I can. He revs and he's gone.

My mum will be up and pottering in the kitchen. She'll remember Luca and now she's more accepting of my, how did she put it, research? I can tell her all about my, erm, date.

It only occurs to me as I plan exactly which details to tell her that I've had sex with two different men on two nights running. If it had happened in Magaluf, that would be believable. It would seem that this little home-girl is rocking it after all. Or a complete slag!

"Morning sweetheart. So, what did you get up to last night?"

I suppose my mum will be the first judge.

***

That night I lie in bed and try to remember my life *before*. Before the new job, before Magaluf and before this attitude that allows me to have causal, guilt-free encounters with gorgeous men.

Did I feel this happy ever? And what about the circumstances that bought me to the very here and now? I don't regret anything, how could I? I don't think *everything* happens for a reason. But there are definitely clues and reasons for certain things- lessons learned, outlooks altered.

I'm moving forward. Next weekend I'm flying to Madrid! And I'm moving into a flat with my best friend!

This weekend I've had sex with *two different men* and I don't even feel ashamed. I'm under no allusion however; this will not be a regular thing, although not really out of choice. If I was in a relationship I might have sex seven nights a week, every week, so what's the difference?

I thought by now I should be married, with kids even! Some of my friends are and there's nothing wrong with it. I suppose I thought it was ultimately what I sought. Now though I feel complete. In a way far differing to what I'd envisioned.

I have things to look forward to, a determined direction. Progress in my job, earn money, travel. And a man to suit every occasion in the meantime. Ashley for the secret weekend visits, Luca for a ridiculously exciting brush with glitz, Aaron for an impulsive city break and Troy, well he can continue to be my doting (definitely sexless at least) work husband.

If he insists on making me drinks, accompanying me at lunch, treating me to long and lusty gazes, who am I to turn it down? I'm not really doing anything wrong. It suits me!

I can't wait to see Alexa again and find out how she is doing in the dating game. She'll be dizzy with desire if it's a touch on my experiences so far. It's easy to forget any niggles. Ashley not wanting to be seen near me, Luca being late and big-headed, Troy being taken! Aaron. What will he turn out to be?

This week is going to be busy. I want to be packed up ready for the big move next Sunday. And I've also got to think about clothing for Madrid. The weather could be anything from twenty to ten degrees which basically incorporates my whole wardrobe!

Plus, I have Belfry to continue sinking my teeth into. I wonder what we'll find out in tomorrow's meeting; just whose behaviour will improve and whose will deteriorate.

Muggy Behaviour

It's Wednesday morning and I'm sitting with Iqbal as he runs through the day's planned lessons. This is a ritual I've become accustomed to. He comes into the hall during breakfast club every morning, except for Friday when I'm with the girls all day, and signals for me to join him.

'Go with dad!' Troy began teasing me at the start of the week.

Everything about Belfry feels more customary. Hearing children swearing, speaking crudely and about sexual organs, crying, hollering, smashing up furniture in fits of rage. Plus, the rules and systems which allow for them to successfully learn and their behaviour to be supported; it's all one huge, well-oiled, intricate process.

"Do you know about this safeguarding thing with Ben?" Iqbal asks me now and I think back to last week's meeting. Nothing more was mentioned this Monday.

"No."

"Ok. Well he's Silver Two now but still not to go anywhere on his own ok? If he wants to go toilet you check nobody is inside first before he goes in, and wait for him don't let anybody else in until he's out, escort him back. Clear?"

I nod numbly not knowing what to think. Harishma told me the whole need-to-know thing is a needless power play and that everybody should know everything about the kids we teach. She hates being out of the loop, I know that, but it does tug on my mind. He seems utterly harmless, daft even- who is he a danger to, himself or others?

"I've got to get to assembly." I tell him fretfully noticing the time. There's light amusement in his eyes but I take my fear of Julie seriously.

"She doesn't like me." I insist.

She makes a genuine effort to make me feel uncomfortable, I'm resigned to it.

"Well you're with me aren't you?" Iqbal soothes. "She can't tell you off when I've asked you to be here."

I think of Lizzy. She asked me to bring in Eve. I think of Julie's comment, *I* am your boss, *I* am in charge.

I itch to leave the classroom but hang around for Iqbal anyway. By the time we enter the hall, the circle is seated and to my dismay Julie watches us enter with a hawk-like glare.

"Get. That. Mug. *Out of here*." She spits at me and I realise I'm holding my empty cup from this morning's coffee. She could also be referring to *me* as a mug of course. All eyes are on me as I turn immediately and retreat. Hot tears of embarrassment form rapidly and I blink them away, furious at Iqbal for convincing me to loiter.

I slam the offending china in the sink of the staff room and march to the toilets for a splash of cold water to the face. Humiliation courses through my veins as rich as if I'd been slapped. Aren't we supposed to be drilling respect into these impressionable boys? Julie has just made me look a complete idiot in front of everyone. A *mug*. I've seen staff members come to assembly with a mug in their hand before. Once again she's used a crap excuse to have a go; shots fired!

I'm in charge of a reading group before I embark on a day in IT and I do my best to pull myself together. The four lads I must coax to read aloud for ten minutes witnessed it and I'm sure will have an opinion! The girls aren't invited to assembly yet. If only I could retreat to the safety net of their unit right now.

The corridor is still deserted and I hang around by one of the doors to the hall. There is NO WAY I'm interrupting! As soon as a class appears, having been dismissed, I'll slide inside to collect my group.

I feel shaky and horribly close to tears still. Julie's appalling treatment of me is so unfair! All I've been since I started is enthusiastic and hardworking.

By the time the three student's faces seek out mine and leave with me for our allocated room, I'm gulping hard to stem the torrent of resentment.

"That was well stink Jodie, you got kicked out of assembly!" Chester is saying wide eyed. I nod and force a smile.

"Get your books." I instruct them croakily and pray they sense my wound and go easy. They aren't a bad group, but this is not their favourite thing and it only takes one to rock the boat.

"Jodie?" Troy peeps into the classroom. "I got Eric to cover me. You ok?"

Now I really want to cry, and I curse him and feel grateful simultaneously.

"Go and take a break." He tells me. The lads, remarkably, stay quiet and I feel thankful of them too.

"I'm alright, we'll be ok." I still sound weary but smile at the students. "Thanks though Troy."

I wave him off and the lads must really feel sorry for me because they begin to take their turns reading without argument.

I don't want Julie to scare me, I've got to be stronger than that. Even though the only reason I turned down the offer of a break is because I was scared she'd catch me. But I'm determined I'll glean what I can from this job. Not only do I owe it to the kids but myself too. The incident was nothing more than a show up on both of our parts and hopefully everyone realises just how callous she actually is. Somebody get a dildo and stick it up her arse! Thinking of Lacey, and the others, cheers me up a tad.

***

That night I begin the task of picking my outfits for Madrid. The upcoming mini-break is a favourable distraction from work-related worries. Aaron is a funky dresser and I'm rapidly realising how in need of a wardrobe update I really am. I need to cover all manner of options; practical, lounging, going out, coffee date, and it's all got to fit into my hand luggage. A shopping spree is not an option and it takes the whole evening to put together a number of items which work with each other and provide a variety of ensembles.

Thoroughly pleased with my efforts I jump onto my bed ready to settle down. Ashley hasn't messaged me this week. The lack of an invite works in my favour because I'd only have to turn it down anyway.

I'm going to Madrid! I can't believe it's actually happening. Unhappy feelings about Julie have been forced into the recesses of my mind and I'm glad to leave them there. Iqbal now takes me more seriously at least. He felt thoroughly guilty and any anger I had towards him quickly subsided when confronted with his regretful apology. He has my best interests at heart I reckon. He told me I should start to write these episodes down. Just in case. Just in case what, I don't know. But I am willing to work closely with him, and Lizzy, to learn what tricks I can about the role. Just in case.

I resolutely won't let Julie impact on my dreams. I'd be gutted, it'd be another hurdle to overcome, but if it really did come to it I would find a new job. I want to succeed, earn more, travel! I refused to bow to pressures from a boss, albeit of a different kind, in Magaluf and I'm not about to start now.

Julie is nothing to me and nothing of significance in my life on the whole. This time next week, I'll have experienced the capital of

Spain, possibly added another couple of orgasms to the repertoire *and* be in my new bedroom at Marshamonvilla.

Perhaps Julie really does need a dildo sticking somewhere. Poor cow must be miserable.

That Need to Know Business

Thursday morning is usually my favourite because not only am I with Troy in Breakfast Club but then it's his class in IT first thing too. Today however, assembly sits between those times like a stinking shit sandwich. Julie was a bitch yesterday and I'm a nervous-wreck against my will. Hopefully she's got it out of her system for now.

"Oh, here's Dad!" Troy remarks gleefully from my side as soon as Iqbal's head pops into the hall, searching me out.

I stem my giggle feeling bad because he always meets my eyes with such genuine cheerfulness.

"Shut up." I give Troy a sarcastic smile and stalk towards the motioning Iqbal.

"Hey!" I greet him. I know Troy will be watching us and resist turning around.

"Good morning Jodie. I thought we could run through a few things…" He says this like it's the first time he's made the suggestion- every time.

He's a good guy though, I like him. "Sure, let's go."

After our little rundown, Iqbal gives me a serious look.

"So Jodie, I wanted to ask you something, it's something, erm…" He is looking increasingly uncomfortable and my already fretful mind doesn't need encouragement to conjure up a number of squirm-inducing scenarios.

What is he trying to ask- is it to do with Troy? Or have I done something wrong!

"It's a bit out there but…"

Oh my god, is he going to ask me out? No! He's happily married, I know that. But how he is acting...

"I wondered whether to take a mug in to assembly this morning and see if Julie reacts? You know, it'd give you a firm example to show she is treating you differently."

"No way!" I gasp disbelievingly. Out of all the preposterous concerns I had, this is more outrageous; Iqbal does not rebel like this. "No, you can't. I mean, thanks so much but she'll know, she'll just know, and she might target you- or me even worse. No, you can't."

It seems he doesn't need much to change his mind and he nods along.

"Iqbal, it's really nice of you, I really appreciate your support but, no, thank you." I give him an encouraging smile.

"It's very unfair though. I don't like that." He tells me quietly.

"I know, but you know what, the world isn't fair. I can handle this."

He snaps out of some thought or another and meets my eye properly.

"Look, I'd better go, I don't want to be late!" I giggle to show him it's under control and he dismisses me with a meek wave. I find the hall in full preparation for assembly time. Tables have been packed away from breakfast and the hatches are down to the kitchens. Chairs are being noisily scraped into the huge circle by mainly staff. Some students are being guided to other places for various reasons, some students are shouting and lively and others withdrawn and tired.

Troy has sat between Keon and Mason. Not because there's danger of them fighting again. Since that episode Keon has taken on a class clown role, still lords it over the others and Mason seems to be the alpha. They're best buddies- if you can't beat them join them- currently the only risk here is they will mess about.

Teachers are lining the walls, I take a seat next to year 7 Jay and he smiles at me. There's a tiny light back in his eyes. It's a temporary placement with the foster family which means more hardship to come for him but I know, for now, he is feeling more settled.

Julie sweeps in and I self-consciously check I haven't accidentally bought anything I shouldn't have but then even bringing myself could cause offence to her. It's then I spot Gilbert. He's looking away, but I could have sworn he had been staring at me. And he's brazenly holding a mug.

My cheeks flush with anger and I wait to see if Julie will send him out but I already know she won't. He's done it on purpose but for what reason? Not the reason Iqbal wanted to, I know it.

Assembly passes without much drama. Obviously, no eyelid is batted at Gilbert for bringing the item which caused my public dismissal yesterday. I know Iqbal noticed from the pointed eye contact he gave me across the room. I know Troy noted it too from *his* sustained and meaningful look. Gilbert didn't mean to help me. I am certain he meant it as a symbol of power, but he unwittingly has because it's clear evidence for my written log. So, thanks, you twat!

Class by class we leave for first lesson and I make sure I have a smile on my face.

***

"Who knows what this is?" Iqbal is at the front of the room, his smart screen displaying a huge sports emblem. He looks around enthusiastically as if expecting the broody lot to jump up and scream the answer.

"It's a Nike tick." Paul mumbles eventually.

"As if you'd know, you can't afford Nike." Keon is straight in with the dig. Paul sneers but doesn't reply. Shay and Kyron giggle loyally.

"I'll think you'll find it's your parents who pay for your named clothes, not you." Iqbal states reasonably.

"Or us!" Troy mutters loud enough for me to catch and I smirk. He's jibing our majority of benefit-claiming parents. I know people need the support but some of these parents wouldn't look out of place on a Jeremy Kyle show.

"What about this one?" A large, red M fills the screen now.

"McDonalds!" Harry yelps despite himself before turning pink and eyeing Keon.

Keon gives him a large grin and nods. "*You* know that one!" He tells him eyeing his bulging gut.

"Fuck off!" Harry is embarrassed but he laughs because he can't let Keon think he is actually challenging him. I catch Troy's eye, I feel sorry for Harry, but he shrugs used to their banter. We can't involve ourselves with every quarrel, that's not how life works.

"We're going to have a quiz," Iqbal tells them all and gives me the signal to begin handing out the sheets covered with little images. "Let's see how well these companies advertise using their logo!"

The boys aren't excited despite Iqbal's continual attempts to engage them. "It isn't a test on you, come on spread out! It's a test on the brand and their marketing plan."

Mason oozes immature arrogance and curls his lip at Iqbal. "Who really cares?"

"Obviously you, you're always wearing Adidas." I quip and Iqbal grins at me. I'm actually looking forward to giving the quiz a go myself!

I hand one to Troy and he catches my wrist when I turn to leave. "Aren't you working with me?"

"No!" I tell him sternly. "Are you afraid I'll beat you?"

He gazes into my eyes and I feel like we are having a completely different conversation.

"I want to be with *you*." He moans.

"Jodie!" Iqbal interrupts making me jump. He points toward Josh. "Just make sure he tries."

I nod and leave Troy alone feeling zingy from the interaction.

By ten past ten I'm shivery for altogether different reasons. I man my post outside, come rain or shine, and today on the hardcourts it is cold. I accompany Lewis and Jess and I love hearing their stories, particularly from Lewis detailing the art exhibitions and festivals he attends in his spare time.

Sometimes we take it in turns to patrol along the edge of the building too, just in case of any stragglers and I excuse myself to do that now. As I turn the corner of the main building I spot Gilbert marching from the opposite direction, straight toward me. He's definitely seen me, I can't turn around and head back now even though I want to and I get the impression I am his intended target.

"Jodie." He barks. "Come with me."

"Now? I'm on duty."

"They'll be fine without you." He snarls gruffly. "Come, we need to talk, now."

He's already walking away, back in the direction he came. Who does he think he is? We need to talk about what exactly? I stare at his back defiantly, and I'm determined not to give Julie another reason to have a go. He's not my boss, that's for sure.

"Gilbert, I'm going to let the others know. They might think something has happened." I don't know why I'm justifying the safeguarding procedure to one of the appointed officers. "Where shall I meet you?"

"My office." He snaps pompously over his shoulder.

"Your office?" I call sounding far more incredulous than I mean to and he stops. If he means the 'BS' room I'm definitely going to laugh out loud. What a load of BS! "I don't know where that is?"

"The *safeguarding* room."

He means *Claire's office* and I nod, suppressing a smirk. Unless she has been moved? Or what if he has made sure she's been moved, stolen her space? I've definitely witnessed an undercurrent between them, it's not a totally irrational thought.

"I'll be there in a sec."

I march back to Lewis and Jess, not explaining in full to them. We're often engaged in break time chitchat but I still don't know them well enough to outright ask about Gilbert; is he a merciless tosser? He seems well liked. I don't want to make more enemies!

On route to the 'safeguarding room'- I can't think of it as *Gilbert's office*- I worry lightly about our meeting. It probably isn't his office, I wouldn't put it past him to have inflated his position there and I assume Claire will be waiting for me too. He's just the messenger boy but what could it be about?

I knock on the door. Gilbert speaks. "Come in."

He's behind the desk and alone.

"Is everything ok?" I ask, anxiety creeping through my chest. He suddenly seems in a far more dangerous position than I initially thought. Bringing his mug into assembly, it was a blatant middle finger. He smiles and his eyes crease. It doesn't put me at ease. Quite the opposite; what if he has got rid of Claire, what if I'm next?

"Why would you think otherwise?" He asks me as though I am in fact guilty of some crime. There's a pause and I'm left gawping at him despondently.

"No Jodie. You've been working a lot with the year 10s." He puts me out of my misery after what feels like an eternity and I sit when he nods at the chair opposite. "We made the decision you should be told about Ben's case."

I don't know who 'we' are but I'm acutely engaged with him.

"The information I am about to share with you cannot be passed on under any circumstances. If you have ANY concerns, you come to me first for direction ok?" He tells me and although I understand this is important I still feel like he is taking the opportunity to stamp his authority.

I nod in reply. I have the 10's today for English and Art after lunch and now Gilbert is about to divulge something that will change the dynamics significantly.

"Ben is being investigated. Allegations, of a sexual nature, have been made by a boy, who is not a student here. We cannot allow him to be alone with any of our students. There is a member of staff assigned to watching him at all times. You do not ever need to mention you know this. Just be aware if he makes any comments that seem unusual. If he begins to tell you anything about this case, try to put a stop to it. Definitely don't ask questions. Remind him he should speak to Claire."

"Where is Claire?" I take the opportunity to pry. What I'm hearing is horrible but I've already desensitised to this level of shock-factor.

"We needed to mix things up. She's got her space down by the laundry room. She is the lead on this case but… she's had to take today and tomorrow off."

His lip curls and he resembles juvenile Mason. I fail to see how anyone could actively dislike Claire. She's nice, harmless and from what I've seen works hard at her post. I feel pissed off at Gilbert for so many reasons. What is his high and mighty act all about, he has a tiny amount of power and he's flexing it sadistically. He got the responsibility of introducing me to this 'need-to-know' business and he's loved doing it in a way that's made me feel uncomfortable and stupid.

I leave the office and break time is virtually over so I head for IT. There is obviously a lot I don't know or understand going on here but I've been trusted with this information about Ben which says something. It is disturbing and absurd, if it is true, but I must keep my mind clear of biased opinion.

Each and every day proves just about anything can happen. Whilst I'm in the Belfry corridors I have to remain open-minded and alert however exhausting.

***

At lunch time I ask Troy about Gilbert and his new office. He says nothing of interest but what am I expecting really? There's perhaps a little work place rivalry going on. Gilbert has an engorged ego- that part's a certainty.

I cast my eyes over to where he's sitting with Julie and Neil. The SLT team except he isn't officially a part of it. I don't dare to watch for long in case Julie looks over and locks onto me with her contemptuous scrutiny.

"So what are your plans this weekend?" Troy asks.

"I don't know yet, perhaps a night out or something."

Maybe a little trip to Madrid a scathing inner voice goads. I don't know why I lie! It's not completely untrue, it's just not the full picture. Just as he is doing to me.

"How about you?"

"I'm off to London, to visit family."

Yours or hers? I don't ask and how can I be mad? When I'm continuing the façade!

"Nice." I smile instead and begin to clear away my lunch. Leanne, the mentor to year 6's, comes over to me whilst I'm at the bin. She's quiet, timid almost; I often wonder how she copes when their students inevitably kick off.

"Jodie? Can I have a quick word?"

This is a much more polite invitation than Gilbert's at breaktime and I smile gratefully. "Of course, what's up?"

"I hope you don't mind me bringing it up." She lowers her voice to an almost inaudible level amongst the hubbub of chatter. "How Julie treated you in assembly yesterday... she was like that with me when I first started. She's just a big, old bully."

I look across and find mellow brown eyes. "Thanks. You've made me feel a lot better! I feel like I'm going mad, paranoid."

"You're not imagining it. She's been better with me since you started. So, I'm sorry, but you seem to have taken the hot seat until fresh meat comes along."

I giggle at her. This is the type of information a newcomer *needs-to-know*! I feel awful but I'm genuinely wondering when 'fresh meat' will come along!

"Who was it before you?"

"A girl called Honey. She left. But don't worry." She adds. "Just keep doing what you're doing, a lot of people round here don't like her. She does a good job in charge though, she isn't here to make friends like us."

"Well thanks for telling me." I tell her genuinely. "I've got to dash to Games club."

I leave Leanne with a tiny skip in my step. I much prefer being referred to as the type to 'make friends', than somebody like Julie. I feel bad for Leanne, Honey and whoever else she has hurt in her drive for ultimate control and also for poor Claire who Gilbert is targeting her with his power trip too.

But just like Harry taking his share of shit from Keon earlier, we're all destined to fight our own battles. There are so many layers to this school and I am happy slowly but surely learning and being friendly with my peers. Overly friendly with one in particular; but it's just harmless fun with Troy.

I can't wait to update Leila; Gilbert is lording it worse than ever plus I'm just one of many who have felt Julie's wrath! Perhaps she can never be fixed. And by the sounds of it she doesn't want to be.

The Trap

A Friday never felt so good in the knowledge that tonight, I'm jetting off to Madrid!

My third full week at Belfry is almost complete and so much has happened already. I'm ready for a break. I've jumped out of the frying pan and into the fire since returning to the UK, something I never thought possible. But it is a good thing, I have no complaints.

I've been with the girls all day and it makes such a change from the main school. Iqbal is funny, geeky, serious and sweet; my time in IT and supporting the 10's is generally ok. Ben was just the same in yesterday's classes even though my mind's eye watched him completely differently. I couldn't help it, I suppose it is a natural response, but I am resolutely keeping my mouth shut that I know anything. I am behaving exactly as before so he is none the wiser, nobody is, I am a professional.

Perhaps it's the double locked doors separating the unit from the main school, separating me from Julie and Gilbert. But I feel so much more relaxed in here. There's an easy-going relationship developing between me, Lizzy, Lacey and Harishma.

Jayde and Mollie are in one pod, and Lizzy and Holly in the other. It has taken until this afternoon for me to find myself with Lacey and no students, now is my chance.

"So, have you noticed Gilbert has got a new office?" I ask curiously.

"No. But did you hear Dom is seeing Leanne now?" She whispers.

"No, that's great news! They're both so cute!"

Lacey rolls her eyes at me but smiles. "And did you hear the rumours about Sean?"

I haven't and my office question is completely side-tracked now, mundane in comparison.

"Apparently he got an official warning because he used a school camera to take topless selfies!"

"Nooo!" I gasp. "Why would he even do that?"

"For a dating site probably." It is slightly hilarious and we giggle guardedly at his idiocy.

Lizzy peers out of a pod, aware she's missing something, so I automatically take over from her and help Mollie and Jayde with their research for an 'Under the Sea' project.

It certainly isn't easier with the girls. Like the boys, they each pose a variety of battles and combined a whole handful more. The intense proximity of the class- always being in here and with the same people- both magnifies issues but strengthens bonds too. The girls unit lives up to its name 'unit'. Despite all of our differences, staff and students alike are gelling as a team.

I've worked more with Holly today but so far I've not sussed a lot out about her. She's like a closed box, giving nothing away. She's barely spoken to me all afternoon but I know she's watching us, judging us maybe, weighing us up definitely.

The sound of the lock clicking on the internal door announces Harishma. She's in a state of feverish delight and dashes towards Lacey who's beginning to tidy up for the week.

"Night out!" She cries. "Night out on Friday in a fortnight!"

"Come on girls. It's time to print your pictures." I check they are actually doing it before leaving the pod to join the gaggle of women.

"What's the plan?" Lizzy is asking rubbing her hands together. "My first work night out!"

"Ours!" I correct her and she gives me a grin.

I want to grab my diary immediately but first I check on Holly and ask her to pack away. Jayde is already to go, as eager as me for the weekend to begin!

"Look at her, with her diary!" Lacey catcalls when I return to the huddle.

"I have to keep a diary, my brain is like a sieve." Lizzy defends me with a wink. I get a feeling in my tummy, like butterflies.

"Right, Boot and Rod at seven." Harishma begins. "We'll probably go earlier. No reason why not! We'll be finished by half three. Do you know it? By the canal."

I nod, hoping Leila isn't working that Friday or can move her shift, and scribble down the details. Taxis begin to arrive to take the girls home, signalling finally my finish time is here.

"Well ladies, I've got to dash. I've got a plane to catch!"

"Lucky bitch!" Lacey says.

I agree!

After I've said my goodbyes I zoom home for a shower, to grab my bags, reassure my mum for the umpteenth time and then leave on another adventure!

***

The airport isn't very busy. I already have my boarding pass and without luggage to check-in I am soon waiting in the departure lounge with only an hour to go until my flight. Aaron and I have been busily messaging each other. He is already there and it's only now that nerves begin to dawn on me.

I cast my mind back to the short time we spent together in Magaluf. There was a spark of chemistry and there were no awkward silences. We chatted and drank and partied happily. He's around my age, has a good sense of humour, and is training to teach English- we should have even more in common now I've started teaching too.

I saw sense in googling his name, trawling his Facebook and associates and eliminated the likelihood of any fishy business. Dad has already text me a warning to pass on;

If my daughter is left damaged in any way, I will find you, and I will kill you.

My glass of wine is going down well and I relax into the book I treated myself to. It's an airport tradition. The last time I was here I'd bought something about three strong, independent women- now I feel like I am one of those characters.

"Welcome to Madrid!" An accented voice greets us as we filter into the airport at the other end. I immediately turned on my phone messaging Aaron and he has already replied.

Waiting for you! ☺ x

My heart does a number of excited leaps. Regardless of how well Aaron and I get on, I'm going to enjoy exploring a new place all the same. Plus, I am moving in to the flat the day I fly home! It could be a rotter of a weekend and I still have something to look forward to at the end of it.

Passport control passes quickly and without a suitcase to wait for I'm free to meet Aaron in the arrivals lounge.

Now I feel my heart racing. I paste a casual smile onto my face and walk towards the doors confidently. As soon as I push these open he could be right there, waiting, spotting me instantly. My eyes will have to wander, try to pick him out. I remember he looks different depending on whether his hair is in a ponytail or down around his face.

There's no more time to consider it, the arrivals lounge is bright, there are bodies waiting *everywhere* holding rectangle name cards and beadily eyeing us as we spill into the area.

I sweep my eyes over the welcoming parties and spot Aaron; deep-set, dark eyes, large manly features, his wavy, brown hair swept back. He grins, and I return it, any lurking apprehensions quashed. He's wearing thick rimmed glasses, adding another 'look' to his selection and I like it.

"Good journey?" He greets me with an extravagant kiss to both cheeks.

"Yes great. I just can't wait to drop this bag off!"

"Here, allow me?" He motions to take it from me.

"I wasn't hinting." I laugh but pass it to him to anyway. He's a strapping build, better suited to a farmer than a teacher!

"So, we'll get a cab to the apartment. And then if you don't mind we'll just walk into town? It's really not far." We stride from the cool building into a darkening evening. "People tend to eat later here, you know ten o'clock onwards. And we can check out the buildings and sites on the way."

"Sounds great!" I enthuse.

He gives my hand a squeeze and leads us to the queue of taxis. Within minutes we're inside and being whisked onto the main roads towards Madrid city centre.

I don't catch much scenic detail. It's mostly inky sky and glittering lights and I tap out texts to mum and Leila. I don't indulge Aaron in my dad's message- just yet- and he lists names of places and museums in impressive Spanish pronunciation. I don't have a hope of remembering them. Good job I bought a notebook along!

We pull up on a road not far from the main extravagant and divergent buildings of town. Having paid the fare, I'm led straight to a single glass door between a run-down theatre and a newsagent. The foyer is pretty dingy with an unattended reception desk and Aaron makes for the lift.

"What floor is it?"

"Third." He replies noting my reluctance. "Prefer the stairs?"

I nod gratefully and he pushes open a door to our side. I feel at complete ease with him already, he can read me like a book.

"Right this way princess."

We exchange shy smiles. In Magaluf we had a proper kiss but nothing more. I wonder now as we climb if he's expecting us to do *more*, as soon we step foot into the flat. There isn't a simmering sexual energy between us but there is a romantic spark. I imagine the chance to flirt and unwind will build a little tension.

He unlocks a mahogany door and we enter a dark hallway. A light flips on.

"Let me give you the tour. Did you want to shower before we go, get changed or something? We don't have to rush." Aaron is ever the gentleman and I follow him from room to room.

"I'll just get changed." I tell him and I can't help it, memories of my shower with Luca race into my mind. I can't compare them; they're from different lives completely.

The flat is cluttered but in an arranged way, lived in and homely. There are trinkets and framed photos, artwork and plants.

"It's gorgeous. How do you know him? The owner?" I finger a plaited throw on one of the mismatched couches. This is exactly how I want mine and Leila's place to look!

"We used to work together." He informs me and takes me to the doors which open on to a small balcony. We don't have this luxury at our Marshamonvilla, but we can go some way to replicate the well-travelled atmosphere.

"He travels a *lot* more now." Aaron confirms my thoughts on the collection.

"So, is Barcelona the city for you or will you move around in the future too?" I'm being instantly nosey but if he's into travelling, he climbs several notches.

"I've actually not long moved." He begins to explain. "I'm out of the city now and I commute to work. It's lovely, I'm right by the beach."

"No way!" I gasp. Several notches climbed.

"How about you, you'll move soon too?"

"It's not quite as impressive!" I giggle.

Aaron smokes a cigarette whilst we're out here chilling and chatting. Once he's finished, I get changed quickly and we pack up a few things ready to go out.

The streets are littered with people in all manners of attire. Trainers and tracksuits, heels and slinky dresses; we're in between with our smart casual jackets and plimsolls. We're right on the outskirts of Madrid centre and fall into step with one another, Aaron holding my hand. Along the skyline I can see the black outlines of gothic buildings and spires, plus chunky rectangles of shiny brickwork. The clothing shops and jewellery stores around us are shut up for the night, and there are plenty of homeless and beggars making me feel helpless. Who to chuck a coin to?

Aaron tells me some are phonies but the fact that some aren't spurs me into eventually parting with all of my loose change. He teases me but does toss a coin or two. Barely enough for a hot drink still.

As the streets narrow, we begin to stumble upon plazas and squares. Street performers adorn corners, music slips through the night air like tentacles tickling our ears. We drift through alley ways and stone arches finding more shops, stalls and restaurants.

"It's brilliant!" I astound. We've just come across a huge statue of a bear and we're surrounded by a large rectangle of lively outlets.

"Puerta del sol." The name rolls off his tongue and a tingle rolls down my spine. "We'll eat somewhere here? Plenty of people to watch!"

"Perfect!"

Aaron speaks in fluent Spanish to a waiter. His voice has a husky edge to it and even English sounds pretty sexy, this is like next level. They conspire, *Barcelona*, he tells him and the waiter is leading us to a tiny table right at the corner of their terrace.

It is washed pine, simply laid. A single red flower and one of those oil candles that smells warm and thick sit central.

"Sangria?" Aaron offers me.

"Please."

"Food menu?" The waiter offers us, and we nod.

We chat and watch those around us. Laughing at the crazy guy with a turkey hat on his head and pointing out a belly dancer juggling. Between us we munch through a tapas sharing platter and order another bottle of wine.

"Does your watch have no face?" I suddenly exclaim when I catch a good look at his heavy silver wristwatch.

He holds it out for me to see, smiling delightedly and sure enough where the circular clock usually sits I can see straight through to his tanned arm.

"Time is irrelevant." He tells me with certainty and I give him an uncertain look. "I know we have to be on time for work and everything but time itself, it shouldn't rule you. Do what you want, when you want!"

I'm mesmerised by this quirky attitude and utterly charmed by Madrid. Aaron with his courtesy and ability to make me laugh out loud, he's lovely, this is all such a treat. At one point he begins singing along to the music in Spanish making my heart do a loop de loop.

"I play guitar." He tells me.

"That's cool! I'd love to play an instrument." I reply genuinely.

"So do you have any talents other than your writing?"

I blush having told him on a night of messaging that I was penning some ideas for a book. "I wouldn't say that's a talent, yet."

"I like that... *yet*! If you enjoy doing something keep doing it. You can only get better. An expert was an amateur once."

Again I'm spellbound by his philosophical insight. I thought conversation with Ashley was good, but this has far more depth. Aaron is patiently waiting for an answer to his original question on special skills.

"Well I used to love pole dancing. I'm getting a pole in my flat." I hadn't mentioned this earlier because of the obvious connotations and his eyes widen significantly.

"Wow." He doesn't hide his approval.

"I'm out of practice. I did get quite good but I haven't done it for a while."

"Why not?"

"Magaluf kind of got in the way." I offer the simplest explanation. No need to go into the real reason that things got a bit crazy with an ex. Time is irrelevant, it's past, and the time is now.

"I like singing." Aaron brings me out of my reverie. "But I think my playing is better."

"Oh I don't know, you sounded good singing in Spanish!" It's an easy compliment to pay being so true.

"Can you sing?" I wonder what makes him ask, that special intuition perhaps.

"Yes! Well, I like to, but I don't know if I really *can*!"

"Karaoke bar it is tomorrow then." His eyes glint excitedly.

"You're on!" I cry. I'm having so much fun and decide to divulge another thing I'd held back on. "You know what, my dad told me to give you a message in case you turned out to be a weirdo!"

Spluttering in entertainment I turn the phone over. Momentarily his eyes flash and I realise instantly it was too much. Too threatening perhaps.

"Sorry." I mumble. "It was just a joke."

"Don't be daft, I'm not offended, it's hilarious! Shall we go on to a party?" He seems unbothered and I breathe a sigh of relief.

"Yes, definitely!"

"Cuenta?" He signals for the bill and I insist on paying half.

"No, no! Please, it's the first night and I'd like to pay for this." He assures me.

I feel a teeny bit guilty for the fact I have been seeing other men on the lead up to this. I get the distinct feeling Aaron has every intention of wooing me. Potentially he is looking for a girlfriend. Do I mind?

We leave the square, again hand in hand, and I tell myself to relax. A long-distance relationship might in fact suit me.

Gran Via, Aaron informs me, is the main strip and as towering buildings adorned with neon signs loom into view I gasp once more. The city has the ability to switch from historic to modern in the blink of an eye and so many of the buildings are extraordinary!

There are numerous venues to choose from. Dance music drifts from doorways adorned by bouncers and we eventually choose a place with neatly clipped bushes lining the walls outside.

Inside is strikingly hot in comparison to the cool night air. We're engulfed by loud music and gyrating bodies. It could be a club in my home town but the signs are scrawled in Spanish. It could be a bar on the strip of Magaluf except the girls, selling shots, are tastefully dressed in white shirts and black mini-skirts.

We're in Madrid! I feel another rush of exhilaration at the realisation I'm somewhere new, and far away from home.

"What you drinking?" Aaron hollers into my ear when we reach the bar through the crowd.

Whisky and coke in hand we make our way to the dance floor. There's a collection of people bopping; groups, couples, locals and tourists. Between pounding beats I hear snippets of French, German, Spanish and I find myself wishing, like I had done in Maga, that I'd concentrated in foreign languages at school.

"Jodie, cigarette?"

I agree, thinking I quite fancy one myself now. I've all but given up but the temptation is always there especially now I have the taste of bitter alcohol firmly in my throat. I follow him to a separate area. Laws don't seem to be the same as back home- either that or they're ignored.

"Jodie, I've got something to tell you."

It's really late and I'm very drunk but I can tell this is something serious and rack my addled brain for possibilities. He *had* looked perturbed when I showed him my dad's message.

"Go on." I encourage him. His eyes look sorrowful. I highly doubt he is in fact a rapist or murderer or about to admit it.

"I lied," he begins slowly and takes a deep puff of smoke.

Don't tell me he's taken as well! Inwardly I groan as he continues. "When I told you my age, I lied, I panicked!"

"So?" I scour his face, twenty-four he told me I think. He can't be older than twenty-eight, I don't see what the problem is!

"I'm nineteen."

The words resound in my head like the clang of a bell and I feel myself sobering, just a tad.

"Nineteen?" I repeat then burst into incredulous laughter. We've been goofing around all evening. He's getting me back for the dad message earlier. "You almost had me there!"

"No, I mean it Jodie. I am nineteen."

I try through slightly sozzled eyes to inspect his skin. It is supple and lineless, but I've only begun to get hints of crows-feet this year. His eyes however are as genuine and intense as ever.

"Really?" I mutter, shocked, and my mind clouds with opposing opinions.

He's nodding, looking crestfallen but not completely defeated, he takes my hands and looks straight into my face.

"You're beautiful Jodie, inside and out. You're kind and caring and modest, even though you have a really interesting life and a good job. You've got talents and you make me laugh! You're like a dream come true!"

Have I ever been told such adoring things about myself? I'm thinking he's the age Jayde pretended her boyfriend to be. He's just three years older than some of the kids I teach! He's six years younger than me, and that's a fair whack when I'm only mid-twenties myself.

But then it adds to the controversy. I'm a sucker for being naughty. He is *legal*! It is legal! He has a full-time job, he lives independently in a foreign country; he is more mature than most lads my own age, for goodness sake.

"Jodie, I'm sorry I didn't come clean sooner. I just wanted you to get to know me first. I knew you wouldn't give me a shot especially when you said you work at a school."

"But, you said you're teaching English?" If he's lied about this too I think I will consider using my credit card and booking a different room.

"Yes, I do. Nothing else is a lie. Everything you know about me is real. I'm training to teach English to all ages using a particular method, it's for a private organisation."

"Ok. Ok." I try to shake my thoughts into place. I was never in this for a relationship from the start; I could never have a relationship with a teenager! But that doesn't mean I have to shelve the plans for the weekend. I really like him, and he's just listed the reasons he really likes me.

"When you showed me that message from your dad, I about shit myself!"

I burst into laughter. It makes sense now. And his idea about time being irrelevant is more significant too. If time *is* irrelevant, then age is just a number.

"I need a drink." I tell him and taking this as a massive positive he smiles widely and jumps to his feet.

"Come on!"

***

By the time we stumble into bed it is close to dawn. I'm sure sex has been on both of our minds since the admission. We've danced closely, suggestively. Aaron can move! I'd forgotten that detail. But now we're in bed and breathing heavily, far too intoxicated for any action. Even at his age! I joke inwardly to myself; I've kept up with a youth.

I know it isn't really a laughing matter but then I can already see the looks on Cat and Leila's faces when I tell them. This is the trap of the century. Aaron was right, had he have come clean at any other point I wouldn't be here.

I'm so glad I am. I thrive on uncovering cultures, I've found inspiration for my new home, plus I am fascinated by the man-boy who tricked me into visiting!

It's strange but I feel at ease in these unfamiliar surroundings and despite the revelation this evening I'm falling asleep blissfully content.

The Omen

"Good morning." Aaron croaks, his voice huskier than ever. I've been awake for ten minutes and amongst other things, taken the time to clear a message from Ashley. It must have pinged through when we got back and connected to the Wi-Fi this morning. It said merely 'hey' from half past midnight.

"It's actually midday!" I correct Aaron watching him from the doorway as he rubs his eyes. "I was about to make us a coffee but there's no milk."

"Shit!" He curses himself. "I'm such a dork! I was supposed to get some…"

"It's fine…"

We trail off as he fixes me with a deep gaze.

"Come back to bed now, and then I'll take us for coffee to make up for my forgetfulness."

His hair hangs around his face in messy waves. The sheet is nestled around his waist and I can see the outline of what looks like a medium sized cucumber. Good god, is that his…?

Clearly noting my gaze he pulls back the sheet with an attractive cockiness, that until now hasn't shown, revealing an almost hard cock. It's massive. What's your luck? This nineteen-year-old is packing.

"Come and sit on me girl. I've been gagging to have you ride me since you got here." This dirty talk seems so out of character but not unwelcome and my groin fires into action.

I match his self-assurance and strip off my oversized tee in one fluid motion, leaving me in just a pair of French knickers. Then I stride toward him, climb onto the bed and swing a leg over his torso.

He grabs the back of my head and a fistful of hair, pulling me down to him and his kiss is also forceful. I rock back and forth over his now solid dick; my knickers are soon sticking to me with wetness.

"Take off your pants." He rasps.

"Have you got a condom?" I hate to halt proceedings like this, but I made a promise to myself.

"No, forget that, I'm clean." His hands are prising down my pants but I'm seated and he can't get them far.

"I've got some, hold on."

"I don't like them. *He* doesn't like them!" He whinges pointing downward.

"*He*!" I giggle as I begin sifting through my bag.

"How would you like having a bag put over your head?" He pouts looking every inch his teenage years and I splutter at the comment.

"Well it's that or nothing." I shrug, undeterred from my rummaging. There's no way I'm putting myself through another check-up. Especially so soon since my last one!

"It's too big. They always split."

"We'll see." His moaning is boring me. It's a turn-off as it is, why make it a bigger issue. And luckily for him I chose to bring regular *and* large- just in case. I toss him the foil packet without another word. His erection has begun to go down and he stares at it dismally.

"Stop being so dramatic!" I chastise him and mount him once again. "We can soon get it back."

After a number of minutes coaxing *him* back to life, Aaron decides he no longer wants me on top and he shoves me off.

"Bend over." He growls, and I do as he says, my heart beating wildly. I've yet to come but this coincides with my statistics of one in three. As he slides his substantial member into me I take a sharp breath. His size definitely makes up for it!

Aaron grips my hips firmly and begins pounding away, his groin smashing into my bum cheeks; I can feel them rippling with each impact. An arm snakes around my waist, still pinning me onto his pole, the other hand finds my clit and begins to twiddle and twerk.

My arms buckle with his added weight and I find myself on my elbows, but his fingers are relentless slipping and pushing, delicious electricity pulses through me. I'm coming within a minute and I relish in how tightly my insides clamp onto his throbbing cock. He pulses, driving himself deep over and over, driven by his own pleasure and then he's yelping and collapsing on top of me with a number of less urgent pumps.

"That. Was. Fantastic." He breathes.

A number of minutes pass before my senses fully return and it dawns on me it is afternoon, we're in Madrid, I'm curious, hungry, thirsty, and in need of a shower.

"Do you drink coffee black?" Aaron asks when he regains enough energy to clamber from me.

"If it's sweet. Black coffee is better than no coffee."

"Exactly!" He skips off leaving me crossed legged on the bed and thinking what a mixture of wrong and right this whole thing feels. Only wrong because of his age! But had that disagreement over the condom been down to his immaturity- or just being a man high on lust.

Last night I'd been enthralled by him. I would never have guessed he is so young! Does it really matter when we have such a connection, so much in common?

By half past three we've eaten in a trendy coffee bar, had a Royal Palace tour and have just left the Plaza Mayor; a square with an entrance of no less than nine impressive archways. I'm blown away by the sights, exhausted but excited for more. We're off to visit the Museo del Prado next. Aaron described it as displaying 'the classic art'.

I've been to museums before and expect a stuffy hush. I'm not disappointed. It lives up to every preconceived expectation with its grandeur and musty smell of age. Photographs are strictly prohibited so Aaron and I get a sneaky selfie shot when there are no porters around to see.

"Can you manage one more? I'd really love to visit the Thyssen-Bornemisza. My mate told me it has some really cool, modern stuff apparently."

"Why not?" I'm dead on my feet and have zipped through cash on entrance tickets but I don't care. Once I'm tied down with bills I won't have this luxury often. "Shall we get a quick coffee first?"

Whilst there's still money in my pocket and caffeine in my system I'm good to go.

"Have you had an espresso before?" Aaron asks.

"No." I admit. "Aren't they like really strong?"

"Well you drank that black coffee this morning, it got me thinking. There's a way to do it properly."

I'm intrigued as we duck into a bar that smells richly of ground coffee beans. And I breathe deeply, gratefully taking a seat. My legs scream with all of the walking.

"Espresso, dos."

We're presented with miniature coffee cups, not much bigger than a shot.

"Ok, so milk and two sugars. Then, down in one." As he says this he tops up our tiny cups to the brim with milk and pours in two sugar sachets each. "Give it a good stir!"

I do as he says. We hold eyes and swig. The coffee tastes sickly and divine and is gone in two gulps.

"Now just wait!" He laughs.

"I'll just use the bathroom before we go." I tell him and follow the signs to the back of the bar. Once locked inside the cubicle I immediately feel the effects of the espresso. My body quivers, the air around me seems to vibrate.

As I wash my hands the water feels tickly, my skin is jumpy and I'm enveloped in a hazy, happy buzz.

"I can't believe this is legal!" I exclaim once we're back out and walking the streets.

"Told you." Aaron says easily and scoops my palm into his. My legs have a new lease of life, my whole body does. My mind is humming with excitement, I'm revitalised; I'm experiencing a massive caffeine rush. I'm intrigued to know if they have the same effect back in England!

***

There were some cool exhibitions at the Thyssen-Bornemisza. I enjoyed the white room with a TV screen that you appeared on when you walked in, except the camera responsible wasn't visible. And there was another room I really liked, large with moving images projected onto every surface.

"I'm so glad your friend told you about that one!" I say again after we leave.

"I know, it doesn't feel right but I enjoy the modern stuff more than the classic."

"That's not wrong. You enjoy what you enjoy! That's the cool thing about art." And I agree with him I suppose; this place was much more fun!

"So back to get changed, then food and a night out. Or straight out for food, go back and get ready for a night out?"

"Let's go back and get ready, then food and a night out. We could get a snack on the way back for now." I suggest.

Aaron looks at me. "You know what Jodie, you really are perfect!"

***

We head to the busier Plaza de Santa Ana for food this evening after another enjoyable session in the sack. The bustling square provides opportunity to people watch and another abundance of street acts. As we linger choosing our restaurant, I spot a strange, tiny cream thing covered in bells. It resembles a piñata and I walk up to it staring interestedly. As I reach for my phone, instinct to snap a picture, the thing lets out a terrified squeal and spins away from me casting a hood over its whole body.

"What the f…"

"Come on." Aaron pulls me away. "We'll eat here, they have an offer on tapas and sangria!"

I'm easily distracted from the creepy object. Tapas and alcohol do their job in dissuading me that it was a bad omen; that the piñata thing put a curse on Aaron and me. But I don't know why I'm even thinking like this. Aaron can't be my boyfriend anyway!

After sharing the bill tonight, he suggests we try out a smoking bar and we head back to Gran Via, the main road.

We immediately stumble upon a place offering all flavours of shisha. It's illuminated in soft neon colours and has real trees growing on the inside.

"How are we meant to choose?" I cry as I scan the long list ranging through chocolate to exotic fruit.

We decide on melon and puff the creamy smoke as more funny and thought-provoking conversation continues. I marvel at how switched on he is. I know he's nineteen but the judgement that comes with it doesn't fit at all.

"So gorgeous, you ready to find a karaoke bar?"

"Will there really be one?" I ask him thinking Madrid seems far too classy for such an establishment.

"You can get anything here! There'll be one somewhere."

As it happens, these are famous last words and we in fact don't find anywhere offering karaoke! This is almost to my disappointment. Aaron was already planning the duets we could sing together, and I was looking forward to showing off my pipes.

Instead we dart from bar to bar and once again find ourselves out dancing and partying until the very early hours. Time is irrelevant! This city just does not sleep!

"Do you want a pizza or something?" Aaron slurs to me as we stumble in the direction of our temporary home.

"No, I'm fine, but if you want one…"

"I don't."

The bedroom is soothingly still, the bed soft underneath my achy body. The day sightseeing has totally taken it out of me and with a head full of novel, new images I fall asleep virtually instantly.

***

When my alarm bleeps initially, I feel like crap! Two late nights of heavy drinking have taken their toll. I lie in the folds of the bed, Aaron groans beside me.

I'm gutted to be leaving today, it seems so soon. Even after only this short time I already know I'll miss Aaron's company and his face. But today, I also move into the flat with Leila! This realisation takes the sting out of the tail that I've got to go. Plus we spoke last night about him visiting me, soon.

"I think we should get ready and make the most of our last few hours." Aaron suggests. "But, first..."

We have sex for the third time, the final time, for now.

"So are you serious about me coming to stay with you?" He asks now we're lying spent beside one another.

"Definitely!" I reply without hesitation. Then I remember the age thing, again, and wonder where he thinks this is going. "You know, we can never be..."

"What?" He looks at me sincerely. "*We* can be *anything* we want baby."

I've got to love his attitude.

Hello Marshamonvilla

The aeroplane jets through the sky putting hundreds of miles between me and Aaron once again. At the airport he told me; 'I'm not spending ages on goodbye, because I'll see you again soon anyway.'

And I much preferred the almost blunt farewell; as if we were just nipping to the shops! We've decided he will visit in November so not that long anyway.

Amazingly by the time I've touched down, all that has filled my mind for the past two days fades away in favour of calling Leila. My car awaits me in the parking lot and I tell her I'll be home within the hour.

Mum is utterly relieved when she sees me in the flesh. I think she genuinely spent the whole time I was away in living fear.

"Welcome home darling!"

I smile at her warmly, I do appreciate how much she cares but don't cry like I did when I came home from Magaluf. This break was a drop in the ocean in comparison. She offers me tea before I leave to meet Leila.

"Sorry mum, I can't wait to see it now the blokes have moved out. I'm going to drive down with a car load of stuff right now!"

"I'll help sweetheart." She tells me kindly. "I'll just get changed and I'll load up my car too."

"Thanks, and I'll tell you all about it whilst we work!"

I approach my new street excitedly. Leila says she's kept her word and hasn't even visited since getting hold of the keys yesterday, so we get to unlock our new home together for the first time!

"Jane said it's all been painted." Leila pants as we twist the keys. I've told her the trip was amazing, but she doesn't know details including the age thing, just yet. There's no time for it all now.

"She said they've put in a new bathroom too!"

"Yes then, that's *sick*!" I giggle using the teenage term.

Now the doors are opened we race up the stairs. Sure enough everything is crisp and painted off-white. The carpets are new throughout, biscuit and hardwearing. We pace through the flat in awed silence and finally congregate in the living room.

There's the manky sofa still, and some other furniture which will come in handy.

"Well, what we waiting for, let's get some stuff moved in!" I squeal clapping my hands in glee.

For the next two hours we haul boxes and furniture and with help from my mum and George we're virtually complete by early evening. It's difficult to fathom this morning I stood in an apartment in Madrid, now I'm in my very own living room back home!

I suddenly remember the purchase I made earlier. I snap a pic of me and Leila amongst the disarray holding the fridge magnet between us and send it to Aaron. It's hardly a gorgeous fabric throw for the couch but it's a start. He sends one back of the view from his bedroom; a grey-blue sky and ribbon of slate sea.

I can't quite offer a sea view when you visit, but I can offer a different type…

I cheekily reply before also sending a message to Jem asking when I can fetch the pole. I suggest tomorrow.

"Cup of tea?" I offer everyone once the final car full has been unloaded.

George shakes his head. "I'm off for a pint."

Mum tuts and eyes him. I smirk over her shoulder, smug because although I'll miss her, I am glad to be gaining my own space.

"*Tea*? I fancy wine!" Leila exclaims. "I'll nip to the shop."

"Oh, I'll leave you girls to it." Mum tells us. "You enjoy your first evening."

To be honest after this weekend's consumption of alcohol I'd prefer a tea, but Leila responds. "Don't be silly, have a little wine with us and toast your hard work! We'd never have been done this quick without you!"

Mum blushes and shrugs persuaded, and I feel eternal gratitude to Leila for encouraging her.

"We haven't got any wine glasses." I giggle when Leila returns from the shop only moments later. "Mugs or half pints?"

"Mugs." Mum interjects. "Then we can pretend we're being sensible!"

I giggle approvingly. There's a side to her we can corrupt yet, especially with Leila on board.

"I'll buy you a set of wine glasses as a housewarming." She suggests.

"We'll have to have more girly nights." I tell them both. "We'll invite your mum too, Leila. And Cat and Chantelle."

We sit at the dining table that has been left in the kitchen on rickety chairs.

"I'll be able to fix these." Mum says. "I bet they just need tightening up."

"Who needs men?" Leila praises. "Can you do other DIY?"

Mum lists her skills and I realise to many extents Leila is so right. And for the things I do want a man for- sex, attention and flirting- I have a number to choose from. I remember and reply to Ashely's 'hey' even though it was a blatant booty call.

Just got your message, was in Madrid for the weekend ☺

I enjoy letting him know I'm not free for him to toy with at his every beck and call.

"Speaking of men," I slowly begin now Leila is done admiring my mum's man-skills.

"Oh yes, tell us about *Aaron*!"

I tell them the age-thing first. Best to get that out the way before my mum starts planning a wedding. Neither are as appalled as I thought they would be.

"So, you still liked him right?" Leila is encouraging, and I wonder if I've been hard on myself. I nod and go on to explain a few things I *really* liked about him.

"I don't see the problem." Mum is huffing, her cheeks flushed with pinot. It would seem a glass- or mug- is enough to loosen her pessimism. Leila too is undisturbed.

"He's an adult Jodie!"

They're right if not a little over-enthusiastic but knowing Jayde's battles and the advice I've been giving her about sticking to our own generation, it seems hypocritical.

Ashley replies long after mum has gone home and I'm lying back on my makeshift bed in my cave-like bedroom. George offered to help me put up the frame but I couldn't be bothered myself and insisted I'll do it tomorrow. For now, a mattress on the floor will more than suffice.

Very posh! Hope you had fun babe x

I don't respond for now. He doesn't need to know immediately that yes, thanks, I did! This has been one hell of a weekend. I feel like I need another weekend to recover from it.

Next door Leila is tucked up. Possibly her mind reeling just as fast as mine at the possibilities our new shared abode poses. Jem has arranged for me to drop in on Tuesday and collect the pole, George agreed to assist me in the installation of it.

We have our Belfry night out to look forward to as well. Leila immediately fixed her shift to allow her to join me. Might we meet suitors? Might we bring them home! We'll definitely get ready together, blasting music and downing pre-drinks.

I feel at complete peace and I chill out, half watching the TV and half imagining the funky style we can stamp onto our pad.

Hello, Marshamonvilla.

Sibling Date

It's a Tuesday and I've finished with IT for the day. I'm now sat in the Girls Unit with Eve. She's attending independently via a taxi, completing a few hours at a time each day.

"What's a *boner*?" She exclaims in her abrupt way. We're working on adjectives for big, small, long... Safeguarding buzzes in my ear. What's made her think of it now? Am I being crude?

"Erm, it's a slang word to do with a man's penis." I try to remain professional, she is thirteen, and her eyes dart to my face suspiciously.

"You can say cock. I know that's what it's called."

"Actually, penis is the proper word." I tell her. "Anyway, we're looking at..."

My eyes land on 'hard'. I rifle through the pages. "Loud. Can you think of another word for loud?"

"My mum talks about cock to me all the time."

Bloody hell! I feel my cheeks flush; at lunchtime Lizzy made me aware social services are investigating her set up at home.

"Which mum?" I have to ask because she calls her auntie 'mum' too.

"Both of em." She shrugs. "They told me what cum tastes like!"

I splutter this time, I can't help it.

"Salty!" She adds smirking.

She could be making it up. Do I tell her off, is she testing me, trying to shock me? It's certainly one of Jayde's tactics. Or do I guide her and try to make better something that's been undone.

"Eve, it's not something people talk about really. Especially during an English lesson!" I add playfully. "Things like that- cum etcetera- it's for when you're really in love. Later in life you know."

I don't go completely 'nun' on her. She should know it isn't a shameful topic but I can't exactly encourage her to go and find out for herself, just yet. An inner voice helpfully reminds me I was trying out such things at not very much older than her, with Luca!

Maybe I am just one huge hypocrite.

"For now," I continue unwaveringly. "You should be thinking about, you know, holding hands and having a kiss and things less *serious*."

"Ewww!" Eve yowls. If the thought of cum didn't repulse her like this, I'm not sure she understands it all yet anyway.

"Holding hands!" She yelps. "No boy is touching me. Why would you think that?"

"Or girl!" I add shrugging, thinking of Lizzy's sexuality.

"No way. Girl? *Jodie!*"

We keep the fact Lizzy is a lesbian private for now but we do rally the attitude of acceptance. In this instance I am relieved she is so opposed to either gender. I will however have to report the exchange and I am aware this will weigh heavily against her home-setting.

I've lost Eve now and she doesn't complete any more work. She's doing so well though! I beam with pride as if I've done the work myself when I show it to Lizzy.

"Well done Eve. You've gained some more points!"

She looks up from her game of Connect Four with Harishma and Bonnie.

"Do I get a smiley?" She's referring to the other reward system tailored just to her.

"You're on the right track." I nod. "You're doing good lady."

She grins and goes back to the game. I watch her and Bonnie and the tiny interactions that are developing between them; a flicker of eye contact, a quick smile.

"Makes you proud don't it?" Lizzy says from my side and leans a hand on my shoulder. "We make a great team."

I meet her eye and she holds it. I'm not sure what I pick up on but I've got to give her the details of our 'cum convo'.

"Hmmm. So, Eve and I covered an interesting topic."

Girls packed off, more safeguarding paperwork filled in, I scoot to the staff room to collect my things. I'm ridiculously excited; I'm going straight to Jem's to pick up the pole. Troy is waiting for me of course and we walk to our cars together chatting. He giggles when I tell him Eve asked me about a boner.

"That'll be me later, thinking about you on your pole."

My heart flutters with genuine glee and I grin.

"I cannot wait!" I admit. I already text George demanding he come as soon as I'm home to help install it. We say bye and part ways and as I drive towards Jem's, the nerves begin to set in.

I don't want to come across as smug when she asks how things are going, because they're going really great. I don't want to talk about Dane, at all. And it doesn't help I love her for the same reasons I loved him. They share extravagant personalities, forthcoming mannerisms and large, dark eyes. It's an inevitable meeting, it has to be done for more reason than the pole.

When she swings open her door it's almost like looking into *his* eyes. Except I feel for Jem still.

"Jodie, you look amazing! I'm so jealous, I bet you had the best time!" I return her hug with warmth. I was silly to be worried! She has two dogs and three kids, all of which are running rampage.

"Maga was amazing yes. But it seems so long ago now!" I have to almost shout to be heard.

"Jodie?" Her eldest is calling me now. "Look at my Viking project!"

She waves a skewwhiff helmet in front of my nose.

"Jodie, look at what I've built on Minecraft!" A control pad waggles in the background, a finger pointing to the screen. The youngest is sat amongst an array of action figures and looks up holding a shiny, red one aloft.

"Leave her alone!" Jem tells them but I cast my eyes over the achievements anyway.

"Keep up the good work." I tell them kindly and follow her into the kitchen where she ushers the yapping dogs into the garden.

"I've packed it all up, you can check all the bits are there. The instructions are inside too." She begins unzipping the long, carry bag.

"It's cool, I trust ya. I just can't wait to get it up!"

"Well the cash will be of more use to me, I can tell you that much! Do you want a cuppa?" She turns to the kettle.

"I've got to go." I put the money on the side. "My brother is coming round to help me put it up."

I pick up the bag feeling a tad ruthless for saying I can't stay.

"You know I'm still your friend right, even though *my* brother..." She trails off and I look at her and smile.

"Of course I know. You're not him!"

Even if she is a spitting image! And admittedly I am making a swift exit to avoid the topic.

"Ok. You know, he's having a real shit time at the moment actually." She divulges. This is exactly the type of conversation I wanted to avoid. It causes an uncomfortable shift within me.

"I feel bad for-"

"No, don't feel bad for anything!" She interrupts. "It's his own fault! She treats him like shit and he keeps going back for more."

I didn't treat him like shit and look how he treated me! I quickly take a firm hold of the reigns and steer my thoughts away. It makes no odds to me, it's irrelevant.

"Thanks for this!" I lift the heavy bag an inch, directing the conversation back to benign territory.

"He told me he'd tried to talk to you and you didn't want to know. I don't blame you!" She continues. "He only ever goes out when they have a fall out. A few weeks ago, she kicked him out and what did he do? Went straight Trap, got steaming and ran up a tab then turned up at mum's-" She stops abruptly perhaps noticing my expression. "Sorry!"

I think about when I saw him, the night we diverted to the Fox and bumped into Shane. I didn't care what had caused him to be there, if anything I was glad but I'm not evil.

"It must be really difficult to, you know, watch it all happening."

"It's my mum I feel bad for." She mutters, and I feel bad for them all. "But anyway, forget him you don't want to hear all of this."

I smile, she's right. I focus on getting home and erecting my pole! "Well, thanks again Jem, it was nice to see you and the kids."

"I'm glad it's you that gets to use it."

"Oh I'll use it!" I enthuse and begin to walk across the kitchen. Naughty visions are welcomed. Who will be the first to watch me on it?

"I'm glad you're doing ok Jodes." She shakes her head sadly. I see it in her eyes, like before, pity. It's misplaced and needless.

"I'm more than ok." I give her a hug. "I hope things settle down with, you know, him."

She raises her eyebrows sceptically and gives me a grimace that says she's sure it won't. If it was my brother and my mum I'd be beside myself with worry. We retrace our steps through the house. The kids do their best to gain my attention and Jem bats them off.

"Take care Jodie." She tells me at the door and I think we both know our paths probably won't cross again for a while.

"You too."

I unlock the car, sling the pole into the boot and hop in with a wave. Jem returns to her houseful and I return to my flat; our very separate lives.

Hearing about Dane is uncomfortable. But however bad it is I can't help it- inwardly I give a shout out to my ex. Thanks for everything! His misfortunes have aided me, perhaps we're both getting exactly what we deserve.

Once home, I text George excitedly to let him know.

***

"Can you take over? My arms are aching!"

George laughs at me but we've been tightening the damn thing for ages!

He switches with me. I stand holding the pole upright as he crouches at its base to continue turning the thin, metal rod which is making the pole a millimetre longer with every rotation. We've an inch or so to go until the circular disc at the top reaches the ceiling.

My biceps are burning with the exertion. "At this rate, I won't be able to swing round it once it's up!"

"Not long now." George mutters as he twists at the stick quickly. He puffs and pants but before long I can let go of the pole and it is holding it-self upright. He grabs his mini spirit level and places it against the rising, silver metal.

"It looks so good!" I clap my hands with glee and he grins.

"I can't wait to have a go." He admits. "Can you carry on tightening and I'll keep it level? Let's hope we've got it lined up with a beam after all!"

"Can you imagine?" I cry. "If we put the ceiling through Leila will go mad!"

"It's your Landlord I'd be more worried about!"

"Landlady." I automatically correct him and think, nope, still Leila's wrath I'm more concerned about! She's at work so isn't here to observe proceedings.

"How sure are you it's lined up?" I double check.

"As sure as I *can* be." He replies.

I drop to the floor and carry on tightening. George builds houses for a living with my dad; if the ceiling collapses they can fix it, plus who better to advise where the beams are running. As if in answer to my thoughts there's a groaning creak as I continue, more slowly now, to turn.

"Is it ok?" I look up at George and he shrugs.

"It's the pressure, it should be ok."

Should is good enough for me! Having the pole up and running is still my driving force.

We've switched positions again now. But this time I'm standing back, sure that plaster board is going to begin raining down at any moment. The squeaky complaining is loud with each forceful twist.

There's a hairline crack in the paint running vertically for a number of centimetres but other than that I'm hopeful I'm just being dramatic.

"Right, test it." George stands up. "I daren't do it anymore!"

I rub my hands together and eye the best purchase I've ever made before skipping full on into a swing. Except as soon as my legs pick up from the floor the pole swings forward with me attached and we both fly forwards, towards the large window.

It all happens so quickly and I place my feet out braced for landing, preparing to take the weight of the pole too. George doesn't have chance to move before I'm on the other side of the room. Luckily the pole hasn't dropped horizontally and crashed straight through the window!

He rushes forwards now to grab it from my arms and we're both howling with laughter fuelled by relief.

"Safe to say, that wasn't tight enough!" He chortles.

Once the giggling is over we're dismayed to realise we have to loosen it to get it back upright, before we can tighten it all over again.

Another gruelling ten minutes later and I'm ready to test again! I'm much more tentative this time.

"Seems alright." I reason.

George watches me timidly lifting my weight off the ground then runs at it himself. This time the pole sturdily takes his weight and he swings round in a clumsy loop.

"Wicked!" I cry. "Let's put some music on and have a proper go!"

"You can buy me some beer first." He retorts. "To say thank you!"

As it happens I already anticipated this request and wiggle my eyebrows. "Already in the fridge my darling!"

"And you're only telling me this now? Jodie!" He wipes his brow exaggeratedly.

"Well, I had to make sure the job was done first." I tease him and prance off to fetch us one.

For all my imagining, George is the first to see me on my pole! Leila won't get home until late. I doubt I'll still be up to give her a demonstration so I send her a picture for now.

"Show me that lift thing again." George has really gotten into it and being strong he's better than me at the more technical exercises. I'm jealous! The annoyance spurs me to keep going.

We take it in turns until we've literally got no energy left. I'd forgotten how good it made me feel! We collapse onto the sofa and although my muscles are drained, my body pulsates with desire to do more.

"It's such a frustrating hobby." I say. "You want to do more, but the more you do the less you *can* do!"

"I can definitely see why you like it. And I'll definitely be round again. I think we should make this a weekly thing. A sibling date!"

"I'll cheers to that!" Lifting my arm to thump the can against his makes my hand shake with the effort. I just can't wait to get stronger and better at it. It might be a more controversial date night for siblings, we sometimes go to the cinema to watch a horror movie and we often go to the pub. But I'm happy to make pole dancing with my brother a regular thing. This sibling date is going to be quite useful!

Party Time

It's Friday and Leila and I have a living room full of squealing girls and guffawing men. Music booms as Alexa casually adorns the pole. Cat had a go and hurt her wrist so she's now cheering encouragement from the side-lines instead. Chantelle and Leila are good, but not as good as me. And I'm nowhere near Alexa's standard. Yet!

There are no males to show off to really. They consist of George, his friends- who are not options sexually- my dad's old advice of 'not shitting on your own doorstep' rings loud and clear. And true. I learned that the hard way of course.

Chantelle's boyfriend is here, who is clearly not an option either! Obviously I don't base the success of a party by the opportunity to shag somebody. But it would have been nice to have Aaron around; or Ashley. Or Luca!

Aaron *can't* be here, and Ashley *won't* come here so I haven't mentioned the party to either during our exchanged messages this week. I messaged Luca yesterday, but I've heard nothing back, he's presumably overseas still. He'll be in touch when he's back in the area, I'm sure. The remaining condom is safely tucked away amongst my knickers and will stay there until it finds its ultimate resting place. On Luca's dick!

Aaron wants to Skype call me tomorrow which I've agreed to, but I dislike phone conversations at the best of times never mind an image to go with it. It's not until the afternoon though so any signs of a hangover can be covered.

"Alexa, show me that lift again, the one where you go backwards." I request and she obliges without question. Her body seems to defy gravity as she stands with her back to the pole and swings her legs up forwards before somehow switching her torso and gripping the pole high up above with her ankles. She's upside down now and then slithers gracefully to the floor.

"Ok, so it's this action?" I can lift my legs out in front of me but I don't know how she gets them to go up and over!

"I'm not strong enough!" I moan releasing the half attempt.

"Giz a go!" George says buoyed with beer. We step back allowing him the space to show off some of the poses I've shown him.

"You're not bad." Alexa purrs eyeing him. "Can you do this?"

She embarks on a difficult combination of three poses executing them with style one after another. He nods suitably impressed.

"I'll try for you babe!"

They're flirting but it's just banter. She's been gushing non-stop about a new man she's met recently. She's seeing him again tomorrow and has already decided he is 'the one'. Alexa is clapping delightedly at George's not-too-shabby effort.

"You try it!" She tells me and I do. I remember trying it when I was still doing lessons and I'm grateful to be reminded of the moves.

"You could make a brother-sister pole team." She tells us now, her eyes glistening how they always do when she's excited. "You should Google the routines for double acts. You'd have something unique, being related."

"Yeah might be a bit weird." George laughs it off.

"Think of the girls you'd get to meet though!" I add, and this instantly changes his expression.

"You're right. Let's do it!"

"Sibling date." I remind him giggling.

"Hey!" Leila overhears us. "I want to learn too!"

"I could come round to teach you two if you wanted." Alexa tells us. "Jodie you can practice with your bro without me. I'm preparing for a very serious relationship, so I don't want to see him half naked."

"Are you sure?" George doesn't miss a beat and again their eyes lock in flirtatious battle. I wonder how she can be so certain about this man she's pinned her hopes on as being 'the one'. But then again Tanya and Chantelle have both made jibes about her ability to quickly and solidly fall in love.

"So tell me more about Arnie, what does he do for a job?" I ask her now George has gone back to Jag and Russ.

"Oh he works as a freelance producer. He travels all around the country. He's already said he can get me tickets to loads of gigs and even backstage!"

"Sounds wicked. I'll be your plus one!" I giggle thinking about hooking up with the stars. I imagine my path crossing Luca's at a star-studded event. His *familiar*, in *his* world; surely a successful blend.

"Definitely!" She enthuses. "I think a life in showbiz would suit me."

"Me too!" I agree with her statement meaning us both but Alexa more so. Even now, dressed only for a house-party she's a complete glamour-puss.

"He's the one, I can just tell, Jodie. He is the one! We are so compatible, and the sex is amazing!"

Judging by her standards I'm building a Top Five, never mind just one!

The night ambles on. Loud music, louder laughter, two more visits to the shop and numbers increasing as word spreads amongst our mutual friends. Even my old mate Micky shows his face. I haven't seen him in ages and it's wicked to catch up.

In the early hours we're finally saying goodnight to those who have stayed longest and locking the main door.

"Well that was fun!" Leila slurs. "I like our friends!"

I giggle tipsily. "That's *why* they're our friends!"

We're hovering in the hallway outside of Leila's bedroom. She scrapes her hands down her cheeks. "I'm so glad I haven't got work until three tomorrow."

"Set an alarm for like ten or something and we'll go to the café for breakfast?"

She nods and loosely hugs me. "Goodnight my beautiful bezzie."

"Goodnight darling." I leave her to get ready for bed. Or just to fall into it. Probably the latter! We're both drunk but she's so right. We do have a good group of friends between us and I'm looking forward to throwing more parties at Marshamonvilla.

I try not to think about the mess we'll have to clear up tomorrow and don't look around the kitchen as I head to my bedroom. It's a price that's worth paying. The legendary flat parties continue! Shane will be so proud.

Saturday Talk

I sit cross legged on my bed, my laptop open and loading in-front of me. Leila has gone off to work, hangover alleviated by our tasty breakfast this morning. Clean-up after last night's party wasn't a bad job. Somebody, Daisy or Chantelle maybe, had bagged up a load of the empties meaning an hour was all it took. Music has been blasting since, but I've turned it down now that my Skype call is due!

My heart flutters. I've never actually used this app although it's second nature to Aaron. He told me how often he uses it to catch up with friends and family. I don't want to look like an old-fogey technophobe so I've gone along with it as though I didn't have to set up an account the moment he suggested it.

I've pushed the age thing to the back of my mind. For now, I'm happy to go with the flow and see what happens. I click on the relevant icon, I'm already logged in with one contact; Aaron. His picture is outdated, he looks young. *Younger!*

But still with the same warm smile that verges on dopey and heavily lashed eyes, thick dark hair. If *the one* is somebody full of life, charming, independent and who can speak a foreign language then perhaps he could top the category. He ticks the right boxes and I'll never know if I'm not at least open to the idea.

A funny ringtone like the sound of popping bubbles begins to warble and the younger Aaron picture hovers in the middle of the screen. I take a deep breath and click on a green circle to answer.

An image is generated of a real-life Aaron and he stares out of the screen grinning.

"Hey!" He greets. "Where are you?"

"Hi! I'm in my bedroom. Can you hear me?"

A message has popped up. *Turn on camera?*

"I can hear you but I can't see you. Ahh, there you are!"

I've tapped the correct button and a small rectangle shows me the image he is presumably seeing in full. Self-consciously I sweep my hair back and try to concentrate on the shiny, black dot of the camera and his picture, not worry about my own.

"It's so good to see your beautiful face." His husky voice and northern accent fills my room. "How have you been?"

"Yeah good! Work's been *busy*... as always!"

We go on to talk about the day-to-day things we haven't shared through messages and I relax back into the cushions on my bed. Before I know it, the call has been going for over forty-five minutes and the battery is draining closer to empty.

"I need to fetch my charger." I tell him interrupting the flow of chit-chat.

"I should be going anyway babe. We're having a barbie on the beach tonight. I've still got to pick up some burgers and shower and that."

"Very nice! I wish I was having a barbie on the beach!"

"Have one in your garden."

I cast my mind to our poky plot which is barely useful for hanging out washing. Not only that, it's early October.

"It's raining." I tell him wryly.

"So what will you do tonight?"

"I don't know. Maybe go out, maybe just chill. Last weekend was a busy one!"

He gives me a wink and smirks. I wish I could reach out and touch him.

"I might have a beach but I'd still rather spend it there with you." He tells me and I inwardly croon.

"So sweet." I grin. "Not long until you can."

"I'll let you know as soon as I get my dates confirmed."

I glance at the battery life. I know any moment I'll get a warning and I don't want us to get cut off.

"Yes do! Right I'm saying bye now then because my laptop is going to die very soon!"

"Ok gorgeous. It was nice seeing you! Let me know if you're free to talk again in the week."

"Ok. Have a nice evening."

"You too! Speak soon."

We smile at each other and I end the call making the image disappear. Well, that wasn't so bad after all! In fact, it really was lovely.

I stand up and stretch. My muscles are tight from last night's impromptu training on the pole. Tonight calls for a hot bath with my book, and then perhaps another go at a few of the swings Alexa showed me. Regardless of whether Aaron is the one, chances are he'll be here within the month. The least I can do is improve on my game in the meantime.

***

When my phone pings at ten o'clock I think it could easily be Ashley, Luca or Aaron although I'm swaying toward the latter. It's Leila though and I click open the message to read;

Word gone round we had a party. You'll never guess what Shane said! Xxx

I think of a number of things that Shane could quite possibly have said and the explanation arrives before I can ask.

His mate told him 'he saw that Jodie walking like John Wayne this morning' and Shane wants to know who you've been banging in his old room!!! Xxx

What the actual hell? I think back to the short stroll through the village earlier. Was I really sauntering like a cowboy? If so it was most certainly not down to a vigorous night in the sack!

Typical cycle of village conversation; we had a party, so this surely means I got it on with somebody. What better way to evoke information than an attempt to catch me out. Walking like John Wayne indeed! I have to laugh. My muscles were stiff from pole dancing! This admittance would likely invoke wilder rumours still. Best to let people think what they want. Regardless of anything I say, they will do just that anyway.

I reply with a number of crying with laughter emoji faces. And;

What a dick!!!

This is virtually the first weekend since Magaluf that I've gone without any dick! And despite wondering whether Aaron is the one, christening my bedroom is on my mind too. There's time yet for Ashley to hit me up but then I'll be scuttling off to his. And I'll be walking the long way around, missing out the busy centre where the Trap is full of sneaky eyes and waggling tongues.

I wake up with a start. Leila is scurrying up the stairs. The front door banging is what disturbed me.

"Hiya." I greet her when she appears in the doorway. "How was the shift? Other than Shane and his fantasies!"

"Oh yeah fine. Busy. Do you want a tea?"

"What time is it?" I ask her.

"Almost one."

"No, thanks." I shake my head and glance at my phone which has fallen to the floor since I've nodded off. There are no messages from any of my boys and I slope off to bed bidding Leila goodnight on my way through the kitchen.

Miss Midweek

The staff room is buzzing with excitement this lunch time. It's been tangible all week and growing with each passing day. Two more days and it's our team night out- plus a week off! This term has only been five weeks long. Next term, I'm warned, is the hardest and the longest stretch this academic year until a holiday. To me it seems ludicrous to have time off so regularly having worked solidly in hospitality, although it's something I'm happy to get used to.

"What you wearing?" Harishma asks me and I shrug nonchalantly as though I haven't been mentally raking through my wardrobe for the last twenty minutes. I've just not got the money to spare for something new. I have to budget more strictly now.

"I'm wearing a leather mini skirt and this silky shirt thing that ties up here." She explains to anybody who's listening. "I've got some knee-high boots; I don't know whether to wear them or strappy heels."

Troy sneakily squeezes my thigh under the table and a burst of lust erupts from his touch. This week he's been as frisky as ever, more so, and I know it's related to this upcoming social event. He still hasn't mentioned his girlfriend and I wonder why he's not suspicious that I haven't made the natural steps of sending him a Facebook request or giving him my phone number.

Perhaps he knows I know. Perhaps he thinks I've accepted it because the cheeky contact between us is becoming more and more regular. Daily he finds excuses to brush my bum or chest or handle my shoulders or wrist. He's not even that subtle sometimes.

"So are you meeting us early Jodie? Are you still bringing your friend?" Sean has fixed me with his stone-grey eyes.

"Yeah she's coming. We're going to meet you about half six." I know he's asking because he's hoping Leila is fit. He's in for a nice surprise there.

"Half six! We'll be well away by then." He chides and looks around the group for support with a screwed-up nose. I won't be encouraging Leila to go there. Not with Mr Topless Selfie! The incident is common knowledge amongst the staff, but he doesn't seem fazed.

Troy scoffs. "Mate, most people will get there about that time. I know me, Lewis and Dom will be there about then. There's no way Del will be out early or Gilbert."

"Is everybody going?" I ask, wondering explicitly if Julie will be there.

"Usually most people make an appearance." Harishma answers. "Iqbal won't and neither will Pav. But only the cool people *stay* out!"

I know who she's referring to as 'cool' and I'm pleased it includes me.

"It'll be a good night." Troy says and he looks me straight in the eye as he continues. "I'm looking forward to it."

A heat fizzes through me. What if he's *the one*? If he wasn't taken I'd be surely jumping about like Alexa declaring to every one of my friends how perfect he is. Is he being taken a sign to move on, or merely a barrier to be challenged?

"Me too." I mutter with a smirk. His current girlfriend might not be *his* one. I can tell how he feels about me; our chemistry is real and as palpable as running water. Does how I feel about him prove Aaron is not the one at least, or does timing play a part. If time is irrelevant, is timing irrelevant too?

"So, your mate's single right?" Sean makes an outright play for Leila. He knows none of the women here are interested.

"Erm, yeah she is." He's put me on the spot and even though she won't fancy him, I don't want to put him down. He's odd and brash but I don't dislike him.

He pats the table as if it's responsible for the good news, smiling downwards inanely.

"Great!" He hisses, and Troy rolls his eyes. Harishma gives him a look as if he is a bizarre insect.

"Right, I'd better get to games club." I jump up. Lacey isn't here to tease me over my good-girl work ethic, she'll be eating in the unit. She doesn't understand my rule-following or know it's also driven by a fear of Julie!

"Have a good afternoon." Troy greets me, and I return the wish to the group.

The others will start to move soon too having posts to get to themselves. The kids have been rowdy today. Most days involve at least an issue of some kind but with the half term approaching there's an opposing mix of excitement and anxiety. It's devastating but some of these kids are dreading being at home for a week. They'd rather be here where they're fed, warm and interacted with.

Games club is the responsibility of the year 6 teacher, Jenni. She's in here every day and hopes to claim a little rest-bite from her class. Although they often choose this club to be around her still! I'm in here along with Eric on a Wednesday and Thursday and I like the opportunity to gossip and watch over Lego creations being formed.

"Are you going out on Friday?" She asks me once the ten or so students are settled and playing.

"Yep, are you?"

"Definitely! We think there's something going on between Gilbert and Julie." She tells me in a hushed voice and I look from her to Eric who is nodding conspiratorially.

"Really!" I gasp and pieces of a puzzle try to slot together in my mind. "Really?"

It's hard to imagine Julie in any other way than terrifying. I bet she's a dominatrix! Actually Gilbert might like this. She's a challenge. She's a meal-ticket because she's the boss! It's all making sense and whereas I thought I'd be worried about Julie coming out, I'm now resolutely looking forward to doing some detective work myself.

"Is he after Claire's job?" The question pops out of my mouth before I can stop it but it seems obvious to me; the staff meeting clash, the threatening 'you mark my words' and his new office- her old office- so soon afterwards.

"What makes you think that?" Eric asks me, but his eyes are alert. He's thinking the same as me but being cautious.

"Well the office for a start! And a few other things. It was weird in that Monday meeting, the first one of the term." I offer the scenario they were both present for.

"I told you!" He hisses to Jenni who's smirking but not agreeing or disagreeing.

"Well, I've heard of women shagging their way to the top..." I mumble. Eric and Jenni both burst into laughter.

"But do you think that's even true? Do women really do that?" Jenni asks me out of curiosity.

Admittedly I haven't 'heard' about anyone specifically doing it, it's a figure of speech isn't it? I just assume it to be that way round.

"I suppose some women might use it to their advantage. And some men too. Just like Gilbert is doing!" I finally answer.

"How much older do you think Julie is than Gilbert?" Eric asks us now. His eyes remind me of Harishma's when we're talking juicy in the unit and I think about if she was here now. She would just burst!

"Gilbert is my age." Jenni tells us. "Twenty-eight. If he gets promoted I'll be mad! He didn't even complete his teacher training. That's why he's in charge of Behaviour and not a teacher. It makes sense because Julie virtually created that role for him. Before Summer he was a mentor like you pair."

"No way!" I gasp. This is far more founded than I realised and if true, it's awful.

"I can't believe you've noticed it too." Eric giggles. "You've only been here five minutes."

Three of the kids have begun arguing mildly but he presses on. "So how old is Julie?"

We hurry our guesses before we have to get involved with the escalating fall out.

"*Forty*!" Jenni poo-poos my guess. "She's older, surely, forty-five?"

"If she's forty-five, she looks good for it!" I say fairly.

We have to break up our own conversation to break up the battle. Jenni takes Ryan to one side to soothe him. He's still seen as the 'new kid'. Eric described me just now as having only been here five minutes. It's been a long five minutes! Both of us have almost completed our first term at Belfry and we're both still finding our feet, fighting our own battles, in differing ways.

The conversation about Julie stays on my mind as I usher Zane away from the dying down commotion. He has IT next with me anyway. Iqbal is present when we arrive and greets us as enthusiastically as always. Axl and Tom are here already tapping enthusiastically at whatever game they're playing.

"Boys, you've got thirty seconds left to shut it down. Else I'll-"

"I know! I know, just shut up!" Axl cries passionately. His voice is still squeaky. We know not to take offence, but Iqbal will speak to him about it, just not now whilst he's engrossed and enraptured with pixels.

Dom, the mentor attached to the year 9's, arrives now too with Archie, Jessie, Reuben and Billy. It's a full house and everyone makes their way to the front, except for Axl.

Iqbal obviously makes good on his word because he lets out a pained screech. "You idiot!"

"Axl." Iqbal begins firmly and calmly. "Come to the front now please."

"I was just about to…" He trails off and looks utterly forlorn before pushing back his chair and skulking to the front.

Iqbal delivers his introduction. I'm used to his routine and I know where to join in and encourage the banter and I know when to help put a stop to it or move a conversation forward. Dom is much quieter than his artist brother, Lewis, but chimes in occasionally when Archie or Reuben get a little too animated.

Once they've been instructed to log in and set up a word document, as I suspected, Iqbal calls Axl to the front for a quick word. Suitably scolded for being unnecessarily rude I am now called over too.

"Dom will be ok for a few minutes, take a seat."

I do as he says and wonder what has brought on this serious expression. Does he somehow know about the conversation I've just had with Jenni and Eric? Is he going to warn me to steer clear of the Gilbert and Julie business?

"Are you going out on Friday?" He feigns casualness and begins checking his emails.

"Erm, yeah." I falter confused. "Are you?"

Harishma already specifically said he wouldn't be, and he looks at me stunned.

"No! No. That's actually what I wanted to tell you." He goes back to his attempt of indifference, looking at the screen instead of me. "I keep work and social life separate. That's why I eat my lunch in here, not the staffroom."

He pauses and I'm unsure if he wants me to say something but really I don't know what to say. Is he warning me after all, about getting too friendly?

"Troy is a good guy."

My skin goes cold. Why has he focussed in on him?

"We go way back, at school." He adds. I pray for a student to shout me over, I feel so awkward, more so because I know the nickname; Eyeball.

"What school did you go to?" I can think of nothing else sensible to say. Eyeball, EYEBALL, EYEBALL!

"Oh, we went to Unity. Anyway, I'm chatting and you should be working, off you go."

I allow myself to be ushered away in a muddled state. He mentioned Troy on purpose and right after he cautioned me about mixing personal with professional. He must have picked up on our bond. When we're together in this classroom there's a constant throb between us. How ironic after what I've uncovered this lunchtime.

Except for me this isn't about climbing to the top. For me, this shouldn't be about anything and Iqbal is right, life would be easier if I put a stop on my growing feelings once and for all.

"Jodie, what should I write?" Axl is moaning and I'm glad to be distracted from my thoughts. They have been tasked with writing a letter and now they've done the initial parts of inserting their address, the date and who it's to, they're all beginning to get stuck.

The rest of the class passes by fairly uneventfully. I'm off to support the 10's in maths next and I'm actually glad to get away from Iqbal.

He showed he cared during the incident with the mug and I liked that. But now I feel like he's crossed an invisible line. Dipped his hand into my private thoughts uninvited and maybe it's because I feel guilty and caught out that I feel so annoyed.

***

I arrive home to a flat that smells freshly hoovered and tinged with chemical cleaning products. Music plays in the living room and Leila skips out of the kitchen at the sound of me climbing the stairs.

"Hello!" She coos. It's been her day off today. "Good day?"

"Yeah! Well, I've got loads of gossip!"

"Ooh brilliant! Well I got us a bottle of wine to share. You know it is Miss Midweek Wednesday."

"Have you just made that up?" I titter at the title.

"Not *just* made it up! It popped into my head earlier when I was shopping. So, are you up for a glass? And you can tell me the goss!"

"Any excuse!" I shrug.

"I was thinking about Friday, and I just got so excited! I can't wait to see this totty you've been telling me about. And *Troy*! And Julie, please tell me she's coming?"

I nod but I'm unable to get a word in edgeways.

"What are you going to wear?" She screeches, and I hold up my hands in defeat.

"I've got nothing, I've been thinking about it all day."

"You have my wardrobe dear. It's been ages since we went out together!"

Of course, why didn't I think? Her wardrobe is still bulging- despite a clear out- all that extra choice!

"I still remember the first time we went out together," I muse. "I borrowed a dress back then too."

"Listen to us, we're like an old married couple!" She remarks.

I laugh and she pours rose liquid into polished globes- our housewarming present from my mum.

"Cheers!" I tell her. "To Miss Midweek Wednesday!"

We smile and chink. I don't mind the old married couple feeling with her, something I don't seem to be striving for with any of the men in my life.

In a way, she makes up part of *the one* because she's who I live with and I do love her. She's nutty and caring, she's keen on a night out hunting fit men, she shares her clothes and she makes up nicknames that allow us to indulge in an impromptu glass of wine. What's not to love!

"Now," she wriggles her shoulders. "Tell me this gossip!"

I decide to begin with Sean and his premature attraction toward her. This evokes plenty of giggling and teasing. I even suggest she download a few dating apps- see if we can find these topless selfies of his! Of course, she doesn't bite.

Iqbal's moral outburst isn't overly scrutinised. Leila doesn't realise the full ins and outs, the implications for me and Troy, and I don't linger on an awkward topic when there's a bigger one to discuss. The history and rumours surrounding Gilbert and Julie! This gives us ample to dissect.

Miss Midweek, I think, might be a two-bottle night.

Fearless Friday

It's Friday so I've been with the girls all day. Spirits amongst the staff are generally high with the half term looming- and of course our night out tonight! But right now I'm experiencing my second ever social worker meeting and it's temporarily put a dampener on things.

Eve is the subject this time and she is here along with her 'mums'. This is the first time I've met either and it is clear where she learns her mannerisms and vocabulary.

Since the social worker, a lady named Gill, began speaking there has been shouting and swearing, accusations and name-calling. I feel sorry for the poor woman, I thought our job could be testing at times, but this is ridiculous.

We've been going for half an hour and so far, got nowhere. Gill has made a couple of notes on her papers and she starts to speak again.

"I think we need to-"

"I frankly don't care what you think!" Auntie-mum guffaws.

"I was actually going to say-"

"All you've said is a pile of crap since the first day you came!" Birth-mum folds her arms across her large bosom.

"Yeah," Eve interjects wanting to support her family. "You're so full of shit, you don't know what you're talking about."

"The meeting is over." Gill sighs. "That's all I was going to suggest. You'll need to take some time to think things through and decide what you're going to say at the next meeting. It will be very important you know."

There's quiet now from the raging women and the girl caught in between.

"Lizzy, can you and the lovely staff here discuss these things? Perhaps it would be better without me present for the time being."

Lizzy nods and we catch eyes both wearing suitably serious expressions.

"Do you all understand exactly what I'm warning here?"

The word 'warning' is a red flag to a bull and instantly Auntie-mum flares up. "*Warning!* You should be thanking me for taking her in and keeping her out of the care system!"

"Vic, there are concerns over Eve's safety."

"SHE'S PERFECTLY SAFE!" She yells in response.

Gill remains unflappable and stands calmly, collecting up her belongings. "Nobody thinks you don't love her. And want the best for her. Sometimes we can't always do what is needed. And that is the time to ask for help. It isn't about winning and losing. It's about Eve."

We all look at Eve whose eyes dart from one face to another as she chomps the tassel of her hoody. I can't imagine being that age and having so many adults surrounding me, talking about such serious things.

Lizzy shows Gill out and I watch Eve closely, trying to guess at what she's thinking.

"Eve?" I eventually say. "Shall we go and chat in the other room and leave Lizzy to talk to your mums?"

Lizzy nods as she comes back over. "We'll look at these concerns together and work out how you can make the social services happy. They don't *want* to take Eve if they don't have to!"

Gill was correct. Without her presence they are all much more willing to co-operate and don't see Lizzy and I as anywhere near the same threat.

I go into a pod with Eve. Mollie and Jayde have been taken offsite. Bonnie has been ill all week- although we suspect she's actually on holiday- and Holly is still not attending as much as we'd like.

"That woman is talking out her arsehole." Eve begins. "I don't want to go into care. They can't take me. I need a think Jodie."

Before I can respond she marches back into the main classroom.

"Mum, gimme a fag." She holds her hand out and without hesitation birth-mum passes over a tobacco pouch and rolling papers. Lizzy and I catch eyes and exchange the same thought; this is exactly the type of thing Gill is highlighting as a concern.

"Guys, you shouldn't be encouraging her to smoke." Lizzy says quietly. "This is the kind of-"

"She wants to smoke, she'll smoke anyway." Vic retorts.

"Not if you don't buy them for her." She is obligated to continue.

"And then she'll steal money. And talk to strangers because she'll get someone else to buy them for her. She'll do it anyway."

My mind flickers along the same path as before. These kids don't stand a chance because nobody is giving them a chance. She is labelled as a tearaway, allowed to be one, almost encouraged and she will continue to behave in the way expected.

"And I'll smash the place up if I don't get them." Eve inputs with pride before licking and sticking the roll-up.

"See." Vic smiles. The mums cross their arms defensively. I feel sorry for them that Eve has become so uncontrollable. I feel sorry for Eve, for being let down perhaps by the system as much as her parents. They do obviously love her but whether they're good for her is what is in dispute.

"You've done really well cutting back Eve." I remind her. When she attends she has to manage without and only starts to complain after a couple of hours now, not minutes like before. I have no choice but to follow Eve. If Julie spots us no doubt I'll bear the brunt of her fury but right now I don't care. I just want to support this young girl in whatever way I can.

"Eve, let's go down to that jitty, out the way."

We begin to walk down the road and I allow the silence for now, hoping Eve is contemplating this afternoon's focus.

I can't exactly remember my teenage way of thinking, possibly irrational and biased. And I know I was never faced with this type of looming worry. Is she able to understand how her own actions could affect the decision? Do even her current caregivers realise their responsibility in all of this?

We come to a stop amid the thicket of trees. This is exactly the type of place I used to come for a crafty fag at her age. My job highlights many occasions when I feel like a hypocrite and I think about my dad, when he found out I was smoking as a teen. He did his best to put a stop to it, over and over. Would I have stopped if I thought there was a risk of being taken into care?

Looking back now, of course I would have. Although it's hard to know if a hormonal rebel understands consequences. I've learnt from hindsight more times than not.

If only it were so simple for Eve; smoking is the very least of it.

She watches me, watching her as she lights her ciggy and I decide not to hound her on the subject right now. It'd be pointless and cause an argument.

"What?" Eve demands with her characteristic aggression.

"What! You were looking at me." I tease her good-naturedly. Before I can approach anything of meaning I have to get on her level.

These kids need me to be all sorts of things for them, maybe even things I can't be for myself. Hopefully it is making me into a better person, not just a two-faced hypocrite.

***

"This bracelet or this one?" Leila shouts to me over our tunes and I nod to one even though they're almost identical. "So that means these shoes. And which handbag?"

I wonder how my choice of bracelet affects which shoes she wears and point to the pink handbag amused.

"A flash of colour." I call out approvingly.

She nods and smiles quickly then plumps her hair for the millionth time. We have a taxi booked for six twenty, in five minutes, and she's acting as nervous as I feel.

I go over to the long wall mirror and once again check my make-up and outfit. I feel banging and I look almost as good in one of Leila's dresses. I smile over at her and she returns it, her eyes bright.

I take a last swig of my alcopop and it has done nothing to dislodge the lump of anticipation lodged in my throat. A flurry of bees buzz wildly in my chest and my forehead feels clammy. I don't know if I'm more excited or anxious. There's Julie to face, her and Gilbert to spy on and Troy to, well, look at! I know I can't *go there* like that, but I cannot wait for Leila to see him in the flesh.

I know she's looking forward to putting names to faces, there's a host of people I want to introduce her to. And she's ultra-restless because she knows to expect totty! Like Eric, Dom, Lewis, Gilbert; even if she doesn't pull either it's going to be so much fun partying with my awesome workmates.

My heart thumps erratically as my phone pings to life alerting us of our taxi's arrival.

"It's here!" I cry out and suddenly feel the need to check my bag again, and pee, again. Leila switches off the music and grabs my wrist forcefully.

"Come on!"

She'd have made a good PR after all, I grin to myself.

We have to delicately manoeuvre the narrow stairs in our wedges before locking up and tottering out to the curb where our car is waiting.

This is it! I think dramatically. Our first night out-out with the Belfry lot! Our first night out as flatmates! We both clamber into the back. I'm breathless when I speak.

"To the Boot and Rod please!"

The Boot and Rod

The Boot and Rod is busy but I spot Troy instantly. He sticks out in my eye-line like a beacon.

"Over there." I tell Leila pointing then smile and wave when Troy spots me in return. His grin is instantaneous and there's flash in his eyes as he looks me over.

"Oh wow." Leila gasps under her breath. He's chatting to Eric, Dom and Lewis. I don't know who she's admiring, possibly all of them!

"Hi!" Harishma and Sean bustle over to greet us and I introduce Leila to the initial group.

"This is Leila." I finish listing the names of those who have encircled us.

Jenni, Leanne and Jess are at the bar; Neil and Claire loiter a few paces away chatting with others.

"Let's get a drink Leila." I pull her away, and my eyes from Troy's.

"Where's Julie?" She hisses as we head to the bar ourselves.

"She's not here yet. There're loads of people not here yet. I can't wait to introduce you to Lizzy and Lacey too!"

"Troy is so hot! And so is Eric, I think he's my favourite."

"Well lucky for you he's single!" I entice her. Unlike Troy! My cheeks still feel bright red from him staring at me like that.

At the bar I introduce Leila to more people. I know she's taking it all in since she's been drinking in the details of them all for weeks. I don't even turn to see if I'm being watched but I don't need to.

"Troy just can't stop looking at you!" Leila sing-songs in my ear and I ignore her, choosing a cocktail from the list instead.

We re-join the expanding group, Troy is lingering close-by and I ignore him coyly in favour of greeting Lizzy.

"Leila, this is Lizzy."

Lizzy the lesbian.

The sentence forms subconsciously in my mind and I balk, as though it hangs visibly in the air between us. It's Troy, he's sending me to pot!

"Leila, I've heard so much about you." She gives her an easy-going hug.

"It's nice to meet you at last, I've heard all about you too." Leila replies grinning.

"All good I hope?" She says turning to give me a squeeze too.

"Of course!" I smile at her.

"I really love working with Jodie! I can see why she's your bezzy." Lizzy leaves her arm round my shoulders and adds. "Don't worry I'm not trying to steal her or anything."

I cringe. She doesn't need to explain herself.

"It's cool, you can have her!" Leila jibes quickly before adding. "Not really, she's mine."

"We're like an old married couple." I enthuse and catch Lizzy's eye as we giggle feeling an undercurrent, unspoken words. It's not unusual really except it doesn't feel like an interaction with Leila- more like one with Troy.

"I'm just going to say hi to Harishma, and I'll be back." She winks at me and leaves.

"She's so nice Jodes." Leila tells me the moment her back is turned, and I nod distractedly noticing more figures sweeping into the bar.

"Here she is, here's Julie!" I gasp. "And she's with Gilbert! And the bald man, that's Del."

He is the only one to look over as they head to the bar and he gives us a large, forced smile like he's holding a banner aloft reading; *Yes, Julie and Gilbert have arrived together...*

He must know the rumours, they all must surely? They'll all know what we're thinking.

"She's better looking than I imagined." Leila comments. "And Gilbert, the blonde one right, he's *nice!*"

Julie *is* attractive and looks more so in 'real life' without the stern shirts, trousers and expression. Ok she's still wearing shirt and trousers but they're prettier and fashionable. Her eyes are darkly made up making the blueness shine out of her face, almost warmly!

"Well don't stare girls, it's rude." Troy swans to our sides breaking the spell.

"It's as if they aren't even trying to hide it!" I giggle agog.

"Why would they? She gets a kick out of being with a young bloke. He gets a kick swanning around with the boss."

"So, do you think they actually are a thing then?"

"Yes." He holds my eyes with clear intent. I have to look away, it makes me blush.

"Do you need the toilet?" Leila rescues me even though I'm not sure I want to be saved.

"Yes, come on."

"Not fair." Troy teases. "Don't leave me, I only just stole you back from Lizzy!"

250

"Ay, she was trying to steal her from me! Not gunna happen." Leila interjects and loops her arm through mine.

I pointedly cast my eyes over the huge group which stand around us and raise my eyebrows.

"I'm sure you'll be fine." I tell him.

We're barely out of earshot when Leila hisses. "Oh my god, he totally fancies the pants off you!"

"Leila!" I chastise. "It's hard enough as it is without you encouraging me."

"I'm not encouraging you!" She states as we enter the toilets.

"So what exactly are you doing?" I lower my voice knowing anyone could be listening from inside a cubicle. "I know he fancies me, and I fancy him-"

"Well, what she don't know can't hurt her." She shrugs.

I flash her a cynical look. I wish I could hide behind that excuse, because that's all it is, and I just can't seem to find one good enough.

When we arrive back Lizzy has cajoled a large number of the staff into playing a drinking game. She is explaining the rules, her eyes sparkling with delight. Julie isn't joining in, she's standing away from us with Neil, Del and a number of others. Gilbert is playing though! Leila and I reconvene, working out what we have to do.

"It's best just to go for it, I'll start. Everybody has to keep this going." She taps the table with one hand then the other, then clicks with each and repeats. A methodical, four beat rhythm begins to resound, thump, thump, click, click, as we all join in.

She then chants, only speaking on the two clicks. Thump, thump. "I name.... to my right... types of... chocolate bars... starting with... Boost."

And away the circle goes.

Thump, thump, "Milky way."

Thump, thump, "Mars bar."

Thump, thump, "Kit Kat." Thump, thump, "Twirl." The beat is hypnotizing. "Snickers."

Dom hesitates but cries; "Freddo!" Just in time and it makes everyone laugh. People are beginning to fall behind.

"Bounty." Leanne smiles.

"Erm, Double Decker!" Harishma yells.

"Twix!"

"Erm, erm..." Lewis looks around helplessly and we're all howling with laughter now.

"Bournville!" Sean shouts from next to him proving he had one ready.

It would have been my go in only a couple more people and I'm relieved he stumbles because I was at a loss myself!

"Your turn to pick a subject now Lewis. So, say the chant, your subject and send it on."

"Ok." He pretends to roll up his sleeves and makes us giggle. "I name... to my right...types of... sex positions! Starting with... reverse cowgirl!"

I chuckle. I should have expected it to deteriorate.

"*Front* cowgirl." Sean beams.

"Missionary." Eric says and Gilbert catcalls.

"Your favourite!"

I nudge Leila.

"Sixty-nine." Troy answers. Leila nudges me in return and now it's my turn. Thump, thump, click, click.

"Doggy style!"

"Wahaaaay!" Sean yells.

Leila looks at me, her turn, she bursts out laughing and misses her cue.

"Drink, drink, drink!" Lizzy chants, others join in.

"I can teach you a few others love!" Sean hollers to Leila with a thumbs-up.

"I can treat you to doggy style." Troy mutters to me. I try to give him a mocking look but I wilt under his steady gaze and even though it wasn't my turn to drink I swipe up my glass and neck the contents.

"I need another before we play again." I announce. "Leila, bar?"

It's my turn to save her now.

"Who's the shark?" She asks as we skitter away.

"The shark?" I splutter. My mind is still reeling with Troy's face. Thoughts of him and doggy style, behind me, gripping my hips.

"Sean is it? Sean the shark!" She snickers. "Don't you think he looks like one? And acts like one. Dur na, dur na!" She sings the Jaws theme tune and hovers behind me threateningly.

"Yes! He is so is!" I agree gleefully. I knew she'd slot right in with the Belfry crowd. "So do you still like Eric the most?"

"Yep. Can we have a jug of Long Island please?" She asks the bartender.

"The strongest cocktail on the list?" I observe.

"Well if I'm going to make my move I just need some Dutch courage!"

I can't help but feel a little stunned even if she is only echoing my own words. This is not the Leila I came out with the first time. The first time my encouragement to 'pull' was interrupted. The first time we were both different people. This time I'm taking full advantage of her confidence.

"You best hope we don't lose too many rounds of this game." I tease as we return. "It's your turn to pick a subject you know. Yay, Lacey's here!"

Fashionably late and dolled up to the nines Lacey's arrival causes a ripple of interest. She's ogled by most of the men but noticeably by Sean and Lizzy as she waltzes toward us and the bar. After a quick introduction we retake our seats.

"What's your subject?" I ask Leila amused at her lack of concern- old Leila would have shunned the spotlight. She taps her nose and there's no time to idle. The rhythm is picking up volume. Thump, thump, click, click, thump, thump;

"I name..." she begins. "To my right... types of... sex toys. Starting with... handcuffs."

I squeal with amusement at Leila's choice of subject. I am so glad to be on her left because I wouldn't want to be under pressure with this topic.

Thump, thump. "Strap-On." Lizzy's answer makes us howl.

Thump, thump. "Dildo." Thump, thump. "Whip."

With each answer the catcalls grow louder. Gilbert's turn and he smirks before booming on the clicks;

"Anal beads."

My sides are aching from laughing. The other punters surrounding us look on in a mixture of amusement and annoyance.

"Blindfold!" Jenni covers her eyes shyly.

"Nipple tassels!" Dom answers and I crease at the image. Leanne is next and either can't think of anything or doesn't want to say it so it's her turn to drink.

We decide to take a break from the game else risk getting asked to leave. Lacey is back from the bar and distracts Harishma. Sean is happy to be distracted and stands right behind, peering over her shoulder and possibly down her top.

"Dur na, dur na." Leila hums in my ear causing me to dissolve into fits once again.

We're being as rowdy as the kids we teach throughout the week. It feels so surreal after weeks of being 'proper' with each other, it's like we're being let loose.

"So what would your sex toy of choice be? We know Leila's is a blindfold." Troy turns to us once again.

"Well we know Gilbert's is anal beads!" I deflect the question and Eric overhears.

"Did you see?" He shouts as if I'm not standing right there. "They came together!"

"Shhhh!" I hush him and look wildly around.

"They just left." Leila interjects.

"Who left? What? Gilbert was just here." I scan our surroundings and can't spot either him or Julie but amongst this rabble that's not hard. Leila nods casually and flicks at her hair as if she isn't enjoying the attention from Eric.

"After the game, Julie's face was like thunder." She leans between our gathered heads. "I turned away to tell you, Jodes, looked back and they were literally leaving! Just now."

"Probably annoyed he blew her cover on the anal beads!" Eric jokes and Leila erupts into flirtatious giggling although it is pretty funny.

"So, sex toys ay." Lizzy sidles over. "I'm so glad you guys liked the game! Do you think I'm fitting in ok?"

"Do you think *we* are mate?" Leila immediately retorts with a grin thumbing over at me. "*I* don't even work here and *I* picked sex toys!"

"Well, we learnt Dom likes nipple tassels!" Lizzy titters.

"And that you like a strap-on!" Troy quips instantly.

"I'm wearing it right now!" Lizzy goofs about and my cheeks feel like they've permanently knotted into balls from all of the laughing.

"So what would yours be Eric?" Leila asks fixing him with her pretty green eyes.

"A blow-up doll." He replies easily, smirking.

"That's not really something you admit mate!" Troy teases him and I watch as his dimples press into his cheeks.

"We're not all lucky enough to have a beautiful girlfriend at home." Eric sniggers. "Or is Beth not putting out? You can borrow it if you want."

I can't bring myself to look across at Troy.

"Oops, hit a sore spot there!" Lizzy laughs wrongly interpreting the silence.

There's a heat in my face that comes from being caught out except I'm not the one who has been caught out. Technically anyway! How would I respond, if I didn't know he had a girlfriend?

"Beth? I thought hoovers were called Henry?"

Lizzy howls at my 'joke'. Obviously I know who Beth is and I want him to answer me. I meet his eye meaningfully.

"My girl. I told you. Do you want a shot?"

"Yeah, of course." I nod, swallowing hard at the blasé reply. "Leila wants one too. She's *my* girl."

I smile at him and then Leila, feeling shot-girl Jodie's attitude zip through me. Why should I be the one feeling choked up, thick with emotion? Get pissed up, not pissed off.

"I'm coming!" Eric yells. He is missing all of the underlying conversation.

"Me too!" Lizzy yelps.

Leila is in complete tune with it all and is by my side immediately except Lizzy comes to my other side so there's no chance to talk about it now.

"What are we having girls?" Lizzy asks throwing me a mischievous grin. "I like tequila."

"I'll have tequila." I agree.

"I *am not* having tequila!" Leila gasps and I catch her eye laughing, some things don't have to change.

We reach the bar and I lean on it, facing away from Troy although I know he is approaching.

"You like a good party, like me. I'm really glad we met, Jodie." Lizzy is gabbling from my side and I smile at her. "I can tell you're like me. You're the hard-core type!"

"Hard-core type ay." Troy says in my ear and a hand rests on my bum cheek. The brazen contact causes opposing feelings and I turn to find his face far closer than anticipated. Lizzy has caught a bartender and is asking if there are any deals on shots.

"So what *type* are you?" I ask him.

"The type you like, hopefully." He replies smirking.

I frown, what a stupid response! I mean what type is that then; too young, too taken?

"Jodie you're having tequila with us aren't you?" Lizzy snags my arm and my attention. There's no time to dwell on whether a guy who has no shame is my type. No boundaries in his conquest to seduce me. *Just* me!

Leila who has missed none of it is in my ear in a flash. "What did he say?"

***

We move on to the next bar, the whole night is becoming a blur. Everybody is getting into their swing, alcohol is loosening tongues and conversation flows. I've spoken with everybody and anybody and the subject of 'work' is absolutely banned. Leila is getting along with Eric in particular and I've given up trying to avoid Troy. He's made it clear he doesn't intend on controlling his intentions towards me and wherever I stand, he's latched to my side.

Now a group of us occupy a corner of the dark dance floor and I bop away any frustration. Let him see exactly what he's missing! I've known all along about her, this is how it should be. Off-limits!

Except Troy easily holds his own in the dance department and he happily moves around me and amongst Eric, Leila, Lacey, Harishma and Lizzy. Sean is circling prey nearby. I can still pick out Lewis, Dom, Leanne, Jess and Jenni amongst strangers around us. Admittedly with each drink, the music grows louder, the atmosphere grows livelier and my resistance fades.

"We're going to the bar." Lacey shouts and her and Harishma leave.

An arm is snaking round my waist and with Leila and Eric occupied with each other, I know Troy is taking advantage of us being left almost 'alone'. We're in the middle of a writhing dancefloor but it is alone enough.

"Let's go to the toilet." It's Lizzy's voice, I was not expecting her. "Don't worry, I won't bite."

I smile at her dopily, embarrassed, I didn't mean to flinch.

"That's not why-" I begin but the music is loud and what can I say? I was expecting Troy to touch me up! She's laughing and pulling me away. I look back at Troy who catches my eyes and raises his eyebrows.

I'll be back! I inwardly holler dramatically and then turn away giggling at my own absurdity.

The toilets are a hive of activity; they're hot and smell sickly. Lizzy wastes no time dragging us into a vacated cubicle.

"Do you want a line?" She says as though she's talking an extra sugar in my tea. "Do you do coke?"

"No, well, no!" I'm knocked off guard. "Do you mind if I pee?"

"Of course not!"

I watch as she hastily shakes white powder from a tiny bag onto a card. I've never done it and I'm curious as she rubs a fingertip of it into her gums.

"Just try a dab if you like." She notices my blatant observation and the choice flashes through my mind.

"Not tonight. It doesn't bother me that you do!" I assure her and straighten up as she tucks the drug back into her bra and slides her card into her pocket.

"I do really like you Jodes." She stares right into my eyes and for just a moment I think perhaps a strap-on would do after all. But before I can consider this wayward thought she leans right in and kisses me. It's strange, soft, I respond but I know it isn't 'right'. I know with certainty I want to kiss Troy!

"Lizzy," I pull away and say shyly. "I really like you, you are really nice and fit and all that, but I'm not gay."

"I know, I know!" She flaps her hand and grins cutely. "I just thought I'd try my luck. Don't worry I won't perv on you or anything in class, I can tell you're not into me like that."

"I am glad we're working together!" I look at her imagining us back at school after tonight. Ludicrous! And she couldn't be a more opposite role model to Iqbal.

"Let's get you back to Troy." She winks. "He'll be getting jealous!"

There's no point telling her otherwise, she's noticed what's been going on.

"Don't worry about it, not your problem." She chatters reading my mind again. There's no need to answer, she happily chunters away as we leave the loos. "Life's too short babe, live for the moment, enjoy yourself!"

My eyes take a moment to adjust to the gloom of the dancefloor. Lizzy is by my side, her hand in the small of my back ushering me toward our original spot. I can't quite believe what has just happened. The coke, the kiss; just wait until I tell Leila!

I spot her canoodling closely with Eric against the wall. Whether she's kissed him already, it is most definitely on the cards and there is Troy dancing still nearby. He sees us and two-steps over, grinning.

Lizzy gives me a shove toward him. Either nobody else I recognise is around or I just don't notice their faces.

"We need to talk." Troy murmurs into my ear taking my hand. Well this I was sort of expecting but still I look around self-consciously. What if somebody sees him holding another girl's hand? But I only find Lizzy's bright face encouraging me.

We push through the throng. I half expect Sean or Harishma to pop out and intercept. I really hope they don't.

"I just can't believe you didn't tell me." My voice is muffled once we're outside with the smokers. I think. My ears are ringing so loudly. Or is it just my head because it's all so mixed up and crazy.

Troy takes my hand again and silently marches us around the corner, away from any other activity.

"I did tell you." It is a forlorn argument and he barely meets my eye.

"You didn't." I tell him firmly.

"I'm sure I told you. Or at least, I wanted to but it doesn't change things." He sighs, and I stare at him incredulously for a moment but it's hard to remain serious.

"You'll never guess what Lizzy just offered me in the toilet…" I change the subject. Common ground, chitchat; let's pretend we're back in the staff room.

"Jodie, I want you. I know you want me. Come with me."

"Where? Come where, what exactly…"

He kisses me. My second kiss for the evening and another I didn't see coming. Well not right here and now and out in the open!

"Troy…" I begin but already caution is leaping into the wind. He stares at me knowing my shell is irreparably cracked.

"Trust me." He pulls me away and I can't even blame a class A drug for the decision or the rush of divine exhilaration as I stumble trustingly behind. *Trust* me!

I silently argue with myself as we blatantly leave the hubbub behind.

"Come on, not far." He says softly.

Too far, a voice warns in my head, but I shut it down. I've come too far to go back now. Leila is fine, Lizzy is holding the fort. I've wanted this all night. She knows it never mind me, us.

The silent footpath we find ourselves on is obviously no accident. On the outskirts of town, I don't even want to think about how he knows it. It is a stark comparison to the pounding mayhem of only moments ago. And it is very, very dark.

He pushes me deeper into the shadows, blackness enveloping me then physical arms. His chest presses against mine. It's hot through his shirt and my dress. His hands are so warm squeezing the base of my back.

"Jodie, I want you. I wanted you from the moment I saw you."

"I really like you." I slur. Alcohol has lubricated my thoughts and disabled my mouth. There's so much I want to say but I can't get the words to come. I can feel his hard cock pressing into my stomach. His eyes are like black holes sucking me in. His hands begin wandering down over my bum, onto my thighs, around to the front of them.

We're camouflaged amongst shrubbery. There's no risk of being seen so I don't stop him from kissing me some more or wiggling up my dress to get a better grope.

My nerves are on fire with the cold and the thrill. What am I doing? Am I going to regret this?

"I really, really like you Jodie." He whispers. My mind spins with lust and disorientating advice. His hands feast on my body, the sensation overtakes rationalising.

"We have got to do it doggy." He mumbles. "The minute you said it, I couldn't stop thinking about it."

I stare at him and like always there is the throbbing connection between us. It's so real I can almost see it pulsating around us.

"Me too." I admit. I feel dizzy. This is meant to happen, we both knew it, pictured it.

"Bend over." He instructs me quietly. "I can't wait any longer for this."

There is no romance just raw passion that has been intensifying for weeks. Nobody will ever have to know, just a one-off. I'm giddy, blood roars in my ears and I reach out to a wall for support. I haven't even held his cock. He fiddles behind me for a few moments, zipping down, strapping up.

It's all happening so quickly. He slides inside of me easily, rocking back and forth and my pelvis is welcoming him, eager.

"Fucking hell." He moans and groans as he thrusts. His fingertips dig into my waist and he's pulling me on to him as much as pushing himself into me.

Moments we've shared flash in front of me in a bitter sweet show-reel. His smile, his eyes, his laugh, his hair, none of it is mine or ever will be. But just for this moment, I can enjoy it right now.

There's a final grunt behind me and it's over. This can never happen again. I clear my mind of depressing thoughts. We've got to head back now, to that busy club. I bet I look dishevelled at least!

"Are you ok?" Troy asks me when I turn around, I'm thankful for the darkness. He's already fixed himself up and sounds completely unruffled. Am I ok?

"Yes." I answer awkwardly and smooth down my dress- Leila's dress! I try not to think about the question too much. *Am* I ok?

"Are you going back to meet Leila?" He's vacated our spot, back on the path. "I'm going to get a taxi. I'll walk you back to the club first though."

"You don't have to walk me back." I tell him and I mean it. I'm choosing to have no permanent man and I'm not scared of walking night-time streets alone.

"I want to Jodie. I'm not just using you, you know."

I smirk and think oh, but I am using you!

We march the streets in quiet and I wonder what exactly he is using me for then if not just sex. What does he want me to expect other than he is using me for precisely that reason? I wonder if guilt is seeping through his pores- or perhaps I'm just one in a string of affairs.

The club is just around the corner. I know I have to cut to business because although he is scarpering, I have to go back and face the music.

"So, if anyone asks I'll say we came out for a fag and then you decided to leave?" Our cover story needs sorting.

"No, say I said I'd got some vodka stashed and we went to find it but then we got chatting to some other people that I knew from school and then the bouncers wouldn't let me back in so that's why I went."

I look at him agog. "Erm, have you heard about keeping it simple? Everyone is pissed, we're pissed, we can't go into all that detail!"

"Well aren't you the expert!" He snaps abruptly.

My mouth swings open and I stare at him. I know this because of the TV shows I watch; How to Catch a Killer.

"What are you saying? I'm some kind of femme fatale?" I giggle. "The expert in the art of cheating and getting away with it."

It's a good title actually, my mind wanders thinking of a possible plot.

"What if they came out into the smoking shelter?" He hisses. "We can't just say that's where we've been. What if someone saw us leave?"

"What like Lizzy?"

His eyes widen in horror. "You can't tell her Jodie, nobody can know, not even Leila."

He is feeling bad for his behaviour, I can tell. He is squirming but also speaking as though I am solely to blame.

"Look," I remain calm because I don't want it to come out either. "Let's say we came out for a fag. If somebody *has* come out to check, we'll say we went off to find your hidden vodka. But if not, I'll just say we had a fag and you left."

"Ok." He stares at me, lips moving, repeating it voicelessly.

"Troy, I'm gunna go. We've not even been gone that long, chances are nobody has even checked. Chill."

"I'm cool." He projects a lazy smile, but his eyes deceive him. "It's cool. I, erm, hope you have a good week off."

"You too, see you next Monday!" I leave him to seek a ride home and march toward the club. There's no time to ponder, I have to hold this together.

I'm cool, it's cool.

I show the bouncers my stamped hand and re-enter. Sean is marching toward me.

"Where you been?" He demands immediately, his eyes flicking around me. "Where's *Troy*?"

He says the name like it leaves a bad taste and I'm confused. They seem to get along just fine at work.

"He left." I shrug. He gives me a long look as if to show he isn't convinced and I feign confusion.

"What? Is Leila ok? I was just heading back up now."

"She's fine. She's with *Eric*." He spits his name too and I suppress a smile. He's annoyed he hasn't pulled her. And possibly saw how Troy was being with me. He's on a warpath for anyone having better luck than him.

"I'll see you back up there." I say feeling confident and leave him behind. I wish I could tell Troy, but I can't contact him. Can't risk even trying, I must wait a week. How to cheat and get away with it.

The club is still busy, the world is continuing unsuspectingly. It's cool, I'm cool. I find Lizzy dancing with Harishma and Lacey. She knows enough. She won't have mentioned anything to them. Eric and Leila are dancing closely and when she spots me I smile- I'm cool, it's cool.

"So, are you going to bring Eric back and christen our flat- again." I call into her ear. Leila's head snaps toward mine.

"Yes! Is that ok? I mean I know-"

I can't fully hear her but I know she's offering sympathy that I can't take Troy home, something like that. She doesn't know, this hoe doesn't need a bed!

"Where *is* Troy?" She finally takes stock of those still in the vicinity. "Ha, there's sharky boy!" She cries, pointing. If only she knew about him too, I think amused. Dur na, dur na!

"Troy's gone," I tell her and she gives me a sympathetic look. "Look, don't react but… I shagged him- Leila! I said don't react! I'll explain it all tomorrow. But forget that for now let's get Eric back home for you, shall we?"

We begin the succession of goodbyes. Lizzy promises she's going to Facebook me her number and I wonder how she will be feeling in the morning. She meets my eye grinning, she trusted me enough to do cocaine in front of me. She fancied me enough to kiss me! I reckon her ability to read my feelings on Troy is safe with her and she doesn't *know* anything, not really.

Leila, Eric and I leave the remaining clan.

"Can I get food before we get a taxi?" I ask but side-step into the late-night takeaway anyway.

"It's a good consolation prize." Eric grins looking smug about his own situation as I clutch the papered package. I smile at him easily and meet Leila's eye. She doesn't let on.

I am being greedy. There really is no need for a consolation.

Distractions Please

I wake up with a claggy mouth and a fuzzy head. My little, grey room is lit with murky morning light. There's a split-second moment when I don't know where I am, who I am. Then it all comes crashing in on me.

I shagged Troy! I kissed Lizzy! Well Lizzy kissed me! And Troy shagged me! A torrent of questions, opinions and thoughts floods me. I'd put off thinking about anything all too much last night and adding to the bedlam; Eric is in the flat! Gilbert and Julie arrived together! Lizzy does cocaine! Dom wears nipple tassels!

The most urgent of my thoughts clamber to be heard. Slut! Hypocrite! Fool! What she doesn't know... Life's too short...

I shouldn't have done it. I'm a girl's girl, I have morals. Or at least I thought I did. It'd seem they don't apply when they stand in my way. I rub at my head as if I could rub out the memory of Troy banging me from behind. In the perfect world I could rub out the attached negativity, not the actual event. I'm not even sure I regret it, I get a tingling sensation *down there* at the hazy recollection making me feel worse and excited simultaneously.

Eric being in the flat is distracting because it means I have to dress before leaving my room in search of liquid. My hangover is limiting my functioning skills and a majority of my focus is being used on manic thought.

He said he isn't using me! That's the most confusing part of all. What does he want me to think, that he actually likes me and sees me in his future? I swore last night it would be a one-off but my heart aches not because I did it, but now because it is over.

I push the Troy dilemma aside and search for a t-shirt and some trackies. I hope Leila had a good night! I feel so proud of her, silly, but I know more about her than ever before and I've realised the timid, reserved Leila I first got to know was a product of a shit relationship. We have been a huge part in helping each other recover. Magaluf has a lot to answer for. Which means Dane played a definite role in both of our lives.

The Dane I despise for cheating.

My life feels like one big web. A chain reaction of events, opportunities and choices connecting to one another. Being connected to Dane led to Magaluf and Magaluf to this- I took Cassie's mistake so personally at first, when she cheated during the holiday. And now, the cheated has become the cheater.

I'm baffled and overwhelmed but finally at least, I'm dressed. I look in the mirror and a pair of confused eyes gaze back.

I look ok enough to risk the living room once I have a drink. Chances are Leila and Eric aren't even awake. Or maybe he's already gone.

I can't wait to tell her about Lizzy! Thinking of her lightens my heart, my newest friend. She is a character! At worst there's the risk of my boss sexually harassing me in the future but I know now, she has been flirting all along. It's a compliment actually. But then she readily admitted using me because she knew I wasn't gay and kissed me anyway. What if I'd been swayed!

It's as I shut the fridge I become aware of the thumping. I think of Lizzy's drinking game from yesterday. There are no clicks. I know what the sound is; Leila and Eric are in her room having morning sex!

I freeze, a silent scream smeared over my face. What should I do?

It's then the moaning starts up from both parties. Oh my god! I stifle a giggle and tip-toe, even though there's no need really, down the corridor, past her room and into the living room. Gently I shut the door. I'll put the TV on to drown them out! They'll hopefully think I never even heard!

There's nothing on but it doesn't matter I won't be concentrating on it anyway. The TV is to save face on the, ahem, banging situation. I can already feel the onslaught of voices I have to appease. It's a conversation I've been dreading having with myself. Maybe I knew all along that it would come to this.

***

Another cup of coffee made and still no sign of Leila or Eric, although all has been quiet for a while, and there's still plenty to keep my mind occupied.

I would be lying to tell myself I'm disgusted at going with a man I know is taken. I know it isn't right, I'm not exactly proud of it but my justification is that I had to take the opportunity. If I didn't feel the way I do about him it would never have even crossed my mind. I know I would've regretted *not* doing it more.

But now my feelings for him are stronger than ever. My chest aches as I think of him. He's with Beth. I'm not jealous because I know, I felt it and then he told me, he has real feelings for me. I just want him so badly.

The past term at Belfry he has made me feel special, acutely different to all the other members of staff and I know some of them notice it too. Iqbal and Sean, definitely Lizzy!

I think of her words, *you only live once*. I am not blaming her for encouraging me or Troy for seducing me. I have my own mind. I just wish he was single and in a position to be doing all of this.

I wonder what he's thinking today. There was that comment he made- something about me being the expert- there's a chance he could hate me right now for jeopardising his relationship.

But he put in all the leg work; he wanted it as much as me. I didn't even need the encouragement from Leila *or* Lizzy. I'm glad it happened. Thinking about it fills me with spiky butterflies.

The shit thing is Beth has the man of my dreams. For now. I've had a short, sweet taste and I liked it. Can I be happy being his mistress? Could I accept just a part of him alongside the other men in my life and be satisfied with that?

Maybe something will give. I'm no longer pretending at least that my feelings don't exist. It'd be senseless to just quit now, the line has been crossed, the relationship risked and surely not just for a one-off sordid fling.

It's almost midday and I decide to go and see Cat. She might have some words of wisdom but at least her busy household will provide relief from the thinking.

***

"Cat!" I dumbly stare at my friend who I have NEVER seen cry as a few tears stray down her face. Gathering myself I quickly pull her into an awkward sitting-down hug.

"I'm ok, Jodie, I'm ok!" She unhands herself and roughly swipes the tears away. "I'm just so tired, I'm pissed off. And I'm worried sick, *all of the time.*"

"I'm not surprised babe!" I cry. "You are doing a sterling job here lady, you have hardly any help other than from Kyle, two kids and Esmay is extreme. I'm sorry but she isn't, you know, the *usual* workload. You go to work. And on top of that you don't know what's going on or when it's going to get better."

"*If* it's going to get better." Cat interjects quietly.

"It will." I tell her and really hope that it will. I trust in the system, I am part of it in some respects and yet I feel useless to her. "Honey, I wish I could help you."

"You do, silly!" Cat manages a watery titter. "You come here to see me, even though it's utter chaos half the time. You bring me all these crazy stories, which missus, you haven't told me about last night and I know there's *something*. I could hear it in your voice when you called!"

I can't help but smirk at her but I'm not ready to change the subject just yet. I arrived to find Cat just short of cleaning up after one of Esmay's 'adventures'. In the process of destroying her own and her parent's bedroom, she ruined all of Cat's make up which has proved the straw that broke the camel's back. Esmay still isn't sleeping well, Cat is surviving on a few hours snatched here and there. And the paediatrician appointment to discuss medication has been cancelled- again.

"Have you looked into respite, or you know, carers who could come in and help?"

As if on cue Esmay begins hollering from the other room.

"I bet her programme has ended, she's been fixated watching Dotty the Cow." I have no idea what this is, and Cat leaves the room. Daniel appears moments later suddenly curious of where his mum has been.

"Ohh deee!" He exclaims initially surprised but then my presence sinks in. "W ay vair!" He totters off in that cute clumsy way of a small person.

Seconds later both he and Cat are back.

"As I thought." She answers my questioning look. "New episodes needed."

"Ohh dee, waj vis." Daniel begins rifling through the book he fetched to show me, singing a happy tune of phonic sounds. "Ta-daaa!"

I burst into rapturous applause laughing at his dramatic ways. "Well done darling, that was wonderful!"

"Now, Dan, come on, back in there with daddy, it's mummy time."

He might be a darling, but attention is paramount in his world and his face immediately contorts. Cat marches over to him and crouches.

"Daniel. Listen to me." But he's wailing loudly and I wonder if it might upset Esmay. This is all she needs. "Daniel be quiet a minute."

His face relaxes into a drooping frown, fat tears hanging from his lashes. His voice is small and squeaky when he speaks.

"Me af choc choc?" It's a tentative suggestion and I curb my giggle.

"Dan, you can-"

He senses it's a 'no' and the face immediately crumples, another huge cry building in ferocity. Cat tuts and rolls her eyes at me, I smile and shrug, can't be helped- he's a kid. She looks at her watch.

"It's lunchtime anyway!" She shouts over his vocalisations. He hushes once again, almost instantly like a switch being flicked, and at that moment Esmay appears in the doorway. She eyes her mum, her eyes flitter to and from her face and she hums loudly.

"You heard me didn't you Es? Are you hungry too? Dan, you can have a yog yog, after your sandwich, ok?"

Kids suitably settled in the living room we return to the subject of Esmay. She might not be able to talk but she obviously understood what her mum had said- suggesting she understands other things too. I love seeing the fire in Cat's eyes as these developments unravel for her.

"There's been a few times I've noticed recently, she really understands, she just can't speak, yet!" She concludes nodding dreamily.

"What about the extra money for the home...*improvisations.*" I stumble over the right word to describe the eclectic list of adaptations and repairs which need carrying out.

"Until she has all of the paperwork we can't get any grants or anything to help us. There's a list of boxes to tick which could take months even years before she'll be classed as, you know disabled or anything like that. There's appointments and assessments, some have huge waiting lists."

"It's so frustrating," I fume. "It is so long winded!"

"I know." She nods helplessly.

I might feel part of the system but I'm not so sure anymore that it is a cure. I only see what is going on at my end of the scale. There must be nurseries and schools specifically to suit Esmay's host of complex needs but all that seems a very distant light at the end of a very challenging tunnel.

Es is calm when she's led in to wipe her sticky hands, beautiful and aloof and she heads off again in search of more Dotty the Cow. Daniel is appeased elsewhere, and Cat sits opposite me.

"Do you have people you can ask, you know for advice and stuff?" I press her.

"The health visitor comes, not often. I forget half the things by the time she's here and sometimes her habits change so quickly! The speech and language specialist will start seeing her soon. And something called 'play therapy'."

"Well, that's good. And are there support groups?"

"Yeah, the family counsellor told us about a few. Although we've finished our slots with him now, you only get them for a few months." She stops and takes a deep breath. I look over at her. I'm worried about her and think, not for the first time, how idiotic and self-induced a majority of my problems actually are.

"I'm embarrassed Jodes." She continues. "I'd love to have more ideas, things to try with her. But the thought of talking to a bunch of strangers about what goes on. Some of it is awful, *you* know!" She bursts into ironic laughter and I smile sympathetically, I do know.

"Can you imagine, does your daughter smear poo all over the walls? Does your daughter pull doors clean off their hinges because she's hanging onto the handles and humping them for hours at a time?"

"Stop it!" I tell her giggling, but she continues in manic amusement.

"Do you have curtains in your house? We don't because our daughter pulls them down, and the curtain pole with it! We go through five mattresses a year because she jumps on them until they're crippled. Are your kitchen cupboards bolted shut so she can't eat you out of house and home?" Cat doesn't run out of ammo, she runs out of breath.

"Cat!" I exclaim suddenly, the idea pinging into my head like a thunderbolt. "You should start a blog!"

"A blog? No." The denial is out of her mouth before she's given the idea thought. I can see her eyes are cloudy; she's tired and caught up in reliving previous instances.

"No, Cat, I think this could work!" I pursue. Usually I allow her to back out of things. She might be confident in my abilities all of the time but she doesn't allow herself the same credit. "Seriously, you could just use it to describe some of the things that happen. Get it off your chest and…"

"And have the whole world judge me as a bad mum who can't handle her child? Because that's how it will be seen. Some people don't even believe in autism."

"Believe! *Believe* in it? That's ridiculous!"

"The world isn't filled with people like you. Accepting, kind, open to new things... it's *true*!"

"I'm not looking at you like that because I don't believe you, there are definitely too many tossers around! But it isn't just me who is those things. You are too, you know! Plus I've seen Es in action. I'd like to invite a sceptic round to watch you just for half a day. That would soon shut them up!"

Cat smiles genuinely. "Want another tea? And then I want to hear about last night!"

"Deal, but please whilst the kettle boils let's just talk about this blog idea? You don't even have to publish it, just write it for yourself."

"You have until the click." She says sternly.

I smile thinking of last night, thump, thump, click, click... But there's time for that. I have two minutes tops to convince her first.

"You never fail to amaze me Jodie! And Leila, I'm so happy for her!" Cat is looking at me with thrilled shock following the complete lowdown. I began with the news of Leila pulling Eric, she was utterly ecstatic. Then me with Troy, her reaction; *I knew it*. I then disclosed the next instalment of Gilbert and Julie- we've agreed it seems they're openly together, flaunting it even. And the news of my almost-coke-induced lesbian kiss came last.

I think this is her favourite part and it feels good to hear her shrieking happily. I came here for a distraction, I'm glad to return the favour.

I give her a proud smile. Not proud of the cheating part but proud to meet expectations as the friend who brings crazy stories. It seems I haven't lost my touch in the crazy department. And Leila, I think she has been just as crazy all along but temporarily deactivated. Something caused us to attract and form such a close friendship in the first place. I check my phone, still no text or call from her. It must be going well with Eric!

"Don't dwell on the Troy thing Jodie. It's happened now and he's in the wrong too you know. She isn't your friend and you don't know their situation. For all you know she's a complete bitch and they're no good for each other. She might be doing the same to him!"

Cat's words are soothing. I haven't dwelled on the uncomfortable thoughts as we spoke, my problems seem petulant in comparison to hers, but as always she knows what's going on in my head. I'm getting ready to leave and have parting words of my own.

"Promise me you'll start writing some of your experiences down." I say to her gently.

"I'll *try*." She smiles but the self-doubt is all there in her eyes.

"It doesn't matter about your spelling." I counter her unspoken arguments. "Spell check will help you."

"*Nothing* can help me!" She giggles as persistent as before when I had until the click of the kettle to convince her.

"Well I can, can't I? I work in a school Cat, I'm not going to laugh when you misspell something. Just write, I can correct it."

"I think I should let you stick to the writing. My head is too mashed up to think straight enough. Maybe one day though, it is a good idea."

I give her a hug before I leave, telling her I'll be around plenty to keep her company over my week off. A whole week off and nothing to do but what I want! It feels like absolute bliss!

I should take her advice and seriously do some writing. Having a job with so much time off- and no money to do anything-could be the chance I've needed. I came here thinking my head is mashed, I'm heading back realising it isn't close to what Cat's going through. And even worse my biggest problem today is utterly self-induced.

Poor Cat. She wouldn't want my sympathy and it isn't what I feel. She's doing an amazing job. I see her patience and resilience and I'm awed by her strength. I just wish she could feel able to relax an inch, maybe even get a little rest.

I know people would love to read about her life and about Esmay. I know there must be families out there who share her challenges. She could probably help them! But I can understand why she doesn't want to go there, yet, and I respect her wishes.

Instead I'll make it my mission next term to find out more about autism specifically. It's another thing for me to glean from my job. I will help her support her daughter in one way or another.

Happy with my resolution and closer to home my mind turns to Leila, and Eric! Still no word, he must still be there. She has work shortly so he'll have to leave soon. If it comes to it, I'll follow her to the Trap so we can still discuss last night properly. It all needs to be spoken about and dissected, it's just the way of the bezzie.

I let myself in and hear Leila squawk from her room followed by a series of footsteps. Her mad, curly red mane appears at the top of the stairs.

"Where is he?" I ask immediately, mildly concerned by her expression.

"Just left. Oh my god, Jodie, I forgot what I was missing!"

I reach the top of the stairs and join her on the landing already giggling.

"It's been like, forever, Jodie, over a year! Probably longer!"

"Definitely longer my dear." I grin. "So it went well then?"

I Am What I Am

I get home from chatting the early evening away with Leila, thinking of my stomach and what to do about dinner.

I already know there isn't much in the cupboards but rifle through them anyway. Single life is so simple at times, I muse. Luxuriously so when armed with the experience of demanding, all-consuming relationships! Being with Scott was fine at first, we were joined at the hip, best buddies. It began that way with Dane too but both became a weighty burden rather than a pleasant passenger in the end, for differing reasons. I have friends to enjoy the ride with now. And seeing Cat today only emphasises the feelings of freedom I experience right now. I love being a part of Esmay and Daniel's life, I can see why people reproduce, but I only have myself to think about and it feels great.

I rejoice and feel a little self-indulgent, but my choices and decisions got me here. I'm child-free and living a bachelorette lifestyle in my own pad. My job has its share of responsibility and stress, I have to work hard- for thirty-nine weeks of the year- and I get paid a pittance. But in my free time I choose what I want to do and when I want to do it.

I am a pole dancer. I am an author. I am a man-eater. I am most certainly fucking crazy.

There's nothing of interest in the fridge but I grin stupidly and spin on the spot in the kitchen overcome with absurd pleasure. *I am what I am*, that old song I've heard being sung on karaoke rings in my ears. I am what I am, and I can do so as I please.

Like last night. I am selfish. I can't help but give that conclusion space. Leila reasoned that I am not doing the cheating. I agree in most part but knowing about her should be enough to stop me, shouldn't it? My morals shouldn't just count when they suit me.

She said I shouldn't be so hard on myself, what I feel is real, I can't expect to be completely unsusceptible to my feelings.

It is selfish of me to act on it.

But I seem to *feel* hard. Perhaps like Alexa, I fall quickly and deeply. In all aspects of my life though I feel hard- work, family, friends and for all my men too. I have feelings for Troy, Luca, Ashley and Aaron. All real, perhaps all could be enough alone. Or between them they offer a blend that equates to one full relationship. Timing *and* time; needed in balance, just the right amount of each.

***

After an uninspiring dinner I take on the pole with a strength building session. Music plays in the background and I go through the routine I've made up for myself concentrating on my arms, legs and core in turn.

It doesn't take long to become zapped of energy and I take a break flicking idly through Facebook. I hardly update my own status but plenty of people do, disclosing and claiming away without shame or care. It's easy to get lost reading the comments of other people's drama or flicking through photos of somebody's day out at the zoo.

I notice an update by Shaun. Luca inadvertently reminded me of him when he spoke of Ibiza. His dad has a boat! He was a nice guy and I banged him *before* finding out he's also loaded. He's booked a flight and is going travelling in Thailand next year. I like the status instantly and linger only a moment before opening his profile page and hitting the message icon.

Congratulations on booking Thailand! Hope you're well ☺

I hit send before I can overthink the wording or change my mind and head back to the main newsfeed.

Ashley's status, about a film I've never heard of, has beguiled a huge number of likes and comments. Curiously I tap to see more. There's a long list of female names who have 'liked' it and more females mainly agreeing with him. Each one leaves a handful of hearts, roses and kisses after their comment and he's replied to them all with a similar array of cute, little emoji's. Mr Tyler has quite the fan club, and one he actively engages with. Intrigued I investigate a number of the females. All are attractive in their own right, some are extremely pretty. I wonder how many he has slept with! Is *sleeping* with even!

Further down I find Aaron has shared something about historical humans and their true evolution. I read that too, almost with the same interest as I scanned Ashley's fan club. How very different they are to one another!

Troy said something about my 'type'- *I hope I'm the type you like*- it doesn't matter exactly, fact is, I don't seem to have a type specifically.

All my men are different, unique and I have feelings for them all. So, stick your type Troy, there is no 'type'.

He is chosen. He's admitted how he feels and I've told him how I feel. This week should give him time to think about things. Will he miss me? Maybe he'll realise his heart is not with Beth, it's with me after all.

I've spoken in depth to two close friends and to neither have I voiced this hopefulness. I'd drop my other men for him in an instant! This is a thought I've tried to ignore too.

Because if he does back off, I'll back off. I very, nearly, almost hope he does. It would save a lot of angst and shut down an uncomfortable chapter before it can get any stickier. I'll await his decision and I'll respect it.

The pole is beckoning for one final punishing. Or rather it is screaming to punish me. I deserve to be punished for my bad, bad behaviour. I plug my phone back into the aux cable of my stereo and flick on a song by the ultimate bad girl of pop, Rhi Rhi.

For an hour I switch between serious practise and pratting around trying to choreograph routines. By the time I sit down, I am exhausted.

As much as I want to improve and indulge Aaron to a glimpse when he visits, maybe Luca too, I already feel fitter, leaner and stronger.

My turn-to viewing tonight makes me think about a part of last night I haven't thought about much today. Troy's attitude toward me when we were thinking up a cover story, how he spoke to me; *aren't you the expert.* Aren't you the temptress? Aren't you just another slag who sleeps with any Tom, Dick or Harry?

No. I know what I am. I am what I am. I am emotional, real, hard-living and free-loving, I'm determined and I'm independent.

Maybe I shouldn't be giving Troy the 'choice' about whether he wants me or not. Maybe I should shut him down before he has chance to do the same to me. You're not good enough for me, you don't respect me.

Respect is important. I give it naturally and I want it in return. But last night he was flustered. Maybe it was the first time he cheated. He certainly makes me feel different from any other.

They all have flaws. Aaron turned out to be nineteen, Luca left me hanging for over an hour on date night. And let's not forget Ashley doesn't want to be seen with me *and* has a harem of adoring women in tow.

Perhaps I shouldn't be giving any of these men a choice. But then see me if you want... or don't... if I don't care which, it's fine. Isn't it?

By the time I head off to my room at midnight, Leila isn't home yet, I haven't heard from Ashley and I realise I'm not disappointed either. A choice *is* ok as long as both outcomes suit me. As long as it's a win-win for me, the choice is fine. I enjoy my own company and have plenty of hobbies to occupy my time besides having sex!

I lie on my bed reading and ache from the work out. I was pole dancer me tonight. Tomorrow I could be author me- I now know what type of character cheats. Very normal characters who don't even have a whole lot of remorse afterwards.

And for the week, I'll be good house-wife me because I'm planning on thoroughly cleaning the flat. And maybe next weekend I'll be back to being hussy me, and who with even!

I am what I am. And I am happy. I don't need *one* man but I am enjoying building a Top Five to play with.

Sunday Feelings

This could quite possibly be the best feeling ever. Sunday evening approaches and the large, living-room window is darkening. I lounge on the sofa with my laptop to my left, a notebook on my knee, pen in hand and an open book to my right. The TV is playing an Attenborough documentary in the background as I flit between writing and reading. This has been the case for numerous, luxurious hours and the best part is, I don't have work tomorrow!

Could Sunday-no-work-Monday feeling be better than Friday Feeling?

Perhaps I'm being dramatic but I have been in author-me mode for the day, tapping methodically for periods at a time or making notes about characters. Before I wrote about a pole dancer, now I'm conjuring 'normal' women, mixing personalities together and cherry-picking habits from people I know.

I've reawakened an old passion. Author me is possessed and unbridled. The words keep coming, the stories conjuring from my subconscious and I let the words flow onto screen and page.

Leila started work at three, after we'd eaten together. At that point I'd felt a little gutted I couldn't go out, meet George, get drunk. But I really am skint. And now I'm glad I couldn't go!

Eventually, I close the blind. It is completely dark outside by now. Another few weeks and winter really will be here. Summer seems far, far away.

My phone pings and I know it's another Facebook message. Aaron has sent me a couple today already but so far I've ignored him. I decide to see what I've been missing. My writing mania seems to have ceased anyway.

There's a message from Shaun, as well as the few from Aaron. I'd forgotten I contacted him and open it, reading;

Hey Jodie, I'm great thanks! Good to hear from you babe, hope life is treating you well ☺ xx

It doesn't scream that it wants to be replied to. Perhaps I'll give it a few days. I flick over to the few from Aaron. He's confirming a date for his visit! The first weekend of November- that's only a few weeks away. I jump up to fetch my diary and cast my eyes around the flat as I do so. It scrubs up alright, but I'd like to paint a feature wall or something before then.

I reply happily to him. I'm already looking forward to introducing him to Leila and Cat, perhaps my mum and George- all of the natural things when you meet someone you like. I quash the Troy-related resentment and instead decide to spend my time browsing for budget ways to do up a house. It's the perfect tonic after all of yesterday's turmoil, something to focus on and look forward to.

By the time Leila comes home at gone eleven, I have drawn up numerous plans for operation spice-up-the-flat. The internet is absolutely crawling with ideas from make-shift lampshades to woven rugs and rag throws- although I only have a few weeks until Aaron arrives and limited resources.

But this week off will prove useful. I have plenty of options and I grin at her as she enters the room.

"What have you been plotting?" She asks suspiciously and plonks onto the chair opposite.

"I'm going to do some upcycling!" I declare.

"Oh-kay. What is upcycling?"

I show her some of the pictures I have screenshot of old furniture that's been revamped.

"And do you mind if we swap the furniture around a bit?" I begin talking her through the changes I have drafted.

"I am very happy with all of this my love. I haven't got a creative bone in my body- fill your boots. Now do you want a cuppa?"

I accept considering for once I haven't got to be up in the morning. And I've still got to tell her what's brought on this sudden motivation. We chat about Aaron and also decide on painting the chimney breast- a splash of colour. She is off on Wednesday so providing Jane gives us permission we can get it done this week.

Going to bed late has always been my preference. I slip between the sheets, TV playing so low it can only be heard once I'm completely still. It will mean budgeting even more closely, but I might treat myself to some new bedcovers too.

The last lot I bought had a sunset on, when I first moved back to my mum's after living with Scott. I dreamed of a holiday but was also happy to be home. Then I had a holiday but not just that, I've had adventures! And now I'm lying in a new home.

So much has happened, has it been in a short space of time because even six months seems yonks ago. And yet six months is not long to completely reshape a life is it? I seem to have spent the past eighteen months remoulding myself. Is my life following a schedule and I am ahead of it? Perhaps time really is irrelevant and it's the changes I should focus on, not how long it all takes.

I *could* kick myself for waiting until I'm in my mid-twenties to start saying yes more! I could wish I'd called time with Dane before things got so messy. But if time is irrelevant I don't have to worry about being a step or two behind as long as I'm having fun along the way!

It is surely impossible to make a plan for life in the same way I have organised the revitalising of the flat. If only it were so easy. Monday: Find life-partner, Thursday: Buy house, Saturday: Have kids.

This plan is outdated and is evolving; get rewarding job, earn good money, travel, buy a caravan, go to festivals, enjoy solid friendships, have many hobbies and master one or two, make good-loving with men who fit the bill...

I'm achieving in some areas but not all and I'm not sure where the caravan part came into it, but I like the idea. It's certainly one way for me to get on the 'property ladder'.

I switch off my thoughts by focussing on the low rumbling from the TV about DNA evidence. I have a whole week off to enjoy. Roll on operation spice up Marshamonvilla.

Saturday Bang

Leila has gone to work for her Saturday three 'til close shift. I will see her later anyway because I'm meeting George there this evening. He knows I have no spare cash and insisted he would treat me to a bottle of wine. I'm looking forward to it! It has been a busy, productive and happy week. A weekend night out with George is the perfect way to top it.

I stand in the 'new' living room and look around appreciatively. I have cleaned *everything* and *everywhere*. The whole flat feels alive with a new energy. Cupboards are organised, boxes have been properly unpacked of things I had from the first time I moved out.

Leila and I chipped in and bought a purple throw with pink patterns for the sofa and I already had some bright, sequinned cushions which are now scattered across it. I've thrown a pink bedsheet over the squashy chair, tucking it into the crevices and underneath. We painted the chimney breast lime green- the smell still lingers- there's a yellow glass vase on the windowsill along with some patterned candles that Leila already had.

I've moved the larger table from the kitchen into here too. I want to decoupage it- stick loads of pictures all over it- and varnish it up afterwards. The long slim table I had stored is now in the kitchen providing an extra work surface, or breakfast bench, and certainly allows more space to actually move about.

I have more to do but they're details. Plus, I need the help of Belfry's equipment- the printer, PVA glue, maybe a canvas and some poster paint. I'll have to be sneaky.

Belfry and sneaky seem to intermingle. Me, Troy, Julie, Gilbert, Lizzy, even Iqbal. There's plenty of sneaky behaviour going on. I resolve I'll be careful not to be caught tea-leafing from the stationery cupboard.

Only tomorrow stands between my reunion with Troy on Monday. I'm so excited I can't think about it for too long. I wonder how he's feeling. Whether he's spent the week secretly making it up to Beth, paying her compliments, cooking dinner, being extra attentive- or has he been pining over me?

There's still one late night to be had though, before school begins and with it all of the thrilling anarchy. I switch on the stereo and load some music before turning up the volume. Marshamonvilla is looking spicy and I'm hoping the same will be true for me by the time I finish preening.

***

The Trap is rammed when I arrive. It's a typical Saturday evening and attracts the typical punters expected. I spot George by the pool table. He's with his usual crowd and I make my way over.

"Good to see you again gorgeous!" Bill jumps into my path and calls out as though we've made a regular habit of hooking up. In actual fact this is the first time I've seen him since I returned from Magaluf! He has an audience to entertain, the ever-loyal crew of butch rugby players.

"Good to see you too Bill." I reply cheerfully and add. "Long time no see!"

"Too long. Now I hear you have yourself a new pad. So when will me and the boys be getting an invite?"

I look on in bemusement as he waits for a response. I might have made my peace with the awkward oddity but there's no way of an invite to my place. For any of them! I leave, shaking my head.

"Just you stay out of that Dane's way." He calls after me and I knew what was coming the moment he began the sentence. I turn laughing.

"You don't need to tell me!"

"Well you're heading for him right now." He shouts nodding over my shoulder. I glance and Dane is, in actual fact, right there. He's looking at me as he's approaching but gives me a small, shy smile and passes on by to the bar. I feel queer seeing him.

"I didn't know whether to message you." George gives me an apologetic shrug when I reach him. "He just turned up about ten minutes ago."

"He's with you?" My lip curls at the realisation but then I catch myself. Who am I to judge now really? "Don't worry about it."

"Here. Get me a pint as well." He passes me a twenty and I head back through the throng seeking out the bar, knowing Dane will also be there.

Cat's working tonight too. She catches my eye grinning as she finishes serving.

"What you having Jodes?" She calls.

"Well I was actually first," Dane's voice booms and the laughter dies on his lips at our mirrored expressions. This makes me and Cat laugh and he mistakes it for acceptance, joining in.

"Ladies first." He guffaws. I ignore him and order. He is still staring at me.

"Where is your lady?" I ask him.

"Fuck her." He replies sliding closer.

"Yes, you did." I smile up at him. There's fire burning in his eyes but it can't seduce *or* burn me and I hold his gaze a moment too long. He doesn't say anymore but I sense that he wants to. He's so close to me I can smell the familiar aftershave, feel the buzz he gives off.

I pay for my drinks, tell Cat I'll chat to her later and leave him waiting his turn.

"At least I've got a job!" Russ is countering Dane who is characteristically ribbing the lads.

"I'll get a new job mate but you'll always have burger nipples!"

This has been going on for some time and again a giggle escapes me. I allow Dane the pleasure of amusing me, he is funny. Russ pipes down.

"Want to go up the road?" George suggests and Jag's head bounces to attention.

"Yeah, I'm up for that." He attempts nonchalance, but I see his mind shift gear, focussing toward gear.

"They won't give me a tab up the road." Dane answers. I feel his eyes search out mine but don't respond.

"I'll get you one." George offers without hesitation. I curse the generosity that I am also reliant on. I've made my bottle last, everyone else though looks sloshed.

"Thanks little bro!" Dane yelps and I ignore him, knowing he's looking at me, waiting for a reaction. He isn't rewarded, by me anyway. George shakes his hand. I shout my goodbyes to the girls behind the bar and we make the short trek to the Sports Bar.

I'm well aware that Ashley could be there, DJ-ing. I want to see him but I'm surrounded by males. And real ones, not virtual, plus one of whom is my recent ex! What will he think? Will he even speak to me?

And if he does, how will Dane react? I've seen regret and lust thick in his eyes all night. There is no reciprocation, of either feeling, but I don't want to cruelly rub it in his face how I did with Luca.

The dimly lit bar is loud and rammed when we enter. Ashley is standing behind the DJ set and he looks up briefly meeting my eye.

I watch his gaze sweep over my company and he looks back at the dials in front of him.

"What you pair drinking?" George asks me and Dane. It's been a long time since we were addressed as a 'pair'. He turns to make the order.

"He's a good bloke, your brother." Dane says from my side and I cringe. I don't need him to tell me so and I don't want Ashley thinking we're back on or something.

"I'm going to the toilet." I turn on my heel and exit the group.

Checking my phone whilst peeing I see Ashley has messaged.

Do you want a drink?

My heart beats wildly and I hastily reply.

My brother is getting me one. Thanks ☺

I've barely washed my hands and the response pings back.

Your brother keeps shit company

I feel a mixture of things. Annoyance and defensiveness, how dare he comment against my brother? But then, it is Dane he is referring to. A swell of heat tells me he must be jealous which means he likes me, surely. He isn't the type to cause trouble, no worries of a scrap.

I quickly type back.

More fool him! I'm not complaining, free drink ☺

I head back into the main room and see Ashley chatting to a pair of brunettes. They're heavily made-up, younger than me I'd guess. George is still loitering by the bar and I join him whilst watching Ashley in my peripheral. He doesn't look but he's holding his phone in one hand, tapping away between flashing the girls his gorgeous smile.

There's vibration in my hand and I look down.

Do anything for a free drink will you?

The message smarts with arrogance and I don't rise, instead I hit send on the cocky retort.

Most things ;)

I put the phone away, let Ashley be moody. There are girls begging to be chatted up after all. I concentrate on talking to George and the clan, minus Dane when I can help it. I can tell he's noticed me distancing myself, he keeps watching me as I ignore the tiny vibrations telling me Ashley has messaged again.

My phone burns a hole in my pocket and I'm sure Dane is trying to do the same with his eyes in the side of my face. Perhaps Ashley is watching me too but I don't give him the satisfaction of looking over. Finally, when at least ten whole minutes have passed, curiosity gets the better of me and I discreetly check the phone.

I hope so.

Now let me buy you one x

"Who you messaging?" Dane's voice is accusatory and slurred, more so since Jay's treat of a snakebite drink. I look up at him, possibly with more anger than I mean to.

"Sorry." He cowers realising his error. "I- I."

He stops and starts as I look back at my phone with more interest than I have for him.

"Jodie, I-"

"Hey, want a drink?" Ashley is right upon us and Dane stares at him dumbly. He knows who he is. He's just shocked that he's talking to me.

"Yeah, sure thanks." I side-step the silenced Dane and push to the bar with Ashley.

"Don't let him talk to you Jodie. He's scum."

I give Ashley an even look.

"I know what he is." I reply. I don't need telling who to talk to, but there's no point being haughty. At least he cares.

"He thinks he's got a chance." He tells me after he's ordered the round; drinks for us and a couple extra, for the lingering twosome perhaps.

"He can think what he wants." I say with a smile.

"Well he *thinks* he's in there." He's like a dog with a bone and I think are you envious Mr Tyler? Aren't you buying drinks for a pair of cuties over there?

I shrug and take the replenished glass.

"Well he isn't. Thanks for the drink." I shimmy away and leave him to get back to his set-up before the track ends. What is it about men and their need to control?

"I can see what's going on there!" Dane exclaims when I arrive back to them. He openly scowls over in the direction of Ashley and his fans. I choose to ignore the comment and I don't look to see if Ashley has noticed. There's nothing I can say- or want to. George senses things getting awkward, catches my eye.

"Jodie, did you see-"

"Well, I'm not hanging around here to watch you give gooey eyes all night!" Dane storms over the top of him. I have to laugh and the lads giggle, startled at the outburst. Dane is looking at me angrily. He wants me to defend myself.

"Go home then." I say carelessly. His head jolts, hurt spreading through his features and he looks at George as if he's going to get involved.

"Seriously, Dane, what do you want me to say?" I didn't want to piss him off but I'm not going to make allowances just because he's here. He huffs and puffs, tries to configure his thoughts. The others, embarrassed by the tiff between ex-lovers, turn away.

I do the same, see Ashley watching us and I smile at him. He raises his eyebrows. There are four girls sitting at the table by the booth now and I cast my eyes over them pointedly, just as he had done to my company when I first entered. An expensive night for you mate! Behind me, Dane slams his glass down.

"I'm off. I'm drunk!" He attempts to laugh off the whole thing and the lads pretend to not hear him. "George, bro, I'm going man. I owe you."

George pats Dane's back, he leaves and I don't watch him go. My phone vibrates. Ashley;

Good riddance ;)

My thoughts exactly. This time he returns my smirk.

"Pool?" George suggests from my side and I nod.

"You know, that Ashley is a bit of a div." My brother is the latest bloke, in a long line it seems, offering me his opinion. He has obviously noticed our consistent interactions all night.

"Really? I didn't know you knew him." I'm interested in his thoughts at least.

"I see him in here all the time, always with other girls."

"Jealous?" I poke fun at him.

"No! I just don't want him taking you for a ride."

"Oh, he can take me for a ride anytime!" I quip giggling. George and I are open with each other, I don't need to curb it.

He shrugs. "Ok, just don't say I didn't warn you."

"Thanks, I won't." I return to another of Ashley's messages and reply simply with a smiley face.

They're all telling me about each other, ironic really because they all think with their penises. Hopefully Ashley's penis will steer him the right direction, toward me!

Dane was certainly thinking with his earlier. He would've dropped his trousers for me tonight with no hesitation, his flare-up only confirmed it. Who knows what's going on with his love-life right now but I know not to take it personally, he doesn't even like most things about me, he told me enough when we were together.

George only warns me from the goodness of his heart although I'm not concerned. I'll take his caution lightly, he is just the same around women. It's not grounds for a psychopath and nothing I didn't suspect already.

The night continues, a little quieter without Dane around, and we play pool whilst chatting to those around us. I subtly check my phone from time to time but Ashley doesn't message again.

"You ready sis? Or are you hanging around for your DJ?" George flashes a sarcastic grin and I don't look over to where Ashley is now sitting with two other guys and six girls in total.

"I'm ready." I return the smile. Mark and Russ just left, Jag disappeared to a house-party a while ago and there are still plenty of people in the bar hoping for a lock-in. I wonder if Ashley will even notice me leave.

We're in the dark, cold street within moments and I shiver as we walk. It isn't far to either of our homes but they're in opposite directions once we get to the end of this road.

"You don't have to walk me back."

"I wasn't going to." He jibes. "Not really, I was going to see if your Leila was up and fancied a late-night drink." He wiggles his eyebrows comically.

"Don't get your hopes up, she met someone last weekend, they've been messaging all week."

George harrumphs in disappointment. "I only wanted a shove."

"George! A *shove*!" I'm not shocked by what he has said but how he's termed it.

"Well what do you call it 'making love'!" He puts on a girly voice and I honk loudly forgetting the midnight hour. "Well?"

"Banging!" I giggle thinking of the original Maga-term. "Shagging, whatever, not a *shove*! It's awful."

We're turning onto my street now and I wonder if Ashley will be 'shoving' someone tonight.

"Did you mean it about a late-night drink because I've got *nothing* in! Well a bit of vodka but nothing to mix it with." We're approaching the house and George has shown no signs of turning around.

"Jodie! School girl error." He rolls his eyes. "Come on, we'll go mine."

I catch up with him as he begins heading back in the direction we came.

"We can't go to mum's! If we wake her up she'll go mad!" We both begin to giggle, I am so right. "Plus I've already messaged Leila, she's just got back and is waiting for us."

"Ready and waiting ay?"

"Ready and waiting to hear my gossip!" I retort. I can't wait to tell her about Dane and Ashley, both have been pretty awful in their own right.

"We'll get your beers and take them to mine." I tell him decisively.

"And I'll woo Leila with my pole dancing skills." He adds.

We pound the streets and in minutes find ourselves at mum's front door. George quietly lets us in and we theatrically tiptoe through the living room, tittering like kids. Once equipped with the almost full box, George gives me a sudden look.

"What?" I hiss warily eyeing the door. Either Keith is coming home, or mum is on her way down. I'd prefer Keith and that's saying something!

"I've got some weed! Do you fancy a smoke?" I laugh quietly and give him the go-ahead nod. "Be quiet! I'll wait on the front."

He light-footedly bounds away and I exit as soundlessly as I can. It kind of feels like we just burgled our own mum but it's all George's property.

"Got rizla?" I double check as we walk away. Leila will be surprised! I know she's smoked it in the past. I have no idea if she'll indulge tonight. "Where did you get weed from anyway?"

"Jag's trying to lay off the hard stuff so we had a joint one night, see if it chilled him out."

"And did it?" I enquire.

"Nah." He laughs. "Don't want to help himself that one."

My fingers are numbing with cold but I quickly check my phone anyway. No word from Ashley. I type to Leila that we're on our way, and come bearing gifts. This Saturday is going out with a bang. Even if it's not the kind I'm accustomed to!

Lindzi Mayann

Praise Monday

I arrive at Belfry on Monday morning amid a flurry of excitement and nerves. I'm looking forward to seeing everyone- even Julie and Gilbert although that's out of sheer nosiness. It is Troy who is obviously on my mind as I park up. A couple of staff members mill in the car park, no sign of him or his car yet and I shut off the engine.

Instead of going straight to the staff room I head to the girls unit first. Lizzy will be there, and we've been messaging throughout the week, I want to see her in person.

"Jodie!" She greets me happily and scoops me into a hug. "Happy Monday!"

She pretends to hang herself and then giggles.

"Happy Monday to you too, cheers to the start of a new term!" Nobody else is in here, and it doesn't feel strange between us just as I suspected.

"I wonder what it's got in store?" She rubs her hands together how I've seen her do so many times.

"Hopefully it will be as successful as the last." I smile and look at the 'All About Me' boards now decorated and lively.

"Well, this term is-"

"Always the hardest." I finish for her with a wry smile. "Yeah, I've heard."

"After Christmas is out the way, you're on the home straight. Summer time!"

I think about Christmas, now on the horizon. I can't imagine what I'll be up to by next summer!

"Yay!" I clap my hands anyway. "Well, I'll see you later, at the meeting, if I don't see you before. I just wanted to come and say, you know, hi."

I meet her gaze. I see her dolled up, sparkly eyed, when she leaned in for a kiss.

"Thanks Jodie. You really are a mate." She rubs my shoulder.

"You too." I grin at her before leaving and calling over my shoulder. "Have a good day!"

Back in the corridor the real edginess to my mood steps in. Troy could be in the staff room by now. My cheeks are already warm at the thought of seeing him. How will he be with me? What if people can tell something has changed between us?

There's no need to use my key because Helen, Jenni and Leanne are leaving as I enter. The obligatory 'hellos' and 'how are yous' are exchanged before I can find my bearings. Troy is beaming at me when I finally look at him. I return it, cheeks growing hotter, and fill my locker with belongings ready for the day.

***

Breakfast club is boisterous. Followed by an assembly which is fidgety at best. Julie sends three boys out by the end, the most I've seen removed yet. First lesson with the year 7's is rowdy and break time on the hardcourt is miserable thanks to the cold, showery rain.

It's the year 10's with us in IT now and they have been more sullen and moody than usual. I think even Iqbal is starting to feel drained, his usual jolly demeanour a tad less bright. It's the year 8's next, meaning Troy, but that doesn't even feed my spirit like it should.

If the behaviour pattern so far today is anything to go by, the 8's will be a handful.

I walk the 10's to their lesson in silence. Ben is noticeably quieter than usual and I make a mental note to mention it at tonight's meeting.

"See you this afto." I tell them, nobody replies. One more lesson, then it's lunch time and my tummy growls hungrily. My lunches are boring, simple and cheap but at least healthy and I already know it won't satisfy me.

I reach the door to IT. I can spy Troy's fuzzy hair through the glass in the window. I can feast my eyes on him for now.

Iqbal barely manages to deliver each sentence of his introduction without some form or another of interruption. Troy and I continually get involved, escorting lads from the room to BS and back again or leaving them there to calm down with Sean the Shark.

"Keeping up today?" Troy asks me when we snatch a minute's respite. The lads, those who remain, are at least looking at their screens.

"Just about!" I laugh and roll my eyes.

"Jodie." Iqbal snaps and I look over, but he motions for me to go to him.

"I think you should go and check on Keon and Josh."

"But- yeah ok." I do as I'm told. Troy literally just got back from checking on them. I think it is a tactical move on Iqbal's part.

I hear shouting from other classrooms as I walk. I hope we haven't got this to look forward to for the next nine and a half weeks! Or perhaps in the week off I've forgotten how mad this place can be.

"Hi." I say casually as I enter the room simply adorned with benches and a desk. I plop onto a seat beside Josh.

"Troy only just left." He pipes up.

"Where you find Troy, you'll find Jodie." Sean smirks from behind the computer. I don't react, and the students don't either.

"Iqbal sent me." I shrug, as though I couldn't care less if they do as I ask. Sometimes this feigned indifference works.

"*Eye*ball." Keon giggles, his hairstyle is a miniature version of Troy's and apparently his humour is too.

I stifle a giggle and chance looking at Josh to see if he's heard, he hasn't. That's two things to tell Troy about, urgently!

"Eyeee b-"

"Keon." I firmly cut him off in his tracks. "No thank you."

He is still chuckling to himself and I flash him a quick smile to show him I appreciated the joke.

"Now are you pair coming back, or what? The task isn't even hard and you're missing out on points."

"Fuck the points!" Josh states and I look at him sternly. He is saving them up for a bike accessory that he's got his eye on, and he knows I know it.

"You'll be stuck in at dinner." I coo before adding. "Boring!"

Keon points at the ceiling. Rain can be heard rattling above on the roof.

"Can't play football anyway!" He says as though I'm dumb.

"Well you can't do *anything* in the time room." I mirror the tone back at him.

"The time room is fun!" Josh says eagerly, and I shoot a glance at Sean who for once avoids it. The time room is where the boys go instead of eating or playing- as a punishment- for however many minutes accrued. It should be silent and tedious, not fun.

"Well it shouldn't be." I tell him. "Now, are you going to get back to class- come on there's like only ten minutes left or something. And it's *easy* work!"

I've by-passed all other techniques for good old-fashioned begging.

"Come on." Keon finally agrees and giving Josh the nod, he jumps to his feet too.

"Good choice." I praise them both. "Bye Sean!"

We leave together and I hope they don't cause uproar on their return. Kyron went off to work with Gilbert and Mason got sent home earlier. Between us, we should manage them, just.

"Is it really only lunchtime?" Troy groans when we're finally dismissed from class.

"Jodie?" Not again, I moan inwardly at the sound of Iqbal's voice.

"Ooh Daddy." Troy trills quietly with a wicked smirk. "See ya in a bit babe."

I scuttle back through the cluster of bodies. Iqbal is sitting behind his desk. "I thought, erm, Jodie I-"

Here we go again! What awkwardness am I due this time?

"Well, I, erm, wondered if you'd like to, you know…"

I *don't* know and silently hurry him along. I still haven't told Troy about *Eyeball* let alone Sean's pointed remark about *us*.

"Eat lunch in here… With me." He adds and instantly looks horrified.

I don't want to reflect his expression and embarrass him anymore than he obviously already feels. But, shit, I do not want to be stuck in here talking software and technology either.

"You don't want to. It's fine." He reads my mind and I feel mean.

"No, it's not that! It's just the other staff, I- they..." are more fun, interesting, exciting? "I want to see them too, you know we've had a week off."

I feel like I'm explaining myself too much. I don't actually owe him an answer but I suspect why he wants me to stay. He doesn't want me with Troy.

"I know, I know, of course." He pulls his professional mask back down. "You know, I warned you about socialising too much, making friends. I don't want it distracting you. You're doing a good job, there are lots of opportunities for you. You have potential."

"Yes, well thanks. I'll be sure to keep trying." I scamper from the room feeling flustered. Fine, I'm glad to hear the reassurance, particularly on a day like today. But recently I feel like men are trying to stake a claim in my life, offering their opinion when it isn't asked for. Is it because I haven't got a boyfriend, they feel somebody needs to be in charge of me?

I reach the staff room. It is a hubbub of activity and I search out Troy once I have my lunchbox.

"What did your dad want?"

"Drop it." I tell him as I sit. The tease feels too close to the truth. Iqbal is not trying to come on to me, I know that. He is around my own age but definitely treats me like I am his charge, plus he's married and oh he likes to remind me of that.

"Anyway, I have got something to tell you." There's no time to dwell on Iqbal's desire to steer my life towards what he thinks is right.

"Sounds juicy." Troy leans closer and adds. "Like your bum."

I automatically look over at Sean. He's watching us and gives me his eerie shark-like grin.

***

Troy is unmoved by any of my news. The 'eyeball' thing he 'expected'. And the run-in pre-holidays with Sean, now tied with today's blatant suggestion, doesn't bother him either. It's a turnaround from the panic-stricken Troy I witnessed *that* night, but what he doesn't know is that Iqbal might be onto us as well.

He squeezes my thigh under the table until we have to part ways and oversee lunchtime clubs. It goes someway to eliminating my angst.

Supporting the 10's in English gives me a breather from Iqbal and I don't face him again until last lesson. We both carry on as if the conversation at lunchtime never happened and that is fine with me.

The Monday meeting is the last thing I want to do now the school day is over, but it is the last thing I have to. And usually it doesn't require much input which makes a welcome relief from being on my toes all day. Troy has already made me a coffee and the chair next to him is free. Everyone knows it is me who will sit there.

"Good afternoon?" He asks casually.

"Not bad." I reply. I look around for Claire, I want to let her know about Ben's mood change but she isn't present. I hope she's just late and I don't have to approach Gilbert. The cat who got the cream sits proudly near to the front.

"Today has been unacceptable." Julie begins coldly. "Fifteen holds, fifty-seven visits to BS. I don't think there were many not present in that time room at some point." She looks at her notes. "Nearly *seven hundred* minutes served!"

She takes a moment to let the information sink in. It would seem everybody is holding their breath.

"Things need to change. Any suggestions?"

Nobody speaks and I think of the conversation with Keon and Josh earlier.

"Keon said he would rather have time to do at lunch because it was raining and he couldn't go outside to play football." My voice sounds tiny in the still room. I wait for Julie to tell me to leave but she continues to stare, and I don't know which is worse.

"Ok." She finally says, dangerously quiet. "So what do we do, switch off the rain?"

I feel my cheeks flush- bitch- but it's a relief she hasn't shouted, or kicked me out. Spurred on I continue. "We could see what the footballers want to do instead? Set up a new club."

Julie actually smiles, and I can't help it, I feel a warm glow in response.

"Any proposals for a new club?" She says to the room. "So we can give them options and not just a free choice."

I relax now the focus has been removed and begin to feel actually proud as the ideas roll in.

"I think we could make the time room stricter." Gilbert proposes after a selection of potential new clubs have been picked.

I nod along with others who stir in agreement. It's odd he brings it up because he's the one who man's it with Sean.

"It should be strict anyway." Julie barks at him. There's no sign of anything loving between them but I wonder if they have unspoken conversations when their eyes meet. "Has it not been?"

"I think it could be stricter." He comments conceitedly.

She looks around the room accusingly and finds Sean. This doesn't bode well especially since the apparent abuse of school property. He looks paler than usual as if her glare has sucked out his blood.

"Has anyone else noticed anything?" She asks demandingly. I feel like it would be pushing my luck to speak again but then Gilbert is right even if he is publicly hanging Sean out to dry.

"Chester said Marley was allowed to go five minutes early." Jess speaks up.

"Shaniq said he ate his lunch in there too." Lewis inputs with an unapologetic shrug. I look at Gilbert who is looking around the room intently. Do I side with the correct man and aid his hunt for power; or the guy in the wrong because he might expose my affair?

"Josh said earlier that it was fun." I add to the evidence. I can't hold back for personal reasons when it would make everyone's life easier if the punishments actually deterred. Both hold power over me; Sharky boy's I can limit, Gilbert's I unfortunately feel I need to earn.

"We'll split the time room whilst behaviour is still settling, make the groups smaller. Del, you'll go in with Sean." Julie actions a precise plan and Terri, the minute-taker, scribbles down details from the corner.

New statuses are discussed- but hardly anybody moves up after a return day of mainly appalling behaviour- and now Julie is coming to a close.

"Safeguarding?" She hands over to Gilbert and I realise I'll have no choice but to approach him about Ben, clearly Claire is not here again.

He pompously delivers a range of points, nothing too severe, and the meeting is being called to a close. I quickly approach him, before he can start talking to Julie and I'd have to face them both.

"Gilbert, could I just mention, about Ben?" He immediately ushers me to the corner of the room. "It's nothing serious. I just thought he was really down. Out of character today."

"The Police talked to him all last week. He's got a lot on his mind. Well done for speaking up Jodie, in the meeting and now. You're really… *flowering*." He leaves the word dripping with sleaze.

"Thanks." I think? More skewwhiff praise from today and this time with a patronising dollop served on top. He nods, conversation over and I leave to find Troy by the lockers ready to go, waiting for me.

"So, I'll see you tomorrow." He lingers, and we thirstily drink each other in.

"Yes, you will."

"Bye."

"Bye then." He turns and I reclaim my own belongings. I exit Belfry and drive home on autopilot feeling utterly exhausted. Not physically really, but my brain is numb, I cannot do anymore thinking. The voices which are usually always present in one force or another are unresponsive this evening. I'll be alone tonight, Leila is working, and I'm glad for the temporary peace in my mind.

This thing with Troy is too fragile to pick at just yet.

And if brownie points were earned with Julie and Gilbert today, and deducted by Iqbal and Sean, it's just something I have to accept. Belfry is a harsh terrain but I am happy enough with my navigational efforts so far. I can't please everyone, and I have more than pleased myself with my attempts.

Once home, I leave my phone in my bedroom. I can't be bothered to communicate with anyone. There's Aaron and he won't mind, I spoke to him all day yesterday. And Ashley is still waiting on a reply to his latest complimentary message from this morning. He was straight in my inbox yesterday, explaining two of the girls from Saturday were his cousins and he was duty-bound to look after them. We chatted on and off since but he can wait for now, he doesn't rule me, none of them do.

I am learning a lot about men. Specifically, that they like to feel needed in one way or another.

And another thing, I am learning about having a casual 'shove' that feelings can't always be protected against. But I just will not let them get the better of me.

Tuesday Medicine

"You fucking lesbian!" Mollie spits for the tenth time. "You fucking tramp!"

Lizzy and I are in a sitting hold, legs stretched forwards, the wall behind us for support as we grip Mollie between us. One sweaty arm each is entwined with Mollie's so she can't continue to lash out. The free hand I am holding to protect my cheek is wet from saliva. Mollie is aiming her anger at mainly me for whatever reason.

"You fucking lesbian!" She cries again in my ear and begins to rock back and forth. We have to tighten our grip, both hands needed again and Lizzy meets my eye over the thrashing blonde head. She flashes the quickest of smiles. I know what's tickling her. The fact I am being called the lesbian.

If only she knew! I can read it in her eyes.

This started over half an hour ago and my body is aching from remaining so tense. Surely she'll tire soon.

"Let me go you bitch. Do you like touching me, do you?" She continues to rage, showing no sign of slowing. The spitting starts up again now.

"Come on Mollie, you know better ways than this." I say tiredly.

"Fuck off." She hisses and continues to sputter but her mouth is too dry to really gob anymore.

Lunchtime started off so relaxed. As usual the unit felt a welcome change from the main school, but it didn't take long to descend into chaos.

They all refused to do any of the work we presented them with, then Holly walked right out. Eve lit up a fag in the toilets and got sent home. Despite Jayde being gobby and Bonnie her usual nervous wreck they handled Mollie's demise ok and are with Lacey elsewhere in the school.

Del is aware of the ongoing situation and keeps popping his head in to check we're managing.

"Is all this worth it Mollie? We don't even know what you're angry about." Lizzy says calmly.

"I'm not angry." She replies her voice shrill. "I'm bored with this stupid school. And your stupid work. And *her* stupid face."

"Mine?" I can't help but titter. "Well thanks a lot."

Her shoulders finally begin to relax. We'll all be strained tonight, I feel sorry for her having to go through this.

"Mollie, we're not mad at you. We want you to enjoy school." I continue and she sighs heavily.

"I will never enjoy school you twat."

I don't bite at the disrespect because I want this situation to resolve and I'm sure Lizzy's cough is a disguised laugh.

"You'll enjoy it a lot more if we go back to having jokes. Last term, we had loads of fun Mol." I tell her instead.

"You might have, saddo." She mutters but her body has given up resisting. We're barely restraining her now.

"Well, we've got half an hour left. What would you do, if you could?" Lizzy asks amicably.

"Minecraft." The response is instant and predictable, I could've mimed it.

"How about we write a Minecraft story?" I offer, conjuring Iqbal-style enthusiasm. There's no way she's being rewarded for this, part of me is angry at her for kicking off but getting back on track is my ultimate aim.

"God, no!" She cries like I've offered her chocolate covered sprouts. We're close to being back to 'normal' and I loosen my grip completely to show I'm trusting her.

"Hangman?" I offer. At least it's spellings! She rolls her eyes. "Come on, let's sit at the table at least."

Lizzy and I stand stiffly. Mollie skips over the room to the desk. I'm accustomed to summoning calm diplomacy when all I want to do is scream, but it definitely makes it harder when her mood switches from vile to cute in a nanosecond.

"She did that for the drama." Lizzy mutters. I nod, agreeing; sometimes there's a trigger, sometimes she just feels like it. Today was impulse, she was bored. And it's meant I haven't actioned my plan of searching for and printing a number of pictures to stick on my table at home. I'm thinking retro posters, cartoon characters and life quotes so the whole top part is a funky patchwork! It will have to wait. I still have a couple of weeks until Aaron arrives- my deadline for this project.

"I wonder why she called you it?" Lacey laughs heartily when we finish telling her about Mollie after they've gone home. "Maybe she can sense it in the room!"

"She's got a gay-dar." Lizzy remarks and we giggle idiotically.

"Don't forget she also said I had a *stupid* face!" I remind them. "And she called me a saddo."

"*And* a twat!" Lizzy adds. "That was so funny how she said it!"

"I thought I heard you laugh, *you twat*, you about set me off!" We're creasing once again. It's a side-effect of being het-up for so long. We're just so relieved day two is down and we've survived it.

"I know everyone warned me about this term, but I was not expecting this!" I admit. "I hope it doesn't carry on this way."

"It won't, it'll settle down again, like before. It's just a long term." Lacey assures me and her mouth curls in humour. "You twat!"

"You lesbian twat!" Lizzy yelps and we all break down giggling again. "If only she knew!"

I return her happy grin. Laughter is the best medicine.

"I must say, I've tried it with a girl, but Lizzy I don't know how you go without a dick." Lacey tidies up the last of the afternoon's carnage.

"I've tried… *it,* urgh, I can't even say the word. I'm just not into it." She responds and catches my eye. I wonder if she *does* use a strap on?

"Me neither." I agree with Lacey but I'm still looking at Lizzy and my face flushes. "I'm not into, girls, I mean. I went quite far with a friend once, ages ago, it didn't feel right." I divulge, so she knows that *she* explicitly didn't turn me off.

"Ages ago," Lizzy repeats a glimmer toying in her eyes.

"A few years." I elaborate and look away from her. The last thing I need adding to my love bow is another string. I'm not a lesbian, twat!

"You're welcome to your field." Lacey comments without malice. "I'm happy with mine. You ready Jodie? And speaking of dick, how is your love-life?"

Lizzy shoots me a mischievous grin. *Troy-* she knows I'm sure of it, but she's totally avoided asking me outright. I know about her drugs, she knows about my affair- it's even Stevens. And we are building a genuine relationship between us, ahem platonic of course.

"See you tomorrow girls." She says and we wave before leaving her to do teacher business.

"Wow, Jodes, I'm impressed, men in faraway places!"

I've just given Lacey the news about Aaron coming to visit. Troy joins us at the lockers now and I hope he didn't overhear!

"What's this?" He asks Lacey nosily and I cringe as she begins to explain about my Spanish boyfriend- who isn't even Spanish- thank god I didn't tell her his age!

"Busy weekend for you then." He states locking my eyes into his chocolate gaze.

"It's not this weekend." I tell him and quickly remind myself I have nothing to feel guilty about. I sense his tension.

"I'm off, see you tomorrow." Lacey darts away from us, glad to be finished.

"When would you have told me?" He asks quietly.

"Told you? Said what exactly?" My mind is whirring and I'm aware of there being other people nearby but I still can't help and spit, "He isn't my *boyfriend*."

"Just somebody you're fucking." He comments in the same soft voice. It goes right through me.

Yes? No?

"I don't know what he is."

He's nineteen, my mind helpfully answers. "I do know he makes an effort with me. And he's *single*." I add in a hiss and look at him.

The soppy, love-filled expression makes me hate him but only for a split second. If he feels this way about me dating another guy, why doesn't he make haste and dump Beth.

"You can't expect me to wait around. What do you want, a second girlfriend?"

"If only it were that simple." He grins, and I look away, grabbing my things together.

"If you were single, it would be simple." I tell him finally and force myself to stalk away.

"See you tomorrow babe." He calls out after me. No shame, I tell myself, he has no shame.

Welcome Friday

The weeks pass steadily and October merges into November. Behaviour settles a little, amongst the students at least, and I look around the work-out club. It was set up in light of my suggestion at the beginning of this half-term, it's loud in here, vibrant and boisterous.

"Go on Mol!" I cheer her on as she manages her fifth pullup. Jay and Chester grin at her shyly- partly in awe, partly concerned there'll have to match her.

"You're nearly as good as your mentor." Troy grins from across the room.

"Yeah, miss, you're well good!" Keon tells me approvingly.

I smile at his little face glad to have made the cut. I can't tell him it is strength gained from pole dancing. Troy knows though and I raise my eyebrows at him sending secret messages.

"You having a go Jayde?" I ask. She gives me a 'durrr' look from where she's lounging on a bean bag chatting to Shaniq and year 11 Jay.

"No Jodie." I answer myself, Keon and Troy snigger.

The girls are finally allowed to mingle with the main school, if they want to, at lunch time. The work out club has proved popular with Mollie and Jayde and I'm more than happy managing their choice twice a week because it means more time with Troy.

Aaron is coming tonight though. He's already in town, sightseeing and shopping, waiting for me to finish. I'm hoping Troy has forgotten about his visit, it seems ages since it was mentioned and I'm not about to bring it up.

Troy might still not be single, but things are fairly simple between us. Our relationship exists solely and idealistically within the protective confines of the school. Nothing is mentioned about other partners; our stories are filtered before they're shared. We make each other drinks, save seats, flirt and laugh together. It's perfect in our cocoon.

"Now, lads. And ladies." Troy begins smoothly. "We're going to try something new now we're warmed up. It's called a Spiderman press-up."

He drops to the floor and demonstrates the exercise fluidly even though it looks tricky. He gets back up after doing three on either side. I'm intrigued, I'll show George this next time he shows up for a pole session.

"I'll try." Mason saunters into the middle of the room. He's barely my height but thickset. I hope he can do it for his own pride but not too many that he gets all big-headed.

He rolls up the sleeves of his Adidas jacket- lime green today. Even Jayde has raised an eye in his direction and he drops to the floor where he manoeuvres into a press up stance.

"Umph!" The attempt to bring his knee out toward his elbow as he lowers himself, results in a slam to the ground.

Troy giggles cutely and spins him over. "Come on try again. It is hard mate, but you'll get there."

Mason takes the advice and I feel pleased he doesn't succumb to an embarrassed tantrum. Mason at the start of term definitely would have!

His second attempt sees him complete one full shaky press-up on each leg before he collapses. His efforts invite a couple of others to try with varied success.

"Your turn Jodie." Troy calls challengingly but I'm sure I can do it. I can do similar plank holds and I shrug nonchalantly before dropping to the floor.

With focussed determination I execute three on each side just as he did and stand up wafting my face bashfully.

"Go girl." Troy's praise rings above that of the students.

Lunch time is coming to an end. It's back to the unit for me, Jayde and Mollie.

"Another thing to add to your wifey CV." Troy coos into my ear as we leave. He touches the base of my back as we shuffle from the room. "Hench females, I like that."

I look over at him. Not for the first time I yearn to take him into my bedroom. Touch him all over and take proper time to get to know each and every contour and crevice. The downfall to our wild affair is it is not so wild. It is trapped, bound by circumstance and time.

"Have a good afternoon." He leaves me and the girls to walk back.

"He's like, well fit Jodes." Jayde remarks. "If only I were ten years older."

I look at her and grin. The last few weeks there's been no talk of her twenty-five-year-old partner. Thankfully she seems to have lost interest since the merging at lunchtimes. A number of lads have been slick enough to interest her rather than the social workers and Police putting her off. But, whatever works!

Just a few more hours to go and I can let Troy go for a few days. Welcome Aaron! At least I'm virtually guaranteed some dick!

I've seen Ashley once in the past few weekends, we're settling nicely into a routine but it means a majority of the time I'm teased by Troy, and left feeling sexually frustrated for weeks on end.

Leila has been getting more than me. I never would have thought it possible before! She and Eric have had a number of dates since their first encounter. At least I get to christen my room tonight. With a nineteen-year-old that's hung like a donkey!

My system is all over the place. I'm getting turned on by ridiculous and illicit thoughts in turn. I love my single life but this weekend I get to make-pretend I have a permanent man around. Regular sex and cuddles, I'm game.

***

"Jo-die! Baby girl!" Aaron's husky, northern voice is filled with joy when I meet him off the bus in the centre of my village. It is a dramatic embrace, he drops his bags to encircle me and lifts me from the ground, twizzling me around.

"Hey gorgeous!" I greet him in return, slightly aware of the Trap not too far away. This will get the rumour mill turning. "Good trip?"

"Piece of cake." He smiles broadly. His dark hair is tumbling around his face and he's wearing contacts not glasses. He sticks out like a sore thumb with his wacky, unusual style.

"I can't wait to see your pad." He grins broadly.

"I can't wait for you to see it! We're getting there with it, making our mark." I won't tell him the renovation was provoked purely because he was coming to stay, although I'm glad for the push it gave us.

Aaron chats amiably as we stroll the short distance. Leila is at work, she begged me to take him in to see her, but I refused. There's no way I'm risking bumping into Ashley *or* Dane with him in tow!

"So, what have you got planned for me sweetheart?" He asks as I unlock the front door.

"Tonight? Alcohol, takeaway, films, lots of chilling out." I answer.

"Sounds perfect!"

We complete the tour, starting with my bedroom so he can dump his bags, before working our way to the living room. The grand finale is not the pole like I thought it would be but the table which is now completely upcycled.

"Mint!" He concludes after examining the overlapping images adorning its large top. He runs his fingers over the central picture, it came from a Carling advert and reads 'you know who your mates are'.

"Only true friends shall sit around this table." I declare and he holds his hand aloft for a high five.

"I love it!" He grins. "Now let me fetch your present!"

"My present?" I'm happily surprised and he skips from the room humming loudly.

***

My present, a duty-free bottle of rum, we decide to save for tomorrow. Leila is working a dayshift so she is free in the evening. She's invited Eric over and Cat is going to come around, perhaps even George and a few others.

We try to watch a film but can't stop interacting. One good thing about the chilly weather is snuggling up under a quilt, our hands wandering and our lips meeting in between varied conversations.

"So when are you going to move to Spain then huh?" Aaron mumbles into my ear. I'm lying back on his chest so it's impossible to see if he's serious. He runs his fingers over my stomach making my muscles contract and I giggle.

"Stop it, it tickles!" I giggle and push his hand downwards.

"Huh, bab, you didn't answer me. I already don't want to leave on Sunday."

"I don't want you to either." I still avoid answering his question which I'm sure isn't for real. Up and move to Spain? I can think of worse things! But with a nineteen year old boy I barely know?

He pulls my chin around toward him so he can kiss me on the lips. I feel his cock hardening underneath me. There's a surge of prickling heat in my groin and I realise how much I'm looking forward to him filling me up.

His kisses are short and forceful, his hands more urgent, delving into my clothing. We can't do it right here on the sofa, I panic as things quickly progress.

His cock is hot and solid in my hand.

"Come on." I pant. "My room."

"No, here." He growls and tries to pull me on top of him.

"The condoms are in my room." I reason between more kissing and grappling. "And I don't want to leave stains on the sofa!"

I cringe at how fuddy-duddy this sounds but he's not deterred.

"Forget that, we'll be careful."

"We need a condom." I tell him firmly and place a hand on his chest. Please let's not have a repeat of before. A mini argument right at the point of penetration is no aphrodisiac. He tuts but jumps up and reaches back for my hand. I take it and let him lead me to my bed.

I've got my new sheets on ready. The picture of a rainbow resembles me following my dreams and hopefully finding a pot of gold at the end of it.

Dancer's Ankles

"A proper cup of coffee from a cropper cuffee pot!" Aaron shrieks his third incorrect attempt at the tongue twister.

"Drink, drink, drink!" I start the chant and he takes a large swallow from his glass before grinning drunkenly. It's Cat's turn next and she rolls the dice.

"All drink!" She yelps after reading the space she has landed on. Leila then rolls after all glasses have landed back down with a thud.

"Blue drink." She instructs. Aaron again! He'll be sloshed at this rate. Eric rolls, yellow drink, that's George.

My turn now and I land on an opportunity to gain a 'pink elephant' point. Aaron just messed up his latest chance; there are only three tries to get the tongue twister correct.

I pick up a card and read it once.

"Say it!" George demands.

"I slit the sheet, the sheet I slit, and on the slitted sheet I shit."

Everyone howls at my error and I try again getting it correct this time with a smug smile.

"Thank you!" I place it by my side on my growing pile.

"I think we should have a dance!" Aaron is yelling as I turn up the music after a few more rounds.

"Here here!" Cat doesn't need much encouragement. She's pleased to have gotten away for a few hours and jumps from the table bopping in the space around the pole. Eric isn't uncomfortable and pulls Leila up swinging her arms back and forth.

"Come on Jodie, give us a move." Aaron beckons to my instrument. I lazily swing round showing off a few poses.

"Wahaay!" Leila cheers me on from where she and Eric have conjoined. George rises to the opportunity and shows off some of the things he has learnt, and it doesn't take long for the men to become engaged in competitive battle.

"You're good." George tells Aaron eventually and I know in that instant he's been accepted. Not to mention they've got on like a house on fire all night.

"In my past life I was a gymnast. I was the school champion!"

I realise for him school was barely three years ago! George is under strict orders not to mention the age thing but he doesn't click anyway and they continue their dance-talk.

The subject of me moving to Spain hasn't been revisited today as we shagged and lunched and chilled and banged. It's an extreme scenario but I've definitely enjoyed having him around. More so now he's met some of those closest to me and they like him. I can tell they do.

"Who wants another drrr- ump!" Aaron had been about to suggest a refill, I think, now he's flat on the floor.

"You ok babe?" I giggle and he jumps back to his feet only to stumble and fall again in the other direction. He hits the wall and slides down it.

"Dancer's ankles, dancer's ankles!" He cries from the floor before righting himself successfully. "I've always had weak ankles, from dancing!"

I can't help but catch Cat's eye and we laugh amused.

"Come on, you're just drunk," I giggle but Aaron looks at me as seriously he can muster in his squiddly state.

"Am not!" He argues.

"Ok, fine, you're not." I shrug. He's obviously just embarrassed. "So, who does want another then?"

When we topple into bed, it's the early hours and Aaron mumbles drunkenly from my side. "I don't want to go tomorrow. Don't make me go. Come back with me. I like you Jodie. I really like you…"

The words- I really like you too- are on the tip of my tongue and I ponder over why they don't easily escape. I don't have to fret though, he's already asleep and breathing loudly.

There's nothing to not *really like*. He's confident, easy-going, complimentary, sexy and strong. He isn't Troy though, no matter how hard I pretended earlier when he was behind me, thrusting away. And he doesn't make my insides squirm like Luca and Ashley do.

But one is taken and the other two are rather popular. Perhaps I should forget about them all and consider the gentle guy lying beside me who speaks a foreign language and is open to travel.

I fall asleep a little confused, hoping that the morning brings a clearer head.

A Pot of Something

Aaron is stirring beside me and I keep my eyes shut for a little longer. My head is throbbing and my mouth is dry.

"Morning." I eventually mumble. "You ok?"

"Morning." He replies huskily. "I'm fine."

"Tea?" I offer sliding from the bed. He nods, and I drag on a t-shirt before entering the kitchen.

"So today's the day." Aaron comments when I return and hand him a mug. I nod, slightly unsure if I'm looking forward to getting my space back.

"Have you had a good time?" I ask taking a sip and climbing back beside him.

"Yeah babe. I've loved it. Just wish I didn't have to go so soon." He moans.

"Well we've still got half a day. How about I show you Hillgate Park? It's the place I told you we use as our beach."

"Nothing can beat the beach." He says proudly and places the mug on the table beside him. "But before we do anything, can we do this?"

He throws back the covers and waggles his enormous member. It's comical but I sense he thinks I'll find it irresistibly arousing so I resist laughing out loud.

"Of course baby." I croon because I do want to do it one last time. Once he leaves, who knows how long it will be until the next opportunity comes along.

***

"Oww!" Aaron howls for the third time and my back prickles. I'm getting annoyed by his huffing and whining which started up the moment we left the concrete path.

"Your ankle again?" I ask patiently and he nods sulkily.

"Another pot hole." He mutters. I resist telling him to look where he's walking- it sounds too parental.

"Not far now. I promise, it is beautiful, there's a lake and rolling hills-"

"I'm not *climbing* a hill after this!" He inserts. "My ankle hurts. I told you last night, I have *dancer's* ankles."

I'm storing up the giggles ready to share them with Leila later on. What happened to the refined, mature gentleman of before? But despite being subtly amused I'm also irritated.

"Don't worry, we'll walk round the lake and it brings us almost home again."

It's a nice day for November, brisk but drenched in milky sunshine. I'm just glad it isn't raining for once. And I feel like I'm back at school trying to appease a moody student. He is my guest, we've enjoyed a morning shove, bacon rolls and this leisurely stroll is my opportunity to show him something of my home. He showed me around Madrid, and I'm sure he'd show me around Barcelona too- if I wanted to go, with him!

"Do you walk down the beach often?" I break the silence, not really wanting it to be like this.

"Of course I do." He snaps and I stiffen. Why is he being so rude!

"Well isn't sand more difficult to walk on than grass?" I snipe. Two can play that game mister. Just who do you think you are? The silence stretches out between us as vast as the open horizon.

"Want a swig?" I offer him the bottle of juice I made up before we left. He ignores me. "Are you hungover? Is that what is-"

"I was barely drunk last night. I can handle my booze." He sniggers snobbishly.

Wow. This time I let the silence string out and tip my head back allowing the snappy breeze to cool my hot cheeks. Aaron is acting like a petulant child and I won't let him ruin *my* day.

By the time we've rounded the lake, we've only been walking for half an hour, and I'm wondering who this person really is. Should I say something by now? I'm a little angry and a little nonplussed. I take a deep breath, still unsure exactly how to word my feelings, unsure what they actually mean.

"Jodie, I'm sorry." Aaron states before I can begin. We're back on the street now retracing our steps to Marshamonvilla, around the centre of the main village. No pot holes to worry about here!

"For what?" I ask. I'm not letting him get away with this easily and I'm wondering if I even want to let him get away with it at all.

"For being a complete idiot back there." He sighs. "I'm just gutted about leaving and I don't know why I'd take that out on you...I really like you, spending time with you and your friends..." He gushes on about emotions I'm rapidly realising I do not feel for him. I was even hoping he might say *sorry, I've realised this isn't going anywhere.*

Because, shit, it's what I've now got to say.

I slow my pace, so we don't reach home too quickly. Leila will still be there and possibly Eric. I can't let them witness this.

"Aaron." I begin, using my stern voice in the hope he'll understand what's coming. "I-"

"Don't say it!" His eyes widen, he knows. "Say you'll come and visit me in Barcelona. Give me a chance to show you *my* home. I could get you a job out there you know, teaching, you'll really love it."

Oh-kay. He is jumping the gun a little and perhaps I have underestimated his feelings toward me. My mind flirts with the idea of teaching in Spain, but not with him- that much is clear.

"Look, I haven't even got the money to book anymore flights. I know they're cheap enough but then there's getting to the airport, money for food and drinks." I falter. I am beating around the bush. We've spent just over a week 'together' in total, spanning *four* months and it's like I'm having to *dump* him. "Aaron, you really are a nice guy. But, it's just…"

He no longer looks at me softly and begins to march ahead, arms swinging and hair bouncing dramatically. I wonder if he knows to cut through the jitty up on the left. He doesn't.

"Aaron," I call after him. "You're going the wrong way."

He halts abruptly, spins on his 'dancer's ankles' and flounces back towards me, scowling.

"Aaron, stop! Listen." I resist telling him to 'please switch on in his listening ears' and instead grab his wrist, swinging him into the alley and out of view. He might be having a full-on teenage meltdown but the last thing I want is to be having a plain barney in the street.

"Just say it Jodie." He simpers. "It's not *you*, it's *me*."

No, it is you. It is definitely you! I don't smirk.

"It's not either of us." I shrug awkwardly as he glares at my face. "We live in different countries Aaron. Now is not the right time for us… to you know, carry on with this. *Timing is* relevant!"

I'm being far kinder than I could be. I could tell him he's acting like a brat and it is in fact very off-putting. And as for the willy waggling… But I at least should end the visit decently. I'm supposed to be taking him to the airport in a few hours!

"I don't get it Jodes. You could come to Spain. To live and work. You did it before." He whines and runs his hands through his hair. "Jodie, this is meant to be!"

"Not now it isn't, not this and not now. Not for me."

"For you." He mumbles head drooping. "What about me?"

"You'll realise the timing isn't right for you either. It's not meant to be with me."

"I don't bloody think so." He mumbles.

I know so, I think to myself but instead say kindly, "You will realise this is the right thing for you too, you have so much going for you."

We return to our slow walk, heading down the narrow path which leads us to my street, and I feel quite bad. I can't believe what has happened during the short time we've been away from the flat. But one thing is for sure; if it isn't right for me in the long-run, it's worth any discomfit right now.

Once home Leila assumes we'll want time to ourselves and leaves us alone. We're sitting in my room, in an almost comfortable silence. The TV is on, Aaron watches and I read. He didn't offer to get a taxi when I mentioned the airport run so I'm biding my time until I can drop him off and place a huge full-stop under this whole thing.

"Want anything to eat before we go?" I offer when an episode of Simpsons ends.

"I'll get something at the airport. Thanks. I'm ready when you are." He gives me a tired smile and I think this must be the worst not-hangover he's ever had!

I can't help but feel sad for him, and guilty because I'm excited for when he is gone. Perhaps if today had gone differently I would have ignored the niggling doubts, the teeny glimpses into his adolescent behaviour. I would have let him fly home on the presumption we have a future. Then I'd have probably ended it via messenger!

"Come on then." I tell him, and we leave hurriedly without saying bye to Leila. She'll probably think it a bit odd, considering the good vibes last night but I can't put him through faking it now.

The airport isn't far and within the hour the deed is done. I'm driving home, music switched up and my heart is much lighter. Farewell felt a little awkward, we even had a hug! But it's over now. One man has been struck off the list! Sorry mate, you don't fit the bill. And I'm in this for me, not anybody else and rightly so.

I've gained from the fiasco. I love the idea of teaching abroad. That could be a possibility if I use my experience at Belfry wisely, develop my skills.

Leila will have left for work by the time I'm back. I'm planning on going to see her and telling her about this whole new occurrence!

***

Leila and Cat are both loitering behind the bar at the Trap when I enter and I grin when they spot me.

"You look cheery. I thought you'd be lovesick!" Cat teases immediately. "He seemed really lovely Jodes."

"Nope, don't go there!" I stop her before she can continue. "It's over!"

I giggle at their bemused expressions and they exchange glances.

"But last night…" Leila says. "What happened?"

"Here." Cat pours me a cider. "I got bought it the other day and I'll never end up drinking it. You know, you never fail to surprise me Jodes!"

I pull up a bar stool, thanking her. The Trap has a fair trade with it being Sunday afternoon so between them serving punters, my story stops and starts until eventually they've both heard it all.

Neither looks overly shocked. Cat nods thoughtfully.

"I did think it was funny when he blamed his dancer's ankles for falling over!" She chuckles and I join in. "He was obviously pissed! Why lie, we all were."

"And the jonny thing." Leila joins in. "That's off-putting. Eric pulled a strop about that at first too, but he's over it now."

"Men ay." I raise my eyebrows. "Can't live with them and can't live without them."

"Well, Jodie, as long you're happy hun." Leila tells me warmly and she is absolutely correct. I am happy, that says it all.

"Oh bloody hell." Cat snags our attention. I quickly see what- or rather who- has caused the exclamation. It's Dane.

Nothing like the presence of a dick-head ex to dampen spirits! I've not personally seen him since the night at the Sports Bar, but I've heard he is part of the circuit again, this split must have lasted. He storms straight to my side.

"Where's George?" He booms and I can tell now, he's really drunk. He physically sways on the spot, his eyes rolling in his skull.

"I don't know. Let me just telepathically ask him." I chunter and so do Cat and Leila. He leans on the bar for support.

"There's no need to be rude Jodie." He slurs with a thick tongue.

"You're the one who just marched right up to me and demanded to know where my brother is. I don't even live with him, why would I know?"

Cat and Leila laugh again before moving away to serve. I can tell from Leila's face she's intently trying to listen in as Dane takes a moment to survey me. I can see his thoughts clamouring within cloudy eyes.

"I saw you with that *paki*!" He slobbers and his face splits into a nasty smirk. "Your new boyfriend is it?"

It takes me a minute to fathom but then I realise. He's seen me with Aaron, Friday maybe, and with his almost black hair and tanned skin has assumed his heritage. I am completely mortified he'd use such a term, regardless he's got it wrong. It wouldn't bother *me* if he *was* from Pakistan and I'm offended by his nerve. What if me and Aaron had seen Dane and he'd said this to his face?

Sorry babe, that's my ex. What a stupid prick! So many things crowd my mouth- spiteful, racist, moronic, selfish- and rage erupts in my gut. Before I know what I've done my hand smacks across his face with a satisfying impact.

Dane is looking at me flabbergasted.

"JODIE!" Chris, the landlord, yells from the other side of the bar and comes flying over. It's the first time he's used my real name in yonks, I'm in trouble!

"It was Dane!" Leila yells at him. "He was a... he was *horrible.*"

"Don't worry, don't worry." Dane who is actually accustomed to being physically attacked in public begins to turn away. "Am leavin', am leavin'."

Cat and Leila have both jumped to my defence, standing either side of Chris explaining how he came in, came straight up to me.

"He was so drunk Chris I was going to refuse to serve him." Cat is saying earnestly. Chris knows me and he's wise enough. We all watch as Dane stumbles out of the door.

"Seems like you did me a favour Soph." He winks, using my nickname once more and ambles back over to his ale. The room is subdued and most people are looking in our direction.

"There's nothing to see here, you bunch of old farts!" He exclaims jovially and talk resumes. I can sense the excitement in the air though and at once feel ashamed and ecstatic.

"As I said Jodie," Cat folds her arms and gives me a mock stern look. "You never fail to surprise me!"

***

Today has been bloody eventful. I get back to my empty, welcoming abode early evening and collapse on the sofa. I'm ravenous, skint, emotionally devoid but far from miserable. I scavenge some scraps from the kitchen, a fridge buffet, and settle down in front of the TV.

Dane really lets himself down and it's a shame on him *and* his family. I think about Jem and his parents and what they'll make of my actions. There's no doubt they will hear about it, possibly know already, too many people witnessed it.

It was long overdue! Maybe they'll even think he deserved it after what he put me through. All of the torment which built up inside of me back then, way before Maga, came rushing to the forefront. Perhaps the fact it wasn't me he attacked gave me reason, or an excuse, to lash out. I don't like racism or bullying. But I don't like losing my temper all the more and he certainly doesn't deserve the energy. His language provoked me but I should've laughed in his face. He's not a racist really, he used the word purely to be cruel.

Perhaps I was more sensitive thanks to the 'break up' today- if it can be called that. I do care for Aaron in a friendly way and I wonder if he is safely home. It's getting late and he hasn't messaged. Did I expect him to? Actually, yes I did but I'm not bothered, as long as he's ok.

I check on Facebook and don't have far to scroll. His recent post tops the newsfeed, possibly because it has had so much activity-almost a hundred likes and thirty comments. Three photos, all virtually the same but they're displayed as one large and two smaller. Aaron snogging, like really snogging, the face off of a petite, peroxide blonde!

What. The Hell!

After all that blithering about me going to visit him, move out there with him! *It's meant to be*, he'd said!

But why am I shocked, he's a man. No, he's a teenager! The shock is quickly replaced by a final bout of laughter for the day. And at his expense again!

I should've known really, nineteen is a bit young. It was over before it really began. But I've not come away empty handed. I have new avenues to explore career wise. I got to visit Madrid and feel like a jet-setter, flying away just for a weekend break. Good sex, good fun, for most part.

No one was harmed in the making of this experience. He's tried to hurt me but I won't let it happen. Better luck next time. What a loser. I suppose that's my comeuppance for messing with a teeny-bop. I click 'unfriend'.

The only thing I regret is letting him sit round our damn table!

Monday Tripping

An excited chatter erupts throughout the staff room and Julie momentarily allows it. Monday meetings have their fair share of tongue in cheek but usually she wouldn't allow such a level of disorder.

An overnight trip to London has just been announced and, predominantly, the mentors look at each other envisioning the prospect. Yes, it is work and there'll be twelve students in tow, but the agenda includes a Christmas fayre, the London Dungeons, Madame Tussauds, Natural History Museum, cinema, turning on of the Christmas lights; the list goes on.

Geek me is invigorated, hussy me already imagining if Troy and I both get put on the trip and responsible me says there is no way I'll be picked!

"If you are available to work these extra hours, sign your name up after tonight's meeting. We'll let you know by the end of the week. There'll be a lot of planning involved. And…" she scans the room smiling wryly. "It is not for the faint-hearted."

"Are you putting your name down?" Lizzy bounds over to us the minute we're dismissed with Lacey and Harishma not far behind.

"Are you?" I ask as Troy declares;

"Yes!"

"I am!" Lizzy exclaims. "We all should, could you *imagine* if we all got chosen."

"Forget that!" Lacey coos. "I just came over to see which of you idiots would agree. It'll be like living in a zoo for three nights! I should've known you'd all be up for it."

"Well," Harishma looks put out to be on the wrong side of Lacey's conclusion. "I'm not doing it for work! I've always wanted to go to the Dungeons."

"Me too!" I enthuse. "And the National History Museum."

Lacey howls and thumbs in my direction. "You're a lost cause."

"Well I'm imagining a few cheeky beers after the kids are in bed." Lizzy says. "I did an overnighter at my last school, it was wicked!"

"Well, they won't take many females. I can tell you that." Lacey tells us and looks at Lizzy. "Least you've got experience."

My heart sinks as I realise she is right. There is no way I'll be chosen. Julie can't even bring herself to look at me half the time, never mind indulge me on an all-expenses paid trip to London. It would be so perfect as well considering my urge to travel *and* lack of pennies. Never mind the opportunities if Troy were to go too!

"How did your weekend go anyway?" Lacey wriggles her eyebrows emphatically at me. She's talking specifically about Aaron, I know it, and presumably Troy clicks on to her gist because he abruptly ups and leaves.

"He fancies you Jodie." She comments and I can feel Lizzy looking at me but I don't return it. "Sooo, come on, how was it?"

I give them the long and short of it- it was good fun, he acted like a fool and now it's over.

"Sounds like something Jayde would do!" Lizzy chuckles when I tell them about the snogging photo.

"Or Sean!" Lacey hisses. I giggle heartily, the whole thing seems one big joke now. "Didn't take him long to move on did it?"

"I know, he must have had her waiting in the wings." I shake my head in mock despair. "He was telling me to move to Barcelona and teach out there. Good job I didn't decide to do it."

Why did he feel the need to feed me with empty words? I ponder about men in general as Lizzy and Lacey both look at me in shock.

"Move out there?" Lacey's face switches to disgust but Lizzy composes herself.

"I did my TEFL. Teaching English as a foreign language," she explains. "I was going to travel Thailand and teach if I liked it there."

I'm committing the initials to memory. T-E-F-L. I will look into this.

"Don't leave us Jodie!" Lizzy compels noting my interest.

"Couldn't think of anything worse." Lacey flicks her hair. "*Travelling*?"

All I can think is, Thailand!

"Don't worry. I'm not leaving now am I." I giggle but I'm definitely thinking about future possibilities.

Lizzy, Harishma and I sign up as possible staff members for the trip, it's just over a month away. I find Troy's name already written and think about any future possibilities with him,   I can't help it.

As I gather my things from the lockers, I note he hasn't hung around, virtually for the first time ever. A lump sticks in my throat. It's daft to feel so upset over his snub, I've only known him a few months. Although, enough for me to know what I feel for him is way more real than anything I felt for Aaron.

But how dare he be annoyed over another man on the scene? What exactly is he offering me in return? A part of him, a share. I want the whole thing, it's him who's stopping that. Maybe I will jet off to Thailand, that would show him.

Leila will be home by six and once back I shower then mope, waiting for her to return and occupy me. The fallout with Troy I'm almost certain is not permanent but it plays on my mind. He doesn't even know I ended things with Aaron. He's at home, being comforted by his girlfriend. It eats away at the corners of my mind.

"Honey I'm home!" Leila bounds up the stairs cheerfully. "How was your day?"

"Fine considering it's a Monday." I reply sulkily from the sofa. Her days off are coming up, how quickly I've become used to having weekends off; Friday Feeling and the Dreaded Monday back at it. I used to love having days off mid-week.

"How was your shift?" I ask her, missing my old job.

"Boring!" She laughs and I remember the customer-less minutes ticking past. No, I wouldn't want to go back to that.

"Any goss today?" She asks. There hasn't been much to report on Julie and Gilbert for a while. She knows most of the day-to-day stuff through Eric anyway. Troy? My taken work-husband is being an idiot, I feel an idiot sharing it, and how can I justify any of it? I could tell her about the trip, but what's the point?

"Not really." I surrender. "Busy, as always. What do you want for dinner?"

"It's two steaks and a bottle of wine for twenty quid up the road…" Leila's suggestion is something we used to randomly do. When I still earned a decent wage! And now the rent, bills and my car literally ties up most of my cash.

"I can't!" I succumb depressed. "I've literally not got a pound spare."

"Well, I have!" Leila tuts and swats the air. "Swings and roundabouts babe, you've treated me in the past."

She smiles and stupidly I feel my eyes tear up.

"Fine." I accept quickly. "Thanks."

I feel pathetic. I should be able to treat myself to dinner at the end of the day if I want to, shouldn't I? There is no budget to borrow it from. I'm barely getting by replacing shampoo and hairspray, I'm just thankful I don't wear expensive make-up.

I haven't even got children to pay for and I share the rent and bills. I can't afford new clothes. I feel like such a loser.

"How long until you're ready?" I ask her hiding the emotion I'm feeling over the proffered steak and wine.

"Do you mind if I have a quick shower? I won't be long."

"Take your time." I tell her and force a smile. Once she leaves the room I scurry to my bedroom and have a short cry. Tears were coming and I let them, quietly sobbing until the emotion is spent.

Perhaps the tiff with Troy, the injustice of his temper and unfairness of his situation, has had a bigger impact on me than I realised. Perhaps Aaron turning out to be a dick head after all has humiliated me.

I look at myself in the mirror and take a deep steadying breath.

The worst thing right now is that I'm skint, but this isn't how it will always be. I think of TEFL, and Thailand- ironically it's where Shaun is headed. I recall these past few months; Magaluf, Madrid, Marshamonvilla, Belfry.

I am stronger than ever before physically and mentally, yet again I am wiser than I was yesterday. My lovely friend Leila is paying for my dinner because we have a fabulous swings and roundabout relationship. When I get home, satisfied by meat, wine and good company, I shall think about my next move seriously- in work and love. My life plan; if it is possible to plan, there's no harm in trying.

Picture It Thursday

It's been a challenging week so far and the IT lessons I supported in before lunchtime were tense. Only one more day to go until the weekend, I console myself as I pull up a chair around the staff table. Troy is the first to join me. Since our fallout on Monday he has been back to outrageously-flirty-normal. Except since then, I've been questioning our 'normal'- it's not quite what I want.

"Troy." Del hands him something as well as Eric and I don't take much notice until Eric begins yelling.

"Yes! Yes! We're in!"

I find Troy beaming and realise at once the London trip staff have been picked- and informed. I at once feel gutted to not be a recipient of the letter. It's like Charlie and the Chocolate Factory except the main character hasn't got a golden ticket. That's all folks, the end.

I stare mutely at my sandwich rather than congratulating either of them. I've felt glum for days, maybe because I'm so skint that's been really pissing me off, but now the trip- or rather no trip. I've not been picked, even though I knew I wouldn't be anyway.

My mind buzzes, telling me it's a sign. Things with Troy are not meant to be. Or at least they cannot just continue like this. I've been paying it a lot of thought and now feels like the defining moment.

My phone pings, thankfully distracting me but it's Lizzy telling me she's been chosen for London too. I tell myself to feel happy for her. Sean comes bounding in, he's also spouting good news, he has made the cut. If I got picked, it was meant to be with Troy. So what now? I don't want it to be over! But I accept it's been weighing heavily on my mood and now it's all coming to a head.

"Congrats." I tell him without a hint of enthusiasm.

"It won't be any fun without you." He seems equally gloomy and for a moment I feel appeased. Then I remember, this *relationship*- or whatever it really is- has got to change.

"It's for the best anyway." I say slowly, goadingly. Troy shifts in his seat, maybe sensing dangerous territory, and despite our closeness being accepted at Belfry, by most, we can't let our guards down.

"No way." He replies and continues to stare at the letter in his hand avoiding my eye.

"Course it is. Where's this all leading anyway huh?"

"Don't be daft." He coos and nudges my thigh with his own.

"Well it's no fun flirting like we do and not being able to act on it. Well, for me anyway, it's ok for you. You've got Beth at home." This is the furthest I've ever pushed it but I'm fuelled by disappointment over the trip news.

"It's not like that." He mumbles. He's not biting at all and I feel painfully rejected.

"How would I know what it is like. I don't know anything about you." I shrug.

"That's not true. I'm- it's," he falters and I wait. "I don't know. I can't just leave her."

"Why not?" I ask forcing calm. I've imagined us having this conversation, of course I have, and it's not meant to be this way.

"I've been with her for five years."

"I *know* that." I hiss losing patience. I cast my eyes around the staff room. Nobody is watching, even Sean is too caught up in animated chatter to notice. Fucking shark, I wanted to go on this trip so badly! "Tell me, why can't you take chance on me, on *us*?"

I hold my breath, it's the ultimate question I've been daring myself to ask.

"How can I trust you?" He asks seriously, quietly.

I explode with resentment on the inside but quickly choke-hold my anger. It's not what I was expecting but then he has an uncanny knack of twisting things on me. Alongside an ability of remaining calm, looking completely composed. I hate him for it. Yet I long for him. What can I do to show he can trust me?

"I would do *anything* for you. To prove it to you." I tell him earnestly. Our emotional declarations have often been abrupt and this time they really need to be. Sometimes I wonder if having these strong feelings for each other is worse than merely succumbing to physical attraction.

"I ended things with Aaron!" I blatantly use Aaron to my advantage, but I'm desperate to prove my point. "You're the one stopping us from going any further."

He stares at me and I ache for him to agree but he says nothing. What does this mean, is it over or is there still a chance?

"Jodie?" Julie is addressing me and in my wobbly state I reel in shock. "A word?"

I quiver and don't dare to look at Troy. Since I printed all those pictures to upcycle my table at home *and* stole PVA glue, I've been waiting for this conversation. She walks me out of the staff room and I feel beyond ashamed. I came into this industry so eagerly and I've totally screwed it up.

I'll have to go back to being a waitress after all. At least the wage would be better. My mood could not be lower as we enter the SLT room and despairingly I spot Neil is in here too; this is so serious!

"In here." Her voice is clipped, and she ushers me into a tiny room beyond, shutting the door. I gulp, this *is* serious! We're completely alone. She takes a seat and indicates for me to do the same.

"Jodie, there has been an incident, in the girls unit."

In my head I tot up the cost of colour printing, it's an expense I can't afford. How embarrassing!

"I'm going to be blunt." She begins and my mind cries, *be honest*, just explain before it's too late!

"You're talking about the pictures," I begin tentatively, and she waits head-cocked. I'm right, how I wish I wasn't, but I have to continue. She's so much scarier up close, I gulp and go on. "I haven't got a printer at home. I know I shouldn't have prin-"

"You printed them off?" She yells and I jump. She looks appalled and I squirm.

"Yes. Well, I wanted to stick them-"

Shaking her head Julie spits. "Jodie are you talking about pictures of Jayde, topless?"

"What?" I cry much louder than I intend. "NO! No!"

"Jayde has sent topless pictures, we think to year eleven Jay, but they're being sent amongst the students. This is a nightmare. What were you talking about?"

"What?" My head is spinning. Jayde is fully formed but ill-informed it seems. Camera phones weren't even around in my day, thank god! Sexting is a new craze and 'revenge porn' is the nasty consequence.

"Jodie?"

"Yes, erm, I was printing things for my All About Me board, I thought I'd hit a limit or something, in printer credits." I blag and she eyes me distastefully. I don't care. I thought I got caught out. And poor Jayde, she has been. Just like Sean was too. Topless picture scandals in common. Although he should have known better being older. I feel sorry for her, it is a mistake I could imagine making in her shoes.

"So what are we going to do about Jayde?" I ask focussing my attention toward our student. Forget all the underlying crap between staff. The kids are who're important.

"I want you to be in with them Jodie. They'll tell you if they have the picture. Convince them to delete it and if they don't- immediately report it to me. I will have the phone removed from them. Silly girl." She adds. "There will be a lesson on Sexting for the students; I've already spoken to Lizzy. Staff training too."

I have a certain amount of awe for the woman I despise serving. To get into her position must have required toughness and a thick skin. She's not here to make friends, she's here to achieve. I want to do both!

"Thanks for telling me. I'll definitely keep my ear to the ground. Is it need-to-know or can I talk about it to the others?"

"Not need-to-know." She confirms. "Tell the staff, warn them! We don't want them looking accidentally, not even realising! You'll be in with the girls tomorrow, do what you can to support Jayde."

This is the first proper conversation we've ever had, I feel almost comfortable.

"Whilst you're here, I might as well tell you, if I could have five Jodies I would have a job for each of you. You have a way with the students."

I was not expecting this and I force a sane smile, feeling floored yet humbled. I'm coming up in the world, it's going to plan! Imagine what *I* could do with five Jodies!

"Thanks. I'd, erm, better get back. I'm supposed to be in clubs."

"Good girl." She doesn't smile. *Good girl!* It can't all be idyllic I suppose.

I leave SLT with a skip to my step. I suddenly don't care about the trip and don't care Troy hasn't left his girlfriend, yet. Julie might have said 'good girl' in that tone but she wants five of me! Iqbal and Lizzy will be well proud when I tell them.

My glee is tinged by the thing with Jayde. I can only hope the pictures don't leak any further than they obviously already have. My part in the rumour mill pales in comparison to the predicament she has found herself in.

We can bounce back though. Learn and move on. I am a product of doing so and now I'm in a position to nurture her through it too. Wiser for next time, that's the best we can do sometimes.

***

Leila is working. I sit alone in the darkened living room my hand hovering on the mouse. If I click accept, I'm tied in to paying fifty pounds a month for four months- and I'll be undertaking a new qualification in the New Year.

Teaching English as a Foreign Language; teach in China, South America, Thailand!

It is a lot of money to commit however and more so at this time of year when Christmas is approaching. At the moment, it is too much. And today with Julie made me think; perhaps a pay rise is on the cards eventually, a promotion even.

I decide to wait, for now, with a sigh. Am I being a chicken? I don't take well to the thought. The courses run regularly. And I've not even been at Belfry half a year, the least I can do is wait and see what's to come. I'm not being a chicken, I am being balanced and grown-up. I feel a responsibility already to the students, Jayde in particular at the moment. I'll be seeing her tomorrow and I hope she isn't too upset. I just can't abandon them now!

A teeny voice echoes in my mind that it would be easier to not be at Belfry at all. But the idea of being away from Troy is inconceivable plus I've worked so hard to get into Julie's good-books.

If I hang on a little longer Troy will get to know me better, he'll see and he might dump Beth. Or is all this talk of not being able to trust me just an excuse to keep stringing us both along?

If only I'd been placed on the London trip with him, I could've upped my game, found out for sure. But that didn't happen. He's taken and he's doing nothing to change that fact.

Actions speak louder than words. I should end it with him.

I've come full circle and shut my laptop on the idea of TEFL, for now. If only it were so easy to cut Troy off. So far any similar conclusion to end things has ultimately been ignored. Tomorrow I'm with the girls for the day so I won't have to see him so much. It'll make the resolution easier to stick to.

The only thing to do now is visit Cat and tell her about today's crazy mix-up over Jayde's pictures. I very nearly gave myself away as a resource thief and I definitely portrayed myself as a complete weirdo! But Julie wants five of me and that fills my heart with hope for my future career.

Dramatic Friday

"Jodie, the girls aren't allowed to mix at lunchtime." Lizzy whispers to me after returning from seeing Julie. We both eye Jayde who's been subdued all morning.

"It makes sense I suppose." I reply quietly. "But will it make her worse? Will she be even more angry at herself?"

I acknowledge I'm gutted there will be no work-out club, therefore no Troy. And I'm pissed off at myself for feeling this way. I distanced myself from him this morning, just a little. I tried not to meet his eye for lingering amounts of times, I tried not to swoon and smirk. I definitely shouldn't be bothered that I can't see him now.

"I don't think she'll mind." Lizzy supposes. "It'll probably be Mollie that kicks off."

I nod in agreement, feeling selfish that I want to kick off too. But seriously, poor Jayde has barely spoken. She's beating herself up big time and I doubt she'd want to have to face the lads. At least she's turned up, not completely avoided her problems and that says a lot about how far she's come already.

"When are you going to tell them?" I ask Lizzy. There isn't too long until lunch time and Mollie is feverish since Jayde told her the news about the circulating pictures. We'd rather she hadn't but one thing about Jayde is her forwardness. Mollie wants to see for herself. I can see why Julie has made the call to keep the girls separate again for now.

"In a minute. I'm just forming a plan." Lizzy grins and I think of my own for today. I wanted the opportunity to see Troy, to prove to myself I'm totally in control. I know half of this is a lie. I'm clucking for contact, like a druggie craving a fix. Two whole days stand between us and Monday when we're reunited.

I hope Ashley messages this weekend. When I'm with him I can pretend Troy doesn't exist and I don't have to pretend anything else. I know I'm not the only one but he isn't my only one either. He doesn't want a girlfriend, I don't want a boyfriend. It's mutual and he's a tidy stopgap.

"Girls." Lizzy addresses the unit and Lacey appears at the pod door. I look at our students and pack my personal thoughts away. They're self-obsessed at best and Jayde needs me today more than ever. She has made her first of many big mistakes. If only she understood there are so many more to come.

"We've decided to all have lunch in here today, together as a unit." Lizzy puts a positive spin on everything and I grin despite of myself. This decision is for the best all round. It's meant to be.

"We're going to do Drama this afternoon and I want us to make a start." She launches her idea and I listen interestedly. "Mollie, you know the most about acting so you're going to be my assistant."

Mollie is on board. Potential protest, diverted!

"Jayde, you get to choose which 'sketch' we try out. Holly? Can you Google the word 'sketch show' please so we all understand what it means?"

Jayde is mildly interested, perhaps happy to be distracted and Holly is glad not to move from the computer.

"Bonnie, could you and Lacey get me some paper and pens please? Bring them over here will you."

Everyone present is engaged and interacted with. It's a shame Eve isn't here to enjoy it, but things are extremely rocky at home and it's affecting her attendance. I watch Lizzy admirably. Her teaching style is something I imagine simulating myself... when I'm a teacher. Well, why not?

The room is a pleasant hubbub of activity and a genuinely lovely atmosphere begins to blossom. I hope Jayde starts to feel better and can go off for her weekend on a high note.

Nobody notices the internal doors being unlocked and Julie is in within an instant observing us immediately. I'm so glad she's 'caught' us busy and productive and grin at the girls encouragingly.

"Jodie?" She beckons. My name was the last thing I expected to hear. She's making a habit of this addressing me thing. I look at Lizzy and she smiles encouragingly, and I dumbly follow Julie out into the hallway.

I almost march right into her. I assumed we'd be going to her office again but whatever she wants to say, here is fine.

"The London trip? Can you still work it?"

"Erm, yes." I try not pounce on her, my mind kicks into overdrive. "Why? I mean, I didn't get a letter?"

"Lizzy didn't tell you? I can't discuss her reasons with you but she pulled out. You were always the female back-up, our next obvious choice."

I tingle all over at the news but I can't show Julie just how much it all means to me. Why did Lizzy pull out, did she do it for me? She's holding out an envelope. The golden ticket! My hand shakes as I accept it but I'm just glad I haven't dissolved into manic sniggering.

"Thanks." I smile at her as normally as I can muster. No wonder she thinks I'm potty.

"Have a nice weekend Jodie." She turns on her heel and leaves me to comprehend what has actually just happened. Is this a sign? Well, is it!

***

The afternoon has actually been hilarious. Jayde chose we re-enact a shop burglary and the ensuing police interrogation. It sounds very serious and in some respects it has been. Bonnie and Lacey, Mollie and Jayde, Lizzy and I, take it in turns to be the shopkeepers, the burglars and the police. We allow Holly to watch because it would make her uncomfortable taking part and she's only just beginning to open up to us. She has been tasked with scoring us in our pairs for each performance. Lizzy and I are winning, we're a class act!

Now it's our turn to be the burglars. The final round! We're standing behind the door to the classroom discussing our angle. Jayde and Mollie are the shopkeepers.

"Let's go IN!" Lizzy giggles. "Like pro robbers. *Get down on the floor*, the whole shebang!"

I agree, laughing at the very thought of what we're about to do.

"Ready? Proper high-profile crims, ok." She checks with me sternly.

"Ok, ok!" I'm on a natural high. I've not had chance to discuss the trip update with Lizzy yet but I suspect she knows the reason for my turnaround in mood. She gives me a nod.

"Let's do this!" She flings the door open revealing the awaiting Jayde and Mollie behind a desk strewn with 'goods'.

"Everybody get down." Lizzy demands as we enter. "This is a heist. Get on the floor."

"Get down! Get down. Nobody needs to get hurt." I back her up and we scurry toward the desk. It's then I notice not only have Jayde and Mollie dropped to the floor, but so has Bonnie. She's not even in this scene; she's a police officer and waiting in the wings. Lacey chuckles lightly, Bonnie is splayed flat to the floor, face down.

"Bonnie, we're not that convincing are we?" I call to her giggling.

"Get the goods Jodie!" Lizzy exclaims. Bonnie has raised her head feeling safe enough to do so and is smiling bashfully, not howling. "Get the goods man, the feds will be on their way!"

"Come on Bonnie." Lacey helps her to her feet. "That's us, it's nearly our turn."

I return to the action amused and proud, to find Lizzy wrapping Mollie up the rug.

"Help me Jodes." She shrieks. "This one tried to make a run for it."

I look over at Jayde who is laughing loudly.

"Stay there and don't move!" I growl in character and she flicks me the middle finger. "Right, that's it!"

I march towards her as Lacey comes bounding toward us, Bonnie in tow, howling 'nee-naa, nee-naa!' It isn't a touch on the entrance Lizzy chose for us- *whoop whoop; it's the sound of the police!*

We make a dash for it but don't reach the door- and our escape- before imaginary cuffs are slapped onto our wrists. Bonnie's job is to read us our rights and I notice how much clearer her speech has got, how much more confidence she has.

The interview is short. Mollie is quickly bored once she's not directly involved. We're convicted for our crimes, The End.

"What's the scores then Hol?" Lizzy asks her, back to her normal, gentle voice. Holly, who's usually pallid, has a colour to her cheeks from laughing at us.

"You pair," she shakes her head smirking. It's so good to see her involved. "I'm giving you ten out of ten because even Bonnie got on the floor and she wasn't even in that part."

"You enjoyed it didn't you Bon Bon?" Lizzy asks her using the sweet nickname. Bonnie grins nodding ardently. Holly gives out the rest of the scores. The school day is virtually over.

What a turnaround. Of course the news I am actually going to London has completely lifted my spirits. I assume Troy will be waiting for me at the lockers when we head there soon. He'll want me to go to the pub. I want to tell him the news!

"Lizzy, why didn't you say you pulled out of the London trip?" I ask her once we're student-free. Lacey is waiting for me by the door.

She shrugs noncommittally. "I've done it before, thought I'd give you the opportunity. Well someone else, I'm glad you got it. It'll look good on your CV."

She's right, it will, and did she know I would be chosen to replace her? Or did she take the risk, in hope?

Troy always refers to my *Wifey* CV; a list of things he likes about me. This is another opportunity to show him. This is good for *both* of my CV's.

"You're going on the trip Jodes, you're mad." Lacey comments and I wonder if I am. "I can't wait to tell Harishma, she'll be gutted! Now come on, it's home time."

"Well thanks anyway." I tell Lizzy and our eyes are locked in private talk.

"You deserve it hun. The opportunity."

I nod. I know what she's really saying, I think. *You only live once, go for it.*

"Let's celebrate!" Troy's eyes are dancing. We're at our lockers and I've just told him; I'm in! "You *are* coming to the pub?"

No. The answer is right there. It's extra money spent and that should be enough to deter me, never mind convictions to shut things down between us.

"Yes, of course! I fancy a half."

The fact I'm going on the trip, three nights in London with Troy, it alters everything. It's meant to be, what are the chances? My very own happy ending!

I follow his car and my thoughts follow my heart. This could be the final straw. I promise myself if he isn't mine by Christmas, I will give up. But at least I'll know I gave it enough time to find out for sure.

***

I'm spending the evening in my living room, sober, alone and happy. My job is tough but so rewarding, this afternoon was just brilliant! And I'm going to London which is an absolute bonus. Troy being there means we'll spend four whole days together solidly. Imagine if we can sneak into each other's room!

I'll go and see Cat tomorrow and tell her the news. And the new plans! She doesn't even know about the option of TEFL yet, or Julie's praising of me.

Leila has tomorrow evening off, but she'll probably be seeing Eric. I don't resent her for dropping me, we should do what makes us happy, live and let live! He is going on the London trip too. He hasn't got a clue about Troy and me though. I'll make sure to tell her again, not to let on, even in the slightest, ever!

We've only had sex that once. Not even a sneaky kiss has passed between us since the October break and that is a month behind us. The trip is less than a month in front. The potential and the possibilities are clear, Troy made sure to articulate in detail earlier exactly what he wants to do to me whilst we're away.

Sean will be on the trip too though and he'll undoubtedly be watching.

He can't stalk us constantly. But even without being physical I know we're technically cheating. We're emotionally tied and bound to keep pulling on each other. Something will give. The potentials and possibilities of what exactly are dangerous and thrilling. I can't wait to find out!

Move On Monday

The main parts of the Monday meeting are concluded and the staff involved with the trip are asked to leave together. I stand with Troy, Sean, Eric and Del, eager at the prospect of beginning to make plans and discussing the finer details.

Iqbal is joining us too, I've been with him for the majority of the day and I had no idea he was involved.

"You coming too?" I ask him as we reach the door.

"Yes. I think it will develop my skills."

"Mine too!" I agree, although possibly not the set he's talking about.

"I didn't know you were, I thought it was Lizzy." He adds. "I'm glad though."

"Me too," I agree again for altogether different reasons. He gives me a warm grin and Troy pinches my bum discreetly as he passes us.

By the time I'm driving home my head is ready to explode with the plans. The days are scheduled out, we've looked at photos of the accommodation and all that's left is for the boys to earn their place. It's going to be mint! I'm about as excited as when I booked to go to Madrid. Four weeks and counting!

Leila is home when I get back. I know she has work at six and she sits on the sofa looking dejected.

"What's up hun?" I ask knowing there is something. Lately especially she's been glowing.

"I finished things with Eric." Her voice is flat.

"What, when?"

"Just now. Well actually, I *had* to end things with him."

"What do you mean?" I'm confused plus I can't tell whether she's upset or angry.

"He bumped into someone this weekend. An old school friend. I could see it all over their faces, there was unfinished business. And now he's on about going to stay with her…"

"What!" I trill infuriated. "You can't just… just *decide* to do that. You're together, aren't you? Weren't you? This is crazy."

"Well, he was honest, at least. He could've just gone and seen her behind my back." It isn't an intentional dig but I feel the sting. "We'd never had the chat about *being together*. I think he knows there's something between him and this other girl, I was just a bit of fun."

"Oh Leila, are you ok?" I sit down beside her.

She nods. "It's ok Jodie. I'm sad but I'm not heartbroken or anything. It's just a shame."

"Well mate, if he wants to take his chances with some other girl over you, you're well clear! What a thicko." My advice resounds in my head, taunting me and I stubbornly ignore it.

"Well at least I got some good sex out of it." She smiles weakly. "I was beginning to worry I'd close over!"

"And hopefully your beer goggles curse is broken too." I add. "You pulled a fitty Leila, it's an improvement on before!"

"Har, har!" She exclaims sarcastically.

I'm glad she is taking this in her stride and grin at her boldly. Selfishly I'm also a little pleased to have her single once again even if I am planning alternative things for myself.

"Let's have a cup of tea." I suggest. I'm annoyed I can't offer to treat her to dinner out before she goes off to work to cheer her up. "Fancy scrambled eggs?"

Eric is not good enough for my best friend anyway I decide loyally. I wonder if things will be awkward between us at work although I can't imagine it will be. He's treated her with enough respect to be honest. I don't miss the irony regarding my own scenario.

"I'll still come out with you guys at Christmas." Leila tells me when I hand her a steaming mug and I laugh.

"Damn right. Show him what he's missed out on! Plenty more fish in the sea!"

She rolls her eyes at me and I realise it's the advice I usually mock hearing. Perhaps I should be taking heed myself.

Suss It Out Monday

December mornings have proven to be bleak- it's still pitch black when my early alarms trill. Usually it's a demotivating way to start the day but even though today is Monday, this morning was different. Weeks and eventually days counted down, it's finally time for the big London trip!

Those who have earned their place, staff and students alike, are contained within one classroom. The atmosphere is electric. A mountain of bags are piled by the door, mine included.

"Jodie?" Lizzy appears motioning to me. Technically she earned me my spot and I still feel guilty she sacrificed the opportunity for me. Even if I don't know it was for me exclusively, but I suspect it was.

"Jodie, I had to come and tell you before you leave."

"What is it?" I momentarily panic, what's happened, are our girls ok? But then she slowly begins to smile.

"I've met someone!" She gasps. "Yesterday! I wanted to tell you in person, I think she's the one, she's everything I've dreamed of."

She gushes and I feel relief and happiness spread through me. My dear friend, I realise our chemistry is purely platonic and I am so pleased for her.

"That's brilliant. The one, ay!" I tease. "How do you know?"

"I just *know*!" She continues to grin. "She's gay for a start!"

She gives me a playful wink.

"That's a start!" I agree giggling. I think of Alexa. She just knew too, how do they just *know* and it all falls into place? But then isn't that what's happened with me and Troy and this big trip?

"Anyway, you feel guilty about going instead of me, so I wanted to tell you. I'm seeing her again tonight, I'm so glad I'm not going. I just knew it was the right thing to do, drop out for you."

My suspicions are confirmed that she did in fact pull out for me. I'm filled with love for her, the friendship type of course. Iqbal wanders over now, my other half to this job. His hands rest in his trouser pockets and he's wearing a self-conscious smirk.

"Hi Lizzy." He greets her then turns to me. "Looking forward to it Jodie?"

"Yes! Are you?"

"Yes definitely!" He agrees. "It's an opportunity. Isn't it, Lizzy? We're always learning."

She agrees seriously with a nod and flashes me a smile when I catch her eye.

"Got to dash." She tells us. "Have fun won't you!"

"And you! Message me, let me know how it goes!"

"I will. See you soon." She disappears and Iqbal raises his eyebrows, stuck for anything else to say. Before he can conjure up an awkward statement or question I divulge.

"Lizzy has met someone. She's seeing them tonight, I hope it goes well."

"Yes, yes, that's nice. A nice fellow is what you all need."

A nice *female*! I decide to not enlighten him right now. He's just referred to us as a collective group that *needs* a *nice* man. We're not on the same wave length, at all.

I *want* the man who is standing not far from us chatting to Jessie and Reuben. I don't know if he can be classed as a *nice* man. Nice men don't cheat do they? But this is wholly circumstantial, everything will be different in a few days.

"Can't wait to see the place." Eric sidles up to us now too. I've barely spoken to him since Leila ended things, much to her disappointment. She says she isn't bothered but I know she regularly checks his Facebook for an appearance of the other girl. Perhaps our forced proximity over the next few days will shed some light on his circumstances.

Would I want to know in her position? I can't say I've been bothered over Aaron. He could've moved another girl to Spain by now and I honestly wouldn't care. As for Ashley I'm privy to his abundance of other women every time I go onto my newsfeed, I don't need to stalk him. And Troy, well I know about his other girl don't I.

"Final toilet visit!" Del calls clapping his hands above the clamour. "Leaving in five!"

***

I ride in the mini bus, along with Sean and five of the boys. Troy drives. We listen to CD's, play crappy games, look at phones, read books and eventually we're arriving!

It is almost the middle of winter and although it's cold, it is dry. We pile out of the van, no sign of the others yet. The large, stately house looks enchanting under the blanket of white sky, surrounded with dark green lawns and foliage. A man comes bounding from the front door.

"Hello! Welcome! You must be the Belfry clan. I'm Mick." He extends a hand to Troy.

"Hi, I'm Troy." He introduces himself and Sean scuttles to his side immediately proffering his own hand.

"I'm Sean." I hear him saying but I'm distracted by breaking up a squabble between David and Brett. They might have worked their little butts off for a place on this trip, but it won't be plain sailing. I hope Mick has been warned.

"Hi." I beam at him widely when I get to give his hand a shake.

"Let's get you settled in. I'll give you the tour?"

"We'll take the tour." Troy indicates to us. "Sean, you walk the lads around the grounds, let them stretch their legs."

"Why can't you?" Sean argues childishly and I cringe inwardly. Troy is being bold, playing Top Dog. He wants us to check out the set-up, Sean possibly suspects it.

Mick might have been told about the nature of the children but what about the staff!

"We don't have the bedroom lists saying who's sleeping where." Troy tells Sean in impatient explanation. "And you can scope out a suitable smoking area for Jon and Mo. Let's have it sussed before the others get here, hmm?"

Sean, who has been making a considerable effort with SLT recently, relents. He has no choice and I pick up on the undertone from Troy. *Let's have it sussed.*

Just like he predicted, the lads have already begun working fidgety legs and are virtually disappearing into the undergrowth. Sean follows after them, rounding them up.

"The boundary is clear, there's a fence. Go and explore!" Mick calls before looking at us. "Shall we?"

We're about twenty minutes from the centre of London and yet I feel like we're off the grid. I try to hear any sounds which suggest the capital city is so close by but I only hear excited, delighted yelps from behind us, the crunching of gravel under our walking feet and my heart drilling in my ears.

"There's a play-gym down there." Mick is explaining. "Goats and chickens. They'll be uncovering it all. Boys, they should be allowed to be wild."

I know he doesn't mean it in a sexist way, I'm glad for his mindset because who knows what the next few nights might bring! Boys, they should be wild. I chance a look at Troy and he smirks.

Inside, it is clear the house is designed to accommodate large groups like us. Aside from the private quarters where Mick will be sleeping, downstairs there is an oblong prep kitchen, a large room with a long, heavy dining table and wooden chairs. And a huge living room area, an array of mismatched fusty sofas lining the walls and an old, bulky TV in one corner.

Upstairs we pace back and forth making note of the layout. There are three large dorms with three bunkbeds in each. Five smaller bedrooms are scattered between the dorms. Two only have space for a single bed and a chest of drawers. These are side by side, right in the middle of the corridor.

I can't look at Troy. There's no way we can risk trying to wangle these rooms. And if we did, the temptation to visit each other could land us in seriously hot water. Perhaps the best thing would be to place ourselves at opposite ends of the corridor.

We did it outside before and we can do it outside again!

"Hello?" Iqbal's voice is unmistakeable when it carries up the main set of stairs.

"Hello!" Mick leaps to attention and ambles away.

"Well, he seems nice." I break the silence but the air between us has intensified. We're surrounded by all of these beds. The intention and frustration is rich.

"Come on, let's explore outside." I suggest and smirk, letting my eyes hang onto his. We can't stay up here, as much as I long to. We might as well be having a quickie if we're going to loiter in the bedroom quarters!

Downstairs is now full of life. Everyone has arrived and bodies mingle in and out of rooms and doors.

"Have a good look around!" Mick is encouraging. "I do have some rules to go through but get it out of your system first!"

I wish we could get it out of our systems!

"Shall we?" I point to the front door. Brett comes galloping through, his cheeks flushed with the cold and exhilaration.

"Jodie, have you seen, there's a goat! Come on, let me show you!"

As is often the case, Troy and I rarely get time to be completely alone. We're both popular amongst the students and wherever we are we often have a circle of kids around us. By the time we've looked at the goat and chickens Jessie, Zane and Paul have joined us too.

"Do you think they still lay eggs even though it's so cold?" "Do you think the eggs freeze, Troy?" "How come a goat has got horns?" "Jodie, watch me on the monkey bars!" "Have you been to London before?" 'Are you scared of the dark?" "Can you do this? Troy! Jodie!"

The talk is continual, and we do our best to keep up with them. It makes a change from the confines of breakfast club and their excited chatter is cute. Hearing them exclaim our names over and over makes me giggle.

"I think Lacey might have been right." I murmur when Troy comes to my side. "We must be bloody mad!"

"It's nice though isn't it seeing them when they're so happy."

I grin up at him. We're like proud parents, watching over our brood as they develop and grow. I've felt it for a while now; our involvement, bringing up children together, it only intensifies our connection.

"Boys!" Del is yelling through cupped hands from the kitchen side door. "And Jodie!"

"Come on lads." I tell them. "I bet we're getting the welcome chat."

The huge living space is homely now it's crowded with bodies. We're squished side-by-side on the settees, some sit on the floor and Mick runs through a list of house rules. The atmosphere is buzzing but respectful, it's nice.

"Nick, Mo. You're going to be head of the two rooms." Del has taken over from Mick's initial instructions and he removes himself with a wave. "Nick, you're in dorm one with…"

He lists who is sleeping where and they begin collecting their bags before dashing off to claim their beds ready for later. The third dorm will be used only if it is needed.

"Now guys, our rooms." It's the moment of truth. We begin to crowd together around the annotated plan.

"I think Jodie would be better in this room." Iqbal is already pointing at his name. "I'd be better where she is, in case the lads are up in the night."

I inwardly curse him when I see Del had in fact allocated me and Troy the single rooms, side-by-side. We're powerless to breathe a word as he scribbles the change because Iqbal is right. I would be better at the end of the corridor and out of the way. Has he suggested it on purpose or just because it makes sense? I'm glad, I tell myself, not worth the risk.

***

"Maybe we could do it in there." I murmur to Troy, slyly nodding at the playhouse and he grins in response. Dinner is out of the way. The boys have been given free-time and even though it is cold and dark, the garden is partially floodlit and occupied by some as we watch on. The Christmas Fayre this afternoon was awesome and completely got me in the spirit. I know the lads are tired though and bedroom curfew isn't far off.

I stem my shivering. I'm loving being in Troy's company, at this late hour on a Monday, even if I am freezing my tits off.

"I'm hoping we'll get the chance later." He whispers and using the shadows for cover traces the curve of my bum cheeks. This time I do shudder but it has nothing to do with the cold.

"We've got to be careful, Troy." I hiss and look around for Sean. He's been lurking on and off, so has Iqbal.

"We will, we will." He soothes. Talking this openly makes my skin crawl with the possibility. This morning seems so removed from all of this. Everything is strange and familiar all at once.

"Jodie? Troy?" Eric rounds the corner. "I'm gunna have a crafty fag, do you want to join me?"

Cunningly I ask him for one, to save for later. It'll be the perfect excuse for me and Troy to get out! I tuck it into my pocket and give Troy a wicked look, knowing he'll understand.

"You really do know what you're doing don't you." He murmurs when Eric's gone again.

"What's that supposed to mean?" I snap thinking about the art of cheating. No, I'm making up the rules as I go along!

"Ten minutes lads. Then we're going in, and it'll be time to hit the sack." He shouts out to our group instead of answering me. I rage, suddenly uncomfortably hot inside my coat.

"What do you mean Troy? You did this before, tried to make out I'm used to doing this or something." I hiss. "I'm not, you know! This is new to me too, against everything I thought I believed in."

"Keep your knickers on." He replies easily. "Or rather, don't."

His attempt to lighten things annoys me. It's his remarks that keep making me feel this way.

"Tell me anyway, how do you know about that little alleyway you took me to on our night out?" I turn to him haughtily, waiting for an answer.

"I photographed it. For my degree. There are a lot of derelict warehouses down there. The topic was 'Damaged'."

It's a candid explanation and I instantly feel like an idiot for my accusatory question. I will be left damaged at this rate. Abandoned, left to rot and only attracting pity.

Except Troy's expression tells me I'm being melodramatic.

"Come on, it's time we went in. Roll on midnight." He winks.

We round up the boys and I think there's no way there'll be asleep by midnight. Six boys in each room will take hours to settle, hence the nine o'clock bedroom curfew. They can chat quietly, read a book or play on a device if they have one, as long as they're lying in bed.

***

Pins and needles are playing havoc with my feet and legs and I manoeuvre myself once again. Iqbal pauses in his story of how he and his wife met. I've heard it before but never in such elaborate detail. He resumes again when I'm still. We're sitting at the top of the stairs on the landing. We've been stationed here virtually since Troy and I returned to the main house, over an hour ago.

I try to concentrate on Iqbal but my mind wanders to where Troy's sitting downstairs with the others. When will Del and Eric come and take over?

"You know she wasn't my first true love." Iqbal is saying, and my ears prick slightly. He's always portrayed his life as simply and perfectly falling into place. Something I haven't found in my own quest. "Beth, she was my first love."

Now my attention is snagged. I know it's a common enough name but there's something about the way he says it.

"Yep, Troy pipped me to the post with that one." He sighs and I'm glued to his face. "He's, well, he's Troy, you seem to like him enough, you know what I mean. I didn't stand a chance, he made up a nickname for me…"

Iqbal's strangely possessive behaviour makes sense now. He's pouring his heart out and I had no inkling of this. *Eyeball*, I knew that part all along. Poor geeky, Iggy the Eyeball!

"Here I am telling you all about me!" He crosses his hands in his lap. "How about you? What do you want out of life Jodie?"

It is a very open question and I don't feel I can portray any of my shady affairs as potential life-partners so I safely stick with work.

"I don't want to have to worry about money. You know, enough to pay my bills. And enjoy myself. I want to travel the world!" I'm not sure he'll understand any of my desires but he nods thoughtfully.

"Jodie, you have to think, you could earn three times what you do now, and your bills could be three times higher- a bigger house, a nicer car, more luxurious food or buying new clothes… you'll still have the same amount left over. Do you see what I mean? Money is only relative to your outgoings." He looks at me wistfully and I expect he's enjoying himself. My work-dad, he's alright really.

"You have to decide how much you want to earn in comparison to how much you actually work." He continues.

"Like a lot of money for as little work as possible?" I giggle provoking a smile from his serious expression.

"Exactly. Most people want that! So what could you do? Start a business, work your way up into a position of power and have minions doing the legwork- but you'd still have a fair amount of responsibility."

"I could incorporate the things I want, into my work. Like travelling." I tell him. He has got me thinking, I appreciate the input this time.

"Aha! You've got it Jodes." He taps his temple and smiles. I realise he has both Beth and my own best interests at heart.

"Do what you love, love what you do." He says profoundly.

There's a stomping from the stairs and Del appears at the top, Eric not far behind him. He sticks his thumbs up hopefully and we return it. So far so good!

***

"You can go to bed now if you want guys." Del tells Iqbal, Eric and me at midnight. Troy is on landing duty with Sean. The lads have been really well behaved and I stretch now, grateful. We've got our alarms set for six-thirty in the morning and today has felt long.

There are four bathrooms upstairs and enclosed in the one closest to my room I brush my teeth and check my phone.

1am, meet downstairs?

The message from Troy makes my heart hammer. I'm a rebel, I accept that, and falling prey to this feeling has led to some of my greatest accomplishments but also some of my worst. I clear my mind, knowing already what the voices will warn and I let them do their job in convincing me.

Too risky. Speak tomo x

I hit send on the reply and lock myself in my bedroom before letting out a shaky breath. How I'd love to go through with it. Possibly before my chat with Iqbal I would have. Did I view Troy slightly differently this evening when we went back down to the living room?

He's lucky to have Beth. That's how Iqbal sees it. He's lucky to have me too! Does he deserve either of us?

Lindzi Mayann

Tuesday Visits

I awake with a start. My room is still pitch black and I grope for my phone noticing the flashing light, indicating I have a message.

Unlock your door

It's Troy, sent only moments ago. Did this jolt me out of my dreams? They were of him anyway. Vivid and sexual, they aren't unusual, they're becoming frequent. I can still feel his body heavy against mine. I am definitely alone though and my body craves for contact. Can we really risk this? It's quarter past five.

Done

I clamber soundlessly back into bed and hold my breath waiting for any signs of movement. It's so dark in here, I think I'm imagining the door as it opens and stealthily a black outline is creeping inside.

"Troy?" I barely breathe. He steps closer and my eyes, already adjusting, pick out his features. He raises a finger to his lips, points to the bed. I lie down, and he lies beside me, almost as quietly as the house itself.

Breathing unsteadily, hearts clattering against our ribs we barely move a muscle and just relish in being close. An eternity seems to pass in what can only be ten minutes. We do nothing but hug and breathe.

Troy doesn't say he's going, he just does. It's only now I can truly enjoy what just happened. Now I know we've got away with it. I'm hornier than ever before. How wrong is to masturbate in a house full of students and work colleagues?

The lurid thought is enough to put me off and I grin to myself in the dark. For now, I drift back to sleep imagining the morning cuddle was not an irregular one-off.

When I wake up at the sound my alarm I feel exhausted. The visit from Troy is hazy and I have to check my messages to convince myself it really happened. I can hear muffled sounds from the other rooms and I lie back down, dozing and imagining I'm part of some huge, unconventional family.

Eventually somebody bangs on my door as they pass making me jump. Then I hear Del calling along the hallway. "Wakey wakey rise and shine!"

Sleepily I drag myself from the bed. Today we're visiting the Dungeons and thinking about what could be in store at the attraction, as well as with Troy, stirs at my insides.

***

Today has barely given me time to stop and think. Lizzy text to say things went really well on her date and they're seeing each other again this week. But it'll have to wait until I'm back to discuss the gory details with her!

The dungeons were amazing. Then it was lunch and then the cinema. We've had our dinner now and I could honestly nod off.

The boys have behaved well on the whole but their general neediness is exhausting. It has been a huge eye opener into the day-to-day life of parenthood. I resolve to give Cat an even tighter squeeze than usual when I next see her. What a job she's doing! I'm not sure I ever want kids after this experience! And we still have another full day to go tomorrow.

This evening, Troy and I grab what time we can to playfully chat and flirt but before I know it Del is calling the students to their dorms and it's time to take turns sitting guard.

I'm paired with Iqbal again and I prepare for stiff limbs as we take a seat. He is easy enough to talk to. Actually, last night he gave me serious considerations regarding my future career and my future potential with Troy! And I politely stifle my yawns as the time slowly ticks past.

Tonight, meet downstairs at 1am?

Troy's message pings through before we've even been dismissed for bed. We're downstairs, he's sitting opposite me and beside Sean. Iqbal is next to me and I'm careful not to raise my eyes and give the game away.

I will be asleep as soon as head touches pillow!

I reply honestly. How can he not be feeling the same? Or is the very thought of bending me over the kitchen table enough to keep him up! I wish I could say the same but for neither love nor money will I be able to keep my eyes open tonight. As for this morning's visit, I just don't want to risk it again.

No more visits! I still have the fag to smoke. We'll try and sneak out tomorrow

I send the second message resolutely.

It's so hard to control myself around you

The message makes me prickle excitedly. Knowing he finds me so irresistible is such a turn-on! But I must remain level-headed. This trip is not about us having a mini-break, as much as we might pretend it's that way.

I climb into bed and try to ignore the resounding rebel's voice telling me I must take the opportunity. I must say yes! It's a stark contrast to yesterday when I told myself I could lose my job and therefore my flat! I stare at my phone from where I lay, arguments rife in my mind but for better or worse I'm asleep in moments.

Smoke and Mirrors

Wednesday morning begins without an early message from Troy to tempt me. Perhaps he listened to sense or maybe he slept as heavily as I did and missed his cue. Other than this, the day follows much the same pattern as yesterday. Breakfast, playtime, museum, lunch, playtime except this evening we're watching a selection of Christmas lights being switched on.

We have an earlier dinner and then set out in our allocated vehicles. Once parked up, we join the bustling wide street on foot which is packed with bodies swathed in woollies and white clouds formed from hot billowing breath. We all have three kids each to keep an eye on meaning our responsibility overlaps and therefore lessening the risk of losing a child.

The fear is real and I can barely enjoy the festivities for scanning hats and heads, making sure *all* the students are present and correct.

"Tonight is the night." Troy whispers in my ear standing closely behind me as we wait for the main event. Amongst the crowds it is easy for him to rub up against me without arousing suspicion. Other things are aroused though. I can feel my nipples as hard as bullets in anticipation for the real main event.

"Jodie, can we have a hot chocolate?" David eyes the stall keenly.

"We've got hot chocolate for when we're back." Del overhears and divulges with a grin delighting him. I smile at the gleeful kids thinking of Troy standing right behind me; my own hot chocolate for when we get back.

We've all gotten closer, staff team and students alike, and I bask in the random family-feeling glow of being around them all. I can't believe it's the last night already, it's flown by! On the other hand it seems like we've been here forever. I'm just getting accustomed to having Troy around so much and soon he will be snatched away. I'm disappointed. And almost surprised we haven't snuck in a cheeky bang already, although he's made it clear nothing will stop him later on.

"Ten, nine, eight…" The countdown begins, and the vivacious crowd soon drowns out the speaker as they yell the numbers. "Three, two, one!"

Lights above, around and beyond us flare into life, cheers rise into the night and *I Wish It Could Be Christmas Every Day* begins to play. I watch our students; their eyes are wide as buttons and reflect the twinkling bulbs surrounding us. Troy gives my hand a squeeze and I swell with festive glee.

Last Christmas I was still with Dane, a waitress and living at home. This year I'm stood in the middle of London, I'm a teaching assistant and (secretly) holding hands with a gorgeous (taken) man. It's an unbelievable difference.

As the crowds begin to disperse we push our way through and back towards the parking lot. The kids chatter animatedly all the way home.

"Do you think there'll be asleep by midnight tonight?" Sean states doubtfully. I smile and shrug, it's Christmas, let them be merry!

***

"I've cleared it with Del." Troy says by way of explanation as he hurries me out of the side door and into the grounds.

My heart begins to race and blood rushes to my cheeks making my face feel clammy against the icy air.

"But where do we go? What if Sean comes out?" I titter worriedly.

"He can't, if we're having a break, they're all needed in there. We'll go over there, in the trees." His voice is breathy, I can tell he's excited and white-hot prickles respond, gathering rapidly in my knickers.

I know there are oppositions to be made, reasons I shouldn't do it but really I'm not thinking straight, with my head or my heart. Some other body part is doing the thinking for me, I feel like a man!

We come to a halt in the thicket of trees. We're still close enough to the house that light from its huge windows licks the ground near to us but we're safely hidden in the black shadows. I look up at him, ready to feel those warm, soft lips upon mine once again. It's been so long!

"Turn around." He mutters. I suppose there isn't the time to be messing about. He bends me over and begins rubbing erratically at my crotch through my jogging bottoms whilst grinding himself into my bum. He is rock hard already. We're both thrilled by the absolute naughtiness of it, which is a good job because his clitoral stimulation isn't up to much.

"Pull them down." He gasps and I do so. He's inside of me, thrusting powerfully and I'm doing my best not to moan out loud with sheer relief.

It's over in barely the time it would take me to smoke a cigarette. I feel as light-headed as if I have!

"Shall I light the fag so we smell of it?" I ask and my voice sounds raspy. Even Troy who is usually unflappable is breathing deeply trying to steady himself. He nods, and I take it from my pocket then remember neither me nor Troy smoke regularly.

"Have you got a lighter?"

"No." He answers and shrugs. "Ah well. We've had what we came for!"

I giggle in agreement feeling bashful suddenly but there's no time for lingering eye contact now. It's an alternative way for a happy ever after to begin!

Inside I tear off my coat in response to the contrast in temperature. I still have the actual hot chocolate to finish drinking but I'm burning up after being with Troy, the stickiness between my legs acts as a reminder and adds to my flush.

Sean saunters over to me as soon as I take a seat amongst the lads playing Connect 4. He plonks himself beside me and I eye him warily.

"Hi." He says.

"Hi." I respond and he makes a point of sniffing the air.

"You don't smell of smoke Jodie, I thought you and Troy went for a fag."

I hesitate because, do I pretend we did have one, or say we hadn't got a lighter? We didn't sort a cover up for this time!

I shrug and smile easily. "Well."

It's my answer, either or. Smoke and mirrors.

I see the glint in his eyes telling me he knows. Or at least *thinks* he knows. Most of the staff at Belfry suspects something is going on between us, just like Gilbert and Julie's age-gap affair, and they can't prove it.

Drinks finished, mugs washed up and the lads have been given thirty extra minutes free time (mainly for them to drain their bladder) and I quickly tell Troy about Sean.

"Why didn't you say we didn't have a lighter?" He's bothered this time.

"Because I didn't know if that's what you'd say!"

"Well, it's what happened!" He harrumphs.

"And then he'd have wondered why we didn't come in to get one from Eric or something! What were we doing outside for so long, hmm?" I'm smarting at his tone.

"I suppose." He fidgets frustrated. "Just forget it now anyway."

Easy to say! I can't forget the romp; my pants are uncomfortably glued to my undercarriage and my groin aches tellingly. I certainly can't forget the look Sean gave me, a mixture of contempt and triumph. And as for Troy and his attitude. It plays on my mind but I bite my lip.

For the final time Del calls the boys and we usher them to their dorms. It is much later than the usual, gone half past ten.

"I'll sit on the landing tonight, you lot chill downstairs. They've been so much better than I expected!" Del says pleased.

Better behaved than some of your staff team, I think wryly.

"I'll keep you company." Iqbal offers nobly. Troy catches my eye and I know what he's thinking but I feel protective over my school-dad. He's just trying to do a good job, in work and at life. Plus, I'm still annoyed about Troy's manner with me before.

"I could do with a couple of days off after this!" Eric announces. We all mumble and agree. I haven't managed to pick up on anything about his relationship status to feedback to Leila. I can't just ask him outright. It'll look like she's bothered. Which she is, but I don't want him to think so.

We traipse into the living room together in amicable silence and shared tiredness, perhaps all lost in our own thoughts.

***

"Time for bed you guys." Iqbal appears in the living room doorway looking drowsy and I notice Eric has dropped off. I couldn't have been far from it and I wearily take to my feet, stretching.

"Night Jodes." Troy calls.

"Night Jodes." Sean mimics.

"Night night everyone." My cheeks burn as I leave the room and head for bed.

Tomorrow we'll be heading back to school, virtually straight after breakfast. Mick has been a star throughout; turning a blind eye to bad language and making jokes when they've been unintentionally rude. And that's just the staff! The house is charming despite being rundown, and I've racked up so many memories from being here, visiting attractions across London. I'll be sorry to leave for many reasons.

Lying in bed, every bone in my body aches. Sleep evades my dry eyes and when I close them I'm greeted with image after image of Troy. What have I learned from all of this? That I can protect myself from STDs but not the onslaught of feelings?

How could I have thought having sexual relations with Troy wouldn't provoke me to want to take action? Single life *could* be so simple. Taken life could be blissful.

But there has been no talk of ditching Beth. Sean put the heebie-jeebies on us both today. And Iqbal's revelation really bought home the reality of what we're actually doing. She's a real girl, just like me with hopes and dreams, insecurities and desires… She isn't my friend though, she isn't *my* responsibility. It still makes me feel sick and I toss and turn for what feels like hours before finally dropping off.

Come Clean

Thursday's journey home is subdued. Assumedly, we're all completely drained but my mood is gloomy for more reasons than just fatigue. Music plays quietly and I'm glad nobody, for once, is trying to make conversation with me. I'm able to get lost in thought.

I no longer feel so guilty about what Troy and I did last night, again. Instead I'm more gutted that it isn't a permanent thing, again. I'm surely closer to snagging him for good. Is it what I want? Regardless of the desired outcome, I've induced more heartache for myself by indulging, again.

We have one week left of term and then it is two weeks off. I should be elated for the break; this term has been difficult. But all I can think is- it's another fortnight without him.

I promised myself everything would be different after the trip. I thought Troy would be wooed by now and convinced to break things off with Beth. The more I think about it the more I have to wonder if he is just using me.

Why tell me any different? He's made an effort to convince me he has true feelings. It just can't be empty words when I can feel it for myself. But if actions speak louder than words and he didn't even kiss me last night, isn't that the rule with hookers? No kissing, purely sex?

We've got the Christmas outing a week tomorrow. A new deadline! How many times can I keep doing this? It's only fair he should go back to his missus tonight and realise that it's me he's missing really. He might come clean to her, guilt might override him! I just have to give him time. Then if it comes to it, I don't want to think about that ending, I'll have to wait and see.

***

"Jodie!" Leila calls out gleefully when she finds me sitting in the living room that evening. Since I got back I've not even unpacked, just sat and stared into space. "Are you ok? Did you have fun?"

"It was awesome babe thanks. I'm just so tired! I can't move!"

"Good job I grabbed some pizzas from the shops. I'll sort you dinner deary."

I grin at her gratefully.

"Do you want a glass of wine?" She offers smiling wickedly.

"Now this is a welcome home!" I joke. "I'll have one but I honestly think I'll be in bed by eight!"

"It's fine, I can't imagine being tied to twelve kids for four days. I don't know how you do your job as it is Jodes." She rattles on then stops abruptly and I look up to find her giving me a beady stare. "What happened with Troy?"

I already told her about the morning visit and the smirk creeping onto my face gives away there's more. I tell her it all, including the parts about Iqbal and Beth and Sean and his comments.

She lets out a low whistle. Amidst the tales I've also let slip my misgivings about the whole situation.

"I think this all started out as a bit of fun. A challenge even! And now you've got yourself in a bit too deep." She theorises, and I wish she wasn't right.

"So what do I do?" I cry, proverbial white flag waving.

"It's up to you what you do hun. You love him don't you? So come clean about your feelings, give him an ultimatum! Or if it's causing you so much pain walk away." She adds shrugging.

"I work with him, that's what's made walking away hard already." I mumble moodily. She makes it sound so easy and I know she's been secretly pining after Eric.

"Jodie, you were so happy when you got this job. Remember, a complete fresh start! You've come so far. Maybe Troy is a distraction you don't need right now."

My sulk crumbles and I feel humbled by her honesty. I can't help but recognise it mirrors Iqbal's advice all along- and he doesn't know the half of it. The job itself did mean everything back then. It still does.

***

"Thanks for everything Leila." I tell her rising to my feet. "Dinner, wine and listening to me moan! At this rate I'll need a new job just so I can afford to pay you back for all these treats."

"Well hopefully you'll get a promotion. Julie is pleased with you never mind Lizzy and Iqbal. You are smashing it. Even if this Troy thing has knocked you back a bit."

I think her conclusion over. Has it knocked me back? Because up until now I thought it was the way forward.

"I'm going to bed hun. I'll see you tomorrow when hopefully I'll feel more human!"

"Erm, before you go, did you talk to Eric? About anything, you know, normal conversation…"

"Sorry babe, I don't know if he's with that girl." There's no point beating around the bush, she knows I understand what she's getting at. "We were so busy, it didn't come up."

"It's fine, it's fine!" She beams hollowly.

"You can ask him yourself next week can't you?" I refer to the upcoming Christmas outing but still feel lame for not finding out for her. I probably could have but I was so wrapped up in Troy and his attention. "I'll try and find out for you before then."

"It's fine." She repeats, her hopefulness leaking through and I smile at her sympathetically.

"Night babe."

I head to my room determined to dwell no further on any love related business. One more day working and then it's the weekend. I'm looking forward to catching up with Lizzy and the girls in the unit. I've actually had enough of boys for this week!

An As Always Saturday

"Hey!" Ashley greets me at the door, standing to one side, letting me enter. I hand the bottle of wine to him and pass by to the living room where I flop onto the sofa. It's inviting and warm as always, the candles are lit, and music plays from the TV.

"How you been?" He asks when he passes me a filled glass.

"I've been on a school trip this week. An over-nighter!" I roll my eyes and take a glug. "It was brilliant, but sooo tiring! I've still not caught up."

"Well I hope you don't plan on getting much sleep tonight." He jibes and strokes my wrist. I smile at him from under my lashes but we both know it'll only be the once, it always is.

"So how have you been?" I return the question. "Feels like ages since last time."

"I know, I thought you'd forgotten about me." He grins gorgeously and I think, *almost*! After spending Friday running from Troy, Ashley's timing of messaging today fell perfectly. I settle down to enjoy an as always, satisfying evening.

***

"I've missed you." Ashley is telling me as he nibbles at my neck and collarbone.

"Mmmm, you too." I float on the cloud of pleasure he's summoning and run my fingertips across his broad back. We're naked, on his bed and now his mouth continues downward, snaking kisses around my nipples and they throb in delight. This is more like it, not just some crafty fumble in the woods!

I watch his head as it moves over my stomach, his lips brushing my skin, working right the way into my pelvis and along the inside of my thighs. His fingers begin sliding in and out of me, I'm hot and wet down there and I groan when his thumb tweaks my clit.

"Grab my cock Jodie." He whispers and I do as he asks gladly gripping the thick girth. The foreplay seems to last for an eternity. He doesn't stop even after my body writhes and spasms when I can no longer fight the delicious sensations. But now, finally, I cry out as he pushes himself inside.

As always Ashley doesn't last long and as always, he makes a form of apology. I get myself comfortable. I always sleep on this side when I'm here. I feel the most relaxed I have in a long time and take advantage of the huge arms enveloping me from behind.

As always Ashley has been a gentleman and made me feel right at home. He surely can't entertain *all* of the girls who actively engage with him on Facebook. I'm of higher ranking than a majority of them. It's just the fix I needed.

Troy wetted my appetite Thursday. Ashley has fulfilled the craving. Maybe, just maybe, I can keep my legs together on the night out next week!

Blog Off Sunday

As promised I squeeze Cat hard enough for her to giggle and squirm.

"Woah! What was that for, I've missed you too but you know, don't break my ribs." She guides me across the threshold into her warm, lively house. "So how was it?"

Dan and Es are individually running riot, there's no point going into specific details of the trip now.

"Yeah it was great!" I smile. "Loved it, saw loads of stuff."

"Getting ready for Christmas?" She asks, kettle loaded and on. "You only have a week left and it's the holidays! Yay, I love this time of year!"

"Yay!" I mirror her shimmy and smile at Dan as he waddles over to show me a dinosaur. "I bet you're excited for Santa aren't you?"

He answers me with a fumble of sounds. I pick out 'toy', 'hero' and 'play', presumably he's telling me his Christmas list and I nod along interestedly.

"So, are you ready for it?" I ask Cat as she hands me a mug, Dan is off again playing, and we sit side by side at the table. She tuts.

"Jodie, I was ready for it by the end of November. We've been stashing food at Kyle's mum's for weeks, out of Es' reach! All the presents are bought *and* wrapped."

I shake my head in amusement. I shouldn't have expected anything less. I've still not even finished buying gifts. Leila and I are having Christmas dinner together at Marshamonvilla, but we've purchased nothing toward it so far.

"I finally looked at all the stuff you printed off for me." She says. "It's really good, Jodes. Thanks."

I grin, feeling appeased that my use of school resources has gone to a worthier cause this time. "Yay good! But not only that, guess what, whilst I was doing the research about Es it made me think about one of our students."

I go on to tell her about Bonnie and her whimsical ways and how I noticed similarities in the way she presents to what I'd been reading online. I showed Lizzy my findings before the trip and on Friday she gave me the news her social worker is putting her forward for some assessments. Perhaps she is on the spectrum, perhaps there are sensory issues at play.

"Well done Jodie! That is so cool. You sound so professional!" Cat remarks when I'm done explaining.

"I wouldn't have been looking if it wasn't for you Cat, and Esmay. Look how you've already helped someone. And you weren't even trying."

She gives me a wary smile, knowing perhaps I am steering the conversation toward blog related talk.

"So I was-"

"No, Jodie, you must put me out my misery and tell me all the details on Troy! You minx, what actually happened then?"

I allow the swerve ball because I do need her genuine opinion despite suspecting her honesty will be uncomfortable.

***

"You need to tell him how you feel." Cat is definitive and in agreement with Leila and although I'd prefer this to walking away I can't help but argue.

"He knows how I feel already." Perhaps I'm scared of the outcome and she eyes me sternly, sensing my reluctance.

"So can you really just put a stopper on it then and walk away?"

She's calling my bluff, there's no point pretending that I can. We both know.

"No." I admit. "But I feel like it's the right choice."

"Right for who, him? This Beth girl who you don't even know? Come on, it's clear this is killing you. It's not fun for you anymore!"

She's right and it's all my own fault. I look at her glumly.

"Have it out with him. And anyway, what have you got to lose, there's Ashley still and that Luca! You're always finding yourself surrounded by fit men, if it's not meant to be with Troy someone else will come along."

"I don't want someone else to come along." I moan.

"Then you have be honest with him don't you?" She has me in her snare, there's no other way out. "You're being fair to yourself Jodes, else you'll never really know. And some men just need a good kick up the arse!"

She shrieks with laughter and thumbs in the direction of the living room. I nod, smiling, trying to imagine me and Troy like Cat and Kyle with two kids and a house. Is it what I want? Or is it because I *can't* have him? *A challenge* as Leila described it and I've taken a step too far.

"So anyway…" I try once again and approach the idea of starting a blog, partly to distract us from the Troy plan but also spurred on after the Bonnie related positivity. And although Cat listens quietly to my ideas, it's clear her stance hasn't altered, yet.

Blog off Jodie, for now.

"It's your work's night out Friday isn't it? I think you should tell Troy how you feel then." Cat gives me a hug at the door and shivers.

"Bloody hell it's cold! And if he won't break it off for you, he isn't worth it." She adds.

"Hmm, yeah." I nod. "I'll try and see you before then anyway."

"Yeah don't worry, I know you're a busy girl." She blows me a kiss and disappears back inside. I march home, she's right it is freezing.

***

Once warm and comfortable I mull over the collective advice I've gathered on Troy. Lizzy was sure it was worth the chance, so much so she pulled out of the trip to pave my way onto it. Leila and Cat favour the idea of being honest. The drawback is his answer might not be what I want after all.

Just five days to go. I should come clean. Then I can enter the festivities and New Year with or without Troy truly by my side. Cat is right, this thing with him left the 'fun' zone yonks ago and I missed all of the warning signs as I drifted perilously out of my depth.

I know one thing for sure, any outcome to this is going to be painful, but to who the most, is yet to be determined.

Admissions Monday

It's the final Monday meeting for the year and I feel all gooey and sentimental as Julie praises our efforts for the term. She highlights me and the others as doing an 'exceptional' job on the London trip and I also get a mention regarding the so-far success of the girls unit. I'm filled with pride and catch Lizzy's eye happily. I am sitting next to Troy and I'm feeling more positive about everything. He told me this morning he and Beth argued *all* weekend!

I'm certain it was a hint!

"Now, last thing for this meeting." Julie is addressing us in her clipped tone. "There will be some new staff plus changes next year. Most noticeably we're losing Claire."

There's a shocked intake of breath around the room and a unanimous 'ahhh'. There have been more random absences lately but I had no idea of this. I look at Gilbert, he's smirking and it makes my skin crawl.

"New staff!" Troy comments when we're dismissed.

"New meat for Julie!" I joke quietly, although I've been in her good books of late.

"It might be new meat for you." He replies and I bristle.

"Jealous?" I venture.

"Yes." He admits.

"So, pick me then." I take the abrupt opportunity. It's an earlier declaration to what I'd envisioned and we stare at one another both taken off guard. I am serious though and he can tell.

"Wifey don't-"

"Don't!" I stand and quickly check nobody is watching us. "I just can't keep doing this. Troy, you've got to decide once and for all. It's me or Beth. I want to know by the end of this week."

I walk away feeling like I've retaken the reigns. There's a huddle of people around Claire and I wonder why exactly she's leaving, how much of this is to do with Gilbert. Who will these new staff be? Whoever they are, I will never bang a workmate ever again despite of Troy's resentful dig. Unless it is Troy of course. What a mess.

But not now; I've delivered the line. We just have this week to manoeuvre. The regular timetable is only running for one more day, there are trips and Christmas themed activities lined up from Wednesday. The mayhem is welcome, it'll keep me busy and entertained for sure. On Friday there's a whole-school turkey dinner and we'll be exchanging Secret Santa presents amongst the staff. I've still got to buy mine, but I have the perfect idea for this person.

And then there's the Christmas night out. I've got it all to play for. Ho ho ho!

Lindzi Mayann

Why Not Wednesday

"Hey girls!" I greet Lizzy and the group when they arrive in the busy hall. I wouldn't usually see them on a Wednesday but I've been timetabled to support with these activities- and now it's their turn. I've been looking forward to them getting in here and seeing what's on offer for them this afternoon. I can't quite believe it myself!

Mollie's face lights up eagerly when she sees the sumo wrestler suits lying lifelessly on the mats and I beam at her childish excitement.

"Can we?" She begins before grabbing Jayde's hand. "Come on!"

"Oh fucking hell, really!" Jayde feigns embarrassment, I can tell she's secretly thrilled and we overlook her bad language. It's good to see her back to her brash self, following the photo incident. The picture stopped circulating fairly quickly and as fickle as teens are it is, thankfully, old news.

They prance off together and I smile, returning to Lizzy.

"So where's Eve?" I ask her.

"Come on Bon Bon, why don't you go on the bouncy castle with Holly? Lacey will go with you." She suggests to the remaining others.

I note her intention to gain us privacy immediately. Eve should be here and something has happened. I'm already sure I won't like it. Holly looks at Lizzy dubiously and Bonnie who is overwhelmed by the unusual commotion clings on to Lacey's hand.

"Can you please go together and watch Mollie and Jayde wrestle then?" Lizzy gives Holly and Lacey an imploring look, my suspicions are confirmed.

"Come on, let's go and watch." Holly says to Bonnie in her quiet voice. She knows it's something serious and is co-operating maturely. Panic rises within me for Eve, admiration for Holly's behaviour. Bonnie nods slowly, fear still etched onto her face. They amble away and I turn to Lizzy, bracing myself.

"Eve got taken into a home today. It all happened pretty quickly, an incident last night, the Police were there today, and the decision has been made to remove her whilst they're waiting for the custody trial."

I gasp and raise my hand to my mouth. The revelation is in stark contrast to the bright atmosphere.

"Oh no." I mutter. "Is she ok? What happened? Why were the Police called?"

"We hardly know any details. That's about the long and short of it. I think Julie, or somebody is going to visit before term is over Friday but we probably won't see her now until after Christmas."

"She's going to spend Christmas in a children's home?" I gasp. "Oh, poor Eve. I hope she's ok!"

"She'll be ok. She's a tough cookie." Lizzy says and we stand side-by-side, our eyes seeking out the girls who are present. Mollie and Jayde are wearing the sumo outfits and are belly bashing one another. Their smiles are large and genuine as are those of the students watching them. Holly and Bonnie laugh shyly from the side-lines. I think of Camden in a cell and Eve possibly surrounded by strangers right now. Is she scared?

My gut aches. News hits hard regularly here, we're told to keep our emotions out of it but it's not always that easy. I feel deeply, I can't help it, and I've formed unique, special bonds with a number of the kids. I can tell Lizzy is like me. She puts a hand on my elbow and we feel for Eve together.

Christmas music can be barely heard amid the screaming and giggling. My mind tortures me with images of Eve upset and alone. The light and the darkness co-exist in the vision before me.

Little year 7 Jay darts past me as if to illustrate the point. He has been reunited with his mum since he was taken into care. I don't know the ins and outs of his case, but I know he'd just begun to settle and recover and then his life changed again. Perhaps the upcoming festivities magnify the scenario. But should Eve be with her family when they place her in danger? I've noticed more often than not a child wants to be with their parent, no matter what the situation. That's what makes it even sadder.

"Try not to think about it." Lizzy rubs my shoulder. We smile at each other. "I know it's hard but we've got to trust in the systems."

I think of Cat, Esmay and Bonnie and the system responsible for their journey with autism. But then there are physical reminders of it working, running amok around us right now. This school is so special. I feel honoured to be a part of it and yet so useless in circumstances like now.

"I don't know. I just wish everyone got the help they deserved. It's like it's a random draw." I sigh.

"Like life." Lizzy shrugs. "We can't all be lucky."

I'm not sure I'd describe those as getting the help they need as lucky but I understand what she means. Life is not fair sometimes.

The day draws to a close and I wave off the girls. Today was just the beginning of a fun-packed end of term celebration. As a unit, and as a school, we've already grown together and there's still so much more to come. The absence of Eve was a bitter-sweet reminder of what we are achieving but also the limitations of it.

Troy is at the lockers as usual. Monday's words haven't been revisited, I wonder if he took me seriously after all.

"Good day?" He smirks and his frivolous tone scratches my nerves.

"Not really." I mumble feeling stupidly tearful.

"Why what's up?"

I blink rapidly before looking at him. His face is soft and concerned and it shreds my heart further.

"Eve has been taken into a children's home." I explain choking. "I have had a really good day actually, so it took me off guard. I don't even know what's actually happened and if she's ok."

I run my hands over my hair despairingly and he takes them pulling my arms around him and giving me a hug.

"Jodie, Jodie." He murmurs into my head. I enjoy the reassuring contact for a moment but then my senses return.

"Troy." I step away.

"Sorry." He looks around but there's nobody to worry over. "You just look so upset. You're cute when you're sad."

I shake my head feigning annoyance but can't help the smile pulling at my mouth.

"I'm cuter when I'm happy." I tell him still trying to sulk. He giggles and mimics me and I can't help but laugh at his ridiculous expression.

We walk to our cars together. I'm trying not to feel for Troy and it isn't easy. I'm trying to keep a lid on this whole Eve situation too, also a task in itself. I bid farewell and shut my car-door wishing it was so easy to lock out the emotions. Dwelling doesn't change things, I tell myself firmly and begin the journey home.

Leila is waiting for me, that thought alone cheers me up and I have some news of a different kind to tell her.

***

"He's single then. He's still single?" Leila's eyes are flicking around the room as if trying to catch her wayward thoughts and view them properly.

I nod giggling, happy, I can tell she's brimming with glee over the news if not a little overwhelmed. It was obvious she had been thinking about him all along.

"I overheard him talking to Lewis today." I clarify. "Turns out they only saw each other once and it just fizzled out."

"And he's definitely coming out Friday? Oh Jodes!" She squeezes her hands in front of her chest. "We need to make a serious plan of action. Me and Eric, you and Troy. We need wine."

"Oh, I'm not going there with Troy." I reply firmly and she eyes me sternly. Before she can press me I add. "Yes to the wine, and we can decide what you're going to wear to win Eric back!"

"Oh I'm not going back to Eric, not now." She tells me just as defiantly. "But yes to wine and sorting our outfits!"

I haven't actually told Leila I already gave Troy his ultimatum two days ago. Partly, I recognise, to save face in the event he tells me it's over. But then I may be going back on my word, *if* he makes his move.

"Cheers to not needing men!" Leila chinks my glass and I meet her eye knowing she is fibbing about Eric. Knowing also, she knows I am fibbing too!

I giggle before adding. "And drinking wine whenever we please!"

"Well why not?" She hoots. "It's Why Not Wednesday?"

I have to laugh at her logic. If we can give it a nickname, we'll drink to that!

"Why not Wednesday it is!"

***

"Fail to prepare, prepare to fail my dear." Leila chuckles. "That is definitely the outfit for you."

I think of all the plans that haven't, well, gone to plan so far but grin anyway. I've raided her wardrobe again and she has borrowed from mine in return.

"Cheers darling. You look fuckin' fabulous too!" I chink her glass. It is ten o'clock and we're standing in the kitchen in our heels and dresses with makeup-less faces, our hair lank, beaming at each other.

"Let's teach 'em a lesson!" Leila roars.

"Let's show 'em who's boss!" I yell. We part ways to change back into our lounge gear and resume in the living room. I suspect we've both agreed to our plans with genuine, alcohol-fuelled sincerity. And we're definitely both hiding our true feelings.

It is clear Leila pined over Eric after they split so abruptly. She'll go back there. Thinking about her ulterior motives allows me to forget about my own. Will Troy get rid of Beth for me? I can't get rid of the thought that he might just do that. Why wouldn't he? Why not Wednesday, wouldn't he?

I'm far more pissed than I'd like to be on a school night and I take myself to bed. Today proved that even amongst the jolliest of times wretched forces are still at work. Tomorrow and Friday are scheduled to be fun and action-packed and who knows what else.

I fall asleep and try not to focus too deeply on my happy ever after with Troy!

Friday Favours

I'm crying and trying to hide it, swallowing hard as I glance around the sea of happy, cherub faces. It feels very adulty to be overcome by children's bright smiles and laughter as they pull crackers and tuck into their dinners. I quickly realise however I'm not the only one 'with something in my eye'. Many of the staff are casually flicking their cheeks and blinking too much.

I expect it can't be a touch on what a parent feels for their offspring and that actually scares me. I look around the hall filled with rows of tables and everybody that can be here, is. Eve isn't far from my mind although we have had feedback that she is 'settled'. It will have to be enough, I have to accept it.

The students I have met have already come on such a journey. I feel privileged to be a part of it. The atmosphere is utterly electric, and it is doing well in fending off any negative incidents this term.

Spirits are high as the adults prance off to the staff room at the end of the day. The students are packed off and it's Secret Santa time!

I've taken part in the anonymous present game before at the restaurant, and when I picked Dom I couldn't resist buying him a pair of nipple tassels. I cannot wait to see the reaction when he opens them. I've been looking forward to it all day, it's far outweighed any excitement surrounding the gift I'll receive in return. Before now I've had edible underwear and a sex position book!

"Has everybody who took part got themselves a present?" Del asks cheerfully holding his squidgy package aloft.

"Yess!" We all call super enthusiastically.

"Right, on the count of three. Three, two, one!"

I have already fingered the stiff rectangle. I imagine the Annuals I used to receive a child as I tear off the paper. It's a thinly framed picture. I stare at the enhanced black and white photograph of worn buildings in varied disrepair. The nettles and thorns in the foreground are black and in menacingly sharp focus. The broken glass in the windows shimmers slightly. Roofs bow under an invisible pressure and the brickwork leans onto one another. Without the support of their neighbours, they'd fall down.

It's a breath-taking print and I look over at Troy who is waiting for me to do just that. *Damaged.* We both bought presents relating to that first night out. This is a picture from his Uni collection, it was taken at the alleyway we visited.

I give him a small smile. Is this a signal? He got me in Secret Santa, what are the odds on that! Will tonight he reveal he is single and ready to be all mine?

***

I feel so apprehensive about this evening, the gift earlier changes everything. We arrive at the venue, adorned with tinsel and towering trees covered in baubles, and we ourselves are done up to the nines.

"We're playing it cool, ok." Leila repeats. I nod, my mouth suddenly dry. I've shown her the picture and told her its relevance. She agrees it's a good sign but that I shouldn't make it easy for him.

Plan. Out. Of. Window. I know it already.

We're spotted immediately by Lizzy and she rushes over with her new girlfriend in tow for a round of introductions. Gem is friendly and pretty. They're 'film lesbians'- another of George's more crude terms springs to mind- meaning they're both fit. We then head to the bar together to stock up on drinks. It's a great start because we easily avoid Troy and Eric without looking like it's purposeful.

They linger and stare, blatantly waiting for an opportunity. Leila and I catch eyes and laugh loudly in the spotlight they're casting on us.

Julie and Gilbert are standing together. She keeps leaning her head on his shoulder in what I suppose should be a cutesy way but it's unsettling to watch. They're definitely 'out' now, unlike Troy and me. The crowd is larger than the half term gathering. People have made an extra effort with it being Christmas, even Pav is here but still no Iqbal.

I'm thankful even though I feel he is missing out. I know religious views play a role for him though, he's unswerving and I respect him for that. And I don't need his judgement tonight. Troy and Eric are making their move and I eye Leila as she squeals and giggles and I think, *play it cool* ay? Not that I can talk. Adrenalin is coursing through me.

"You honestly didn't fix it?" I repeat.

"Honestly! I never even usually take part."

I just had to check the Secret Santa was a genuine fluke. "Well I really like it. So thanks."

"Well I really like you. So I'm glad."

"Troy, this whole, whatever we are." I sigh. Now is the moment, has he, hasn't he, will he, won't he?

"Jodie. I love you." He whispers and I wonder if I've heard him correctly above the chaos of my mind exploding into a thousand pieces. It's what I've been waiting to hear since I clapped eyes on him and I can't believe I'm really hearing it now.

"I think I love you too." I tell him warily. "So what exactly are you saying about us in the long-term?"

He shrugs and my heart sinks.

"What needs to be said?" He deviates. "We love each other, we've got to trust each other it's the right thing."

"Trust?" I ask cautiously. "So you do trust me now then?"

He nods but it's all backwards in my mind. He hasn't answered my question, has he? He wants me to trust him now push comes to shove.

"So you and Beth?" I continue, gnawing the bone.

"Jodie, I will ok. It is all going to be ok."

I stare at him. I know what he's really saying but I don't want to think about it.

"Shot?" Lizzy declares from elsewhere on the table. I seize the interruption and jump to my feet.

"Shot?" I ask him avoiding my conclusions for now. He nods, capable of answering that question clearly. I need to talk to Leila and I need to get drunk.

***

"So, I'm going to go back to Eric's." Leila tells me when we visit the club's toilet. "Do you mind because it'll mean you getting a taxi back alone?"

"Or will it?" I scheme aloud an idea taking over me. Troy has been very vocal about his feelings tonight, well now is his chance to prove it.

"What are you thinking? Take Troy back to ours?" Leila's eyes glisten with excitement for both of us.

"Yup. He thinks you don't know about us. So I can say it's the perfect opportunity."

"Well everyone will know about you soon if he means what he says!" She gushes.

"I *know* he loves me Leila. But he hasn't exactly said he's going to leave Beth."

Leila raises her eyebrows doubtfully. "Jodes, I'm sure-"

"I'm not so sure." I admit finally to myself and to her. "I know what he's like by now and I can tell by the way he's avoiding my questions."

"Well, Jodes, should you be going back there then? You said your-"

"I know what I said." I cut her off quickly. "It'll be the last time. A goodbye. And anyway you said the same about Eric!"

"Touché." She giggles but then her eyes clear. "Just, be careful."

"I'm always *careful*." I refer to my condom habit because I can't say the same for not catching feelings.

We finish up in the loos and swing open the door revealing thumping music and strobe lights once again. Our group has dwindled by now and we return to find Sean leering over a bunch of girls, the rest still bopping heartily.

I dance up to Troy and shout in his ear. "Leila is going to Eric's tonight. You should come back to mine."

Stepping away I check his face. It is alive at the prospect and my heart jumps hopefully.

"Ok. Yeah ok!" He agrees nodding and I raise my face to the smoked filled ceiling, stomping my feet giddily. This is going far better than I planned. It wasn't even the plan at all!

"Shall we go for a fag?" Troy calls to me miming the action.

"Like actually just go for a fag?" I yell back grinning and he nods, automatically holding out his hand. I take it, fuck it. I'm an inch away from victory, I can feel it and we leave the others behind without a word.

They loved gossiping over Gilbert and Julie before their relationship materialised. This time it's just going to be about us.

We push and shove through the throng to an outdoor area which is freezing but still jammed. And then we push and shove our way over to a darkened edge.

"Jodie!"

I freeze. I'd literally recognise that voice anywhere. No, no, no, why does it have to be him?

"Jodie!"

I turn, hoping Troy walks on and isn't bothered by the bloke calling out to me. Dane sways right there and he smiles awkwardly.

"Am sowry about, about everyth…" He stops his slurring and his eyes come to rest on somebody just behind me. Troy, it must be. The last time I saw him I slapped him because of something he said and I can only hope he doesn't do it now. "Sowry, al leave you…"

To my shock and delight he stumbles away. Disaster averted! I can't believe it and I turn to Troy happily. He looks angry.

"What the fuck was that?" He demands.

"What? Who, that? Oh, it's, erm." I stutter drunk and confused, we've always avoided this type of subject. These worlds have never crossed paths before.

"Please tell me you haven't slept with him?" He gasps and I think, what business is it of yours? But admittedly I am embarrassed. Dane looked an absolute mess! My mouth opens and closes and he continues fuming.

"He looks like a fucking crack head! Oh my god Jodie, tell me you're clean! When did this happen? Have you been fucking him all along?"

"What the fu-" I can barely make the words come, my head is spinning, I feel sick to my stomach. *Tell me you're clean* rings in my ears. What does he mean?

"I need to know Jodie, what the fuck have you been doing? Or rather *who*!"

"What do you mean, *am I clean*?" I struggle articulating the words, my mind is ringing and my heart is pounding.

"If I've taken something back to her. I'll- fucking hell I feel sick! TELL ME!" Even above the clamour in my head I know he's yelling.

"I am *clean*. You used a condom didn't you?" I'm racking my brain as best I can but it's all so hazy. He did, I'm sure he did! He was behind me…

"No, I fucking didn't, thank fuck for that. Are you *sure*?"

"Yes." I spit and I don't know how I don't slap him now. I know I'm capable of a nifty whack. Hatred courses my veins, love and hate are close and the switch flips. He runs his hands over his afro momentarily flattening it, still muttering under his breath.

"Thank fuck, thank fuck."

I'm insulted, embarrassed and furious. What have I been thinking! What have I been *doing*? Bile is rising in my throat making me want to heave but I steady my breathing ready for what has to be said. If I projectile vomit all over his shirt in the process, it's not such a bad thing.

"Troy? I have never been so disgusted in all my life and that really is saying something." My voice is shaking but it's getting stronger. "Now you need to fuck off before I find that fucking *crack* head and ask him to bite your fucking ear off."

He stares at me and I return the glare, Julie-style, icier than the night itself then he turns on his heel and is gone.

I'm light-headed, everything is happening so fast I can barely comprehend it. I lean against the wall behind me, it is so cold but revitalising. The adrenalin surging around my body is sickly. That man, my *type*, risked infecting his girlfriend! Could have given something to me! I'm repulsed by both of our actions and I swallow a number of times, closing my eyes against the reality.

Come on Jodie. Finally, I'm feeling close to in charge once again.

I need to tell Leila I'm leaving and also prove to those inside that Troy and I haven't snuck off for a dirty shove. It's the last thing I want people to be asking about in the New Year, now. I shudder and know my senses have returned.

I can't let it all fall down on me. I take a shaky breath and begin to make my way back to the door. Sean appears up ahead looking frantic, what now! He is swinging his arms around gesticulating and talking animatedly to whoever he is with. As I get a little closer I can see Leila looking panicked, Eric, Lewis, Dom and Lacey are all with him.

Realisation dawns on me.

"There she is!" Leila is squawking, barely suppressed surprise in her voice. She obviously didn't actually expect me to be here. The group smile and begin to laugh, relief visibly spreading through them.

"What?" I feign confusion which isn't all that difficult considering my current state. "What is it?"

"Sean told us you and Troy had gone off for a shag!" Lewis pipes up giggling at the absurdity. "I knew it wasn't true!"

I chuckle hollowly, only Leila will notice it's all an act.

"I came out for a fag." I tell them coolly. "Troy left ages ago."

Sean is gobsmacked and timidly looks around the group. I feel a tiny bit sorry for pissing on his parade but equally thankful for the unprecedented turn in events. Dane's favour! We might have deserved to be outed.

The whole last twenty minutes have been bewildering. I want to go home and collapse into bed. Or dance my arse off. For now, I have to do the latter, let everyone forget what has just happened.

"So, are we going back in?" I suggest. Leila notes the wave in my voice and her eyes are fixed on me.

Sean doesn't apologise for being 'wrong' and I can't expect him to. His mission to expose us however spiteful didn't succeed but it wouldn't have anyway ironically, we were actually just supposed to be going for a cigarette.

And then there was Dane, again. Oh Dane, what are we going to do with you?

***

"Hoes before bro's!" Leila is arguing with me in the loos once I've given her a quick low-down of why Troy has gone. "I'm not going back with Eric!"

"Don't be daft, Leila, I'm fine. Honestly, I'm only going to go to bed when I get back anyway, what's the point in you missing out?"

"I'm not sure I am missing out though." She admits wearily. "I think I built him up to be a God and now I'm noticing he's got a bit of a beer belly and his hair is thinning more than I remembered."

"Leila!" I giggle at her brutality. "So what, you don't want to go back anyway?"

"Nah," she shrugs. "Not that much. And it'll really show him won't it, like you can't test out another girl then come crawling back to me!"

I laugh bitterly. If only I'd had the same resolve the past few months!

"Can we get food?" I ask. Tonight, I feel like I need a consolation prize.

Blah, Blah, Blah

I awake on the Saturday and it's a wakeup call on a whole new level.

What the actual fuck have I been playing at with Troy? I lie in bed replaying our encounters to date and the room swims in and out of focus. I actually fell for the whole mistress call-card. It is a hard pill to swallow.

I thought I was different and special. I can see it now though, in black and white. The pieces slide neatly into place. At best he actually fancied me, at worst he risked mine and Beth's sexual health for a fling to suit himself. He used me all along to satisfy his needs. What a top plonker I have been!

I roll over and stare at the picture. My impossible-odds Secret Santa present. It's been a damaged relationship from the start. It really is a striking print and I'll enjoy it even if it did come from him; from this horrible, sticky mess. I cast myself into the dregs of my memory. There was a time I knew I shouldn't pursue this and I did so anyway.

I wanted my cake and to eat it and now I've had my ultimate just desserts.

The photo makes me think of best friends holding each other up so they don't fall down when they begin to crumble. That's the thing about the best relationships, they work both ways.

It reminds me of the good influences in my life as well as the negative. They will *all* always be part of the scene because they're all busy teaching me so much.

Dane is on my mind. In my head, and on paper, I grew him into a villain and yet another chance meeting has resulted in my seeing the light. He turned another favour; the flat and now with Troy.

He really is a prick at heart, but he's not the devil. The devil's brother perhaps.

But ultimately, WE have made mistakes. WE *ALL* DO.

This goes some way to ease the culpability. But I know I deserve the discomfit. I've tried not to wish bad things on Dane, but they happened anyway and I didn't care. The universe could choose now to turn on me too or it could give me time to put things right again.

Maybe when I cross paths with Dane I'll put his mind at rest and tell him he can forgive himself for being a twat to me.

Definitely when I cross paths with Troy I'll be graceful yet unmoving. It's over. I promise, it is over!

I have led myself down a jolly path with my eyes wide shut, priding myself on being so open. I never thought I'd fall for this! I totally fell for it and it feels grim.

I resign I must remind myself of the positives in my life. There's plenty of them and I have two whole weeks off to enjoy some of them in. It makes me feel even more ungrateful. I've got all this going for me and I honed in on him. Pathetic.

Let the hangover from hell begin.

Resolutions

"Cheers girlies!" Alexa chinks all of our glasses one more time and swigs the last of her champagne. "It was great to see you. Now you have a fabulous New Year. I know I will!"

She blows extravagant kisses to us as she shimmies to the top of our stairs.

"See ya babe, happy New Year!" I call and she disappears down them. Leila, me and my mum remain and giggle as we wait for the front door to slam.

"She's nuts." Mum exclaims and I nod replenishing the glasses once again. "You all are really."

"I'll cheers to that!" I grin raising my glass. It's New Year's Eve and Alexa dropped by whilst waiting for her latest squeeze to pick her up. Yes, turns out 'the one' actually wasn't the one. This one is.

"I must say though, it obviously works. You're all crazy but look how well you're all doing. I'm so proud of you all!" Mum muses tipsily and I giggle at her. We both look at Leila who recently received the news; she's been officially promoted to Assistant Manager!

She hugs herself bashfully and I beam. Being crazy doesn't always lead to the best decisions but the journeys are worth it, I reckon both Leila and Alexa would agree on that! Alexa has been telling us the latest developments of her booming business. And all the sordid details of her latest affairs too, mum had listened agog.

"I don't know how that Alexa fits in all her shagging with that much work!" Mum comments and I splutter into my drink amused.

"Work hard, shag harder." Leila snickers. Mum smiles, her shyness loosening. She gives me a look as if to say- *that's you!*

·   ·

"Leila's been getting more than me." I hold my hands up in surrender.

"Jodie!" Leila yelps. "That is *not* true!"

I nod emphatically at mum who is smirking. "Is so!"

"You're both getting more than me anyhow!" She erupts cheeks pinkening.

"Well I was off the horse for almost two years." Leila howls. "And I'm off it again now."

"The horse!" I snigger.

"Well, I don't know the donkey, the wagon! Jodie, shut up, anyway you should never have to go without sex. It's a human right. If you want it, that is." Leila continues undeterred. I smile snidely, glad mum's hearing this outlook from a woman other than me. Maybe it'll mean more coming from somebody unrelated.

"Come on mum, let's see what you can do on the pole! Before you get *too* drunk." I suggest raising an eyebrow at her. She looks at me in utter horror.

"Jodie. I am *not* drunk!" She huffs. She smooths her chiffon top and looks at me with a lopsided grin. "And anyway, who do you think you got your dancing skills from? It certainly wasn't your dad!"

With that she stands, albeit a little unsteadily, and strides toward the pole.

"Put me on a good song then!" She demands. Leila shrieks and whoops at her from beside me.

"Go on Zoe!" She yells.

I do as my mum asks only partly shocked. I wish she'd show this rowdy side more often. It just takes a few bubbles to release it. Mum, as good as her word, walks around the pole wiggling up and down to the music. She brushes her hair up from her face and lets it fall again around her shoulders and runs a finger down the length of the pole seductively. Leila and I catcall enthusiastically before she steps forward and points to me narrowing her eyes. I see myself briefly in her features, it is a strange feeling. My mum is actually damn sexy and it gives me eternal hope for becoming a future cougar.

That inevitably seems my destiny. Concentrate on my career and then bag a young man; I'll be following in the footsteps of Julie more so than I intended at this rate.

"Let's see what the expert has got then." She challenges me.

"Are you sure you're ready for this?" I tease her standing. We have the same eyes and smiles but I'm shorter than her and she looks down at me.

"Awww, shorty." She mocks and I laugh gleefully.

"The last person to call me that was Justin!" I cry and Leila cackles loudly.

"One of your many men, you little tart." Mum giggles and slaps my bum. "Now get up there and dance!"

I titter delightedly, mum is completely out of her shell and I totter off to do as I'm told.

"I must say!" Leila bellows. "I thought you and your brother pole dancing was a selling point but you and your mum!"

"Never!" Mum squeals. "I would never dance to men for money!"

"Then do it for free!" Leila retaliates.

"Imagine, brother, sister and mum, triple act!" I yell as I put on the first of my favourite 'pole dancing' songs.

When Leila told me she had New Year's Eve off I was worried she'd be disappointed that I couldn't afford to do anything fancy and after last year I did not want to spend it in the village pubs. If she was however, she didn't show it and then mum mentioned she'd be alone, again. I suggested we spend it together, in our living room.

And it's panning out to be a top night!

"Wow, you *are* good!" Mum looks at me amazed when I collapse back at the table, two and a half songs in.

"Why thank you!" I raise my glass to be chinked yet again. "Leila's turn!"

"No way!" She shakes her head. "Zoe's well better than me and I've been practicing on and off! That's gunna be my New Year's resolution, you've inspired me."

"Nice one." I grin and sip the tangy liquid. "I've got so much better since practising regularly. It's not a miracle."

"So, what's yours going to be?" Mum asks. "You've already done more this year than I've done in a lifetime!"

"Don't be daft!" I swat her. "I haven't had kids. Don't worry! That's not my resolution."

I notice the look on her laughing face. It is no joke, Belfry is more than enough on the child-front and I'm happy to keep it that way.

"I want to focus on my career. That's the only way kids will be in my life." I chuckle. "And carry on with the whole saying-yes-more thing. That's all my resolution had been so far."

"For better or worse!" Leila inputs. I'm not sure I could take my mum's judgement on the example of 'for worse'.

"Well, saying yes isn't without its drama." I explain carefully. "But I've been places, met new people, done things, exciting things, I've seen so much and it's all come from saying yes more!"

My mind flickers to Luca, I sound like he did that night he boasted about his great life. Mum giggles knowing some of the stories, but the sadness is there still, resting at the back of her mind. It breaks my heart, stopping me in my glorified tracks. This is down to feeling unappreciated, unreciprocated in an excuse for a relationship. She's *too* selfless, it's directly oppositional to my selfishness at times.

"So what about you, mum? Me and Leila have aims. We're proof of meeting them when we try. What are you going to change?"

A rabbit caught in headlights she stares and shrugs. "I don't know. I don't know what I want to change."

"Ok," used to rephrasing for the students I find an angle. "How did you feel this time last year? What did you do?"

Her cackle is sharp. "Sat and watched the TV until eleven and went to bed."

"Well this is an improvement." I jibe. "More nights with Leila and Jodie, resolution number one! So what else is different?"

"Nothing." She states. I feel guilty for exposing her like this but my intentions are sincere. Defensively she mutters, "I don't want anything to change. I just want to live in my house and do what I want to do."

"Like cook and iron and clean?" I probe.

She rolls her eyes. "Like sew and crochet and watch the soaps and read." She retorts. So she does remember she has hobbies then.

"So kick Keith and George out and buy yourself some cats." Leila interjects before glugging her drink.

"Brilliant." I commend and clasp my hands. "Resolution number two sorted!"

I don't mean it harsh on my brother but he's old enough and earns enough to take care of himself. Keith too, he's an emotional leech.

"Hmm. Sounds good." She says.

I'm glad for her minor acknowledgement but I'm under no allusion. This time next year she won't have taken that plunge. But I'll remind her of the conversation if she's still blatantly unhappy. Resolution number one however firmly stands. She'll spend time with us, we'll show her what can be achieved, actions speak loudly.

Conversation deteriorates with alcohol consumption and as my mum joins in with stories of her own cringeworthy dating mishaps I realise she did play the game, once upon a time. There's optimism in the air!

"Too young, I could've told you that Jodie." She croons now referring to the Aaron mishap. Leila is howling as we relive the dancer's ankles story.

"Well you didn't tell me that did you, for once!" I tease. "If I remember rightly you were all for it. We were here, drinking wine the first day we moved in."

Mum casts her eyes around the living room. "It does look nice in here."

"Why do you say that so surprised?" I chortle.

She points at my latest project, the small side table which is now bright pink zebra print.

"That!" She exclaims pointing. "With a lime green wall! And the purple throw, those red curtains and all these mismatched candles. None of it matches! But it works somehow."

"That's why I like it." Leila nods. "Your daughter is a genius. It's organised chaos."

"Kind of like my life then." I giggle. Mum snorts knowing I can be scatty but I think of Troy. Thoughts of him have been reduced to a pinprick in my mind the past week, like a star in a night sky.

I love a New Year. It's the chance to begin a whole new chapter.

When the clock strikes twelve we've already cheered and cheers-ed umpteen times. I'm happy and more so because mum has a glow in her cheeks that I hadn't even realised I missed.

We walk her home despite of her protests. It's not long past midnight and there are still fireworks banging in the distance. The frosty air is tinged with the smell of smoke.

"Doesn't it all feel so wonderfully fresh and new?" I say.

"You are a strange one Jodie." My mum answers. "But I wouldn't have you any other way. You always see opportunity in everything."

I squeeze my arm which links hers pulling her into me. "Thanks mum."

A secret resolution crosses my mind. I will help coax her into more fulfilling circumstances, whatever they may be, whatever way I can. Seeing her this evening so full of life has only made me even more determined.

We all hug and declare our love and then Leila and I are retracing our steps through the dark streets. There are people about despite the late hour, music can be heard in the distance, tyres screeching and voices calling out.

"So resolutions from now!" Leila lists on her fingers shivering as we walk. "Be a great manager. Get good on the pole. Learn some more new hobbies."

"Like what?" I ask her intrigued.

"I don't know, you like to read and write and get crafty. I might begin with those and see where it takes me."

"Yeah man!" I reply enthusiastically. "It was only six months ago you made the decision to upgrade your job. Just imagine what you could be doing by next year!"

"You should be thinking that yourself."

"Oh I am, babe." I tell her grinning.

We let ourselves back in at Marshamonvilla, the heating has been on and we're engulfed in a stifling cloud.

"One for the road?" Leila asks picking up our empty glasses.

"Do you even have to ask?"

We sit back around the table. The 'you know who your mates are' table. I've loved sharing this New Year Eve with my mum and my best friend.

"Thanks for tonight." I tell Leila. "I think my mum appreciated hearing somebody else's point of view."

"She thinks I'm nuts Jodie." She giggles. "But you don't need to thank me. I really like her! Maybe I'll add being able to do DIY to my wifey CV." She claps a hand over her mouth remembering where the term 'wifey CV' originated.

"Don't worry." I giggle. "It is a good name for it. But don't lose focus of the CV overall. Searching for a man ain't the be all and end all!"

"Cheers to that!" She scoffs heartily, and we chink glasses a final time.

I go to bed feeling a little like I've been born again. Stuff I knew all along has been steadily fusing together and the bigger picture is forming in my mind's eye.

Mum's presence tonight struck a chord. We might look the same, in some ways resemble natures, but in other areas our moral codes completely differ. She wouldn't be payed to dance, she won't even go to see a male stripper for feminist reasons and she's happy to go without for a simpler life.

I realise I don't feel apologetic for ever having followed my heart and appeased my own appetite. Yes, that sometimes feels selfish and I love the selfless quality my mum has but it's making her unhappy. Plus there are things I think she should try. New hobbies, new friends and nights out. I have paid good money in the past to see men peel off uniforms and waggle their engorged members to music and crowds of leering women! It's fun but I still doubt she'd say yes to that.

I'll start her off slowly, invite her round for dinner. We'll see where it goes!

My other resolutions include building my career CV and my *life* CV. I'll continue to take measured chances and risks, grasping opportunity where I can. Even this thing with Troy had boundaries; I didn't sneak into his room on the trip, I never messaged him or met up with him out of school hours. I accidentally fell in love and knew all along it was wrong. A condom, or rather lack of, became the definitive barrier and actually it could have been a lot worse.

Beth is none the wiser and there is little point enlightening her to cause inevitable pain. Saying yes to Troy, letting him in, has evoked all manner of negative feelings within me, it's senseless to cause more now that it's over. I still don't quite regret it but I want to forget it, leave it behind.

I just need to keep my head down next week when school resumes and hope Troy has enough decorum to do the same.

With good there is always bad, life is unfair and I suppose even my mum's life isn't simple- she's an unpaid maid. Whatever our choices there will be consequences.

I'm still none the wiser to what really makes a man tick! But I'm not going to stop myself from meeting new ones and possibly falling into the sack with a few. I came home from Maga feeling like I was invincible and perhaps I'm naturally an optimist but I've managed to get myself burned, again. Even if I deserve nothing less this time!

But possibly it won't be the last time either although I'll be steering clear of taken men. It's a resolution I never thought I'd have to make. The universe works in strange old ways.

It is a new year, a fresh canvas, what mistakes and lessons will I paint now?

Back to School Tomorrow

I put away my washing and eye the dreary collection of work clothes. Two weeks off have passed seemingly in the blink of a merry eye. Indulgence has proved remedial in the course of forgetting Troy. He hasn't contacted me even though I'm sure he could have found time to. Actions speak louder than words. And I didn't think I was bothered but the thought of seeing him again tomorrow makes me feel itchy all over.

I sit on my bed and stare at the black and white picture for not the first time. A new thought rumbles across my mind and I begin to undo the tacks on the back of the frame. I slide the picture out and sure enough a scripted message.

Jodie,

Some people see the beauty in damaged.

T

My heart thuds and I breathe slowly and deeply allowing the words, in Troy's voice, to replay in my mind. Is this his final dig, he thinks I'm damaged but I'm still *beautiful* to him?

I stare a little longer, zoning out. Then replace the photo and affix the frame. I don't actually care what he thinks. The little stab in my gut will soon fade to nothing. Experience tells me that, if I just sit out.

If I am damaged, it's from the likes of him toying with my emotions. I don't pretend to be anything I'm not. I do not need him to validate me with his judgements that have so often been wrong anyway.

I look at the brick buildings, interlacing vines connecting them. They're my supporters. Leila, Cat, mum, George, Chantelle I am lucky to be able to name plenty.

He can think what he wants. Actions speak louder than words. I'm going to be the best possible version of me at work and at home. I'll work hard, play hard and shag harder as Leila said. I will not waste energy on shame but I'll take what I've learned and move on.

I lie on my bed. How have I got work tomorrow? This has got to be the worst Sunday-Feeling EVER!

Get a grip! Inner voice scolds. I've had some wonderful days and evenings to myself and now I must pay the price. Work tomorrow. Last year I worked non-stop shifts over this period, now I'm mourning going back after two weeks off. This is the perspective I need and my mindset shifts.

I think about all of the drama that comes with Belfry. The staff and students, daily commotions and weekly bombshells. I wonder how Eve got on over Christmas? It's my new normal to be involved with these things. How quickly I've gotten used to it. I wonder where I'll be next year and what my circumstances will be this time then!

It's only eight o'clock, I'm halfway through the book mum bought me for Christmas already so I decide to take a break and flick through Facebook. Ashley is active online as usual, I saw him last Friday and click like on his most recent status. Luca has uploaded some promo shots of him as a backing dancer. This guy has fingers in every pie! He messaged before New Year but we didn't manage to meet.

A status of Shaun's catches my eye. He's off to Thailand this year and my mind flickers to the TEFL qualification. We've exchanged the odd messages since my initial 'congrats' and I open the contact.

Happy New Year! I bet you're on Thailand countdown now! x

Nothing wrong with a spot of fishing I tell myself wryly. And then I get set to be immersed in the pages of somebody else's tale.

Lindzi Mayann

Back to School Monday

It feels a little surreal pulling into the carpark this dreary Monday morning. I can't imagine what it will feel like after six weeks off! As Lizzy said, we're on the home straight to summer now with another couple of holidays dotted in-between. It makes me ridiculously happy to think about all that time off to come.

I clamber from my car just as Troy rolls into the carpark. Usually I would wait for him. Last year's usual would be to wait for him. This year, I stride confidently into the building. I want to go and see Lizzy but I also want to be in the staff room before Troy so I can get myself settled.

I make a coffee and slide into a seat at the table. Lacey is already here, Sean, Leanne, Lewis, Dom and a few others. I don't recognise one guy; he must be a newbie!

New staff, fresh meat!

Julie was alright with me toward the end of last term, I want to keep that momentum going and now I am no longer the new girl either! I focus on chit-chatting with my peers, aware that Troy will enter any minute. There's plenty to discuss and I listen to Lewis as he tells us about the Festive Fair he smashed with his artwork. It's amazing how many talented people I'm surrounded by here, I find it inspiring.

"Good morning!" Troy announces himself. I hadn't even noticed him enter which I'm taking as a firm positive.

"Morning!" Everyone replies, and conversation easily includes him without us having to specifically greet one another.

"How was your holiday Jodie?"

STOP

I knew it would be only a matter of time until he directly addressed me.

"Brilliant thanks!" I enthuse. The last thing I want to do is further arouse suspicion around us. "How was yours? Did Santa bring you everything you wanted?"

"He sure did. I must have been a good boy!" He exclaims giggling. He might know about Sean and the witch hunt he led, Dom or Lewis could have told him, but he doesn't let on. He is his usual self and I don't think it's an act. His eyes happily glow when they catch onto mine.

"Have you seen Lizzy yet?" Lacey leans over to ask me.

"No, not yet, I bet she'll be down in a minute for the welcome brief." I feel like a pro using the correct terms.

Lacey beams at me. "Yep, she'll be down. Just you wait!"

"What?" I ask her intrigued and glad for the interruption, but she shakes her head biting her lip.

"I can't tell you, she wants to tell you in person!"

"Oh Lacey, why even say anything then?" I moan. "I'm going to look for her."

I jump up, overcome. Plus it gives me the perfect opportunity to get away from Troy. I can tell it's something exciting, but what! Surely not a new job because Lacey wouldn't be so pleased about that. And she's only just announced about her new girlfriend, so it can't be love-life related.

I round the corner almost upon the unit and collide with Lizzy. We both begin squealing at once talking over one another and asking questions.

"How are you?" "How was your break?" "What's new?"

"You go first!" I tell her eagerly.

"Oh Jodie, I'm engaged! Gem Gem asked me to marry her!" She cries.

"She did! Wow, that's amazing, you said yes right?" I double check because it's very quick, yet she seems so pleased.

"Yes, of course! Look." She shows me a dainty ring. "We're having an engagement party. It's the nineteenth I think. I can't remember, two weeks Friday anyway. Say you'll come! Sean plays in a band and he's going to play for us!"

I can imagine Sean in a band actually, with his leather jackets and big buckled belts. I wonder what instrument he plays. Another talent in the staff pool!

"Congratulations Lizzy!" I tell her warmly. "Of course I'll be at the party!"

I think of my tight budget but it's worth it, I want to celebrate with her.

"And Leila. Make sure to ask her too."

"I will, I will!" I agree, it's a given she's my plus one.

"Come on, anyway, staff briefing." She says. "Ay, we won't be sister newbies anymore!"

"*Never* sisters and no longer a newbie!" I quip. Harishma's dislike to the nickname is so very relevant.

"We're *work*-sisters." She grins at me and I nod satisfied. I'm down on a work-husband and work-sisters is safer than work-wife with our history. She'll be a real wife soon enough! Lizzy unlocks the staff room door and I'm aware of the silence straightaway.

"Miss the memo ladies?" Julie drawls sarcastically looking at the clock above the kitchen area.

"Sorry Julie. It was completely my fault." Lizzy tells her brightly. "I wanted to double check the targets I've made for the girls. Jodie has worked so closely with them."

Thanks sis, I tell her with my eyes when she smiles at me. Julie gives us a glare and lets the silence linger.

"As I was saying," she eventually resumes.

I spot another new face, a girl who looks possibly younger or my age and very pretty. I try not to think of Troy and his judgement on her. She looks on, solemnly, paying attention to Julie. I almost hope she doesn't lay off me in favour of her, I actually wouldn't wish her wrath on anyone. Being intimidated by my boss isn't the worst thing. I'm virtually getting used to it- finding it motivating and keeping me on my toes like an inconsistent lover.

Getting told off again isn't exactly the best start to my 'smash career' resolution but I'm determined to succeed anyway. And I will one way or another, regardless of anyone else.

***

Breakfast club is loud and Troy, Sean and I watch the students as we discuss the latest news. Lizzy's hasty engagement has taken a backseat to finding out that Gilbert is in a new role.

Between Troy and Sean gossiping I understand he hasn't got the correct qualifications to take over Claire's old role completely. Instead another teacher has been given some of that responsibility and a new title has been created- just for Gilbert.

It was done before, I remember Jenni telling me that in games club. I lose some of my rather new-found respect for Julie. Being a shameless cougar is one thing, but it is clear she is favouring him and there are definitely personal reasons for it. Maybe her tirade to belittle me has reasons behind it too, or perhaps she merely dislikes me. But I don't care about that. I've decided more about my next career move since this morning than I did with two weeks of pondering over the Christmas holidays.

"I'm just so annoyed." Sean fumes. "I've been asking for a new role for ages. And a pay rise! I've been here longer than Gilbert and working with behaviour improvement for longer too!"

I nod along considerately, my feelings toward him shift in light of this injustice. As do any hopes of a promotion for myself.

"Oh, here's Dad. Bet you've missed him." Troy exclaims teasing me as if nothing has changed. But then Sean is present, he could be as intent as me on keeping up appearances.

I smile at Iqbal's face and approach him.

"Hey Jodie!" He grins warmly. "I wondered if we could have a little catch up?"

"Yes of course." I agree and follow him out of the hall. I'm glad he hasn't changed.

***

Monday passes by. The meeting is brief because there isn't a lot to discuss other than a few changes to the working days. Eve is still in a home, tomorrow I'll be going to visit her and I genuinely can't wait. I'm taking her the Christmas present she didn't receive from Belfry before the holidays, it's chocolate and I hope it cheers her up.

I've text Lizzy to tell her again how pleased I am for her. It might be a bit soon but who am I to judge what other people want to do. She's an impulsive person- you only live once! And if she's happy, I'm happy. Plus there's another party to look forward to just as I thought I'd been partied out.

Leila agreed immediately to be my plus one. I spoke to Sean about his band at lunchtime, they sound really cool, covering a mixture of mainstream artists. I've decided to let the incidents between us from before go. They're irrelevant now that Troy is out of the frame and I feel sorry for him about the job thing, it's not right.

The world is an unfair place.

I click through the screens on my laptop. I'm booking the TEFL course. I'm already strict with my money but the fifty pounds a month I keep back for luxury items and/or socialising can be lived without for four months. It's the bigger picture I have to think about.

With this qualification and the continuing experience at Belfry I'd be able to go abroad and teach. Not in all countries, for some I'd need a degree but there are a few, plus perhaps a degree is next.

I hit the confirmation button and scribble the training dates for Feb into my diary.

I'm already feeling productive after a successful return to school. Plus I worked with Troy and didn't reciprocate any of his playful banter. I've subtly made it clear that whatever happened between us is now over. He'll get the message.

And I've taken a step already toward bettering myself career-wise. I enjoy my cup of tea with a peaceful mind and don't feel guilty for my pride.

Thursday News

"Anymore incidents with Julie?" Iqbal enquires politely as I get set to leave for lunch. He didn't miss Monday's episode and made it clear that was my own fault. I didn't need telling.

"Nope thankfully. I've been on my best behaviour." I add jokily and salute.

"Good. And I'm really pleased you booked your TEFL course. You have a lot of potential."

"Thanks dad. OH MY GOD!" My cheeks flare bright red immediately. My sarcastic inner voice slipped out. "Sorry, I'm tired, first week back!"

Luckily Iqbal thinks it is hilarious and also has no idea of Troy's jibes; to him it's an innocent slip of the tongue.

"Jodie!" He wipes his eyes as he calms down and motions me closer even though we're alone. "You could never have known this. I'm not supposed to be telling anyone yet, but, well… we're expecting! I'm going to be a father!"

Saved from embarrassment and filled with pleasure for him I gush. "That's amazing! Congratulations! Ahh, Iqbal, I'm so happy for you both!"

"Erm, Jodie, whilst you're here?" His face has filled with confusion and I slowly switch from glee to dread as he continues on stumbling. "I, erm, I saw, erm, Lizzy has gotten engaged. And, erm, I heard it's, erm, to… *another woman*?"

He whispers this part and looks at me expectantly. I can't help my wide smile. In some aspects he's so wise and in others completely clueless.

"Yeah, yeah she's a lesbian. It's another woman. I met her just before Christmas, she's really lovely."

"Is it who she had a date with? When we were going on the trip?"

"Yes! Good memory." I wonder if he'll mention the speed- or the sexuality- but his face has cleared as the information processes.

"It must be love!" He nods. "Send her my best wishes won't you. I don't, you know, socialise much."

"I will. She's rarely in the staff room either, she's almost always in the girls unit."

"Hmm. Committed." He says approvingly and I think, it isn't by choice! She's hoping Julie will rota other staff members into the unit at lunchtime soon so she can get a bit of a break.

"Ok, enjoy your weekend anyway." I tell him making to leave. "I'm with the 10s this afternoon and the girls tomorrow."

"I notice you have been keeping yourself to yourself more this week." He comments and looks at me evenly. Troy might still not be taking the hint, but Iqbal hasn't missed it and I'm for once pleased with his borderline nosiness.

"Yep, I'm learning." I smile. "Congrats again on your news, it really is lovely."

"Don't tell anyone!" He calls as I leave.

"I won't. See you next week."

I walk toward the staff room, his secret is safe, but I'm gutted I can't tell Troy about the dad slip-up. It will make us laugh. I miss his dimples and I miss our friendship. It would be mixed signals though.

I console myself that I have a work sister now instead. And I can't wait to tell her how Iqbal asked if she is gay, bless him.

Harishma is amidst a debate between some of the others when I enter. Topic: Lizzy's engagement. She has been openly aghast at the timing and it is no surprise to hear her venting her feelings at the table.

I collect my lunch and take a seat amongst the row. The more opinionated of the group battle out their reasoning for and against. I listen and watch as I eat. I don't feel bad, I'll give Lizzy the gist of it tomorrow. She'll find it funny. Harishma hasn't exactly been shy about telling her just what she thinks about it all. Plus Lizzy knows that since the poster went up announcing the celebration there have been mixed reviews.

She doesn't care and why should she? She isn't do anything wrong and anyway I reckon she likes the controversy she's causing, I know I would.

Troy is sitting almost opposite me. I've been gradually sitting with other people so the change hasn't been abrupt to anyone other than us. He catches my eye and smiles. I return it then look away.

Carla, the very pretty new girl, is by his side. She's been flirting with him all week, I've seen her. Initially I was interested in case Julie treated her any differently, I didn't mean to notice her always making a beeline for him and tossing around her silky hair. But I try not to obsess. And from what I can gather he isn't responding anyway. He's still trying with me. I wish he wouldn't and yet I'm glad Carla isn't getting his attention either.

Clubs don't start for another ten minutes but I leave the table now anyway and force myself to ignore Troy as I do so. I'm supporting Arts and Crafts with Leanne and Helen, I doubt they'll be there yet, but I can get us set up ready.

"Hey!" Leanne startles me from my arranging of felt shapes. "Looks good."

"Just messing about." I shake them back into the pot. "I got here early so I set up an activity."

"Has Julie been on at you again?" She teases.

"I don't want her catching me late again!" I use the excuse, dramatically rolling my eyes.

"There's a new girl for her to pick on now anyway." She giggles and I nod smiling.

I think of Carla and her pretty pixie face, possibly still chatting with Troy. A small ear-battering from Julie wouldn't be so bad. It's character building after all.

"Good afternoon!" Helen trills as she enters. She dumps her bags on a desk and turns to us. "So, what do you reckon about Lizzy getting engaged then? And so soon!"

I let them have their fun with the trivial but think about what I'd rather hear discussed. It's a moral issue not just mere attitude and I take the plunge.

"So what do you think about Gilbert's promotion?"

"Very naughty." Helen surmises instantly. "No internal position was even advertised."

I hadn't even thought about it like that and look from Leanne to Helen. "But isn't that against the law?"

"Probably, it's all corrupt, these systems. Just got to work hard and hope for the best."

Hope for the best doesn't seem entirely appealing. I'm feeling more positive than ever after booking onto a new qualification but it's not going to fix anything in the short term.

"Sean wanted a different position. Like Gilbert's. He told me he even asked about it?" I pursue.

"Sean's an idiot." Helen laughs. "But even so, Gilbert should watch out too. You know, Julie has been married three times before."

"Three times! I thought it was only twice." Leanne giggles.

"Three! How has she found *three* men to marry?" I giggle. "Once would be nice!"

"Once is enough!" Helen quips nodding knowledgeably. "Rumour has it, her last one was shooting blanks…"

She lets the suggestion hang in the air before wiggling her eyebrows. "I'd bet she'll be up the duff by this time next year. He has no idea what he's letting himself in for."

Well, I think it seems Julie has plans all of her own! And they scupper my own plans. There's no hope of a promotion for *me* here, let alone a pay-rise. Sean might be an actual idiot but Julie probably thinks I am too plus I have nothing to offer her. Unlike Gilbert and his strapping, young sperm!

We settle down as students begin to arrive. There are a range of lads who choose this option and I look forward to working with Billy because he wants to be a graffiti artist when he grows up. I've been working on my own canvas alongside his. If only I could have my youth all over again, what different choices I could make. That is the beauty of hindsight and it's the hidden message in the image I'm creating to display at home.

***

The school day is over and Troy is waiting at his locker when I enter the gently humming staff room.

"We need to talk." He mumbles.

"About what?" I already know but I don't want to be presumptuous.

"About us!" He hisses.

"There is no *us*." I reply quietly and firmly, glancing around. Nobody is watching.

"I know." His agreement surprises me but I'm careful not to show it.

"So, what is it then?" I huff.

"I want to clear the air." He tells me genuinely.

"Ok. Well," I quickly check nobody is close enough to hear. "What you did, not checking about the contraception thing was downright dumb! If I hadn't been on the pill-"

"You didn't exactly say anything either!" He cuts in defensively.

"Yes, there is that." I didn't check, so no hypocrites here- when it can be helped. "But anyway, it was never meant to be. We should forget it happened. For both of our sakes."

He nods, and I swallow the lump building in my throat. If he is dumb, I have been dumber. Dumb for thinking he really cared, dumber for acting on it and dumbest for believing I could click my fingers and get over it.

"So anyway, see you tomorrow." I rush the words just wanting to get away.

"Jodes. You know I did, *do*, really, really like you. But. Well I could just never trust you, not now, so we can't be together anyway."

I look at him as a wave of freezing emotion rolls over me. His eyes are almost pitying, amused.

"You understand don't you?" He pushes. I do understand far more than he'll ever realise. I know what he's doing, trying to lure me in and I won't satisfy him.

"Whatever Troy." I turn on my heel but just can't resist throwing over my shoulder. "I think you need to learn a bit about trust yourself."

Didn't he ask me to *trust* him before the holidays? I *have* trusted him, look where that got me. And now he's turning it around to be my fault. He scurries out of the room after me and falls into my stride. Any interaction is better than none to manipulators and I curse myself for biting.

"I know how it looks babe. I just want you to know I never would've risked me and Beth if I didn't really believe in us. But I'd just always be thinking you were off seeing these other men behind my back."

Babe! My mind reels as he talks. He's making this out to be *my* problem? How dare he!

"So basically I haven't been a loyal enough mistress." The sarcasm oozes from the statement. I'm biting again, I know it, I should just leave.

Our eyes feel connected by Velcro as I rip them away painfully, fumbling for my car key.

"No, no, no Jodie. You're better than a mistress. That's what I'm saying!" I've unlocked the door now and open it creating a barrier between us. "If I left Beth for you, you'd leave me for the next guy that comes along and takes your fancy. It's just what you're like."

He shrugs and smiles and a hollow cackle escapes my lips.

"You don't know what I'm like." I grimace darkly. "You'll never know me now. And that's fine with me."

Troy looks frustrated and I'm glad.

"See you next week, I'm with the girls tomorrow."

"I might see you in clubs." He says still not moving. "I don't want things to be awkward between us."

"They won't be." I inject sweetness into my tone. "I'm a professional babe."

I swing the door shut and he walks away knowing he can't make a scene. I'm rumbling with anger as I pull away and I turn up my music, belting out ballads all the way home.

Leila has left for her evening shift already and I get changed and continue expending pent up energy with a serious of vigorous pole moves. Music plays, my mind whirs and my surroundings blur as I spin and spin.

Finally I am burnt out physically and mentally soothed. I'm ready to eat and relax.

Troy does not know me if he thinks I am a sly, disloyal person. And therefore, simply, he is not worthy of me or my emotion. He has no idea what I am capable of. Yet!

I'll climb this ladder (and my pole), I will be successful and happy and if I find somebody worthy along the way I will make a loyal wife too.

Troy will fade into the background in the grand scheme of things and if he wants to, he can watch me from afar.

This fall-out has brought me to singing my head off in the car and dancing my arse off all evening. And perhaps now I'll write some more too. I feel like I've learned a lot more about the complexities of character since the last time I picked up a pen.

Turn Up Saturday

I sit at Cat's kitchen table and scroll through my Facebook.

"Anything interesting on yours?" She asks. "Mine's all mummy talk. There's another bug going around." She rolls her eyes and smiles.

"Just everyone else going on nights out. And I'm too skint to join in." I answer wryly and continue to read the taunts.

"It's a shame your pay is so crap. You've been thriving since you worked there but you should be able to live! Have you searched to see if there are other similar things that pay more?"

"It's a bit too soon to be jumping ship." I tell her. "I'm still very new to it all."

"And a promotion is out of the window because you can't shag the boss!"

I giggle at her. I've told her about Gilbert and also that Julie could be using him as a sperm-donor.

"It makes me so angry!" Cat continues screwing up her fists.

"I wouldn't shag the boss anyway even if I could. Especially not to climb the ladder anyway." I add. "I'd want to earn it. And anyway I'm being silly. I've got Lizzy's engagement party to look forward to. I can cope for now."

"Will Troy be there?" She asks.

"Yeah, I assume so. I think just about everyone is going, she's been the talk of the school!"

I've told her how everyone has been gossiping like mad and she laughed heartily when I told her about Iqbal and the dad incident! My eyes snag on a status by Luca.

Home is where the heart is

My own heart thuds. Is he in the area? Our last messages exchanged only a few weeks ago amounted to nothing. Without thinking I send him an inbox.

U home? Hola ☺

"What are you smirking at lady?" It doesn't matter how worn out Cat is, she always notices.

"Probably nothing. I've just messaged Luca in case he's about."

"Ohh I hope so! I love hearing your stories Jodes, I live my life through you!"

We whittle away another hour and I decide to stroll home. Leila doesn't finish until late, so I've got the flat to myself and Luca has read my message but not replied. It's freezing outside and I decide to have a bath and read a book.

***

I'm snuggled up on the sofa feeling like an old woman but actually loving it and then my phone pings. If it's Ashley expecting me to leave the warmth of my nest for his, then he's right, I probably will.

But it's Luca! I grin and push myself into an upright position.

What you doin

It's a simple enough question but saying *nothing* on a Saturday night sounds a little sad and suddenly I'd very much rather be doing *anything* with him.

Chilling at home

I reply hoping it makes me sound cool. I'm doing quite the opposite, I'm roasting!

You free?

I scan the text, smiling now inanely but tap casually;

I'm not up to much. Are you free?

Within ten minutes he has my address and is on route. I jump to my feet and dash to my room in search of some perfume and after tidying myself up, I set about doing the same to the living room. I'm so glad we jazzed it up before; mum was right it looks wicked!

***

"You gunna be a pole dancer then?" Luca teases me, his eyes dancing playfully. He looks larger than life sitting right there in front of me as I mess about dancing to his playlist.

"You think I'm good enough?" I mount into a more daring pose which ends with me buckling unceremoniously.

"With practise!" He grins as I climb from the floor laughing. "Do you want another drink, it might help."

"Why not." I smirk and plonk next to him on the sofa. I changed into shorts to be able to grip the pole and he runs his hand down my bare thigh.

"Leila, my flatmate will be home soon." I tell him, and he pours us up another large measure each. "You met her when you came to the Trap that time."

I actually messaged her the moment he showed up with a bottle of Grey Goose. I can imagine her running up the street as we speak, she'll be finished anytime now. I don't mind her invading us for a bit, share the love!

"When was I there last?" He asks nonplussed and shrugs not waiting for an answer. "So we having a threesome?"

This question is not rhetorical. Did I really mean share the love? I giggle at his hopeful face. I'm not offended, it's not like we're pretending to be exclusive to each other.

"Sorry babe, I don't think Leila will be up for it. But I'll ask her if you want." I add when he looks unconvinced. I already know she'll say no. Not that I'd be all that bothered if she said yes. Especially if I continue drinking at this rate!

"You worked in Magaluf?" Luca looks impressed when Leila drops in the story involving me.

"I told you that." I tell him but he's caught up in his own memory.

"I loved it there." He coos narrowing his eyes at Leila and beaming. "So much pussy!"

She giggles shrilly not used to him, like me.

"I'm off to bed." Leila announces after a second drink.

"You don't have to go to *your* bed you know." I give her a worse for wear wink.

"Jodie!" She chastises and her cheeks colour.

"True dat." Luca grins from me to her. "Don't be shy girl."

His charm is instant and he beams at me approvingly.

"Sorry Leila." I giggle. "He is *really* good though."

"Ooh girl let me take your body…" Luca is singing, he's pretty decent and I watch through giddy eyes as Leila stumbles away unable to take anymore.

"You're such a clown." I tell him when his focus is back to me.

"It's why you love me."

"Not just that." I grin. He wraps his arms around my shoulders and stares into my face.

"You should really think about pole dancing, there's money to be made out there for girls with your body. It's better cash than waitressing."

"I don't waitress." I tell him. "I work in a school now."

It's a backhanded compliment. I'm starting to wonder what he does know about me, other than the shape of my body. There have been a few instances this evening which make me realise he doesn't remember our meetings with anywhere near the same detail I do.

I was chuffed when he praised me for knowing the real him. And yet he doesn't know me at all in return.

I stare into his thickly lashed eyes. I'm a little hurt but not all that bothered about it right now. Luca coming tonight has been a very pleasant turn-up. I take a steadying breath and let him draw me in.

Sunday Education

I wake up to find Luca sitting on the end of my bed in his boxers.

"Morning." I mumble. My head is pounding. We drank a lot in a fairly short time. Last night's sex fuzzily replays in my mind. "What time is it?"

"Six." He answers. I roughly calculate four hours sleep.

"Why are you up?" I gasp. "Are you coming back to bed?"

"Gotta go." He replies bluntly dragging on his socks.

I sit upright and rub at my eyes, scraping my hair from my face. He told me last night he'll be working away for the spring and summer. Chances are I won't see him, at least in the flesh, for a while again.

"Well, I'm glad you came to see my flat." I comment and slide from the bed naked. Let's make sure he remembers me, in the flesh. I take my time looking for a tee-shirt to put on.

Luca gives me a hug at the front door and smirks. "I'm gunna be real big after this summer you know."

"I know, you told me last night. Good luck."

"I don't need luck." He laughs. "I'm smashing it. So, anyway, I probably won't be around for a while. Keep doing your thing Jodes, I'm sure you'll work it out." He pats my shoulder smiling and saunters away. I shiver in the chilly morning air and shut the door as he unlocks his car.

I already have worked it out. I'm smashing it too you know Luca! A voice wails in my head but I hush it. He doesn't see it, yet. He's too wrapped up in himself, last night made that much clear. It might take me a little longer for me to get *real big* and I'm not sure what I'll get real big in either- pole dancing, writing, singing, upcycling, teaching, travel, blogging?

The potential avenues swim before my eyes. I think I'm still drunk and I should go back to bed for a while but I'm filled with sickly sweet emotion that won't allow my brain to switch off. I'm elated, satisfied, disenchanted and restless all at once. I need to drink tea and allow my thoughts to settle like glitter in a snow globe.

***

"I can't believe we didn't hear you!" I repeat wiping away tears of mirth, my stomach is aching as Leila and I chat.

"I was so worried Luca would come to the toilet and find me crawling along the landing."

"You were crawling?" I squeal, and she nods, her own face screwed up with the giggles.

"I already felt sick, I drank too much too fast, and I'd had a glass of wine whilst counting the tills. And then he started singing to me, I just couldn't take it."

"I can't believe he made you sick! I'm gunna tell him!" I howl with laughter.

"No! No!" She cries. "I'm so embarrassed, I wasn't even going to tell *you*!"

"He'd think it's funny." I giggle. "He wouldn't even think it was in an offensive way, he's way too big-headed! Didn't you notice how much he talks about himself, he never listens."

Leila raises her eyebrows seriously.

"One, Jodie, men *never* listen. Two, I wasn't thinking about anything other than how fucking fit he is! And then you said about the threesome!" She remembers and points a finger at me. "It was your fault!"

"I'm sorry, I couldn't resist. And you know, I actually wouldn't have minded! He has had sex with so many other women, why should you miss out?"

Leila is choking on her tea and holding up a hand for me to stop. "Jodie, I know you like him though. I wouldn't go there for that reason-"

"I know he can't be my boyfriend though-" I begin to explain.

"-but anyway, he is way *too* fit! I'd be just thinking, shit, he's shagged models before me."

I giggle at her reasoning and remember how I felt with him in the hotel room last year.

"I understand but I don't think men see it like we do. They think with their dick and they like boobs, ass and fanny in every shape and size!"

"Hmmm." She sips her tea. "Even so. I'll leave Luca for you."

I sip at my own mug. I drank two cups before she even got up at around ten and my thoughts finally make some sense.

"I don't think I'll be seeing him again."

"What? Don't be daft-"

"Leila, he's going away with work. His world is so different to mine, we're nothing solid. He doesn't even remember the last time he was at the Trap!"

I know this will put it into perspective for her because she's recalling that very time right now. For us it was quite a big thing but to him it was a mere drop in the ocean.

"He didn't know I'd worked in Maga or work in a school now, even though we spoke about it all the last time we met. Look, just because Luca is fit doesn't mean he's perfect."

I just want her to understand he isn't better than her or anybody else just because of his looks.

"Did you bang him though Jodes? Tell me everything!"

She is not deterred by my wistfulness so I take full advantage of this attentive audience and decide once she's gone to work I'll nip down to also tell Cat everything. My stories are entertaining to them. Sometimes they're fulfilling for me and most of the time at least enlightening. Casual sex has not, in fact, been casual at all. It has led to all kinds of feelings. Catching them has been accidental. Dealing with them has been an education.

Monday Requests

"Jodie! Jodie?" Lizzy looks unusually flustered as she approaches me at break time.

"What is it? Why aren't you-"

"I left Harishma and Lacey in there. I had to come and find you. Didn't you say you like singing?"

"Erm, yeah but I'm not singing in class! I'm talking karaoke and alcohol." I imagine she has formed a crazy plan for lessons tomorrow afternoon.

"No, my party. Will you sing at my party?"

"What! *What*?" My mind reels.

"The lead singer can't do that date. Sean just came to tell me. He's gutted but he said if we can find other singers it could work, and I thought of you!"

"Oh my god, *why*?" I don't know how I feel about any of this and I'm worried I'm bloody going to agree.

"It would be so perfect Jodes. You are a real friend, we've been through so much already and it would give you a chance to try something new. How many people can say they've sang on stage really?"

She's blatantly playing to my weakness, my love of saying yes!

"Ok, ok, yes." My mouth is dry and I swallow feeling on the verge of being sick. Can I do this really? Except Lewis and Jess have both heard and are cheering looking thrilled.

"Yes then Jodie!" Lewis enthuses.

"I knew you would Jodie! Yes!" Lizzy is clapping gleefully. "I'll tell Gem. And Sean. You can practise with the band a good few times before the party, it's still almost two weeks away."

It's really beginning to dawn on me what I've just done and I wonder how many songs I'll have to learn, what songs, have I really got a wide enough range to pull this off? Amongst the terror there's a flutter of excitement.

"Tell Sean I'll chat to him at dinner." I muster feeling bemused.

"I will! Thanks Jodie, you're the best!" Lizzy gallops away.

I almost want to cry but with thrill or sheer horror I'm still unsure.

"Well!" Jess gasps.

Well, indeed!

Thursday Catch-Up

I check for the umpteenth time that I am replying to the correct 'Shaun' before I hit send.

This week I've been in contact with Sean regarding songs and band practice and Shaun about travelling and frankly, sex. Something I don't want to be accidentally raising with Sharky Sean!

We should hook up before I leave xx

Sexy Shaun's reply pings through and I take a final look in the mirror before leaving the flat. I'm off to Chantelle's for dinner, she really is a good cook and my mouth waters already in anticipation. I don't rush to reply to him, it's icy out and I brace myself for the stroll.

"Something smells *amazing!*" I enthuse when I'm welcomed into Chantelle's warm home.

"Oh I just threw something together for a bit of a starter. Thought we could have that first and a few drinks before the main."

"Perfect. So how you been?" I take the glass of white from her, condensation already forming on its surface and we head to her table for an overdue catch up.

***

"I just don't know how you do it!" Chantelle tells me frankly. "If me and Perry split up and I had to start dating again I'd just die! I don't know what I'd do!"

"You'd be inundated, let me tell you!" I take in her kohl lined bluey-green eyes and flawless olive skin. "Anyway, I love it, it's so much fun!"

"It doesn't always sound it Jodes." She tells me smirking. Unlike Leila and Cat, Chantelle is not enchanted by my craziness. "Between you and Alexa it's enough to put me off for life!"

"You and Perry are ok though right?" I probe and she nods genuinely.

"Yeah we're fine, thank god! So who have you got left in the running now then, just Ashley?"

"He's not exactly in the running." I chuckle.

"Well maybe it's a sign. He outlasted the others I mean Aaron came and went. This shit with Troy, well stay clear of him. And Luca, I never liked him, even when we were younger he was always so bigheaded!"

She knows the deal with all the men in my life and makes her disapprovals clear.

"It's part of the thrill I suppose, the not knowing what's around the corner." I try to explain because I do feel guilty about the Troy thing especially when she's in a relationship. If somebody did it to her I can only imagine how I'd feel. I've learned a lot about where my moral responsibility should end- or shouldn't end even.

"I've been messaging a guy called Shaun." I divulge. "I met him in Magaluf too but he's going travelling in Thailand so we're thinking about hooking up before he leaves."

Chantelle giggles and puts her head in her hands. "What will we do with you ay! What if you really like him and then he's leaving anyway?"

"Well after my TEFL I might be able to go and teach out that way. So you never know." I defend the decision.

"I suppose that's just it." Chantelle looks me square in the eyes. "You like the excitement of not knowing. I feel like I have to know exactly what is happening next else it stresses me out. I need everything in order."

"Fair enough." I tell her. "But don't forget we can't always truly know what is round the next corner!"

"But we can try and plan for it!" She responds and I agree to a certain extent. "Fail to prepare, prepare to fail."

It's what Leila was saying before Christmas and I smile, I failed whilst prepared and definitely wasn't prepared for failing.

"Well, I'm planning to do my TEFL and hoping it will open up new career paths. But then I could sing next Friday and get talent spotted! I know that's not likely, but what I mean is, I'm open-minded to my plans changing."

She nods thoughtfully. "I suppose I could benefit from chilling out. But I still can't believe you're going to be singing! Well, actually I can, it's you. Seriously, you've got some balls mate."

"Bigger balls than most blokes I've met." I agree grinning, thinking of my first acapella sessions singing to Shark-boy Sean this week. I could've crapped myself with fear, but I took a deep breath and took the plunge. It's gotten easier as the evenings have gone on.

"When is your TEFL face-to-face training? Because you never know, maybe you'll meet a bloke there! And you can teach and travel together."

"It's next month. I do hope so!" I tell her.

"Well, you never know!" She throws my own sentiments back at me.

We devour our main course, it's scrumptious as expected and it's already getting late. But there's another few cans left for us to drink yet, Chantelle and I don't do our catch-ups by halves.

"That is so cool!" I tell her after she explains her next career move. She's buying shares of her business, something that totally goes over my head but she's always been financially savvy. "I need to do something about my money."

My head droops at the very thought of the upcoming months. TEFL best be worth it in one way or another is all I can think!

"In the future Jodie, I can imagine you flying high with this teaching thing." She tells me warmly. We're tipsy despite the heavy food and I grin at her.

"I'm glad you think so. I'm going to bloody well try."

"You should try and sell some of the furniture you upcycle. Or your arty stuff." She gestures to the trainers I'm wearing. Cheap, white plimsolls except they're now adorned with graffiti of my own hand.

I shrug and stare at them and think of the small projects I've been working on so far.

"With social media these days Jodes you can sell anything. Just take pictures of it as you do it. If people like it they might buy it eventually."

I think of Lewis attending Art fairs, Troy with his photography, Sean playing in a band- just some examples of people earning extra through their creativity. It's food for thought.

"Thanks so much for a wonderful dinner and fabulous evening." I gush, hugging Chantelle as Perry waits patiently in his car. "And congrats on buying some company or whatever it is you did!"

She giggles as she releases me. "And well done you for booking your TEFL. And for still being sane and single. At least I think you are! Now go, message me soon."

I blow her a kiss and hop into Perry's car. He is used to doing this for me, I think Chantelle pretty much makes him, I don't know whether he wants to and I always thank him profusely when he drops me off. It's not far to walk but they both say they'd rather know I'm back safely which is sweet.

Leila is in bed and I creep with blurred vision to my own room. I'll have a hangover tomorrow but it's been worth it. Great food for the body *and* for the soul! I'll get the singing out of the way next weekend and then I'll think properly about what I could do to turn an extra penny. Luca suggested I pole dance for a better wage and I'm glad to realise this is not my only option!

This time next week, it will be the eve of a different kind of live performance! The thought makes me vibrate with nerves and excitement. I'm certain Chantelle wouldn't do it and likely most of the people I know wouldn't dare either. That thought alone is enough to spur me through it, I hope.

Lindzi Mayann

Be Brave Saturday

"That was really great, Jodes you smashed it!" Sean cries as the instruments cut. My ears ring and I physically shake.

"Thanks!" I'm breathless. This is my first practice with the full band and it's a lot easier with the drums and guitars keeping me in time- and drowning me out. The nerves I felt before singing with these guys were nothing on that first time singing alone with Sean.

"I loved it!" I tell him honestly wiping sweat from my brow.

"I could tell." He grins. "Now try and learn the lyrics, but we don't mind you having your papers with you, so no pressure."

The countdown is on and although I know the songs such as Sex is on Fire and Price Tag I don't quite know all of the words. Yet!

"We'll all meet again Wednesday night. Jodie, me and you can practice Tuesday and Thursday too after school. And then Friday…" He slings his balled fists into the air. "Let's be having you!"

My heart beats erratically. I still can't quite believe this is going to happen but there's no getting out of it now. I'd be letting too many people down and never mind myself!

"What you doing for the rest of the day then?" Sean sidles up to me as we tidy and get ready to leave.

"I'm seeing my friends later." I lie. I don't want him to seize an opportunity and ask me out!

"Ah, ok. Going out? Like in town?"

"No, no. Just at a mate's house. Just dinner, you know."

"I'll be out." He tells me sternly, maintaining the eye contact. "You know, I never did take those topless pictures on the school camera."

452

"Oh. Erm, I hadn't heard..." I drift off because it's more insulting to deny it surely.

"It was Gilbert who sent the rumour round." He hisses. "I'm certain it was."

I cast my mind back. The rumours surfaced just as Gilbert got his new office. I've spent more time chatting with Sean recently and I believe him when he says it's untrue- he's the type he would just admit it, however embarrassing. And probably he's right that Gilbert did spread the gossip- to remove the limelight from his own activities and propel things in his favour for the future.

"He'll get what he deserves eventually. And anyway, it's old news about the pics." I tell him and don't add, like the pictures of Jayde's boobies.

"Well, I just didn't want it to you know, put you off or anything. Or Leila. Is she still single?"

"Yes she is erm, right I've got to go anyway, see you Monday!" I wave and dart to the car shamelessly. I like Sean, mostly. He's weird but he's alright and if Gilbert did send that rumour round it is childish and spiteful. I don't know for certain he'll get his comeuppance, but I sure hope he does. But neither me nor Leila are interested in Sean, like that anyway. He makes it clear anybody will do. None of us could ever feel special with him!

I drive home thinking about next week and the party. This week has consisted of cutting off any thoughts on Troy before they can creep into my gut and take hold. But the thought of singing in front of him makes me shiver. I know it will be difficult facing him out of work but I do trust myself, I'm feeling stronger and getting over him. I've been messaging Sexy Shaun still and although we've not arranged to meet up yet I'm seeing Ashley tonight, and at least I know what to expect with him.

***

The difference is noticeable almost immediately. Ashley keeps disappearing off upstairs for long periods of time leaving me to sip my wine alone.

I try to relax, play on my phone but notice that he is doing the same when he re-enters the room. It's rude and I'm annoyed but I place my phone beside me and catch his eye. He smiles and I try to make conversation but the chat is stilted.

The bottle is empty now. I'm alone again so I helped myself to the last glassful. My thoughts creak with irritation. I don't come round here to feel like this. He is really pissing me off but I decide I will finish this drink before taking any action. Give him that chance to sort it out.

I check Facebook once again and note it doesn't say Ashley is 'online'. What is he playing at up there?

I need the toilet anyway and I climb the stairs purposely. Ashley is in his room, I can hear him talking. His words are muffled and for a split second I think there's another woman in there with him but when he pauses it is silent. He's on the phone.

I use the bathroom knowing he will already have heard me. When I come back out he's on the landing, phone pressed to his ear.

He holds up a finger to me and mouths something, *one minute*, maybe. I look at him questioningly but he shakes his head and goes back into his room, laughing at something the other person has said.

I prickle as I descend the stairs. It's completely disrespectful and back in the living room I wait, and drink, and wait and my mind impatiently rampages. What is he doing? What should I do?

The last drop of wine swallowed I go back to the doorway and can hear him still talking upstairs.

"Ashley?" I call. "Ashley? I'm going."

He appears with the phone no longer at his ear.

"Why are you going?" He asks innocently.

"Erm, because you're up there on your phone and I'm sitting down here bored."

"Oh well." He begins to come down the steps smiling shyly. "I've got something I need to tell you anyway."

"Oh, what?" I move back, letting him pass and he takes a seat on the sofa patting the space next to him. He looks so sweet, boyish. Perhaps I am overreacting and I sit beside him waiting for him to speak.

"So, you know, I've really enjoyed spending time with you and getting to know you. You're a really, really nice girl. And I want you to know that I'm really happy now. I've got a new girlfriend!"

"Ahh, what?" I'm a little befuddled, the line doesn't make sense tacked onto the end of that spiel. "A new *girlfriend*?"

"Yeah, she's lovely. So that's who I've been talking to. I hope you don't mind."

I stand abruptly, stammering. Should I smile or shout?

"W- why did you even invite me here tonight?"

He looks at me confused. "I don't know. I suppose I didn't expect this all to happen so quickly with her." He nods to his pocket where his phone is, or perhaps it's his penis he's gesturing towards.

"I've got to go." I tell him. "I'll see you around."

"You don't have to go!" He follows calling my name after me but I'm already opening the door to be greeted with a rush of fresh night air.

"Jodie are you ok?" He asks and I step outside, turning to look at him backlit in the doorway and force a smile.

"Yes I'm fine, bye." And with that I'm hurrying away.

Well that did not go to plan!

I am ok, I decide as I pound the pavement. I'm a little shocked and upset, embarrassed too, but ok. I think I assumed Ashley didn't want a girlfriend. Full stop. Now I've realised he did, just not me. I believed I was some kind of higher ranking to the other girls, deluded I now realise. Is it because I slept with him on the first night?

It's almost midnight and I know Leila will be home from work soon, if not already. Can I admit to her what has just happened?

***

"I don't know why I'm crying!" I giggle but the tears continue to pour. "I'm not even that bothered!"

"Oh Jodes. I wish we had wine!" She cries. I've just finished telling her what happened between Ashley and me this evening. We're still standing in the kitchen.

"I don't need wine. I've had enough wine, I could've done with a shag. It's what I went round there for!" I moan.

"Can't help you there mate." Leila says smirking.

"No, I don't have a strap on." I continue the joke, momentarily forgetting my woes. "I wonder whether lesbians have to put up with all this shit? I bet they bloody don't, it's men that are the bastards."

Leila goes to flip the kettle switch and I carry on my with my patter.

"Troy made out I was just a hussy in the end. Now Ashley too." I ponder. "Even Luca really, I know he just uses me for a shag."

"No, no it's not like that! They like you Jodie. Luca does else he wouldn't make the effort when he does. Troy does but he hasn't got the nerve to leave his bird after so long, just in case. It's like your mum isn't it. Not everyone is as brave as us!"

I point at my own eyes smiling. "Brave? And what about Ashely hmmm? He's chosen someone else over me, I would've been his girlfriend."

"Would you though?" Leila asks and I take a moment to think it over.

"No. You're right." I frown.

"It's that thing. You didn't want him but you're pissed off he wants someone else."

I giggle as I see it for myself. I am annoyed at the rejection. How very clear yet confusing this all is.

"Ok, I didn't want him as a boyfriend I don't think. But I am pissed off my pool has dried up! Who the hell am I going to turn to for sex now?"

"Welcome to my world!" Leila giggles.

"Oh bloody hell, I am not going two years! But I don't want a boyfriend either. Shit." My tears have dried up but I do feel genuinely sad at the conundrum. My Top Five is completely empty! Leila gives me a weary look.

"Jodie, you could get a bang at the drop of a hat if you wanted to."

She's right but not because I'm insanely irresistible. The Trap alone attracts enough dogs that would lie with anyone. I'm not about to settle in desperation and I give her a sarcastic sneer to communicate this.

"Get onto meeting up with Shaun that'll take your mind off it." She tells me as she makes our hot drinks. "And anyway, more will come along, perhaps at this party when you're singing your heart out on stage... you know... it's never quiet around here for long!"

She doesn't say what I think she's going to- *there's plenty more fish in the sea*- and I'm glad. We've outgrown the term. I don't think either of us are particularly looking for a boyfriend but when I began casting my net I didn't envision it dragging up all of this extra stuff either.

She is right, I think, as I take a steaming mug from her. It is never quiet for long. And I'll keep approaching new corners without fear of what is around them, just like I told Chantelle in the week.

Forget Ashley, forget Luca, forget Troy! Forget making men such an important feature in my life. It's onwards and upwards, Jodie, business as usual.

Skip to my Step Sunday

I'm walking back from Cat's and decide to swing into the Trap to say hi to Leila and my brother who I know is in here too. It's a regular Sunday afternoon crowd. Bill and the rugby lot are nestled into one corner and I'm treated to the usual jeers as I pass.

"Hi, hi." I call good-naturedly over my shoulder to them and wave at Leila behind the bar. My spirits are high, and I grin at George even though he's with Dane.

"Hey sis." He smiles. "Glad you came."

"Not stopping. Just wanted to say hi." I wave at him stupidly and chuckle. "Just went to see Cat. She's had so much good news about Es, I'm so happy!"

"Well let me buy you a half ay? Just one?" He waggles a fiver and I note Dane watching me.

"Go on then." I give in. "Just one!"

I prance to the bar and fill Leila in on the good news from Cat as she serves me.

"I'm so pleased Es' health is all fine. And let's pray they don't cancel these next set of appointments."

"I know, I know." I tell her crossing my fingers. "They've got to come through sooner or later! And even so, all the other stuff is fantastic."

"We'll have to see if Kyle will watch the kids for an evening and cook her a dinner! Well you can, you're better at cooking than me!" Leila chats as she hands me the change.

"Well maybe cooking could be one of your new hobbies to try out." I tease her picking up the drink. "We'll sort something."

An hour passes quickly between talking to George and his mates. Dane is brash but funny as usual and I realise how my feelings even toward him have changed subtly over time. I don't feel an empty nothingness but just calm and indifferent. He is what he is. Live and let live.

He catches my eye and smiles, and I return it hoping my eyes show I've truly moved on. We can forget his mistakes, and mine, that's what forgiveness is all about. We'll never be friends but we were so close once and for almost a year. I don't want to view that time with bitterness.

I say my goodbyes to him, George and the other lads and trot to Leila one last time.

"I'm off mate. I'll probably be in bed by the time you get home."

"Okey doke my love. I will see you tomorrow."

"Oh, Soph, give me a hand would you?" Chris appears and shoves a bag into my arms. It's stuffed with material and is heavy.

"Oomph!" It knocks the air out of me and I take a step-back regaining my balance. It's old curtains or something, they smell fusty pressed right up to my face and I eye him over the top pleadingly. "What am I doing with them?"

"Take it out the back to the carpark, I'll grab another sack. I'll be coming up the rear." He winks and I know he meant the innuendo. I smirk at the old man, although he's obscured by the load in my arms. His daughter is my age and just as crude and witty. I nod and stumble on my way.

"In here please chick." He slings his own package into the rusting yellow skip.

"Having a clear out?" I eye the wooden shelving units as he relieves me of the burden.

"The missus is making me spend my money ain't she kid." He answers rubbing his face before making to go back inside. "Thanks for your help! Plenty more to-"

"Chris, could I take those shelves?" I ask him but I'm already sure he won't mind. He turns from the doorway and his head crinkles up.

"They're damaged!" He cries laughing. "Look."

Agilely he jumps onto a bench and hoists the tall slim set up for me to see. The backing is loose and he flaps at it.

"And that one is the same." He indicates the second stubbier set. Both are painted white, scuffed but my mum's voice says, *only take a few nails to fix it.*

"That's fine! I want to upcycle them." I tell him confidently imagining the possibilities already.

"Well I don't know what that means Soph but I'll help you take them up the road now if you like? Frees up more space for me in the skip!"

"Are you sure? I could go and get my car if you'll help me load them up."

"No, no, there's life in the old dog yet. Whatever you might think." He begins to shift my new projects out with relative ease. "And a girl as fit as you, you can manage this one."

I work up a considerable sweat in the cold night air and after a steady gait we're placing the damaged furniture at my doorstep.

"I'll help you get them up the stairs Soph. Wouldn't want you falling and breaking your neck for these old things."

I've unlocked the door and he continues his chuntering as we drag them up into my flat.

"Lord only knows what you think you can do with them." He mutters shaking his head. They're blocking the door to the living room like bouncers of opposing builds and I smile at them.

"I'll show you photos when I've done them. I hope you don't mind but I might try to sell them." I admit now. Well, he was chucking them out.

"Good luck to ya. Who knows, I might be buying 'em back off ya one day. But I doubt it." He adds grinning. "Good night me ode fruit."

I watch his bald head bob back down the stairs and wait until he's closed the door below to skip down after him and lock up. His description of the shelves, *damaged,* didn't go unnoticed. I saw the beauty and potential in damaged goods, perhaps this is how Troy meant his message. He is the damaged one and I still loved him.

Not anymore. It is over, I know it. And I feel like this whole thing panned out exactly how it was meant to be. I've forgiven Dane even though I didn't realise I still held his cheating against him. By making my own mistakes with Troy I've been brought down a peg or two.

I realise all I can make count now, is my reaction in light of my mistakes. This still makes both Troy and Dane first-class dickheads of course, but I won't hold it against them.

I have way more to focus on in my life than just men. I suddenly have two substantial pieces of furniture ready to work on for a start. I see beauty where other people see damage and if I can earn a nifty buck in the process it's an added bonus.

Far better than trying to fix a broken man!

I gaze lovingly at my newest acquirements and realise I had better text Leila to warn her what I've done this time, if Chris hasn't told her already. Perhaps I can get her on board too and we can start our very own upcycling business. Maybe that will be her new hobby.

After dragging the shelves into the edge of the living room so they don't look quite so imposing on space, I make myself a tea. I was going to read but now I might trawl the internet to see what cool things other people are doing with their furniture. My phone album is already full of screenshots from previous research.

I lie in bed that night feeling satisfied and at ease. Certain recent conversations replay in my mind; my mum, Leila, Chantelle and Cat. The New Year is still very young but I already feel productive and like I've morphed and grown yet again.

I came home from Magaluf still on a high, immersed myself in relationships- back then I thought they were harmless- and since then I've realised I need to take more precaution than just a rubber.

The next guy, because I'm not sworn off men altogether, I will not allow myself to become so attached to. I didn't realise I had been until it was too late. And I honestly realise now I'm not even ready for a relationship just yet. I'm excited about so many things and they all require time. Soon I'll be studying too. There isn't enough room in my life for a full-time man.

I wonder where Leila has stashed her Sex and The City DVDs. I could do with channelling some Samantha and Carrie, all of them in fact. How I adored that programme when she first introduced me to it and didn't realise back then I was using the characters to heal and grow.

When, if, someone comes along and blows my mind, I'll know then the time is right. Hopefully I'll just *know* it.

I won't hold it against Ashley for how things panned out. Or Aaron or Luca. I've been using them all as much as they did me and I won't let the hiccups slow me down. Somebody once said all is fair in love and war- do whatever has to be done to be a winner. I don't think things are fair and I don't think people should play dirty to get what they want. But then over the past few months I have succumbed to doing just that.

I should be number one in my own life, I am important. But I don't feel good for letting this thing with Troy get out of hand. Some things are uncontrollable, but some things can be helped.

Love and war, just like positive and evil, entwine with one another daily. I've got to continue being me, my lessons learned and packed tightly in my mind. I'll make the most out of whatever trail it all weaves.

This Is It!

It's Friday and the party is tonight. The fact is vibrant in my thoughts and I haven't been able to forget it, never-mind that Lizzy has been manically excited all day. Honestly I have veered back-and-forth from feeling absolutely sick with nerves to overwhelmingly hyper about the prospect.

I keep reasoning with myself that I have conquered things just as daunting in the past- but I'm not sure whether this does actually top it all.

I remind myself that I wanted to say yes more and this is just part of the quest. And it has, at least, given me something far better to concentrate on than the despairing state of my sex-life.

I'm driving home after school, playing the CD Sean gave to me at the start of the week, singing each of the songs that tonight I'll be *performing live*. It seems so surreal to think of it like that. Me, Jodie, performing!

I already have my outfit sussed, obviously. I've been obsessing over it all week and have finally chosen an oversized tee and sequinned trainers. I want to be comfortable and blend in with the band vibe.

Sexy Shaun has messaged. I've told him what I'm doing and he's sent a gif stating, 'break a leg'. Perhaps I could do just that by throwing myself off the stage instead of going through with the whole thing!

Once home, I sit down to message him back but immediately my body is filled with restless energy. I can't concentrate, I need to just get ready. Time to take a shower.

***

"Jodie, you need to have a drink, it'll loosen you up!" Leila follows me around with the glass. "And the sugar will help, I promise."

I take it from her and neck it finally. My hair and make-up are done, I'm dressed and we're waiting for a taxi. I've been reading and re-reading the lyrics over and over but there are two songs at least I can't remember word-for-word. Seven tracks in total, they have some bloke covering some others. I can do this.

"I don't think I've ever seen you so nervous." Leila comments observing me like I'm an unknown specimen.

"Not helping." I say through gritted teeth and try to smile.

"Here, drink some more." She says topping me up looking worried. My stomach is doing somersaults. I've never experienced nerves like it but there's still the smallest hint of excitement.

I take a shaky deep breath and swallow down some more Dutch courage. There's no way I want to go on stage drunk but Leila is right, it does make me feel a bit better!

***

The venue is a smallish pub with two rooms and we're in the back. There's a poster on the door stating, 'The Key FEATURING Jodie' and it makes my heart pounce with the reality of it all. We're early, the band are only just setting up but there's already groups of people chatting and drinking.

I can't see either of the engaged couple and we head over the dance floor to Sean.

"Hi Leila." He croons and she giggles. I nudge her, reminding her to be nice. I've told her the latest in Gilbert double-crossing him.

"Hiya Sean. Excited?" I ask him.

"Absolutely buzzing for it! I can't wait for the Belfry lot to hear us!"

"Me too!" I say honestly. Now I'm here I'm feeling better by the moment.

"Jodie! Leila!" Gem spots us first and dashes over. "Jodie thank you, thank you for doing this!"

"You don't have to thank me, I'm erm, really glad." It's the truth, my nerves are dissolving, I'm enjoying the stream of adrenalin. Lizzy appears and makes a beeline for us with a huge smile on her face.

"Let me buy you a drink." Gem dashes off without waiting for an answer and Lizzy scoops us into a hug in turn.

"How are you feeling? Are you ok?" She asks beaming.

"Yes, actually, a lot calmer than I thought I'd be."

"You should have seen her before we left!" Leila adds helpfully.

"The drink must have worked." I tell her with a smile. Gem comes back over clutching a bottle of champagne and four flutes.

"Couldn't resist!" She tells us thumping the items onto a nearby table. "We have got a lot to celebrate after all."

Gem and Lizzy gaze at each other and I admire the genuine love which passes between their eyes. How they feel about each other is clear and written in their body language. I know I might find it one day, the elusive 'true and reciprocated love', and I'm happy to wait and see. Happy ever after can be forged with or without a prince by my side!

Bubbles poured, I sip and I'm reminded of New Year. My heart swells with happiness and my body fizzes in excited anticipation. Mum has begged that Leila films at least some of my performance. I told her she'd have been welcome to come along but her courage didn't stretch to a night out. Yet.

"Jodes, you ok to have a quick warm up?" Sean interrupts the chatter between us girls and I nod leaving my drink with Leila to watch. One, I don't want to spill anything on the equipment and two, I genuinely daren't drink too much. Until afterwards!

Guitars and drums rumble into life. I recognise the rhythm instantly and Sean passes me a mic.

"Just sing until we cut, we're just tuning up and getting the volume right."

It all feels very surreal, but I like it. I know I'm good enough to blast out the chosen songs tonight but I'm not harbouring fantasies of a career in music anytime soon. I'm not *that* good and that's fine. Upcycling furniture, writing books and teaching, they all come above it in no particular order.

I begin to sing casually, eyeing Leila and grinning. She gives me a thumbs up. Lizzy and Gem hold hands, looking between me and each other with pride. For me or themselves in finding each other, I don't know, perhaps both.

"Can you hear her?" Sean calls over to them when we break.

"Oh yeah, she sounds wicked!" Lizzy calls. I blush and busy myself wiping the sweat from my palms. A number of the Belfry lot have begun to trickle in, but still no Troy. I wonder fleetingly if he won't come and feel a flutter of disappointment because I do want tonight to be a clear full-stop.

Nothing is going to happen. I know that because I know how I felt the time when it still did. I was playing myself a string of bullshit, well I'm not this time!

"Get yourself a drink for now." Sean says. "Drink water on stage but we've got half an hour. A beer won't hurt."

I turn to smile at him and catch the drummer's eye. He grins coyly and looks away.

"Cool." I tell Sean and lurch over to join Leila.

"Can I just say babe, you are amazing." She turns to me, eyes shining. "You're completely pulling this crazy stunt off. Yet again. And I love you for it!"

"Well thanks friend. I love you too! Now, do you think that guy in the red shirt is fit?" I nod in the rough direction of Blake.

"The drummer? Yeah he's alright in a hippy, rock kinda way. But you like that *different* look don't you?"

"Yeah I suppose I do." I laugh and look over to where Blake is looking back. He holds his drink aloft and gestures toward it.

"You'd better get over there. I think he wants to buy you a drink!"

***

I'm climbing onto the stage now and admittedly I'm starting to feel extremely shaky. The room is heaving, which Blake said is so much better because people get stuck in with chatting and dancing therefore not paying too much attention to us.

The lights are focussed on our square platform, they're warm and limit my ability to clearly see who is in here. Troy still wasn't on my last check and I swallow the lump. I just wanted the opportunity to *not* go there and really show him. Oh and of course shine like a superstar in front of him for just one night! Perhaps he decided he couldn't take seeing me like this. Or he thought I'd be made a fool of.

I'll make sure it isn't the latter!

Behind me Sean counts in and with that the band are thrashing out the introductory notes to our first song. I made sure I wouldn't need my lines for this one and confidently belt out the words allowing the atmosphere to engulf me.

I'm doing it, I'm really doing it! It's so much better than karaoke and I'm thrilled with the rapturous rounds of applause we get at the end of every tune.

I'm five songs down with two to go when Sean puts on a recorded track and tells us to have a quick drink. Sweat is pouring down my spine and I'm sure my makeup must be obliterated but I just don't care! I've loved every second of it; the crowd cheering and dancing and me on stage jumping around like a possessed maniac.

I look for Leila as I gratefully gulp down my water and spot her pushing her way toward me.

"Have you filmed some of it? Please tell me you have, my mum is going to go wild!"

Leila looks at me a little wildly and I continue to sip waiting for her to explain. Maybe Eric is making his move on her.

"Oh Jodie. I don't know how to tell you this." She cries over the noise.

"What?" I yell looking down at myself just knowing my t-shirt dress is going to be tucked into my pants or something equally as embarrassing.

"Jodes, Troy is here."

I look up, initially pleased but then spot her expression.

"He's with Beth babe."

My heart thuds as the realisation dawns on me. I wanted him to feel rejected. How I had. I understand that, and now it is impossible because he bought his girlfriend along. Lacey said he *never* brings her out. Well he has tonight. A shield or a message. Probably both.

I look around trying to spot them but I'm on level ground and can barely see over the cluster of shoulders around us. Once I'm back on the stage the lights will make it impossible to find them.

"Jodie?" Sean is calling me.

"Are you ok?" Leila asks and I nod.

"Yes, I am." I grin really meaning it. "And did you film it already? Make sure you get some of these songs too because I'll be giving it my all."

I wink at her and crush the last part of Troy out of my system. Whatever his reasons for bringing Beth, it's given me the final nail I needed. Men are not the be all and end all. I have to forgive to be able to forget. I've learned this along with so much more and I'll use it all to firmly stick a line under things with Troy. Now it's time to sing my fucking heart out.

Epilogue

"Jodie so good to see you." Alexa coos as she enters Chantelle's living room and kisses me on both cheeks. Chantelle has gone off to fetch her a glass and she turns now to Leila and greets her in the same way.

"How are you?" I ask her enthusiastically because I've already heard the latest gossip; Ronaldo has asked her to move to Spain to be with him! And I'm still a little shocked that she's apparently going for it, she made it clear when we were in Magaluf she would never jeopardise her business by doing what I'd done.

"In love!" She gushes not afraid to get straight down to the brunt. "Did Shan tell you, I'm moving to Spain to be with my fabulous lover!"

"Wow!" Leila respectfully fakes surprise. "That's amazing!"

"Definitely!" I agree thinking of Lizzy's whirlwind engagement which is still going strong. "So what about your business?"

"I'm leaving my assistant in charge for now." She says breezily, relieving Chantelle of the wine glass. "Thanks darling. So yes, anyway, it's going to be just amazing. I'm leaving in two weeks!"

"Well cheers." I hold my glass aloft genuinely pleased for her. Why not take the leap, I'm all for her going for it especially when she's got things covered here.

"So, Jodie you were saying about your painting?" Chantelle returns to our latest topic before Alexa arrived.

"Yeah, Chris is paying me to paint him some pictures for the pub! So who knows, maybe it will generate interest." I conclude. He'd been so impressed by what I did with his raggedy, damaged furniture he immediately suggested it as a way of him supporting me and I've been waiting for the May half term to make a start.

"And what was this about a new job?" She presses. It's difficult usually to talk about ourselves with Alexa around but Leila knows all this gossip and keeps her engaged in other conversation.

I tell Chantelle about the informal interview with local business guy, Harry. It was Bill of all people who helped me to make the connection and we'll be discussing a potential position working with challenging teens. It's more money than Belfry and even though I don't *need* to get away from Troy, I want to. I'm ready to.

The night I sang, back in January, he introduced me to Beth. The audacity! As if I needed any more evidence to show me how rid of him I was! Her adoration for him was clear. Will their relationship stand the test of time? It's not my business and never should have been. And as for Ashley; he and his girlfriend broke up within weeks and he was blowing up my inbox just as quickly. I turned him down. Over and over! And yes, it felt quite good to show him that's not how it works with me, at least not anymore.

"So, Jodie, how is *your* love-life? I've heard about Leila's!" Alexa can be distracted no longer.

"Didn't take long to tell all!" Leila giggles shrugging apologetically.

"Shut up, what about Tom?" I ask her.

"Yeah she told me about him." Alexa chimes in. "What about you? Seeing anyone?"

But before I can decide whether to mention Blake- who is only a casual bang but the only bang I currently have- she begins telling us all about Ronaldo's massive member and the things he does with it! I giggle as I listen and resolve I'll tell them about Sexy Shaun, who I might be going camping with soon, later on.

I'm glad I'm not the only one with relationship gossip and listen intently to Alexa, I always manage to pick up hints and tips from her. I admire her for not caring what people think of her escapades. I probably wouldn't go into the detail she does but it has certainly taken having flings to help me find out a thing or two about the world. I understand a little better who I want to be and my own self-worth.

I don't regret my past and I'm happy to covertly bang when the opportunity arises. A small part of me admits maybe a proper partner is on the cards for the future. He'll have to match up to a long list of attributes though.

And I'll continue to say yes to new opportunities and build on my *life* CV in the meantime. Maybe along the way I might meet a Mr Right. But I certainly don't *need* to. I'm just happy enough to admit a tiny part of me is open to it.

"So, you didn't meet anyone on the TEFL course then?" Chantelle asks after she's finished detailing her horrors at the thought of camping.

"Well there was one guy he was kind of cute and we've been messaging. But he was going off to China as soon as he qualified so, nothing serious like."

Chantelle shakes her head how she has done a fair few times before and chuckles.

"Well, I'm so glad you passed, you deserve it." She lightly chinks my glass. "So, you're not planning on jetting off around the world just yet."

"Need to get my money together first. Never say never!" It's an idea I give a lot of credit to but for now the extra qualification did its job in snagging the attention of my potential new employer, Harry. As for my old employer.

"Shan, did I tell you my headmistress is pregnant?"

Chantelle looks at me with intrigue but before she can comment Alexa is interrupting us again.

"So, girlies! Who's excited about my upcoming burlesque show?"

"Me!" I tell her eagerly, we can pick up that gossip later. Alexa is dancing on stage next weekend, having taken up an eight-week crash course. I really loved the stage and I'm already seeing the event as an opportunity to scope it out for me- and maybe Leila- to try. She never did stick to any of the hobbies she tried out (cooking, reading, upcycling) perhaps this is the poke she needs.

"I can't believe Zoe is coming." Chantelle comments. She knows how shy my mum is and I grin at Leila who had a huge helping hand in convincing her.

"I'm pleased too! It's a start." I smile at them. She won't pay to watch men fling their willies around but as this is in the name of art she's succumbed to the likelihood of nipple tassels.

"I have something for us to celebrate with!" Alexa drawls and raises an eyebrow. She pulls a few bottles from her bag and disappears into the kitchen.

"What is it?" I ask when she's handing me the glass of almost black liquid moments later.

"Espresso martini!" She declares. "I swear it is the *best* cocktail *ever* made!"

I take a swig and it tastes delicious! It's the first espresso I've had on English soil. I've been meaning to have one for so long and with vodka added to the mix it's definitely 'the *best* cocktail *ever*!'

"Cheers!" We chink glasses. It seems there's been a lot of that going on this year and we're only a third of the way through. And hopefully, there'll be lots more of it to come. It's my birthday soon enough. I'll be celebrating that in style, in my newest home. Things have *really* changed!

Perry drops us all off home later on, Alexa first, then Leila and I climb out thanking him genuinely. He flashes us his huge smile and drives away.

My mind is still humming, presumably with the rich coffee cocktail. We let ourselves in and I begin my night time routine, lost in thought.

I have another week off from Belfry soon and I have more plans to paint and write. I've shelved one novel attempt- The Art of Cheating- and I'm now planning 'Damaged Love' instead. Alexa proves so inspirational in fuelling a fanciful personality and drawing on my experiences to scribe stories is a process that I not only enjoy but benefit from. It's cathartic; providing a release and a way of making sense out of the madness. The truth I've realised, is far crazier than fiction. I know it will take years to master this particular hobby; creative writing is a work in progress. Just like me really.

I also have another project ready, alongside the paintings for Chris. It's an old school desk. I had to ask Julie if I could take it, which I did with confidence. I'm glad I haven't had to add to my 'workplace bullying log' for a while now but my experience with her has set me in good stead. I'm more self-assured than ever and never imagined our relationship would become as amicable.

Even though her pregnancy isn't 'common knowledge' her prominent bump is causing rumours to run rife. I think she likes it. And a taste of his own medicine for Gilbert, perhaps, who has definitely been meeker lately.

Iqbal's own happy news is out in the open and I've been working on a little present for him. It's just a drawing but it will be partly congratulatory and partly a goodbye gift. If I get on with this Harry, it'll be new beginnings yet again.

I've learned so much at Belfry and it's given me a perspective I didn't know was possible. In my bedroom I stare at the black and white photograph from Troy. It's a lasting impression which continues to remind me of the important things in life and who I have become so far. My graffiti canvas- influenced by the painful beauty of hindsight- is pinned up beside it.

I look at the Belfry lanyard and ID badge. The photo I stuck over at the very start of the school year is peeling, eight months ago and yet it seems an age!

I already feel gutted at the idea of leaving the students behind even though leaving is not a given. But then I've already achieved so much with them and I could have the opportunity to work with even more young people. Plus, I'll finally peel that picture completely off, a completely different Troy took that photo, and me and Leila shall shriek with laughter at the hidden beetroot beneath.

A completely different me.

The future looks bright and for those around me. Esmay almost has her complete diagnosis and Cat and her family continue to battle another day with renewed hope. I hope she'll blog, I hope she'll let me help her but I'm happy to be supporting her however I can for now. We're attending an autism info session together soon. Who knows, meeting others in her situation, realising she isn't alone, it could be the confidence boost she needs.

Leila is a successful assistant manager, loving every minute. Chantelle officially part-owner of a thriving business. I've made new friends too, Lizzy who I've watched blossom as she's fallen further in love. I never succumbed to trying a dab of cocaine with her- the opportunity has arisen- but never say never and all that.

There're possibilities for us all and no doubt enough lurking on the horizon too. But we've got each other. We all have traits, some we share, some which complement and some which oppose. I enjoy meeting new people and trying new things. I like uncovering what's hidden out there and seeing through the damaged exterior when I must.

My life felt like one big web before, but I know now it's more like an intricate ladder. Those I cross on the way up I'll treat with openness, acceptance and forgiveness, if it's called for, because a tumble back down is not impossible. I know all of this now.

I get to choose who I share my journey with. I'm thankful for who I've chosen to be around me still and who has chosen me to be a part of their own experiences. They accept me for me, crazy and all.

I accept me. My morality has strengthened and stretched, and I realise more now than ever I am not a person who wants to hurt others through my choices- regardless of whether I personally know them, or how they have treated me. Maybe that is the most important lesson to date. Or perhaps it's knowing any manner of Happy Ever Afters could be just around the corner, waiting.

Happy Ever After might not involve a dashing prince and there's no rush to get there even if it does. I'm glad for the stories I'm creating en route, and I know it's all just been part of my education so far.